HEART OF VANRIS

THE WARDEN'S SON
BOOK THREE

NIKKI McCORMACK

ISBN: 979-8-9903922-3-6
First Edition 2024

Published by
Elysium Books
Bellevue, WA

Written by Nikki McCormack (https://nikkimccormack.com/)
Cover Design by Robert Crescenzio (https://robertcrescenzio.artstation.com/)
Map Design by Melissa Nash
Typesetting and Design by Brian C. Short
Editing by Alexander Lockwood

•

To all the book lovers of the world. Without the imagination you bring to these pages, this world would forever be only half alive. Thank you.

•

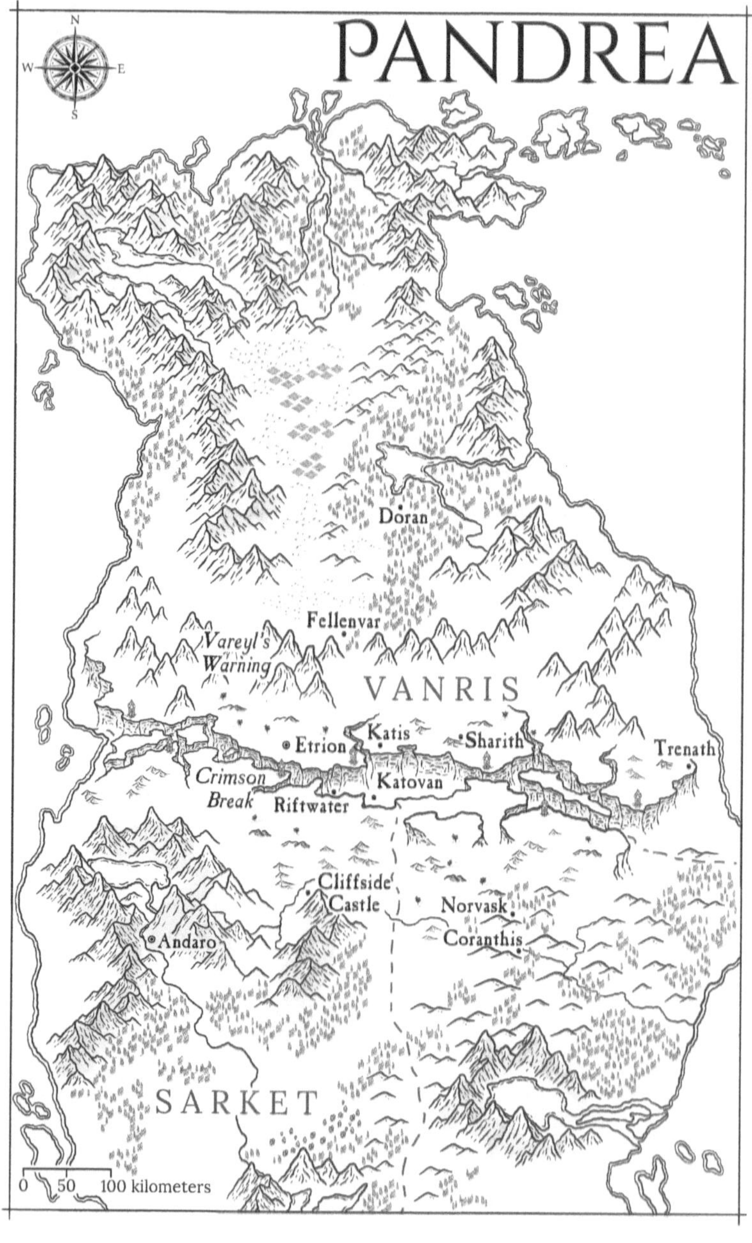

N
W E
S
PANDREA
Doran
Fellenvar
Vareyl's
Warning
VANRIS
Katis
Etrion
Sharith
Trenath
Crimson
Break
Katovan
Riftwater
Cliffside
Castle
Norvask
Coranthis
Andaro
SARKET
0 50 100 kilometers

Kasiel ducked back, narrowly avoiding the arc of Dhomen Farren's swinging sword. He darted in behind it, attempting to take advantage of a brief opening. The instant he committed to the attack, he knew it was going to be too slow. Too slow and too clumsy. Farren's parry and retaliation were lightning quick and anything but awkward. Kasiel's practice sword hit the ground, the strike that had disarmed him leaving his wrist stinging despite the protection of the bracer.

"This is impossible!" He followed the declaration with a string of curses in a blend of Vanrian and Pandrean Common as he tried to shake the feeling back into his fingers.

Farren watched him. A couple of braids hung behind his pointed ears, keeping his long white-blond hair back out of his eyes. The sharp red lines of his ke'hanoath tattoos climbing up his throat added an edge of threat to his countenance even when he was still.

The dhomen remained silent until Kasiel ran out of vulgarities. "Are you finished?"

"No," Kasiel snapped.

He kicked the training sword, sending it skidding across the sandy practice ring until it hit the low border at the side. Irith, his cliff cat companion, leapt the outer fence and sprinted after it, pouncing on the weapon when it rebounded toward the center. With the sword securely pinned under his front paws, the big predator sat and began grooming one shoulder. He paused with the tip of his tongue still hanging out to look at Kasiel, the expectation in his bright blue eyes making it apparent that some recognition of his valiant efforts should be forthcoming.

Kasiel stared at the cat for a second, trying to rein in his temper, then he faced Farren. "Why are you wasting your time on this, sir? Any inren in the city could hold their own against me right now." He was being generous. Even a child could probably beat him in single combat now.

Farren drew a deep breath and released it before answering. "What you are trying to do is extremely difficult, Ahninveth. Learning to fight left-handed is not something you're going to master overnight."

Kasiel clenched his right hand at his side. Three months since the battle in Sharith and the arm remained weak, the nerves still not responding normally in places. "That doesn't answer my question. Why are *you* doing this?" He strode over to collect the practice sword, paying the toll of a scratch behind Irith's ears to get the cat off it.

"Maybe I want you to have the skills to defend yourself when you're out running your beasts in battle. I believe you can do this. Besides, the dhomvalen didn't give me a choice." He passed his practice blade to his left hand and flowed through a few elegant combat forms with it. "My being left-handed might have played a part in his decision."

Kasiel stared at him. The man wielded a sword in his right hand like he had been born with it there. This was the first time he had seen him use the other. "Why don't you fight that way?"

"I do, against my enemies. Most people aren't

accustomed to fighting a left-handed opponent, so it can give you an advantage if you're good at it. I don't fight that way with my students until they're more advanced because they'll typically be facing right-handed foes."

A flush of shame warmed Kasiel's cheeks. This man trained with both hands to better prepare his students. Here he was, complaining about having to train with his left hand when what he was actually angry about was being injured in a fight he shouldn't have gotten into to begin with. Although, several residents of Sharith might feel differently, given that he had stalled the Delaphinian general long enough to save their lives. Regardless of the outcome of his actions then, right now he was being bitter and ungrateful.

His temper was too quick to rise. Maybe losing Sylaryth and almost losing Jethan played a part in that. Those experiences still weighed on him, sometimes haunting his dreams. Watching them execute the man who had raised him might also contribute to the problem. Not that Edmund hadn't deserved it with everything he had done to Kasiel and to the Vanrian people, but his emotions around all that remained a tangled, confusing mess. It could also have something to do with the way they forced him to abandon Danica after being foolish enough to bring her to Etrion for help. He still didn't know if they had cured her nightmares before sending her back with the Alliance messenger. No one would talk to him about it.

Not a full year in Vanris yet, and so much had changed.

With a thought, he sent Irith out of the ring and faced Farren again, raising his blade.

"Ready?" Farren asked.

Kasiel nodded.

The combat instructor came at him like a lethal whirlwind. When Jethan showed up an hour later, Kasiel was bruised, sweaty, and struggling to keep his temper leashed, but he had made progress. In the final twenty minutes, Farren had failed to disarm him again, despite the numbness in Kasiel's fingers from all the hits he had taken on that arm.

A woman wearing the simple black and purple attire of a palace attendant accompanied Jethan. Her gaze focused on Kasiel as they approached.

He urged Irith to his side, putting a hand on the cat's head when he sat there. The bond they shared wasn't as strong as the one he'd had with Sylaryth, but maybe it would get there in time.

"Ahninveth Kasiel." She inclined her head. "You and Lord Jethan are required in the palace."

Farren held out a hand to take the practice sword. "You did well today, Ahninveth. I expect more improvement next time."

Next time. Not tomorrow. Farren must think the summons heralded a journey of some kind. A ball of dread formed in Kasiel's gut. "Of course, Dhomen." He handed Farren the sword, then faced the attendant. "Lead the way."

She started back toward the palace, trusting them to follow.

Jethan fell into step alongside him. "You look tired, tehnaak. You want to skip the Twisted Vine tonight?"

Kasiel gestured to the woman in front of them with his chin. "We may not get much choice depending on what this is about."

"True."

He watched the woman for a moment, his thoughts turning to Nerith. She had been an attendant in the palace when he first met her. The khevarin orchestrated that encounter so she might spy on him, but something genuine had grown from it.

"Are there rules about who can marry who in Vanris?"

As the question tumbled out, he realized how it would sound, but it was too late to stop it.

"You mean, do nobles have to marry nobles or something like that?" Jethan grinned and bumped him with an elbow. "Why, are you already thinking about making a certain someone your future bride?"

His cheeks were instantly ablaze. "No. I..." His gaze rose to the towering black pinnacles that speared up from the rooftops of the palace complex as he collected his thoughts. "I guess I don't even know what I am here."

"You're considered military nobility, given your father's status."

Kasiel looked at him, unnerved by the comment. Why did the concept of being nobility of any kind make him so incredibly uncomfortable? "Really?"

"Would I joke about such a thing?"

"Is there anything you wouldn't joke about?"

Jethan chuckled. "Well, I'm serious this time."

They followed the attendant to a side entrance into the palace. It didn't rain often in this region of Vanris, but it had been chilly enough in recent months that when it did, they occasionally got snow, though the coldest part of winter was past. While fighting Farren, Kasiel hadn't noticed the chill, but now that the sweat on his skin had cooled, it felt good to get inside. The cliff cat, with his heavy blue-gray coat, seemed to enjoy the brisk weather, requiring a little mental encouragement from Kasiel before he would come through the door with them.

"You're royalty though, aren't you?" he asked as the cat stepped inside and shook dust from the practice ring onto the polished marble floor.

Jethan shrugged, his interest in the conversation waning the moment Kasiel brought up his status. "I am. Part of the extended royal family."

"So, are there restrictions on who we can be with?"

"Not really. Not unless you have far more influence on the future of Vanris than either of us do, though arranged marriages aren't unheard of regardless of rank or status. It depends on the circumstances. But Nerith is a healer now. That puts her in a well-respected position."

Kasiel's face warmed again. He stared hard at the back of the woman guiding them. Did she find their conversation amusing? "I didn't say anything about Nerith."

"Not by name."

Jethan's teasing tone didn't help Kasiel's composure. "We'll talk about it later."

"All right, tehnaak. Whatever makes you happy." A faint, self-satisfied grin lingered on Jethan's lips.

Kasiel rolled his eyes. Jethan wasn't wrong. Nerith was the reason for his questions. She was a healer now. Vanris highly valued its healers. Was that enough to make her an acceptable match for the son of the dhomvalen of Vanris? Did he care if it didn't?

The woman stopped outside the war room adjacent to the large council chamber that he had been summoned to on several occasions. The first time for the results of his assessment testing and many times since to face Khevarin Seylin's judgement for various incidents over the course of the year.

The attendant stepped to one side, and one of the guards by the doors nodded to Kasiel and Jethan, his eyes lingering a moment on Irith before he opened it to allow them entry.

Dhomvalen Arhk was notably absent, but Adnar, his blond hair hanging loose over his shoulders, stood at the far end of a long table across from a stern-looking dhomen Kasiel hadn't met yet. The new man's dark blond hair, pulled into braids along both sides of his head, had streaks of gray through it, and his blue-gray eyes were hard as steel. The only other person there, aside from guards positioned around the room, was Khevarin Seylin, ruler of Vanris, her white-blond hair pulled into a single loose braid that showed off both finely pointed ears. Her cool blue eyes focused on him as he entered. Not once in the seemingly endless walk from the door to the end of the table did her gaze shift to Jethan or the cliff cat.

Kasiel absently touched the back of his right hand, where two more symbols had joined the original tattoo that showed her appreciation for catching Nerith's attackers. Of the newer ones, his entire unit shared the first. A recognition of their service to Vanris in destroying Edmund's research and bringing the man to Etrion to face judgment. He thought of it rather cynically as the symbol of his obliterated childhood. The other, he alone received to honor his efforts in Sharith, getting them into the city without losing more than a few of the citizens the Alliance force had been using as human barricades.

The way the corners of the khevarin's mouth curved up in a brief, covetous smile reminded him of their conversation after Sharith.

"Remember, Lord Kasiel, weapons are forged in fire."
"Is that what I am now?"
"Do not doubt it."

Her response had left him ill at ease. Becoming a soldier was never his ambition. Edmund would have done his best to discourage such notions if he had ever had them. Now that he had a growing number of people he cared about in his life, he had that many more reasons to hate this war. Perhaps fear of losing them was another thing that contributed to his sharp temper of late.

When they stopped at the table near Adnar and knelt, Seylin finally released him from her gaze. She gestured for them to rise, then glanced at the Feral ahndhomen.

Adnar inclined his head to each of them. "Ahninveth

Kasiel, Lord Jethan, this is Dhomen Sorval."

"Dhomen." Kasiel and Jethan acknowledged the other man together, both bowing their heads.

"You run tethdraks, Ahninveth?" the dhomen asked, eyeing Irith curiously.

"Yes, sir."

"This is the first time I've seen a Feral whose companion wasn't one of their preferred beasts."

"This was Irith's idea." The cliff cat's purr filled the room when Kasiel set a hand on his head.

"I see. You were responsible for getting Vanris's force into the city in Sharith?"

Where was he going with this? "Yes, sir."

"Our scouts recently reported a small company of Alliance troops gathering southeast of Etrion at the Sarketi border. We had driven them out of Katis and our base just before you took Sharith back. From there, we kept after them, pushing them out of the ruins of Riftwater in the Break. They had been using that location as a base for some of their operations in Vanris. It now looks as if they are preparing to go back in there. What I need to do is figure out what they're after in Riftwater and, if necessary, keep them out of the town while I accomplish that."

His hard gaze shifted to Adnar for a moment before he continued. Did that mean this was the ahndhomen's idea? Had he recommended Kasiel's unit?

"Etrion is light on troops with so many out providing defense and helping rebuild after the Alliance's invasion. There should be units returning within the next few days, but I need to move on this now. I could use the combat power of your beasts and your unique scouting abilities. I understand you are still recovering from your injuries, but Ahndhomen Adnar assures me you have excellent fighters in your unit who can provide you protection while you run your tethdraks."

A dark unease stirred in Kasiel's chest. "Does that mean you want my full unit, sir?"

"Not your healers," Seylin answered. "Dhomen Sorval has enough of our healers already. There is no reason to put yours at risk for this mission."

Relief washed away some anxiety. Nerith and Tath would get to stay out of the fighting this time. He was more than happy to stand behind that choice. "When do we head out?"

Respect found its way into Sorval's slow smile. "The company departs in the morning."

"We'll be ready, sir." Kasiel might have appreciated Adnar's firm nod of approval more if he hadn't noticed the satisfied smirk that tugged at the khevarin's lips.

After they received the details for their coming mission, Seylin dismissed them. Irith's tail switched back and forth as they strode down the halls, the big cat picking up on the fresh tension in Kasiel. As happy as he was that Tath and Nerith weren't going, the rest of his companions would be back in harm's way, Jethan included.

What had his father said?

"You can't save everyone, Kasiel."

The truth in those words haunted him as unceasingly as the moment Itana's mace struck his arm. Whenever he did the exercises to strengthen it, he could see that powerful blow sweeping down again and hear his father's words.

"I guess we should go tell the others."

An uncomfortable edge in Jethan's tone pulled Kasiel's from his morose thoughts. Maybe it was the prospect of possibly heading into combat again that made Jethan sound uneasy, but he got the feeling there was more to it.

"What's wrong, tehnaak?"

Jethan shook his head, his nose wrinkling as if he

smelled something foul. "It's just the way my aunt was watching you, like she'd found a new favorite pet."

"Ah, that. I'm kind of getting used to it. From where she's standing, I'm just another tool in her arsenal." Another weapon to be deployed.

"Yes, but you're so much more than that. I hate that she can't... that she *won't* see you for who you are outside of your potential as a weapon."

Kasiel smiled at his tehnaak. "Usually, I'm the naïve one."

Jethan shook his head at him, a reluctant grin cracking his features. "True. I prefer it that way."

When they arrived at the tavern, the rest of the unit was already there. Tath sat at one end of the bench against the wall, Darro's arm wrapped around her shoulders. Then Kince and Wedro with Etris at the far end, the Speaker looking ill-at-ease among them. She was a welcome part of their unit now, but Chander's loss still hung heavy over the group, and her discomfort made it clear how obvious that was.

Merrin, Avris, and Nerith sat across from them. The three women had become closer since their mission to rescue Jethan, though a slight tension rose between Avris and Nerith whenever Kasiel was around. He suspected Nerith knew he and Avris had slept together. It hadn't been a manifestation of romantic love, just a dash of attraction and the intense need for comfort. Still, it had changed his relationship with Avris, creating a closeness and physical ease between them he didn't share with the other women in the group. Something Nerith appeared to have noticed.

Jethan claimed a spot next to Avris, bumping Nerith down to sit between him and Kasiel, who took a seat at the end of the bench to accommodate Irith. Once they settled, each with a mug of Vanrian Black Mead before them, Jethan turned to Kasiel, waiting for him to break the news. It was an odd thing, considering this unit had been under Jethan's command when he first met them all on their mission to bring him to Vanris from the southern kingdom of Fallend. Now they were his unit.

"We're being sent out." With just a few words, he captured their full attention. "We'll be going into the Break to the ruins of Riftwater under Dhomen Sorval's command. There's an Alliance company gathering south of there. The goal is to keep them out of the town and see if we can figure out what they're after. We leave in the morning." Nerith's fingers wound through his, tightening on his hand. Dread twisted in his gut. She wouldn't like what he was going to say next. His gaze moved to Tath. "The dhomen has enough healers in his company, so they want ours to stay behind."

"What?"

It wasn't clear whether Nerith or Tath exclaimed the word first, but Nerith aggressively extracted her hand from his and both women stared at him as if this were his fault.

Kasiel cringed inwardly. "The khevarin doesn't want to risk more healers if it's not necessary." At least he had someone else to place the blame on. An individual they couldn't argue with.

"That's horseshit," Tath snapped. "We're a unit. We should go out together."

"Do we get to take your kanodrak?" Kince asked, ignoring the tension at the table.

Kasiel seized on the question, eager to escape the anger of the two healers. "I assume so. I won't go without Niske."

Nerith hit his arm. Slight as she was, she packed impressive power into that swing. "You won't go without her, but you'll leave me here?"

Kasiel rubbed his arm and looked at her, catching Avris's smirk from further down the bench before she hid it behind her mug of mead. Jethan leaned back a fraction and gestured to Nerith's head, raising his brows as if to ask whether Kasiel would like him to use his Charmer ability on her. Kasiel negated the idea with a subtle shake of his head, trying not to chuckle at his tehnaak's audacity. That would only raise Nerith's ire.

He met her eyes. "You know I would rather have you with me."

"Do you think I can't tell when you're lying?" Nerith countered, her sharp tone making it clear how she felt about that.

He drew a deep breath, his gaze flickering to Darro and Tath, who were engaged in a quiet conversation punctuated by several light kisses. Tath was smiling. He sighed and met Nerith's eyes again.

"You're right. I'd rather not put you in danger, but it isn't because I doubt you. I've seen you fight." He leaned in and gave her a light kiss, encouraged when she didn't avoid it or pull away. Drawing back a fraction, his lips still almost touching hers, he said, "Can we talk about it later?"

"It had better be a very compelling conversation." She kissed him then, a soft lingering kiss that reassured him they would get past this.

After an hour spent enjoying the unit's company over tavern food and a few rounds of mead, they split up earlier than usual. They had responsibilities the next morning that required them to be awake and alert. Kasiel, Jethan, and Nerith went to drop Irith at the cliff cat enclosure together. Jethan split off when they reached the private quarters in the palace.

By the time Kasiel had pulled out his clothing and equipment for the next day, Nerith was curled in the bed, her eyes closed. She looked peaceful. Knowing how fierce she could be, he found the image endearingly deceptive. He stripped down, snuffed out the last wall sconce, leaving one candle burning next to the bed, and climbed in beside her.

"Kas?" she murmured.

Good, she was still awake. He didn't want to leave with this conflict hanging between them. "Yes."

"If you find yourself compelled to try saving anyone out there, could you do me a favor?"

He rolled onto his side and brushed a lock of hair away from her eyes. Those unusual lavender eyes that he could contentedly gaze into for hours on end. "What favor?"

"Before you go charging in, make sure you'll be able to save yourself too. You're still recovering from the injury to your arm. You're not in any condition for heroics."

She was right, but he couldn't promise her that. If someone in his unit was in trouble, he knew himself too well to believe he would stay out of it. "Would you even like me if I didn't try to protect the people who are important to me?"

"I don't like you, Kas. I love you." She traced a line of the tattoo on his cheek with one finger. "And I love how you care so deeply, but I don't want to lose you. Promise me you'll remember that."

That was something he could give her. He doubted he would ever forget the way she was looking at him, or the words she had just said. "I promise," he whispered, taking her hand and pressing his lips to her palm.

"And Kas?"

"Hmm?" He leaned in to kiss her neck, sliding one hand down her side to the curve of her waist.

She turned her head to the side, giving him better access to the soft skin there. "Do you love me?"

"Of course." He kissed down her neck to her collarbone, moving in toward the hollow of her throat.

"Of course, what?" she asked, the question punctuated

by a soft gasp as his hand slid over to her belly and down.

He drew back to look at her. "Yes, Nerith." He placed a light kiss on her lips. "I love you." It felt unexpectedly good to admit that and see the resulting sparkle of pleasure in her eyes. He gave her a mischievous smile and slid his hand lower, drawing another gasp from her.

She pulled him in for a deeper kiss.

Niskenya shifted restlessly as Kasiel soared along behind the eyes of a raptor above them. He had his tethdraks gathered at the back of the company. Dhomen Sorval sat his mount alongside them. The man's horse was over a foot shorter than the kanodrak, forcing Kasiel into the uncomfortable position of having to look down on his commanding officer when they spoke. It didn't appear to bother Sorval, perhaps because he was too busy staring at the blade-like front fangs that dipped below the huge predator's jaw to have noticed the disparity.

The rest of the company waited on them, also mounted on horseback. Kasiel controlled the horses closest to his tethdraks and the kanodrak to keep them from panicking around the predators. Irith lurked alongside him, the big cliff cat dwarfed by Niskenya.

"Check to see if the ruins are still empty," Sorval advised. "We need to know if we're going to have to fight our way in or not. If the Alliance isn't in the town, do a sweep to see if they are making their approach yet."

Kasiel nodded, investing himself fully in the sand-hawk so he could see through its eyes and hear through its ears. Adjusting to the altered color spectrum and field of vision was almost instantaneous now. He located their company first, waiting at the entrance to a narrow valley between two towering plateaus. Using that to orient himself, he sent the raptor to the opposite end of the valley toward their target, the ruined town of Riftwater. The mostly frozen trickle of a creek that ran down the center of the valley gave the location its name. A hint of snow dotted the tops of the plateaus. Almost a week had passed since the last snowfall in the area, but lingering cold, dry winter air preserved those patches of white.

The first thing he noticed as he soared over with the hawk was that the town was about to be occupied. A company of around fifty Alliance soldiers was entering the south end of the ruins. They had an empty wagon in their midst, which suggested an intention to fill it.

Curious, he dove in closer, swooping down to perch on a half-collapsed rooftop as the soldiers rode past, numerous spears, bows, and crossbows among them. Weapons that were more useful against beasts than swords were. Not a surprise, since the success of the campaign to drive the southern forces out of Vanrian territory could largely be ascribed to their Ferals. No matter how much of Edmund's elixir Pandrean Alliance soldiers used to shield themselves from mind-crafters, it couldn't protect them from a pack of rampaging tethdraks or cliff cats.

A man riding to the right of the wagon, with three red and gold braids on the shoulder of his surcoat marking him as an Alliance captain, shouted orders to his soldiers. "I want two scouts to ride to the north end and keep an eye out for company. Our target should be in the cellar of a house toward the center of the town. We find it, get it loaded, *carefully*, and get out of here."

Whatever they were after was fragile. That was interesting.

Without the slightest warning that he had noticed the sandhawk, the captain gestured in its direction. A soldier in front raised his bow and fired at the bird.

Kasiel got it airborne fast enough to avoid a fatal strike, but the arrow clipped one wing, sending a flash of sympathetic pain through him as the raptor tumbled to the ground. The bird struggled to its feet, dragging a broken wing that refused to fold in properly. The captain halted his horse and dismounted, his company stopping with him.

"Remember," he said, drawing his sword as he approached the hawk, "we have reliable information now suggesting that the Warden's son can see through the eyes of his beasts. We're not sure about other Vanrian Ferals, but it's safer to assume that they can as well. That leads to the obvious conclusion that they could use creatures like this sandhawk as scouts. Don't take chances out here. Kill any beasts you see lurking in the area."

He raised the sword. Kasiel released his connection to the raptor before the blade fell, guilt twisting in his chest. Another bird dead because of him. If they knew he could see through the eyes of beasts now, then it wouldn't be the last to die, either. But how did they know? Unless...

He ground his teeth.

Danica.

They would have questioned her after she returned with the messenger, assuming she had. Or perhaps an Alliance source on the Vanrian side sold the information, but Danica had plenty of opportunities to watch him using his ability when she was traveling with them. He had been a greater fool than he realized for taking her to Vanris with them.

He faced Sorval. "An Alliance force is entering the town. About fifty soldiers, many with ranged weapons or spears. They have an empty wagon with them, so they're expecting to collect something."

The dhomen gave a stern nod. "A few more soldiers than we have, but your beasts should balance the odds even with their weaponry. Return to your unit, Ahnin-veth Kasiel. Keep an eye on our friends in the town and have your Speaker alert me if anything changes. When we get close enough to charge, weave your tethdraks in with the front line." Raising his voice, he shouted a quick recap of Kasiel's report, finishing with, "Our goal is to keep them from getting whatever they're after. Let's move!"

A nervous flutter spread through Kasiel's chest as he let the company go ahead of him and moved back with his unit. Heading in so closely matched in numbers didn't make him feel good about the situation, but Sorval was right; one tethdrak was equal to several soldiers in combat, and he had twenty. Niskenya and Irith could have been the same creature for the eager energy passing through his links with them. He didn't share their excitement.

The company increased its speed to a controlled canter or extended trot for most of the horses. For Niskenya, it was an easy lope. A pace she could keep up for hours. Kasiel grabbed the saddle grip with his left hand. His right arm didn't have the strength to hold on for long periods. It had begun aching insistently within a few hours of getting on the road after leaving Etrion.

As they moved, he reached out with his ability, searching for a bird to give him a view of the town. He didn't want to risk another one yet, but he had his orders. At some point, he needed to tell Sorval their enemy knew he could see through the eyes of his beasts, but that would have to wait.

"What are we looking at?" Darro asked, coming up alongside him.

"Around fifty soldiers, many armed for beasts. We'll need to watch out for ranged weapons, though being in the back should help with that." Kasiel found a smaller bird this time. Its size would make it a harder target for Alliance archers. "They took down my sandhawk. They know I can see through the eyes of my creatures now."

"How..." Jethan trailed off when Kasiel gave him a dour look. "You think it was Dani?"

"It's certainly possible."

"It was going to get to them eventually with or without her," Kince said, being uncommonly supportive for him. "There's always someone willing to feed information to the other side for the right price."

Darro glanced at his tehnaak. "You all right?"

Kince gave him an irritable sneer. "What? I don't have to be a calloch all the time."

"That's news to me," Darro countered.

To Kasiel's shock, Kince chucked a dagger at his tehnaak, unconcerned by the fact that they were moving along at a good clip. His gut squeezed into a tiny ball of panic, but somehow, Darro caught the weapon by the hilt.

He tossed it casually back to Kince. "Nice try, calloch."

Kince chuckled, catching and sheathing the weapon.

Kasiel glanced over at Jethan who rolled his eyes and asked, "What do you think the odds are of our entire unit making it through the battle alive?"

Kasiel let Niskenya and Irith's wild energy move through him. He grinned. "I'll be impressed if we make it *to* the battle."

He began moving his tethdraks into position, sending a calming influence out to all the horses as he did so. Riftwater was visible at the end of the valley. Using the new bird he had sent toward the town, he spotted a rider come up around a building near the north end. The man turned to stare down the street that opened onto the narrow valley they were advancing through. The Vanrian company broke into a full gallop.

Kasiel's bird dove in close enough to see the alarm in the Alliance soldier's eyes as the man spun his mount and kicked it to a gallop. He reached for a small horn tied to his belt. When he raised it to his lips, Kasiel slipped into the mind of his horse, making the animal skid to a stop and rear, going up high enough that it tipped over backwards, falling on top of its rider. The horse flailed for a second, then righted itself and surged to its feet. The soldier lay staring up at the sky, wheezing bubbles of blood between his lips, the horn crushed on the ground next to him.

Kasiel's stomach turned, and he sent the bird deeper in, not wanting to linger over the damage he had done. Even without the horn's warning, it was a matter of seconds before the sound of their approach alerted the Alliance force gathered near the heart of the town. He hoped they would run, but the captain ordered them to defend their position. A bold, but foolish move, considering he couldn't know yet what they were up against.

Someone blared a horn near where the captain was, and another answered from the south end of town. The Alliance soldiers were too far from the north edge of the ruins to get there before the leading line of the Vanrian force charged through. Kasiel bounced between his tethdraks, getting different views as they sprinted ahead of the horses and took out the first enemy riders. In seconds, his beasts alone had neutralized no less than nine Alliance soldiers, already balancing out the odds.

His unit hung back with him, letting the rest of their force go in with his tethdraks. They weren't here to ride into the fray. They had a job, and that was to keep their Feral ahninveth safe while his beasts tore through the enemy, leaving carnage in their wake. This was what he hated about being a Feral. The gruesome devastation. Then again, it had helped him keep his companions alive on more than one occasion.

"Why didn't the captain retreat?"

"What?" Jethan asked, moving closer.

Kasiel didn't respond. He wasn't looking for an

answer. He was merely pondering aloud while he had his focus split between controlling the tethdraks and scouting with the bird. What if the Alliance captain had a reason to believe holding their ground wasn't a foolish move? What if he knew something they didn't?

Kasiel sent the bird up, scanning for more troops in the area. He soared out past the edge of town to the south. When he spotted nothing that way, he swept around toward the west. Almost immediately, he saw a dust cloud rising from one of the larger slot canyons outside the southwest edge of town.

"Etris!" Deepening his connection, he took the bird out and over the canyon and found another Alliance unit plunging along the passage at full speed.

He sucked in a sharp breath as the pain of one of his tethdraks taking a spear in the shoulder lanced through him. Pulling that beast back, he let a couple of Vanrian soldiers move in to continue the fight.

"You needed me?"

Kasiel drew back from the bird and tethdraks enough to give Etris some of his attention. "Tell the dhomen's Speaker that there's another unit about twenty strong coming up through a slot canyon approaching the west side of town."

Etris was silent a moment, her gaze turning inward. While he waited, Kasiel moved through his tethdraks, helping them pick targets and trying to keep more of them from getting injured.

Etris finally turned her attention back to him. "Dhomen Sorval says to take your unit and intercept them. You can pull half your tethdraks if you need them."

Kasiel nodded. "Let's go! We've got a flanking unit coming in around the west side," he shouted.

It surprised him how many eager, almost predatory grins answered him as he turned to lead them out of the valley around the edge of the town. Along the way, he drew on half of his tethdraks, taking them out of fights where the Vanrian company appeared to have the upper hand. The injured one he moved to the back and made it stay there where it would be out of harm's way until a healer could tend it.

Darro and Kince took point, pulling ahead of him, followed quickly by Avris, Merrin, and Wedro. Jethan stayed beside Kasiel along with Etris whose primary purpose was to serve as a means of communication with the main company, and Irith, who he saw no point in risking for now. The Alliance force was emerging from the slot canyon as Kasiel's unit arrived. The confidence with which their opponents charged out to meet their small group of only eight soldiers turned to alarm when nine tethdraks raced out of the town to join the fray.

Darro and Merrin raced into the heart of the fight, blades moving with impressive speed and accuracy. Kasiel brought a tethdrak in to take the horse out from under an Alliance soldier trying to flank Avris. Like him, she probably shouldn't be in the middle of a fight yet after the injuries she sustained in Sharith, but she had a stubborn streak, so he settled for assisting her with a couple of his beasts rather than trying to order her back out.

Kasiel released the bird when an arrow narrowly missed his head, turning more attention to his immediate surroundings. Another arrow flew past, only this one was going in the opposite direction, finding a home in the neck of the Alliance archer who had fired on him.

Turning, he saw four riders galloping toward them, all wearing black leather armor with dark metal reinforcements, like his own. His father rode in the lead on his impressive black stallion, the woman next to him in the process of lowering her bow. Kasiel extended his influence to their horses as they came up alongside Niskenya.

Arhk looked over the battle. "I see you found a way

to put yourself at risk again."

"Someone had to keep them from flanking our force," Kasiel snapped.

"And you assigned yourself that responsibility?"

Kasiel's lip rose in a silent snarl that Niskenya and Irith both reflected. "I'm following orders."

Arhk nodded as if he had known that. He glanced at Kasiel's injured arm, seeming unconcerned by the fight raging several yards away. "Are you applying yourself in your training with Farren?"

With Kasiel's hackles already up and the bloodlust of the tethdraks flowing through him, there was little chance of the conversation going well. "I don't need your supervision. I'm not a child anymore. You missed that part."

Arhk narrowed his eyes, black starting to swirl in at the edges as a sense of pressure moved across the battle-field. "Pull your beasts back and go help in town, Ahn-inveth. We'll finish up here."

At a nod from Kasiel, Etris sent out the order. He kept his tethdraks out to run interference while his unit pulled out and Arhk's group moved in, flinching when another beast in the town took a hit.

The area grew darker, as if a thundercloud had rolled over. Several enemy soldiers, realizing what was happening, turned their mounts and fled. Arhk and his guards gave chase.

Once his last tethdrak was clear, Kasiel turned away, leading his unit toward town. A quick bounce between his tethdraks among the buildings told him the fight there was nearly done.

Jethan trotted up beside him. "You know, your father could actually be trying to establish a relationship with you."

Kasiel shrugged it off. "If so, he's terrible at it."

"He may not be the only one."

A red flash of rage swept across his vision. Irith, responding to his temper, snarled at Jethan, startling his horse, even with Kasiel's influence calming the animal. Fortunately, Jethan was an excellent rider. He moved with the animal, pulling it quickly back under control. He flashed an angry glare at Kasiel before trotting ahead. Kince, Darro, Merrin, and Wedro went with him.

"Nicely done," Avris said as she followed them.

Etris rode up beside him. "What just happened?"

Kasiel's anger with himself pushed aside his frustration with his father. "Go with them. They have the right of it."

Etris shrugged and trotted after the others.

Niskenya sent a sharp snap of disappointment across their link.

"Yes. I know. I'm an ass."

The pressure continued to increase as their surroundings grew darker, his father's Frightener ability overflowing beyond its intended area of effect. A chill of dread came along with the memories of what that ability had once done to him. He might not remember the initial incident, but he recalled the nightmares that tormented him whether he was asleep or not. With a mental nudge, he urged Niskenya to move faster.

If anything, he was acting more like his father. That wasn't who he wanted to be. He wanted to be kind the way he was raised to be. The problem was that Edmund had been the one to encourage that in him, but the professor's kindness proved to be nothing more than a wall to hide his lies behind. Everything the man did revolved around making Kasiel his docile test subject, all so he could find a better way to fight Vanrian mindcrafters. Not even for the sake of saving Alliance lives, but for the riches he stood to make from it. How was he supposed to embrace anything Edmund taught him now that he knew the truth about him? And how was kindness going to help him survive in war?

When they reached the rest of the company near the center of town, Dhomen Sorval sent them all out to search for survivors hiding in the ruins. Most people dismounted and struck out in groups of two or more. Kasiel went off on his own. With Niskenya and Irith, he had plenty of help. The kanodrak moved amongst the buildings at a casual pace, her nose and Irith's to the ground around the ruins, hunting. Kasiel let the two beasts guide their efforts while he moved his uninjured tethdraks through more of the broken-down structures.

Irith stopped outside a building, raising his head and letting out a soft chattering sound as he peered through the doorway. Kasiel hopped off Niskenya. He drew his sword and followed the cliff cat inside. Barely past the door, he had to duck under a collapsed portion of the roof. Borrowing Irith's keen hearing, he caught the sound of someone trying to muffle their panicked breathing. Irith continued to the next room, his stance sinking into a predatory prowl. He growled and Kasiel heard a quick hitch in the breathing.

Following the cat, he saw someone's leg partly visible behind a broken standing wardrobe. The cliff cat bunched as if to pounce, and Kasiel stepped out beside him.

"Irith, no." It was his intent that stopped the cat. He only said the words, speaking in Pandrean Common, for the benefit of the young Alliance soldier tucked in alongside the wardrobe, eyes wide with terror.

When Irith relaxed, the young soldier's gaze shifted up. He wasn't any older than Kasiel. He swallowed twice, shaking hard enough that the sword he held trembled in his grip. Kasiel met his eyes and gestured to the weapon with his dark metal blade.

The youth dropped it, raising his hands in surrender. "Please, don't kill me. I don't want to die like this."

He licked his lips, his gaze darting between Kasiel and Irith. "You can understand me, right?"

"Everyone in Vanris speaks Pandrean Common." Kasiel answered. "Why are you in Riftwater?"

The youth's gaze moved to take in the braids in Kasiel's hair and the winged ear cuffs that symbolically completed his cut ears. His eyes widened again. "You're the Warden's son. The one raised by Professor Danovan."

Kasiel wasn't sure why that made the youth look less afraid. Maybe he thought being raised in the south created a connection between them, one that would help prolong his life. Kasiel wasn't in a hurry to kill him, but that had nothing to do with it. It could easily be him or Jethan standing there pleading for their life. He should have let Irith take care of the youth, but now, after looking him in the eyes, how could he kill him?

"That's why your company's here, isn't it? There's a store of the professor's elixirs somewhere in town?" Kasiel didn't need an answer. They were after something fragile. What else would be worth the risk of coming back out here?

The youth hesitated.

Kasiel lowered his sword. It wasn't as if the weapon was his primary defense when he had Irith standing between them.

The Alliance soldier watched the blade sink. Then he met Kasiel's eyes. "The troops stationed here didn't have time to collect the elixirs before they were driven out. I think the council in Sarket is hoping our alchemists can use them to figure out how to make more." When Kasiel narrowed his eyes at that, the youth took off the satchel slung over his shoulder and tossed it to the ground. "Please. I don't have any on me. You can check. I just want to get out of here. I can't die like–"

Irith's ears flicked back an instant before a crossbow bolt plowed through the youth's throat, passing out the other side to sink deep into the wall. He fell back, grabbing at his neck. Blood spurted around his fingers. His lips moved, but no sound came out. Slowly, his legs gave under him, and he crumpled to the floor, his eyes glazing over.

Kasiel's chest constricted, sorrow and shame warring for dominance there. He glanced through Irith's eyes when the cat turned around to face Kince, who was lowering his crossbow.

Kasiel couldn't look away from the young soldier's face. He had hazel eyes. "I'm sorry. I just thought, maybe..."

Kince's hand rested on his shoulder. "Your heart is why we all love you, Kas. It's not something you should ever apologize for or consider a weakness." He walked over to pick up the satchel from the floor. "Now get out of here. Go find your tehnaak. You owe him an apology."

By the time Kasiel found Jethan, Arhk and his three guards had already departed for Etrion, leaving him to wonder how and why the group had shown up there to begin with. Dhomen Sorval's company had scoured the ruins of Riftwater, then gathered back near the center where several smashed-apart crates of Edmund's elixir burned. When the substance was completely destroyed, the dhomen had a group of soldiers ride down and place a banner outside the south end of the ruined town. It bore the symbol of a sword in the ground with the sun setting behind it in silver on a deep purple background. It was, Darro explained, a promise that the Alliance could come collect their dead without fear of attack. A courtesy being offered because they were in the Crimson Break and not within the borders of Vanris. And because, with Edmund gone, Vanris had quickly regained the upper hand.

Jethan, in his typical fashion, shrugged off Kasiel's apology. From his pensive silence during the ride back to Etrion, Kasiel got the sense that the hurt caused by his actions still needed tending. A problem better addressed at home perhaps, where they could discuss it in private.

As soon as they reached the towering black gates of the city, Dhomen Sorval dismissed the company. They had, he said, earned a break with their crushing victory over the Alliance force in Riftwater. Kasiel didn't follow the rest of them through the gates. He needed to ride around the side of the city and return Niskenya and the tethdraks to their proper habitats. By some unspoken accord, his unit stayed back with him. They had come out of the encounter with nothing more than a few shallow cuts and bruises. Some others hadn't been as fortunate, though there had at least been no fatalities on the Vanrian side.

Avris absently scratched the base of her horse's neck, glancing around at them. "Shall we meet at the tavern in, say, two hours? That should give everyone enough time to wash off the stink. Especially you, beast boy," she added with a teasing smile for Kasiel.

He patted Niskenya's shoulder. "I see not everyone appreciates your delicate perfume, Niske."

The kanodrak answered with a huff that earned her several tired chuckles.

"Two hours," Darro agreed, getting nods from the others.

They split up, and Kasiel returned the tethdraks and Niskenya to their habitats. When that was done, he went to the palace with Irith. The big cat expressed no interest in retiring to his habitat. He preferred running around the palace and city with Kasiel. Niskenya no doubt would have chosen the same if she were small enough to navigate those spaces.

It was a pleasant surprise to find a hot, scented bath prepared in his bathing room. The heated water eased his aching muscles, freeing his mind to think about what had gone wrong in Riftwater. His interactions with his father and Jethan. His failure to deal with the Alliance soldier hiding in the house the way he should have. Though he couldn't convince himself that Kince's handling of it was right, either.

Irith attempted to drink from the tub, forcing Kasiel to chase him out with a sharp mental poke. When he came out to get dressed, the big cat was curled up on the bottom two-thirds of his bed.

"That's not for you either." He nudged the beast back to the floor with a thought as he pulled on some trousers.

Someone knocked on the outer door, the firmness and cadence telling him he wouldn't have to waste time looking for Jethan.

"Come in."

The other youth entered the sitting area, scratching Irith behind the ears when the big cat trotted up to greet him. Kasiel scowled at the scars on his arm where they had opened it to align the compound fracture from Itana's mace before pulling on a simple ivory shirt. Jethan wandered past him into the bedroom without a word and went to sit on the far side of the bed, leaning against the headboard.

Kasiel laced his shirt as he walked over and sat on the opposite side. "About what happened in Riftwater—"

"It's not a big deal."

"It is," he snapped, frustrated with Jethan's avoidance. Then he checked himself. This was exactly the kind of behavior he was trying to apologize for. "I lost my temper and I let it manifest through Irith toward the one person who means more to me than anyone else. I shouldn't have done that."

Jethan arched a brow at him. "Anyone else?"

Kasiel gave him a well-deserved eye roll. "Yes. Granted, I'd rather not have to choose between you and Nerith, but you are my tehnaak, and the person who keeps me going even when things get overwhelming. But even if that weren't the case, I shouldn't be letting my temper influence my ability."

"That's true." Jethan shrugged his shoulders, avoiding

Kasiel's gaze. "Still, you are a Feral, Kas. The moment we found out what you were, I knew it would make things difficult. I don't like how much of you I lose to Niskenya and Irith, but your beasts are part of who you are. I have to accept that."

Kasiel itched to smack sense into him, though he wasn't sure which of them needed it more. "You also have to accept that I care about you too much to be pushing you away. Don't let me do something I'll regret for the rest of my life, Jeth. I need you to keep calling me out like you've done before. I will get it through my thick skull, eventually. It's easy to retreat into my links with Niske or Irith when things get hard, but you're my tehnaak. I need... I *want* to be here for you."

Jethan looked at him, tension working the muscles in his jaw. "If that's true, then open up to me. Tell me why you're so angry lately."

He held up his right arm. "This doesn't help."

"It's more than that," Jethan insisted.

Kasiel leaned back against the carved headboard and closed his eyes. "I've been thinking about my life in Fernwallow. Days spent practicing reading and writing. Learning to recognize herbs and brew medicinal teas. Helping around the house and garden. Finding my first love in Danica. I hated having to hide my cut ears so no one would know what I really was, but aside from that, life was so much simpler. So peaceful."

He drew a deep breath and opened his eyes, not wanting to see the memories that accompanied his next words. "How many people have I killed with my beasts? With my own hands? With plans I've helped make? In less than a year, Jeth. I have so many people in my life I care about now, and I worry every day about losing them. The people I've killed had someone who feared losing them too.

"And it's not just that. Now I'm expected to be

an officer, making calls I don't feel qualified to make. What if taking the beasts in first in Sharith had been the wrong decision? What if I had missed something critical while scouting over Riftwater? Being a Feral is incredible, and yet sometimes I hate it so much. I have a constant storm of anger, guilt, and fear riding on my shoulders, looking for any excuse to break free. I don't know what to do with it."

Irith leapt onto the bed and sank to his belly between them, pushing his nose into Kasiel's arm. Kasiel sighed and shook his head at the cat. "Don't worry, you big calloch. I don't hate you."

Jethan smiled at him. It was an expression rich with sympathy and affection. "See, all you have to do is talk to me." He reached over to scratch Irith's head along one of the two slate blue stripes that ran from his black nose all the way to his tail. "I can't change what you are or stop them from calling on us to fight. I can say that how much you care is part of what makes you the remarkable person you are, and a good leader. Anytime you face a problem, you consider the lives of the people around you when coming up with a solution. It's why you have that pool of people you love who love you in return. People who don't want to lose you either, which is why we have to turn to each other to get through these things rather than push each other away. And remember, you may never meet some of them, but there are many people alive today who wouldn't be if not for some of the choices you've made."

Kasiel scratched behind Irith's ear on the near side. The big cat's purr vibrated the bed. "Maybe that's all true. I guess it's just hard to weigh intangible knowledge against a pile of mangled bodies stacking up in front of me."

"I know, Kas, I hate that part too. I'd worry about you a lot more if you didn't hate it."

"Like Kince?"

Jethan shook his head. "Oh, Kince does hate it. He also hates himself. Every person he kills is a piece of himself he's destroying."

That was a darker response than Kasiel had expected. Much darker. "You're serious?"

Jethan nodded.

"Why?"

"You can't tell him I told you about this."

Kasiel nodded, his curiosity piqued.

"One of his first missions was a night battle in a town like Sharith. He became separated from the rest of his unit and got spooked while moving alone through the dark streets. When a figure came running out of the shadows at him, he panicked. He shot them with his crossbow. It turned out to be his older sister. She was part of the same unit and had come searching for him. He's always been a lethal shot with that thing. Darro's the only reason Kince didn't kill himself after that."

Kasiel swallowed. What had happened with Danica was bad enough. He couldn't imagine trying to live with killing your own sibling. How hard must that have made it for Kince to shoot Ahrin that night outside of Andaro? His friend. Tath's tehnaak. And Kasiel had screamed at him for it. It was a wonder the man didn't despise him.

"I can't believe you let this beast get on your bed."

Kasiel looked down at where Irith had joyfully kneaded his claws clear through the top layers of his bedding. He sighed. "I don't."

Jethan laughed and hopped off the bed. "Come on. It's early yet, but maybe we can get our table at the tavern. If we're lucky, we'll find a palace attendant along the way who can swap out what's left of your bedding."

Kasiel got up. Not wanting to be left behind, Irith leapt off the bed, scoring a few more runnels in the fabric in the process. Jethan looked away, failing to fully hold back another laugh.

When they arrived at the tavern, the only thing Kasiel wanted to see less than Jhanik sitting there behind a mug of mead was Nerith sitting with him. The other Feral kanodrak rider and his unit had stayed behind in Sharith to help secure the area and start rebuilding. Kasiel had dared to hope they would send him back north when that was done, since the Pandrean Alliance appeared to have abandoned their offensive.

Instead, here he was, the sides of his head freshly shaved to show the black symbols of his ke'hanoath tattooed there. He had the rest of his long blond hair pulled back into a loose braid, showing his perfect Vanrian ears. Nerith responded to something he said with a light laugh, her beautiful silvery hair left mostly down today except for one braid pulled behind her right ear.

Kasiel almost checked to be sure his long red hair covered his ears. He occasionally wore braids in it now, but unless he was in battle, where he wore the winged ear cuffs the khevarin had given him, he kept his hair over his cut ears.

"Ahninveth Kasiel! Lord Jethan!" the barkeep, Nok, greeted. "I'll get your table cleared."

"Always appreciated, Nok," Jethan called back.

A few of the other patrons nodded to them or lifted a mug in greeting. That was one thing that had changed in the last few months. After his unit brought down the professor, effectively destroying the Alliance's new advantage, the number of people who questioned his loyalties had plummeted. Stories of his role in the battle in Sharith had also earned him a bit of renown among some of the other soldiers.

The best thing that recognition had gained him so far, though, was this moment and the way Nerith turned the instant Nok called out to them, her face lighting up with a beautiful smile. With a quick word to Jhanik, she bounced to her feet and ran over to Kasiel, flinging her arms around his neck. He wrapped his arms around her waist to lift her, letting his left arm do most of the work, and captured her mouth in an ardent kiss. For an instant, it occurred to him she might not appreciate him being that forward here, but she opened her mouth to him, the taste of mead on her lips and tongue, and slid her hand into his hair.

As he eased her back to her feet, she pressed her forehead to his and whispered, "I hate you being out there without me."

He breathed a laugh. "I hate not staying here with you."

"You two are disgusting," Jethan remarked, though his smirk said he didn't mind.

She turned to smile at his tehnaak. "You're just jealous that I chipped a tiny piece of his heart out of your hands."

In the instant Jethan had Nerith's attention, Kasiel dared a glance at Jhanik. If hatred alone was enough to kill, he would be bleeding out on the floor. Since it wasn't, he grinned and offered a slight nod to counter the other man's glare. When Nerith turned back to him, he caught her lips in a soft, more chaste kiss this time.

She disengaged after a moment and slid her hand into his. As they walked past the table Jhanik was at, she stopped and picked up her mug. "Why don't you join us?"

Jhanik stood, meeting Kasiel's eyes over her head. Kasiel hoped his icy stare was adequately discouraging. Next to him, Irith's ears flattened back, the cat catching some of his irritation with the other Feral's presence.

"I've got better things to do." Jhanik lowered his gaze to Nerith, a half-hearted smile briefly lifting the corners of his mouth. "Thanks for the company. It was nice catching up." He finished his drink in one swallow, smacked the mug down on the table, and strode for the door.

Kasiel watched him leave. "Why didn't he return to Doran?"

Nerith gave him an indulgent look. "Because we might still need him down here. He may not be the most pleasant person, but he is a good Feral."

"Not the most pleasant person? I see you've upgraded him from the horse's ass you told me he was before."

"Kas." An edge of warning hardened her tone.

"Sorry. I don't like him."

"Don't like him around me, is what you mean." She squeezed his hand and continued toward the table where Jethan had settled on one end of the back bench.

"Both, if we're being honest," Kasiel answered.

He disliked that the man was a Feral kanodrak rider who ran tethdraks and that he had a long history with Nerith. It irritated him that they were similar in so many ways. What he liked even less was that, when it came to the ways in which they were different, such as Kasiel's cut ears and years of missed training, Jhanik surpassed him.

Trying to shrug off his annoyance, Kasiel claimed the spot at the end of the bench across from Jethan. Irith settled on the floor next to him and began grooming one foreleg. Nerith sat on his other side and slipped her arm through his, holding on as if she feared he might vanish.

Over the next ten minutes, the rest of their unit filtered in, finding places around the table. When they had all settled with food and drink, Tath asked for a report on the mission in Riftwater.

Kasiel glanced down the table, catching Etris's eyes. "Why don't you tell it, Etris? You were in an excellent position to see most of what happened."

The woman shifted on the bench as if unable to get comfortable. "I don't know everything that went on with your beasts."

Darro chuckled. "Does anyone know that?"

Wedro glowered at his mug, his facial scar adding to the severity of the expression. He didn't smile or joke much anymore. Kasiel desperately hoped to see that re-emerge someday, but losing Chander seemed to have broken that part of him.

"I'll fill in if necessary," Kasiel said, holding Etris's gaze. If she was going to become a genuine part of their unit – of the family it was outside of battle – she needed to interact with them more. Her voice in his head told him he was a terrible person, then she looked at the others and began recounting their mission for Nerith and Tath. Kasiel smiled and took a drink of his mead. Nerith squeezed his hand under the table.

The others quickly warmed to the telling, jumping in to add to Etris's accounting and turning it into a group effort. By the end, they were all chatting together amiably.

Avris turned to Kasiel in a brief lull. "What's our next mission, Ahninveth?"

"I'm hoping we won't have one for a while. I could use more time to train with this useless thing." He looked down at his left hand.

"I'll help you practice." There was an unnervingly dangerous edge to Merrin's voice as she made the offer.

He met her eyes. She was their unit's best fighter. He could learn a lot from her, assuming he lived through it.

"Why don't we take turns? I've got a few things I could teach you." Darro's crooked smirk promised it would be a painful process.

Kasiel nodded. "I could use the help."

Their answering smiles made him feel a little like a quail that had wandered into a pack of wolves. But he trusted them both, and there was much they could teach him.

Jethan shook his head, grinning at him. "You're asking for it." Then his eyes caught on something else in the room and his expression darkened. "You've got to be kidding."

Kasiel turned to find a palace attendant coming up behind him.

The man inclined his head. "Ahninveth Kasiel, Lord Jethan, you are required in the palace."

Some distant part of Kasiel marveled at how his limbs suddenly felt weighted down with lead. Reluctance held him to the bench like a powerful magnet. It would do him no good to ignore the summons, though, so he leaned over and gave Nerith a quick kiss before extracting himself.

He glanced at his companions. "We'll be back soon. Save us some mead."

A few minutes later they were standing in the war room before Dhomen Sorval and Khevarin Seylin, the usual smattering of guards posted at the doors. They waited inside the entrance for several minutes while Seylin and Sorval conversed in hushed voices near the table. Then a side door opened and Arhk strode in, his long black jacket with its dark metal trimmings rippling out behind him. Seylin met his eyes, and he responded with a subtle nod as he joined the two at the table. After another moment of quiet conversation, amongst all three of them now, Seylin finally acknowledged them.

"Ahninveth Kasiel, Lord Jethan, please join us." Her elegant voice had a knife edge of authority to it that cut across the distance, making a command of a politely worded request. Before they reached the table, she started speaking again. "In three days, a company will depart for Doran to escort my daughter, Khesran Velara, back here to Etrion. Your unit, Ahninveth Kasiel, will make up one half of that escort."

Before Kasiel could react, Jethan partially raised one hand, catching her attention.

She arched a brow at him. "Yes, nephew."

"It's not that I don't want to go north, Khevarin, but aren't there plenty of soldiers already in Doran who could escort Vel to Etrion?"

"Khesran Velara," she corrected, tapping her long silver nails on the table. "Perhaps if you listened to all the information before speaking, you would not need to ask that question."

Jethan lowered his gaze. "Apologies, Majesty."

She nodded and met Kasiel's eyes. "This is more than just an escort. It is an opportunity to please our people by sending a hero out among them during a time of celebration."

There was an uncomfortable tightening in Kasiel's chest. Irith pressed against his leg. He wasn't certain what she meant to imply with her mention of heroes and celebrations, nor was he sure if he really wanted to know.

Whatever she saw in his face caused a slow smile to cross her lips. She looked at Arhk, whose expression remained carefully guarded. "Your son is delightfully naïve. Perhaps he does not realize what he has done?"

Dhomen Sorval, gruff and confident as he typically seemed, shifted his feet as if her comment made even him uncomfortable.

"Perhaps that is because he did not engage in heroics for the sake of fame, Majesty," Arhk said, his tone as guarded as his expression.

"Hmm." Seylin arched one precisely shaped brow at him, then turned her gaze back to Kasiel. "Perhaps not. Regardless, we intend to parade you in front of our people, Ahninveth. The young Feral kanodrak rider whose unit destroyed the greatest weapon the Pandrean Alliance has ever brought against us and delivered its inventor to face our justice. With your tragic past, stories of your deeds – and misdeeds in some cases – have quickly captured the hearts of our people. We feel it is time they met you."

Kasiel felt like throwing up. He couldn't think of anything to say. It was as if his entire vocabulary had abandoned him.

"Fret not, young Cavenos." The fingers of one graceful hand unfurled like the petals of a flower opening to point toward Sorval. "Although Dhomen Sorval will lead the escort, we are sending Dhomvalen Arhk along to make certain you do not embarrass us."

The muscles in his father's jaw tightened, the faintest swirl of darkness moving at the edges of his eyes. Arhk left Etrion with some regularity that Kasiel had seen, so it seemed unlikely that being sent away had gotten his ire up, but something clearly did.

Kasiel found his voice hidden somewhere within his father's discomfort. "If I may ask, Majesty, who will make up the other half of the escort?"

"Ahninveth Jhanik's unit will make up the other half."

Kasiel tried to ignore the sudden foul taste in the back of his mouth. "Why?"

A flash of irritation tightened her eyes, and she cast a quick glance at Arhk. "We would hope everyone here is mature enough to set aside old rivalries for the sake of their country." Her icy gaze drilled into Kasiel. "While this mission does provide a convenient opportunity for us to lift the spirits of our people, its primary purpose is still to bring Khesran Velara to Etrion. An escort of two kanodrak riders and their revered beasts will not only keep her safe, but will also be dramatic enough to appease some of the discontent she may experience at being summoned thus."

"Why is Khesran Velara coming to Etrion, Majesty?" Jethan asked. He deflated when her sharp gaze cut into him, her lips pressed together in a tight line. "Never mind. I'll assume that information is above my rank."

"Far above."

"Aren't we needed here, Majesty?" Kasiel asked, a small part of him hoping she might have forgotten they were at war.

She gave him a long, measuring look. "The Pandrean Alliance has been hobbled, thanks in no small part to your efforts. Now you are free to provide a different service to your country."

She dismissed them a short time later with assurances that Dhomen Sorval would fill them in on the relevant details over the next few days and orders not to discuss the purpose of the mission with anyone outside of the two units involved.

They had barely stepped out of the war room when Kasiel spotted Evoker Setera walking down the hall. One of the few people who could tell him what had happened to Danica. He had tried several times to get that information out of her, but now he had another reason to ask.

"Ahninveth Setera."

She stopped and faced them. The fine pale blue lines of the tattooed symbols running down the center of her forehead to the tip of her nose added a sharpness to her appearance that was countered by her unexpectedly welcoming smile. He would have thought she would be sick of his pestering by now.

She brushed back her long, honey-colored hair and tapped an insignia on her shoulder as they approached her.

"Ahndhomen Setera," Kasiel corrected himself.

"Congratulations," Jethan added, inclining his head respectfully.

"Thank you. How can I help you, Ahninveth Kasiel? I hope you're not still trying to open closed doors."

He ignored the comment. "When I was scouting the enemy troops on our last mission, I overheard their captain talking about my ability to see through the eyes of my beasts. It occurred to me they might have learned about it from Danica, assuming we sent her back. I was concerned about what else they might learn from her if that were the case."

Setera breathed a laugh and shook her head at him. "I'm not sure whether to be impressed or annoyed by your persistence. Regardless, isn't that a risk you should have been concerned about before you brought her here?"

Kasiel absently kicked at the floor with one foot, wincing when the sole of his boot squeaked against the polished marble. "I suppose it is."

Her expression grew stern. "I know it is. With my new rank, I now have more authority to decide what information I share with you. I will tell you that, given the number of traitors we have found within our own walls, it is highly likely they got the information from another source. Knowledge that useful is hard to contain. I did extract some of the girl's memories of her time on the road with you, though that is certainly no guarantee that she was not a potential source for that information."

He tried not to feel guilty about them meddling in Danica's head, but it caused an uncomfortable aching in his chest despite his efforts. "By some, I assume you left the memories of me and Nerith," he guessed. "And the one of me choosing Jethan and my freedom over her."

Jethan placed a supportive hand on his shoulder.

Setera offered his tehnaak an approving smile before returning her solemn gaze to him. "It is better if the girl hates you, Kasiel. Now she can let you go and build her own life back where she belongs. It's a chance she's extremely lucky to have gotten."

He exhaled, the weight on his shoulders easing a fraction. "At least I know they didn't kill her."

"We were going to. It would have been the right choice, but Dhomvalen Arhk asked that we adjust her memories and send her back with the Alliance messenger instead."

Kasiel wanted to check his ears to see if they were

working right. "My father saved her?"

"Not for her sake, I assure you." Setera gave him a tight smile. "Now, I have duties to attend to. I strongly advise you to forget her, Ahninveth."

Kasiel stepped to the side and bowed his head. "Thank you, Ahndhomen."

He stayed there, staring at the polished floor after she had disappeared down a crossing hallway. That Danica lived was a relief, whether or not she hated him. As was the fact that information about his abilities was something they had expected to lose control of, regardless of the source. Those weren't the revelations that left him stumbling uncertainly through the jumbled mess of his thoughts. He was distantly aware of Irith's abrasive tongue scraping across his hand. A quick mental nudge discouraged the cliff cat from grooming him.

"Are you all right, Kas?"

He looked up at Jethan. "Do you think what she said is true?"

"About Danica?"

He gave a sharp shake of his head. "No, what the khevarin said."

Jethan shrugged and gestured down the hall with a wave of his hand, waiting until Kasiel started walking to fall in alongside him. "Why would she lie?"

"I don't know, but I'd like her to be lying. I have no desire to be a hero."

Jethan smiled. "Excellent. That makes you perfect for the role."

"This isn't a joke."

Jethan was silent.

Kasiel half-turned toward him for a few strides, holding his arms out. "Do I look like a hero to you?"

"More so than you might think, especially on your kanodrak wearing those great earpieces." He used one finger to mime the shape of a wing over his own ear. "I mean, Kas, the khevarin had special ear cuffs made for you. And you have three tattoos of recognition from her. Do you know how few people can say that?"

He scowled, which he suspected by the wrinkling of Jethan's brow wasn't the expected reaction. "Maybe she planned this all along."

"Would it matter if she had? It wouldn't have worked if you hadn't risen to the occasion. This isn't something that happened to you. It's something you did."

"With a lot of help." He felt a gentle, concerned prodding in his mind from Niskenya. How could he explain this to a kanodrak? He pushed back with a touch of reassurance. Yes, something was bothering him, but it wasn't anything she could help with, and he wouldn't die from it. "And this horse shit about my tragic past."

"Kas, I think anyone would agree that you have a tragic past."

"Maybe, but I didn't even know it was tragic until less than a year ago." Ellaris. His mother's name danced across his thoughts. One day, he would find the courage to ask someone about her, but, in a way, it was easier not knowing what he had missed out on.

"Are you sure that doesn't make it more tragic?"

He threw up his hands. "I don't know."

A scoundrel smile curved Jethan's lips. "Well, maybe you can just embrace this hero stuff for your tehnaak's sake. There's this girl in Doran I'd love to impress."

Kasiel breathed a laugh and punched him in the shoulder.

"Ow." Jethan laughed as he rubbed his shoulder. "Some people have no sense of humor." His expression sobered. "Do you want to invite everyone to your rooms since we can't talk about this in the tavern?"

Kasiel glanced at the cliff cat. "Can you go get them? I think I'll take Irith back to his habitat for tonight."

Jethan gave him a slight, jesting bow. "As you

command, Ahninveth."

They parted ways at the palace exit. Kasiel struck out for the entrance to the cliff cat enclosures beyond the building that overlooked the canyons where the kano-draks and tethdraks were. The cliff cats liked to climb and were fond of small shelter caves, so their habitat was in a set of less impressive canyons, with natural and artificial shelters dug into the walls. He watched for a few minutes while a new litter of cubs mauled Irith near the entrance, dragging him into their play. It surprised him how gentle the large predator could be.

Unlike some wildcats, the cliff cats nurtured the young of their species regardless of relation. They were solitary creatures much of the time, but they sometimes cooperated for hunts and the enrichment of the next generations. Working with Irith gave him the opportunity to learn a great deal about the creatures, despite them not being his specialty when running beasts in battle.

He almost stopped by the other canyons to visit Niskenya and check on the tethdraks injured in the fighting in Riftwater, but he knew he would linger even longer than he had here. Growing up, he had never noticed a particular affinity for creatures, but since the awakening of his Feral ability, he found himself consistently drawn to them.

A hero?

He shook his head, negating the idea, and reached out to Niskenya for the simple comfort of her powerful presence. She tugged at him, encouraging him to visit, but he answered with images of sunrise, promising as best he could that he would go see her in the morning.

When he reached his rooms, the rest of the unit was there. They had acquired a second couch and a few more chairs from somewhere. Two platters of food, already heavily picked over, sat on the table along with mugs and four stoneglass bottles of Vanrian Black Mead, one empty and another halfway there.

"If it isn't the hero of Vanris," Darro declared, lifting his mug.

The others followed suit. Kasiel gave Jethan a sour look that his tehnaak answered with a wink as he also raised his mug.

Avris bounded over to Kasiel and took his face in her hands. Her eyes were bright with excitement. "We get to go to Doran!" She punctuated the exclamation with a firm kiss before twirling away. Then stopped herself mid-spin and looked back at him, an enormous grin on her face. "Oh, we need to teach Kas some of our dances."

Still trying to catch up, Kasiel looked at Nerith where she stood near the fire, hoping Avris's enthusiastic welcome hadn't gotten him in trouble. She set her mug on the hearth and walked to him, sliding one arm over his shoulder. Bringing up her other hand, she brushed her thumb across his lips, then kissed him possessively as if to reassert her claim over the territory another woman had briefly invaded.

She stepped back and met his eyes. "You finally get to see what we're fighting for."

Around them, the others were pushing the chairs to the edges of the room. Kince wandered through with a stoneglass bottle, checking that everyone had a full mug of mead. By chance, the changes in their unit, the losses of Ahrin and Chander, left them with an equal number of men and women. Avris paired Kasiel with Nerith and Tath with Darro. Then she put Kince and Etris together, and herself with Jethan. Wedro and Merrin volunteered to make some dubious semblance of music using a combination of utensils, platters, and the wooden table.

For the better part of the next two hours, they turned his sitting room into a dance floor, teaching him an array of exhausting Vanrian festival dances. There was more laughter and cheer among them than Kasiel had ever seen. Nerith eventually convinced Wedro and Merrin to abandon their musical performances and join the dancing. For the first time since Chander's death, Kasiel saw Wedro crack a genuine smile. He even laughed when he and Merrin careened into Tath and Darro during a particularly lively demonstration, ending up in a tangle on the floor.

Once all four stoneglass bottles were empty, Jethan *persuaded* an attendant to bring more. He then led them through several court dances, the last of which turned out to be as lively as some of the festival ones. When those were done, Kasiel, who had never danced so much in his life, collapsed on one couch. Nerith flopped down next to him, smiling and breathing hard. He took her hand and rested his head back.

"I think it's time we called it a night," Darro said, pulling Tath against his chest and kissing her flushed cheek. She leaned into him and closed her eyes. He met Kasiel's eyes. "Since we'll be heading out of town for a while, Merrin and I will join you for your session with Farren tomorrow and find out how he'd like us to manage your training."

Kasiel sank back into reality, the high from an evening of revelry slipping away. He didn't know enough about where they were going to share their enthusiasm, though seeing them all this excited did a great deal to lift his spirits. "Thank you. I appreciate it."

Merrin reached down to pat him on the shoulder, a wicked smirk curving her lips. "We'll see how long you appreciate it once we've started training."

The others wandered out, leaving him with Jethan, his feet up on the table alongside one empty platter, and Nerith, sitting next to Kasiel with her eyes closed as her breathing gradually slowed to normal.

Kasiel stared up at the ceiling. As much as he loved everyone's energy for the journey, he still didn't like the implication that he was some kind of hero. Seylin's words suggested he would be an object of curiosity and fascination on this mission, under constant scrutiny. Not a prospect he was especially comfortable with.

"Do you think the khevarin encouraged stories to be spread about me?"

Jethan started laughing. "Please, Nerith, take his mind off this."

Nerith opened her eyes and answered with a crooked little smile. "I can do that, but you may have to leave first."

Jethan hopped to his feet and strode to the door. He stopped with his hand on the lever. "See you in the morning, tehnaak. Don't stay up too much later." Then he winked and left them.

Nerith straddled Kasiel's lap and tilted her head to one side, smiling at him. "What do you think? Can I get your mind off this hero thing?"

He stared into her lavender eyes, bringing one hand up to brush some of her hair behind her ear. "You already have."

The next three days they spent preparing for departure. Merrin and Darro joined Kasiel for his combat training with Farren. The enthusiasm with which they took up the mantle of torturing him with his limitations made him wonder if he had made the wisest decision by accepting their help. Still, he had to learn. His right arm might never work again the way it had before the unplanned encounter with General Itana's mace.

He and Jhanik were to run a small unit of five tethdraks each, plus their kanodraks and companion beasts, along with the soldiers who supported them. That meant Jhanik would have six tethdraks, whereas Kasiel had the odd addition of a single cliff cat. He had worked with Kenna enough after she first brought Irith to him to be comfortable managing the cat's needs over the journey. The animal was intelligent, though not to the extent Niskenya was, and the tethdraks tolerated him. They weren't above reprimanding him with a firm nip when he got too close the way they might a juvenile, but Irith was a lethal fighter in his own right. His superior agility helped him perfect the art of dodging around the bigger beasts.

There was a different feel to his unit when they struck out this time. Excitement animated them. They smiled and joked as they followed the road north toward the black crags that made up Vareyl's Warning and the lands beyond. They weren't heading into conflict for once. Instead, they were going away from the fighting to more peaceful parts of the country. Jethan, Nerith, and Wedro had all grown up in Doran, so they had family and friends there. The rest, except for Etris, had lived close enough prior to being stationed in Etrion to feel at home in the northern capital.

For Kasiel, every step they took north of Etrion would be new. He was trying hard to embrace curiosity and excitement instead of trepidation, but the khevarin's talk of heroes didn't help with that. Implied expectation hung over his head like a storm cloud. He did his best to keep that hidden, though, not wanting his mood to bring down that of his companions.

They had been on the road for an hour now. Jhanik's unit had moved ahead, staying close to Dhomen Sorval at the front. Kasiel and his unit hung back behind a division created by Arhk and the three black-armored guards who accompanied him on his forays outside of the city. The four rode in a loose formation, with one guard on either side of the dhomvalen and the third behind. Kasiel had yet to see any of them engage in casual conversation with each other the way soldiers in the two Feral-led units did.

"You know..." Jethan trailed off as if still contemplating what he wanted to say.

Something in his thoughtful tone struck an alarm in Kasiel. He followed the direction of his tehnaak's gaze to the same group of four riders he had been watching and shook his head. "No."

"Come on, Kas, this is the perfect opportunity to talk to him. We've got hours of dirt ahead of us before we even get close to the crags. Apologize for your temper in Riftwater to break the ice. Find out if he really is interested in bridging the gap."

Kasiel stared at Arhk's back for a few strides. It was more than a gap between them. More like a gaping chasm. "Why would he want to?"

"Because you're his family. The same reason you want to."

Kasiel scowled at him. "What makes you think I want to?"

Jethan grinned. "Because I know you. And because you haven't stopped staring at him with your brows all pinched together since we left Etrion. What have you got to lose?"

He didn't answer, but Niskenya, apparently sensing that he was considering the idea, increased her pace, trotting up toward where Arhk rode. Irith loped along beside her. Kasiel's nerves danced to life, but he let her go. Maybe Jethan was right. The time had come to see if there was anything there to build a relationship on.

As soon as he got near the group, the three guards moved in closer around Arhk, blocking Kasiel out. With a flare of irritation, he slipped into the minds of their horses and moved the animals back out of his way. All three put their hands on the hilts of their swords, drawing them about an inch from their sheaths in an unnervingly synchronized warning.

Back away if you value your life, Ahninveth, a man's voice ordered in his head.

At the same moment, Kasiel's vision started darkening, the sounds around him growing muffled.

Arhk cast a glance at him and held up one hand to signal his guards. The three settled their weapons back in the sheaths, though they didn't remove their hands from them yet. Kasiel's vision and hearing snapped back to normal as his father gestured for him to approach.

"Not an appropriate use of your ability, Ahninveth," he said when Kasiel was beside him, the corners of his mouth curving up a touch. "They would merely have been fulfilling their duties had I allowed them to subdue you."

Kasiel glanced around at the three guards, catching their calculating stares as they slowly took their hands from their weapons. "If that was such a dire infraction, then why do you look amused?"

"I would encourage you to follow the rules as they are given to you and ignore what you might learn from the expressions of a man who has spent much of his life breaking them. Did you require something, Ahninveth?"

The words would never come easily, but they needed to be said, so Kasiel forced them out. "I wanted to apologize for my behavior when you joined us in Riftwater."

"Did you?" Arhk kept his eyes on the road ahead, denying Kasiel any revelations he might find in their depths. "Your hostility toward me is not unwarranted. However, it would do you well to remember that, when you are acting in a professional capacity as a soldier of Vanris, you need to show respect to your ranking officers, regardless of how you may feel about your father."

"And no one outranks you," Kasiel muttered more to himself, working hard to curb another flash of irritation.

"Only the khevarin."

He cast a sideways glance at his father. Was there ever a time that Arhk wished to be anything but the dhomvalen? Did he never just want to relax and shake off his responsibilities? "When am I not acting as a soldier?"

Arhk glanced at him, the briefest hint of sorrow shifting behind gray-green eyes a few shades lighter than Kasiel's. Sunlight caught on the curved line of silver symbols tattooed under his left eye. A small piece of his ke'hanoath. "I imagine it feels like never."

Kasiel looked away, jaw clenching as his father's words hit too close to the mark.

"Perhaps," Arhk offered, "as we get farther from the Break and the conflict there, you will find opportunities to cast off some of that burden for a time."

"Perhaps." He hoped so. If his unit had anything to say about it, he believed he would. "Regarding what you said a moment ago. You're the most powerful man in Vanris, but it almost sounds as if you're advising me not to try following in your footsteps."

Arhk gave him a stare that cut through to his core. "I will only ever say this to you once. When they first brought you before me, I doubted you had it in you to be a decent soldier, let alone follow in my footsteps. Seeing what you have accomplished in such a short time, I now believe you could do far better by continuing to forge your own path. So, no, I do not think you should try to follow in my footsteps." His jaw tightened as he turned away. "Return to your unit, Ahninveth."

Kasiel drew a deep breath, unsure how to process Arhk's words. Did that mean his father was proud of him, or was he just dissatisfied with the path he had chosen for himself? Could it be both? Either way, the conversation appeared to be over. "Thank you, Dhomvalen."

Arhk answered with a slight nod.

Niskenya slowed, letting the dhomvalen and his guards pull ahead. It struck Kasiel then that, somehow, despite being on the back of the massive kanodrak, he hadn't once felt like he was looking down on his father while they were speaking. How did the man manage to have a presence that could defy physical reality?

As they fell back in beside Jethan, he glanced over at his tehnaak. "In answer to your last question regarding what I had to lose, my life, as it turns out."

Jethan chuckled. "Well, *I* didn't advise you to take control of their horses. Those three are elite among elite guards. The woman on the right's a Dampener, the one on the left is an Evoker, and the man riding behind is a

Speaker. They're also three of the most respected warriors in Vanris. The only ones that might be as good are my aunt's personal guards."

"Now they know to be more cautious of Ferals." Kasiel answered, a slow smile creeping across his lips. He knew he shouldn't find pleasure in disrupting his father's guards so easily, but he couldn't help it.

Jethan gave him a sideways smile that had a glimmer of pride in it. "One Feral in particular."

By the end of that first long day in the saddle, Kasiel was ready for a break. The unit ate together and settled around a fire to ward off the chill in the air. The sun hung on the horizon, as if reluctant to leave them to their own devices in the cold dark of night.

Kasiel watched his companions relaxing and bantering with one another. In this setting, he noticed more how often Tath and Nerith glanced at Wedro, who ducked out of most of the conversations, deftly pushing attention onto someone else whenever it came his way. Not something he would have done back when he had Chander always at his side. The three shared a common bond in that they had all lost their tehnaak within the last year. Tath hid that lingering sorrow better than the other two, but she'd had more time to adjust to the pain, and he suspected her relationship with Darro helped.

Was there anything he could do to make it easier for them?

Merrin caught his eye and stood, walking over to offer him a hand. When Darro also got up, Kasiel heaved a sigh and accepted her hand. He let her help him up to get a feel for the strength hidden in her lean frame, so he could properly dread the coming session. It wasn't at all comforting.

"Stay here," he said when Nerith and Jethan started getting up. "Enjoy the fire."

Jethan leaned closer to Nerith as Kasiel turned to

walk away. "He just doesn't want us to watch Merrin beat the shit out of him."

"Oh, don't worry, we'll stay close enough that you can all see," Darro said, much too cheerfully.

Darro found a flat spot and kicked some rocks out of the way while Merrin drew a large ring in the dirt with one of the practice swords they had brought with them. They spent a few minutes warming up with an easy back and forth. Then Merrin laid into Kasiel, catching him with several bruising strikes and disarming him twice in the first few rounds. After experiencing her speed and power one on one, Kasiel suspected she might surpass even Dhomen Farren.

Once she had him sufficiently humiliated and frustrated, Merrin let Darro bump her out and take over. Wedro joined her at the edge of their makeshift ring, standing beside her in companionable silence as they watched. Unexpectedly, Darro approached the process with more patient guidance than aggression, walking Kasiel repeatedly through different forms until his clumsy left arm started getting a feel for the motions.

Despite his patient teaching, Darro brought plenty of his own skill to bear when he got around to testing Kasiel on the forms they were practicing. For a few minutes, it went well. Then Kasiel's left arm seemed to stop listening to his brain and his sword was suddenly skidding to the side of the ring near Wedro and Merrin. As he walked to collect it, he spotted Jhanik and his tehnaak, Keryk, strolling past. Jhanik glanced over, the amusement that lit his expression causing a sinking feeling in Kasiel's gut.

"My two-year-old nephew can fight better than that, Cavenos," the other Feral called out.

Before Kasiel could generate a comeback, Merrin turned to look at the two. "Careful, Jhanik, your little insecurities are showing again. Might want to tuck those back into your trousers."

Jhanik started looking down, then caught himself. "Bitch," he snarled.

Wedro took a step toward the other Feral, but Merrin stopped him with a hand on his chest, pushing him back. "No, Deathwish," she said, softly enough Kasiel barely heard her, "you stay right here. He's not worth the trouble."

Deathwish? What kind of thing was that to call someone? Unless...

Kasiel looked at Wedro, forgetting Jhanik, who continued toward where his unit had camped with sharp, angry strides.

Darro's hand settled on his shoulder, and he leaned in close, speaking in a whisper. "Don't worry about it, Kas. Merrin and I are taking care of Wedro. He'll be all right."

"Did he try—"

Darro's grip tightened. "He doesn't want anyone else to know about it."

Kasiel's chest constricted, a sickly churning in his stomach. He wanted to help – to not feel useless – but this was Wedro's battle. Forcing his way into the middle of it wouldn't make it any better. "If I can do anything..."

Darro nodded and took his hand away. "Let's call it for tonight."

Early the next morning, Sorval advised Kasiel to don his symbolic ear cuffs and braid some of his hair in the Vanrian style. They would reach the first town today, and he needed to look his part. It started him off in a sour mood to be reminded that he was here at least partially to be paraded around like a prize bull. Still, with help from Nerith and Jethan, he made quick work of preparing and tried not to dwell on it after that.

Within an hour of setting out, they passed into

Vareyl's Warning. The jagged stone formations shot out of the ground, towering above them. Exposed black stone became more prevalent than dirt, but only for a short time. The roadway wove among the crags along a surprisingly level path, allowing them to move through quickly, as if the broken landscape had planned for the needs of its future human residents while it was forming.

On the other side, they passed a modest barracks with two small guard towers before entering a vast forest of evergreens with dark, reddish bark and even darker green needles. The black rock strewn around the area soon gave way to a softer, gray stone. Sparse grasses began eking out an existence alongside the roadway and the occasional river or creek they came upon was far livelier and more robust than anything Kasiel had seen on the southern side of the crags.

They skirted around a small village about noon, Dhomen Sorval choosing to avoid interruptions and focus on reaching the larger town of Fellenvar by late afternoon. Arhk and his group galloped off on their own about half an hour before the rest of the contingent reached the town. Any question of where the four had gone vanished when they found many of the townsfolk waiting in the street at the edge of Fellenvar when they arrived.

What Kasiel could see of the town itself as they approached was brighter than he had expected. The buildings were constructed of wood, light mud or clay, and gray stone. There wasn't a black structure to be seen. Many had window boxes or hanging planters full of decorative plants, some of which appeared to be developing early spring blooms. The people themselves were wearing a wide variety of attire, from dresses to trousers, drab to colorful, with no military uniforms or armor in sight.

Dhomen Sorval called Kasiel's unit to the front,

advising him to keep his tethdraks farther back, away from the civilian population. A few of the villagers pointed at them, or him in particular, smiling excitedly. With Jethan and Irith on either side of him, Kasiel continued until Niskenya stopped about ten feet back from the crowd. A woman who looked to be in her late twenties walked forward, leading an older couple along behind her.

"Ahninveth Kasiel?" she asked tentatively, a hopeful light in her eyes.

"Yes." He hopped off Niskenya and moved out in front of the kanodrak, the rest of his unit dismounting behind him. Irith followed and sat beside him, the big cat's presence giving a boost to his courage. He never would have imagined that facing a gathering of towns-folk could be as intimidating as riding into battle.

The trio came a little closer, and the woman turned to the older couple. "This is the soldier who saved my life," she told them.

The older man approached him. "Our daughter lived in Sharith. She was bound by the southern gate the night you led the retaking of the town. She would not be here today if not for you, Ahninveth."

Kasiel considered telling them he hadn't actually led that effort, merely made it possible to breach the gates without hurting the prisoners. But then, that appeared to be the part that mattered to these people. The man took Kasiel's hand, his gaze lingering a moment on the khevarin's three interconnected tattoos on the back of it. He pressed his forehead to those symbols, then looked up to meet Kasiel's eyes, his own brimming with unshed tears.

"It is an honor to have you here."

The older woman came forward and wrapped a hand around Kasiel's arm on the opposite side from Irith. "Come. Let us serve you a drink and a good meal." She started guiding him toward the town.

"You don't need to do that," he protested, heat climbing up his neck.

"Nonsense. It's the very least we can do." The man beckoned to Kasiel's unit. "Come along. No soldier achieves such greatness alone."

The heat rose into Kasiel's cheeks.

As the crowd closed around them, Niskenya pulled him into her mind, letting him see through her eyes. A sense of amusement bubbled up in her as she watched Jhanik scowling at them, him and his unit forgotten. Kasiel grinned. Maybe this wasn't so bad after all.

Dhomen Sorval had them up and on the road again early the next morning, not allowing any recovery time from the evening's festivities, which had included much food, drink, and music provided by the townsfolk. The mild headache and exhaustion weren't all Kasiel regretted about the evening of revelry. There had been another downside to being the subject of all that attention. While the people occupied Kasiel and some of the more gregarious members of his unit with questions and requests for stories of their various undertakings, Jhanik took advantage of the opportunity to spend time with Nerith.

No matter how often Kasiel reminded himself that he trusted her, he couldn't help remembering how she had lied to him for the khevarin. Every smile or laugh she gave to the other Feral was a dagger in his chest. Telling himself it was fine because the two were childhood friends only made the feeling worse somehow. They were heading to Doran, where Nerith and Jhanik had grown up together with parents who hoped to see them become a couple. What memories might the journey bring up between them? What feelings? The smug looks Jhanik had given Kasiel whenever Nerith wasn't watching told him the man knew exactly the effect it was having and relished every minute.

Growing animosity toward the other kanodrak rider coupled with a lack of sleep put Kasiel in a less-than-pleasant mood heading out. A few sanity checks from Jethan throughout the day had him almost convinced to put the entire experience behind him by the time they stopped to set up camp.

After they settled and had eaten their evening meal, Kasiel spent an hour sparring with Darro and Merrin. When they finished, tired and only mildly frustrated with his performance, he wandered out to check on his tethdraks. It was gratifying how much enthusiasm he got from the big reptiles whenever he spent time with them. Most welcomed his presence physically and mentally in their space without hesitation now. Keeping them fed out here was easy enough if he didn't dwell too long on the dubious morality of luring wild deer to their deaths.

On the way back, he spotted Nerith walking between the two units' campsites. Smiling, he quickened his pace, hoping to catch up. The smile vanished, and he stopped the instant Jhanik came out of the trees to intercept her. The other Feral didn't appear to have noticed him.

"Nerith." Jhanik reached out to touch her arm as she stopped and faced him. "There's something I wanted to talk to you about. It involves your parents and a conversation I had with them a few weeks before I left for Etrion. Nothing bad. I just thought it was something you should be aware of before we reach Doran."

Kasiel felt his ire rising. Nothing bad indeed. It was probably just another of Jhanik's transparent attempts to get her to spend time with him.

Nerith looked at him, a hint of concern in her drawn features. "Of course. Let me take care of a couple of quick things, then I'll come find you."

His smile had a faintly self-satisfied edge to it. "I'd like that."

She continued toward their camp, unaware of Jhanik's predatory gaze following her. Irith growled softly next to Kasiel, staying close as he stalked out of the trees.

Jhanik's tethdrak faced them, letting out a low growl that drew his companion's attention.

"Stop throwing yourself at Nerith," Kasiel snapped without breaking stride. He didn't intend to hang around and chat. "There's got to be some desperate woman out there who'd make a better match for you."

Jhanik stepped into his path, stopping him, and leaned in until his face was all Kasiel could see. "Just because you've shoved your prick into her, doesn't mean she belongs to you."

Kasiel didn't think, he just swung. Unfortunately, he did so instinctively with his right arm. His fist caught Jhanik in the mouth, and though it did send the man reeling, it also sent pain shooting through Kasiel's arm. He managed to dodge Jhanik's return swing, but not the slug to the gut that came flying in behind it. Staggering back, he narrowly avoided the other man's attempt to grab him, swallowing hard against the sudden need to throw up. Then a different pain hit him as Jhanik's tethdrak slammed into Irith. Its claws raked the cliff cat's side when Irith tried to twist out of the way, sending sharp agony spearing across their link.

In that instant of distraction, Jhanik's fist caught Kasiel in the jaw. He hit the ground, his ears ringing. He needed to focus. The tethdrak would kill Irith if he couldn't stop it, but the punch left him dazed. Another presence moved into his mind then, clearing his head and soaking up some of his pain. Niskenya. The kanodrak's intervention enabled him to dive into the tethdrak's mind and shove Jhanik out. Taking control, he pushed the beast away from Irith.

Jhanik let out a howl of rage. The other Feral's boot caught Kasiel in the side before he could move to get up, pain bursting out from the point of contact. He rolled away from the next strike, vaguely aware of shouting as others in the company came running in their direction.

Then Jhanik's big male kanodrak came charging toward them, the beast homing in on Kasiel. Terror swept through him. This was one opponent he stood no chance against. Right before the beast reached him, Niskenya lunged into its path, letting out an earsplitting roar. Jhanik's kanodrak skidded to a halt and dropped to his belly, pressing his head down on his forelegs in a posture of submission.

Niskenya turned on Jhanik and snarled. The other Feral sank to his knees, hands up in a gesture of surrender, visibly trembling. No one among the many now watching, not even Arhk and his guards, two of whom had their weapons out, dared to come any closer with the enraged kanodrak there. Jhanik's kanodrak stayed down, making no effort to challenge Niskenya despite the threat she now posed to his bonded rider.

Spitting blood to one side from a split on the inside of his cheek, Kasiel climbed to his feet. He put one hand over his tender ribs, struggling to catch his breath. The other he placed on Niskenya's shoulder. He could feel Jhanik trying to get back into his tethdrak's head. It took little effort to block him out.

"Niske." He tried to sound soothing, though the tremble in his voice didn't help.

The kanodrak growled, her nose inches from Jhanik's forehead.

Kasiel could feel Irith's pain, a blazing beacon that overshadowed his own. He passed the cliff cat's need along to her. "Niske. Let him go."

Finally, she retreated a couple of steps, shifting closer to Kasiel, her milky eyes still locked on the other Feral.

Jhanik scrambled to his feet, brushing at a trickle of blood that ran from a split in his lower lip. He moved back several steps, putting some distance between them. "Give me back my tethdrak, you half-eared calloch," he growled under his breath.

Niskenya answered with a growl of her own and Jhanik flinched, casting a sullen glance at his kanodrak, who still lay on the ground near the subdued tethdrak.

Sick of the other man's mental presence pressing in on his own, Kasiel released the tethdrak to him. Niskenya relaxed, retreating another step, and Jhanik's kanodrak rose, backing away with his head lowered. The threat at least moderately controlled now, Tath and Nerith hurried over to Niskenya's far side where Irith stood, blood running from the deep gashes along his ribs. The cliff cat cowered and hissed at them.

"Kas, we need you to control him," Tath called out. "Now."

With one last glare at Jhanik, he went around to kneel beside Irith. Wrapping an arm over the cliff cat's shoulders, he pulled the beast's head against his chest, passing calm and a sense of safety through their link. Niskenya stepped closer, hovering protectively over them and earning anxious looks from the two healers.

"Are you all right, Kas?" Tath asked as they inspected the cat's wounds.

"I'm fine." He wasn't exactly fine, but he had suffered much worse.

"That's unfortunate," Nerith muttered, a cutting edge to her voice.

This would require a lot of smoothing over. For now, he focused on stroking Irith's head and taking on some of his pain. Nerith's anger could wait. Irith was the one who had suffered the most for his actions.

"Come with me, now," Dhomen Sorval ordered somewhere behind him.

Kasiel suspected he was talking to Jhanik. They weren't likely to bother him until the healers finished caring for Irith's injuries. If they did, he would ignore them.

"Can you get him to lie down?"

Kasiel urged the cliff cat to the ground, stretching out there with him. Irith pushed his back against him, a faint tremble moving through him from the pain.

"Nerith's going to pour something into the wounds. It'll sting for a minute, but then it will numb them so we can stitch him up without hurting him more."

Kasiel nodded. He closed his eyes and pressed his forehead to Irith's head, opening himself to more of the cat's pain. The sudden intense flare of agony as Nerith poured the solution into the wounds made him groan. Irith tensed against him, trying briefly to pull away until Kasiel tightened his hold, both physically and mentally. Then he felt Niskenya move in, her breath warm on his shoulder as she took some of the pain from them. Kasiel clenched his jaw, cruel memories dragging him back to those last moments before Sylaryth died. A few tears slipped free, sinking into the cliff cat's blue-gray coat. He didn't deserve these remarkable creatures.

"I'm sorry," he murmured.

*

The next three days were awkward. Dhomen Sorval warned him and Jhanik that another incident, even a minor one, would see them both being demoted and pulled off the escort entirely. They received orders not to interact with each other for any reason short of an emergency until further notice. Separation between the two units was now an imperative instead of a choice. They bartered for an open wagon in the next village to carry Irith, who couldn't walk without risking the stitches, let alone lope along with the company over long distances, given the severity of his wounds.

Nerith avoided Kasiel as much as she could while still being part of his unit. The only comfort there was that she stayed well away from Jhanik too. Tath and Jethan advised him to give her time, so he did. Despite his bruised ribs, he insisted on continuing lessons with Darro and Merrin. He needed to practice until using his left arm became instinctive to avoid hurting his right one again the way he had when he punched Jhanik. In the wrong situation, that could be a fatal mistake. Besides, there was something cathartic about the pain. He deserved far worse.

They stopped in one other town for two hours in the middle of the fifth day. Dhomen Sorval permitted Kasiel and his unit to enjoy the generosity of the locals that his status earned them, but members of both units received warnings to partake of no more than two drinks each. The rest of the time, they stayed on the road. They would arrive in Doran later than planned on the sixth day, long after most people would be asleep. Sorval pointed out that this was due to them being slowed down by the distinctly avoidable injury Irith had sustained, singling Jhanik and Kasiel out with hard stares as he spoke.

By the time night fell on that sixth day, the forest bordered the eastern side of the road with more open grasslands and rolling hills stretching to the west. The distant lights of the capital formed a fallen constellation on the horizon. Kasiel decided it was time to approach Nerith. There might be too many distractions once they entered the city, and he didn't want to leave things as they were. The rest of his unit conveniently moved away when he eased over alongside her on Niskenya. She made no sound or gesture to acknowledge him.

He drew a deep breath. "Nerith–"

"I can't believe you. Either of you." She glared death

at the dark road ahead of them.

"I know I messed up."

"What gave you your first clue? That, maybe." She gestured to where Irith lay looking miserable in the wagon.

Kasiel lowered his gaze. He didn't have to look to know how much the wounds still hurt the cliff cat. He had never stopped absorbing as much of his companion's pain as he could bear. It made sleeping hard and the days unpleasant, but he refused to let Irith suffer alone.

Niskenya huffed, and Nerith looked over, staring at the kanodrak for a long moment. She finally breathed a soft sigh. "I'm too tired to control my temper with you right now. We'll talk once we're settled in town, all right?"

He didn't want to wait, but he wanted to argue with her about it even less. It made no sense to pile another argument on top of the existing conflict. After a few seconds, he nodded and let Niskenya move them back to the front of the unit.

Sorval brought Kasiel's unit to the lead behind him and Arhk's group when they approached the wall that surrounded Doran. It was a much smaller wall than the one around Etrion, made of a pale stone with iron spikes topping the battlement. The gates opened, letting out a group of fifteen armed and armored soldiers. The leader, a woman with her shoulder-length blond hair braided back against her scalp on one side, signaled the others to wait as she rode up to Kasiel's father.

"Dhomvalen Arhk Cavenos, it is always a pleasure."

"Likewise, Dhomen Aleren." Arhk offered a respectful nod.

Her gaze moved to Kasiel. "This must be your remarkable son I've been hearing so much about lately. A Feral kanodrak rider. You must be quite proud."

"Indeed." The look he gave Kasiel then was any-thing but. "I can show myself to the palace." He kicked his mount, his three guards following him as he cut through Aleren's soldiers and let himself into the city.

Aleren watched him go, an enigmatic hint of amuse-ment in her smirk, then her gaze moved back to Kasiel before finally settling on Sorval.

"Dhomen Sorval," she greeted. "I sense some ten-sion there."

"Yes." Sorval took a deep breath, his gaze stalling briefly on Kasiel and then Jhanik as it swept over the company. "Shall we get them set up for the night?"

Her curious gaze went to Kasiel again. "Divided en-closures have been prepared for the beasts. We'll split the Ferals off here so they can get them settled. My soldiers are ready to escort the rest to their quarters."

"If you don't mind, I'll accompany my Ferals and see that they don't have any... difficulties." Sorval's hard gaze shifted between Kasiel and Jhanik again.

That only appeared to entice Aleren more. "Of course, I'll show you to the enclosures."

Most of the company left with her soldiers. Listen-ing to Sorval and Aleren talk along the way to the habi-tats revealed that Aleren was Khevarin Seylin's tehnaak. Despite her apparent curiosity around Kasiel, the two dhomens spent most of the ride discussing recent events near the Break. Aleren also asked after Seylin's well-be-ing. It seemed strange to Kasiel that the khevarin and her tehnaak would live so far apart, but perhaps things worked differently when you were the ruler of a country at war.

When they had the beasts settled in the prepared enclosures, Jhanik and his tehnaak broke off with a separate escort from Kasiel and Jethan, who continued to the palace along with Irith. Given his injury and his smaller size compared to the tethdraks, they decided the cliff cat could stay with Kasiel for now.

As they approached the massive, beige stone and wood structure of a palace as extensive and complicated as the one in Etrion, Kasiel lost interest in listening to the two conversing. What he wanted was to have that talk with Nerith, but he wouldn't find her in the palace.

"Dhomen Sorval?"

"Yes, Ahninveth Kasiel."

"Won't we be staying with the rest of our unit?"

Aleren glanced at him, her eyebrows rising slightly. He noticed, now that they were on foot, that she wasn't much taller than Nerith. "The khevarin's nephew and the dhomvalen's son will not be sleeping in the barracks."

But Nerith would be, and Jhanik would be.

"I'd actually like to be with my unit."

The frosty look Sorval gave him could have stopped an army in its tracks. "It's better this way, Ahninveth."

"I—"

Jethan interrupted him with a touch on his arm. "We appreciate the hospitality, Dhomen Aleren."

"Just Aleren, Jethan. I've known you since before you could walk. Back when you were the short one," she added with a teasing wink.

Kasiel could learn to like Aleren. She seemed grounded and approachable for someone so closely tied to the khevarin. But all he could think about right then was how, somewhere in the city, Jhanik might be getting his chance to smooth things over with Nerith.

CHAPTER SEVEN

Jethan didn't give Kasiel time to dwell on things in the morning. Before the sun had fully risen, he showed up at the rooms assigned to Kasiel for their stay. Rooms that, while a little smaller than the ones given to him in Etrion, were no less finely appointed. When the palace attendant showed him to his quarters in the night, she had pointed out a small selection of clothing in the wardrobe. Items that were tailored for him per instructions apparently received over a week ago, which told him this trip had been in planning for a while.

They made quick work of a tray full of mouth-watering sweet and savory pastries that arrived in the early hours. As much as he enjoyed the soft bed and excellent food, he would have happily given it up to stay with his unit where he might have gotten to speak to Nerith.

Jethan, far too energetic for the little sleep they had gotten, hopped up and started toward the door. "Come on, I'll show you the barracks."

Kasiel's last bite felt as if it had become lodged in his throat. "What if..." He wasn't sure how to ask what he was thinking. Or if he really wanted to ask it, since that would open the door to answers he might not like hearing.

Jethan leaned on the back of a chair, giving him the patient instructor gaze he was disconcertingly good at.

"What if Jhanik convinced Nerith you were the one in the wrong? What if she decided in the night that he's a better match for her and they reconciled their differences between the sheets?"

Kasiel felt as if someone had punched him in the gut again. "Was putting my fears into words for me supposed to help? Because it really didn't."

"Have a little faith in your relationship." He stepped back from the chair. "Come on. I'm sure you'll find that she's just as in love and angry with you today as she was yesterday."

"Right. Still not a tremendous help, but sitting here won't fix anything and Irith needs to go outside." He walked to the big cliff cat, ready to step in if the injured beast needed assistance standing up.

"Exactly."

In the morning light, Doran was a bright city. The antithesis to Etrion, it had none of the aggressive angles or black buildings that made the southern capital so intimidating. In a strange way, Kasiel missed that dark, militaristic environment, if only because he had gotten so used to it. But he quickly came to appreciate the frequent small garden parks that created pockets of nature amidst homes and businesses, and the many hanging planters that gave a splash of living color to the streets.

Decorative streamers hung from several houses and shopfronts, bringing a festive atmosphere to the city. The residents who were out and about dressed in clothing of all kinds, in all qualities and colors. Outside of some local guards, very few people wore uniforms, and far more than he was used to left their hair hanging loose without the braids that were so common in Etrion. One thing he noticed right away was that he and Jethan with the cliff cat received a lot of long, curious looks.

"I don't see many braids here," he remarked as they

strolled along, keeping their pace measured for Irith's sake.

"The style developed to keep our hair out of the way when we fight. It also happens to show off our ears. Down near the border, where we're so close to people who hate us, we wear it often to show pride in who we are. It's good for morale."

That made sense, even if it left him in the uncomfortable position of feeling out-of-place most of the time. He still had a strong aversion to letting his cut ears show. "Are the streamers normal?"

Jethan shook his head. "No. It's near Awakening when we celebrate the reawakening of nature after the winter sleep. A lot of mind-crafter Trials are run this time of year too. The Vanrian silver, purple, and black mixed in with some streamers tells me they may also be planning something special to honor our arrival here."

"As long as they don't expect anything too impressive out of us." A young girl walking with her parents smiled and waved at them. Kasiel waved back. "What do mind-crafters do here?"

Jethan chuckled. "You know, we may be good at war, but there's actually very little of it in Vanrian history prior to our conflict with the Alliance. Dampeners are incredibly useful for things like blocking pain from injuries to enable wound care in emergencies. Fishing boats always have a Speaker on the crew to provide quick communication between vessels. Ferals mostly manage livestock and companion beasts."

Kasiel glanced at him. "So, if we lived up here, I could just be a cattle farmer or something."

Jethan grimaced. "With your skills, I doubt you could escape to a job that mundane. Helping run one of the tethdrak or kanodrak habitats might be an option someday, but as long as we're at war, even that's unlikely. You can scout using birds and run the best combat beasts remotely. You've proven to be far too valuable as a soldier."

Kasiel fell silent, resting a hand on Irith's head. Being valuable didn't seem to have a lot of upsides.

Jethan led him down a side street, the end of which opened on a large dirt courtyard that contained a series of fighting rings in various sizes and an arena big enough to practice mounted combat. A bunch of low buildings spread out around the perimeter appeared to be mostly barracks, judging from the uniforms of those moving between them.

Striding through the area with confidence born of familiarity, Jethan led them to a pair of buildings reserved for visiting soldiers. Inside the first one, they found Darro, Kince, Tath, and Etris all engaged in various tasks. The minute they walked in, Tath went for Irith's injured side, peeling back the bandages while Kasiel placed a hand on his head and passed reassurance through their link.

"Where's the rest of the crew?" Jethan asked before Kasiel could open his mouth to blurt out some poorly worded, dread-laden inquiry about Nerith.

"Wedro went with Avris and Merrin to a smithy they wanted to visit. Nerith went to see her parents," Kince answered, his feet kicked up on a table next to the remains of toasted bread and porridge that made Kasiel feel instantly guilty for the breakfast he and Jethan had enjoyed.

"Nerith went alone?" He tried to sound nonchalant, but Kince's smirk and Tath's arched brow told him how completely he failed.

Tath grabbed a container of salve off a side table and crouched back down next to Irith. "She left here alone." She began spreading the substance over the stitched wounds.

Kasiel focused on keeping Irith calm and absorbing

some of his pain for the next few minutes until Tath finished wrapping a fresh bandage around the cliff cat's midsection. Then Darro walked over and clapped him on the shoulder.

"Why don't we get a little sparring in and burn off some of the angst I see built up behind your eyes?" He pointed to a set of practice armor lying on the end of one bed. "That should be about the right size."

Kasiel eyed the armor, considering the value of some distraction, then nodded and picked it up. Darro led them outside to an empty ring. They stood in the shade of a small shelter while Jethan helped him fasten on the armor. He was buckling the last bracer when a practice sword landed at his feet. Kasiel looked up, expecting to see Darro there. His breath caught in his throat when he saw Arhk standing there instead.

Darro, who had stepped off to one side, just shrugged.

"Shall we?" Arhk walked out into the ring without waiting for an answer. He wasn't wearing armor.

Kasiel had seen him fight. He was fast and efficient. A living weapon designed to terrify and kill.

He looked at Jethan. "Should I die out there, tell Nerith... Well, you can figure it out."

Jethan patted him on the shoulder. "Just try not to take a blow to the head. You can probably survive anything else."

Kasiel encouraged Irith to settle next to Jethan under the overhang. Then, his heart pounding in his ears, he walked out into the ring.

Arhk tilted his head forward, the gesture making him more intimidating somehow. "Are you ready?"

Absolutely not.

"Yes, Dhomvalen."

In two swift movements, his sword was gone and the stinging in his fingers made him grateful for the protection of the practice glove. Frustration already rising, Kasiel retrieved the weapon and stalked back into position. Arhk smiled. This time, he came at Kasiel a little slower, giving him a chance to defend and attempt an attack of his own. An effort that somehow ended with him sprawled face-first in the dirt.

When he flipped over, Arhk was there, offering a hand down to him. Merrin, Wedro, and Avris had returned and were standing outside the ring with the others. A couple of strangers stood near one of the barracks now, also watching. Kasiel drew a deep breath and accepted the offered hand.

Arhk leaned closer once Kasiel was on his feet again, speaking in a low voice. "You are thinking too much."

"I'm not supposed to think?" His frustration made his tone sharper than he intended, but his father either didn't notice or didn't care.

"You worry about failing because you are using your non-dominant hand to fight, and you make it happen. Overthinking is a human problem, Kasiel. You are a Feral. That can be a significant advantage, even when you are not using your beasts. The creatures you work with are lethal, in part because they do not question their instincts. Embrace that. I have been watching you with your kanodrak. You are part of each other. Let her in. Let her guide you. Her instincts will help you get out of your head and move the way you need to when you need to."

Kasiel met his eyes, surprised by the confidence he saw there that said his father believed he could do this. That was all the encouragement he needed. Reaching out with his ability, he drew on Niskenya, vaguely aware of Arhk's slight smile as he stepped away. The kanodrak responded instantly, her presence moving through him the moment he offered her entry as if she had been waiting for this. Her wildness, her raw animal power, threatened to consume him for a few seconds. Then she settled, and he let himself merge with her, an unfamiliar hunger rising in him.

Kasiel grinned at Arhk and raised his sword. In the distant enclosure, Niskenya bared her teeth, claws flexing into the dirt.

Arhk lunged in. Niskenya reacted, her instinct guiding Kasiel's blade – his claws – confidently into the path of the oncoming weapon, catching it and sweeping it aside. They swung into the resulting opening, but Arhk twisted agilely out of the way. The dhomvalen stepped back in with a slash, the tip of his blade barely brushing the armor over Kasiel's ribs as Niskenya guided him clear. They moved in with a similar attack, only higher, going for the throat, for the kill. Arhk parried, staying just out of reach.

The violent dance continued for several minutes. Kasiel and Niskenya shared each other's space, the kano-drak maintaining a deadly calm, guiding every strike and counter with instinctive speed and precision. Arhk held them at bay, a fierce light shining in his eyes, the barest hint of a smile curving his lips.

Arhk's attention flickered to the edge of the ring for an instant then, but when Kasiel moved to take advantage of the distraction, his father slipped in a clever feint and disarmed him. He almost continued the fight with fangs and claws, but remembered in the last second that he didn't actually have fangs or claws. Stepping back, he tried to catch his breath while Niskenya prowled through his mind, displeased with the lack of a kill. He felt almost too wild to form words.

With a gentle nudge, Kasiel encouraged the kano-drak back to herself and withdrew most of his awareness from her, trying to be human again. "How did you know that would work?"

Annoyingly, Arhk didn't appear half as winded. He

casually twirled the practice blade in an elegant circle. "I have an exceptionally gifted Feral friend in Doran. I asked him about your situation after we got in last night."

Last night, in the middle of the night, his father had gone to visit a Feral to talk about him? Still riding high from the experience of fighting with Niskenya's guidance, this new revelation made Kasiel break out in a giddy smile. "You have friends?"

Arhk raised his blade, scowling along it at him. "Keep practicing. Next time, I will not be so gentle." A hint of amusement lit his eyes, belying his expression. "Now, go get cleaned up. There is someone you need to meet in the palace in half an hour."

With that, he walked to where one of his three guards stood waiting with a palace attendant. They left the barracks courtyard together.

Jethan trotted out to Kasiel. "By the Break, Kas, that was amazing. You just held your own with the dhomvalen. No one does that."

"He was holding back." Though his response was dismissive, Kasiel soared with pleasure on the inside, and not just because he had performed well. His father had gone out of his way to help him and had even sparred with him. He had acted like a father.

"What did he say to you," Darro asked as the rest of them walked out, "because it made an enormous difference?"

Kasiel glanced around, noticing groups of unfamiliar soldiers who had gathered to watch and now stood talking outside the various buildings. The one person he most wanted to see wasn't there. Neither was Jhanik, though some members of the other Feral's unit stood near their barracks.

"He told me to tap into Niskenya's instincts to help me get out of my head and react the way I needed to instead of overthinking it... basically."

"That's a handy trick," Kince remarked.

Merrin slid an arm around Kasiel's shoulders and leaned into him. "I guess this means we don't have to take it easy on you anymore."

Kasiel chuckled, his cheeks warming. "I mean, you can if you want to."

Darro mussed his hair like he might a child's and laughed. "Not a chance, danro."

"I don't think you can call him that anymore." Avris gazed at Kasiel fondly. "He's kind of proven he belongs here."

"I'll call him whatever I like," Darro countered, "unless he wants to call me out on it." Challenge flashed behind his eyes, and he raised the practice sword he was still holding.

"I *will* take you up on that later." Kasiel handed his sword to Merrin. "Right now, Jethan and I are supposed to clean up and meet someone in the palace. If anyone sees Nerith—"

"Don't worry, Kas." Avris reached out and gave his hand a squeeze. "We'll tell her you want to talk."

"And regale her with tales of your battle prowess," Wedro added, almost smiling.

Kasiel met his eyes, delighted to see him interacting. "Be sure to embellish." He called Irith over with a thought. The big cliff cat nudged the others out of his way as he moved to Kasiel's side.

Merrin's lips curved in a faint smirk. "I don't think this one needs any embellishing."

"See you all later," Jethan called as they strode from the ring.

They had just enough time to clean up and change into more palace-appropriate attire before an attendant came for them. At Jethan's recommendation, Kasiel had donned a pair of charcoal trousers and a dark blue-gray shirt with sparing silver embroidery on the cuffs and collar. A fitted black jacket that hung down to his knees completed the ensemble.

The female attendant eyed them both with a look of approval that vanished when she saw Irith. "Your beast is—"

"Injured and staying with me until the stitches are ready to be removed."

"Yes, Ahninveth." The tight line of her lips made it obvious she didn't approve, but she guided them out into the palace halls with no further objection.

Kasiel left a hand resting on the cliff cat's shoulder, soaking in some of the pain that walking still caused him. Irith reacted to his effort with a calm sense of gratitude and affection. The cat didn't seem to realize that his injuries were Kasiel's fault, or maybe he did, and it just didn't matter to him. Either way, until he finished healing, Kasiel was determined to take away as much pain as he could.

They walked down a long hallway floored in a stone of swirling ivory and beige. The curved walls were a pale cream color that somehow amplified the light of the sconces along the way. It was bright and spacious, the soft tones giving it a warmth that was quite the opposite of the palace in Etrion. Oddly, he once again felt unexpectedly nostalgic for the familiarity of the military city.

As they approached a door near the end of the hall, a guard beside it held up one hand. "The beast can't enter."

Kasiel opened his mouth to respond, hesitating as a woman's raised voice reached out to them from within the room.

"No! To the Break with both of you, and to the Break with my mother too!"

The door flew open, and a woman around his age

ran out, slamming into Kasiel, who instinctively grabbed her arms to keep her from falling. She looked at him, tears brimming in storm-filled silver eyes. One lock of dark, blood-red hair fell into her face, pulled free of an intricate webwork of fine braids. Her elegant features twisted into an expression of outrage. She shoved him, stumbling back when he didn't budge.

A tear slipped free of one eye as she glared at him. "And to the Break with you!"

She darted around him, racing off down the hall, an attendant and a palace guard hurrying after her.

"Be right back," Jethan said, before he too took off in pursuit.

"Ahninveth Kasiel," Arhk said from within the room, "now that you have had the pleasure of meeting Khesran Velara, do come in and meet her father."

Khesran was the title given any child, male or female, of the Vanrian ruler. The equivalent of a prince or princess in the Pandrean Alliance kingdoms. Similarly, khevarin was the ruler and khemron their spouse, regardless of gender. Kasiel hadn't figured out yet if those terms translated equally to the role of a king and queen in the southern kingdoms. From what he had learned through his studies, in the current state of conflict, the khemron oversaw everything north of Vareyl's Warning, while the khevarin acted as ruler and military leader to the south.

Whether this man was the actual ruler of Vanris or not, one word came to mind when Kasiel met Khemron Genyith. Strong. Strong in physique, in character, and in presence. He was tall and broad-shouldered, with long red hair several shades lighter than his daughter's, though his eyes were the same striking silver as hers. A set of four thick scars ran across the left side of his neck and jaw that reminded Kasiel of the scars the werdyn cat had left on Jethan's shoulder. Given how effective Vanris's healing salves and tinctures were, he hated to imagine how severe the wounds must have been to leave such marks.

Genyith rested one hand on the back of the ornate ivory chair he stood beside. "I see you wondering about my scars."

Realizing he had been staring, Kasiel quickly lowered his gaze. "Apologies, Khemron."

"I am not upset. I would have to be quite fragile to be offended by staring at this point in my life, Ahninveth. These were the outcome of a falling out with a Feral when I was twenty-three. A fight I was winning until his companion, a cliff cat," he said, his gaze moving to Irith, "came to his defense."

Receptive to Kasiel's unease, but not its cause, Irith stepped protectively in front of him. Kasiel gave the cat a quick mental nudge, moving him back to his side. "I'm sorry, Khemron, I wasn't aware—"

Genyith cut him off with a laugh. "He is far too polite to be your son, Arhk."

Arhk glanced at Kasiel. He had adopted that unreadable expression that he was so infuriatingly good at. "Not always."

To Kasiel's relief, Jethan returned then, though he came with Velara on his arm. Her tears were gone, and the lock of dark, blood-red hair tucked back into the webwork of small braids that held the rest in place. A sable liner around her eyes called attention to their silver color. Red paint upon her lips, as rich in color as her hair, made them compete for attention with those stunning eyes. Her pointed ears had a series of delicate dark metal cuffs and rings affixed to them, some studded with gemstones. Though refined like her mother's, her features bore a hint of her father's strength in the sharp lines of her jaw.

"Khemron Genyith," Jethan greeted with a bow of his head as he escorted Velara to Kasiel.

"Nephew," Genyith answered.

Now that Kasiel had an opportunity to see her standing still in the light, he noticed part of Velara's ke'hanoath tattooed across her forehead. The symbols were a pale cream color that might have been almost invisible if not for a hair-thin border of silver edging each one. Interwoven as they were, the gracefully rendered symbols created a permanent tiara upon her brow.

"Vel," Jethan started, pausing when Genyith pointedly cleared his throat. "Khesran Velara," he amended, "this is my tehnaak, Ahninveth Kasiel Cavenos."

One corner of her mouth quirked up in a beguiling smirk. "Yes, we have run into each other before."

Her wry humor brought a slight smile to his lips. "Moments ago, in fact, though I believe you did most of the running." After he said it, Kasiel realized maybe he shouldn't be bantering with the khesran in front of her father, or his for that matter, but the words were already out.

Her smile sparkled into her eyes. "I did." She removed her arm from Jethan's and reached out to place her palm against Kasiel's chest. Her fine brows pinched together. "You proved to be an unexpectedly solid barrier."

Unsure how to handle her breach of his personal space in this situation, Kasiel uncomfortably stood his ground. Jethan reached for her arm, but she moved again before he could get hold of it, this time sinking to crouch in front of Irith in a way that somehow infused elegance into the posture.

"Velara." An edge of unease entered the khemron's voice.

"Relax, Father. Just because beasts don't appreciate you does not mean they will find me equally offensive."

Genyith scowled, his features darkening.

Kasiel looked to Jethan, hoping for guidance, but his tehnaak only shifted his feet and shrugged.

Velara moved on to scratch behind Irith's ears, eliciting a deep purr from the cat. She leaned to the side to peer at his bandage. "It looks like someone has been mistreating this poor creature."

"There was an... incident." It was Kasiel's turn to shift his feet, wishing he could leave. He didn't know how to handle this woman who somehow came across as elegant, composed, and aggressively bold all at once.

Velara looked up at him, silver eyes flashing with a mischievous curiosity. "Oh, I really must hear more about that." She stood so abruptly that Irith flinched. "Father, I wish for my cousin and his tehnaak to be my escorts at the festivities this evening. I would like to get to know those I will be traveling with."

"That sounds like a reasonable request, unless you object, Dhomvalen."

"Not at all," Arhk said, his face still as expressive as stone.

"The matter is settled, then. We have events planned this evening and tomorrow to celebrate your arrival and the recent victories at the border. Tomorrow morning there is to be a parade in which your units and beasts will ride along with the royal family. The kanodraks too, should they consent to it. For now, you will join us for an inaugural afternoon feast to begin the festivities." Genyith started for the door, offering his daughter his arm on his way past. She flashed them both a quick smile before sliding her arm through her father's. Arhk followed the pair from the room.

A weight landed on Kasiel's chest. How would he ever get to talk to Nerith if he was stuck playing escort to the khevarin's daughter?

"Sorry, Kas," Jethan whispered as they moved to follow.

The feast was extravagant and drawn out, with five types of meat prepared seven different ways and so many other varied dishes that Kasiel quickly lost track of what he had and hadn't tried. The city's elite joined them, few of whom were introduced by military titles, though Jethan explained that they didn't default to military rank here as they did in Etrion.

Dhomen Aleren sat to the left of Khemron Genyith with Arhk, Kasiel, and Jethan to her left. Velara sat on the khemron's right between her two brothers and their tehnaaks. Khesran Karith, the eldest at twenty, had mid-back length, light red hair that exaggerated the narrowness of his features. As heir, he sat closest to Genyith, alongside a fine-boned woman who was his tehnaak and wife. An arrangement, Jethan explained, that, while uncommon, happened occasionally. On Velara's other side, Khesran Nakhul, the youngest of the three, chatted with his sister, his white hair a striking contrast to the deep red of hers. The two grinned conspiratorially as they spoke, receiving disdainful sneers from their older brother whenever they broke out in barely contained fits of laughter.

They had been there over an hour when Velara disappeared, returning a short time later in a long dress, disturbingly similar in color to Kasiel's shirt, with elaborate silver embroidery along the bodice and sleeves. The skirt of the dress split open from the waist down in front, revealing a pair of matching fitted pants underneath with more silver embroidery on the lower legs. She collected Jethan and Kasiel and led them from the grand dining hall. Khemron Genyith informed them on the way out that he was entrusting his daughter into their care for the remainder of the day, though he also sent two personal guards and one of her attendants with them.

Once they were clear of the feast, Kasiel considered Irith. "If we'll be walking around much, I should take him to the recovery area in the habitat. I'd rather not hurt him by dragging him around the city." He also didn't want to be parted from the cat, but making him walk all afternoon would cause him unnecessary pain.

Velara gave him a long, penetrating stare, then she

nodded. "We can take him there together." She started walking, the practiced grace of her movement screaming royalty. The guard and attendant went with her.

Jethan stayed with Kasiel when he didn't follow. "That's unnecessary. I can meet you all somewhere when I'm done." A plan that might provide him an opportunity to seek out Nerith before he rejoined them.

Velara strode back and looked him in the eyes. "I am in your care. Father might not appreciate you splitting up my escort."

He clenched his teeth, fighting the disconcerting urge to growl at her, encouraged by the kanodrak hovering in the back of his mind. "Fine." He stepped around her. "Let's go."

Velara hurried to catch up with his brisk strides, cutting Jethan off. "Are you annoyed with me, Ahninveth?"

"No."

"You are." Her delighted smile struck him as entirely inappropriate to the situation.

"Vel." The edge of warning in Jethan's tone drew her gaze to him. "Don't push him. I love you, but he's my tehnaak, and I will take his side."

Her eyes widened a fraction. "Even against my father?"

"Yes." There was no hesitation in Jethan's answer.

Kasiel smiled to himself, touched and a little surprised by his tehnaak's unequivocal support.

Velara moved around on Jethan's other side and slipped her arm through his. "You know, Cousin, I think having your tehnaak back might be good for you."

"Where's your tehnaak?" Kasiel asked, his thoughts going to Wedro. Perhaps it was an inappropriate question to ask. He had no way of knowing if she might have lost her tehnaak, as several of his companions had.

"Keyla is getting ready to perform in the dances tonight." Velara's gaze lingered on Jethan. "I'm surprised you weren't the first to ask after her, Cousin."

"Why?" Kasiel asked. Then he noticed the hint of color rising in Jethan's face. "Oh, is she the someone you were hoping to impress?"

The hint of color blossomed, reddening Jethan's cheeks.

Velara laughed.

When they reached the cliff cat enclosure, the ahn-inveth watching over things was unexpectedly more excited about meeting Kasiel than she was at having one of the khesrans visiting. She bombarded him with questions regarding his unusual situation, having a bonded companion that wasn't the same species as the beasts he ran in battle. Velara managed to fend her off, insisting that she had places to be and required Kasiel as part of her escort.

Prior to leaving Irith in the woman's care, Kasiel sank to one knee before the cliff cat. "Don't worry, my friend, I won't be far. I'll come check on you in the morning."

Irith rubbed his face against Kasiel's purring loudly. Kasiel closed his eyes, passing affection and comfort to the beast. Velara and Jethan were speaking in hushed voices, though he couldn't quite make out their words, at least not until he slipped into the cliff cat's mind and borrowed his ears. Scratching under Irith's chin, he lingered a moment longer to listen.

"He cares deeply for his companion, doesn't he?" Velara asked, her tone oddly pensive.

"Of course he does," Jethan answered.

"You say that as if it is a given, but we both know it is not."

"With Kas it is."

Uncomfortable with the direction of the conversation, Kasiel straightened and rejoined them. Velara watched him approach, her head tilted to one side, gazing at him as though she had found a particularly interesting puzzle to solve.

"Where to, Khesran?" he asked, avoiding her eyes.

"There is a cart they bring out at every festival where they sell the most beautiful handwoven crowns using vines, leaves, and flowers. The hard part is finding it. It is never in the same place."

Kasiel started reaching out with his ability as he spoke. "Isn't the tiara you wear all the time lovely enough?"

A faint blush colored her cheeks. "Thank you, Ahninveth Kasiel, but I like to change things up now and then."

"You can call me Kasiel." He held out his hand and Velara let out a squeak of surprise when a bright blue and black songbird landed on one finger. He struggled to smother a satisfied smirk. "Any distinctive features I might spot from above?"

"And you, my enchanting Feral, may call me Velara," she said, before proceeding to describe the cart in question.

Jethan, standing just behind her, allowed his crooked grin to show.

Finding the cart using the bird proved easier than getting Velara to it. Once they entered the festival area, she stopped every few feet, insisting on showing Kasiel this art display or having him taste that traditional food or drink. Jethan was no better. The celebratory atmosphere and his cousin's enthusiasm infected him until he was also dragging Kasiel from one place to another to show him some fantastic local metalwork or have him try a game of skill or chance that left them laughing until the next stop. Kasiel quickly regretted eating as much as he had at the feast, and the many drinks they gave him to try were making him giddy and disconnected. Still, the excitement of his companions was infectious, and he found himself loath to try reining the two in once they got going.

When they finally found the cart, Velara purchased a crown of vines woven together with bright green leaves, yellow flowers, and ribbons of gold and green that hung down almost to her waist in the back. She bought similar crowns of woven vines with darker leaves, evergreen needles, and purple flowers worked through amidst ribbons of silver and black for him and Jethan. Then she picked out three simpler crowns for the two palace guards and her attendant, insisting they shouldn't be left out. Once they were all decorated to her satisfaction, she sent the attendant off to enjoy the festival with her family.

From there, she drew them into a crowd of revelers dancing along the street from which they extracted themselves several blocks later. Jethan somehow emerged with three wooden cups of strawberry-honey mead in his hands, passing one each to Kasiel and Velara. They thirstily downed the sweet brew.

With a glance skyward, Velara took Kasiel by the wrist and pulled him with her. "Come. It's almost time."

Sunlight was fading, the sky darkening. He let her lead him through the crowds to a sizeable square not far from the palace. An elaborate statue of a kanodrak with three frolicking juveniles at her feet stood on a large rock in the middle of a decorative pool at the center of the square. Enough people milled around the statue that it felt like half the city was there.

Velara moved them through the crowd with practiced skill, finding a spot along one of two streets heading toward the palace on either side of the square. People around them eased back from her and the guards, providing more space for their party to slip into.

The crowd quieted, a sense of anticipation hanging over them as people cleared the street. Velara stepped between him and Jethan, taking their hands in hers.

Haunting music from some kind of wind instrument filled the air. It was distant at first, growing gradually louder. Two more joined the first, creating a sweet, sorrowful harmony.

Velara's fingers twined through his, her hand soft and warm.

Three figures dressed in simple shirts and trousers of a dark reddish-brown came up the street, moving in a solemn, elegant dance as they played their instruments. Behind them, a second trio in matching outfits began strumming lutes, adding another layer to the slow, evocative piece. Four individuals in the same attire danced into view, carrying drums that varied slightly in size that they weren't using yet.

Behind the musicians, seven more figures moved along with the music, all wearing masks that were stylized renditions mostly of tethdrak faces, though the two in the front were kanodraks. They all wore the same dark clothing and had their hair in braided rows, the long ends hanging loose. As the performers passed, soft, breathy vocals joined the instruments, rising gradually in volume.

The crowd closed in behind them, moving with the music as darkness sank over the city. Velara pulled Kasiel and Jethan out with her, the presence of the two guards helping make room for them directly behind the dancers. Some of the crowd began vocalizing with the singers, surrounding them with the surreal, haunting melody. The drums joined in then, adding a rhythmic beat, all of it getting steadily louder as they advanced. Niskenya's wildness moved within Kasiel, increasing that sense of disconnection from normalcy.

The music rose, the beats growing steadily stronger as the procession took them up the steps to a large, ornate building alongside the palace entrance. They continued through double doors that stood open, awaiting them.

The performers danced across the floor and up onto a large stage, those with instruments going to stand at the back, while the rest continued moving with the music.

More guards met Velara's group at the door to escort them upstairs to three divided balcony sitting areas that reminded Kasiel unfortunately of Edmund's execution. Khemron Genyith, Dhomvalen Arhk, and Dhomen Aleren occupied the center section. Velara's brothers sat in one of the other two, Karith with his wife on his arm. The guards led their trio to the third balcony where Velara then dismissed them, along with the original two, to go stand watch outside the curtain at the rear of the section. She then sat in the center of three chairs, placing herself between him and Jethan again.

Once the crowd finished funneling into the building, the doors boomed shut. The music stopped at exactly that moment and attendants snuffed the sconces in the seating areas, casting the crowd in darkness. Dim light around the stage focused them upon three figures frozen in different poses. The rest of the dancers had moved off to the back with the musicians.

Velara took his hand in hers again. In the dark, he could only assume she did the same to Jethan.

Soft, staccato huffing, intermixed with faint melodic humming, came from the back of the stage. It went on for several seconds before the dancers began moving, all three wearing tethdrak masks. Kasiel leaned forward, mesmerized, as they came together with wary movements, heads tilting in a manner that suggested curiosity. More voices joined the huffing and humming. The figures started pushing tentatively at one another in a strange dance that hinted at aggression. More tethdraks moved out to join the others while the vocalizations increased in volume. The drums picked up, light and slow at first, rising in intensity with the huffing and the soft cries that had taken the place of the humming. The fluid movements of the dancers turned fierce and sharp, suggestive of combat, and yet still beautiful somehow.

Velara's fingers twined through his again, her grip tightening. His head spun, too much mead and the wildness of the performance pulling him further from himself. He was becoming part of the music.

The dancers cast each other about, tumbling upon the floor as if locked in battle, but with a body control that brought extraordinary grace to even the most violent of movements. They continued until none remained standing, all writhing on the floor with music that became suddenly slower and quieter. The two kanodraks moved out, gazing down at the others, their masked faces tilted curiously. One by one, they reached out to them, lifting them, supporting their weight with fluid displays of strength until all were standing again. The music stopped.

Kasiel remembered to breathe again. Applause rang out. Attendants relit a few sconces, revealing that Velara held only his hand. He extracted it, using it to adjust the opposite sleeve of his shirt, though it wasn't necessary.

Wine was delivered to the balcony seating areas and a second remarkable performance erased the momentary discomfort from his mind. When that dance ended amidst enthusiastic applause, Velara leaned over to Jethan.

"Cousin, could you find someone to bring us water?"

Jethan smiled, affectionately indulgent. "Good idea. I'll be back."

Kasiel rose and walked to the rear of the sitting area, moving out of view of the crowd as he stretched his shoulders. Velara touched his arm. When he turned, he found her standing rather close, her bright silver eyes drawing him in.

"Ahninveth Kasiel," a faint smile curved up the

corners of her mouth as she spoke, her voice soft and captivating, "you would like to kiss me, wouldn't you?"

A distant part of his mind tried to form an objection, but, as her smile broadened, it faltered, spiraling away. Still, he shouldn't... for some reason.

"I can't do—"

Her index finger slipped inside the collar of his shirt, tracing the chain of his ke'hanoath. He drew a sharp breath as the contact sent a surge of desire through him.

"Of course you can. There's nothing wrong with one little kiss, is there?"

The noise of the crowd faded away. He fell deep into her silver eyes. She was right. What could it hurt? He leaned in. She tilted her head back. The scent of her – the honey mead on her breath, the floral crown, a hint of perfume – washed over him, a wave of longing making him dizzy. Their lips were a hair's breadth apart when Niskenya's fury slammed into him like a punch to the head. His mind cleared abruptly, and he jerked away from Velara.

She stumbled back, one hand going to her forehead as if it pained her. "What just happened?"

The kanodrak's rage merged with his own now. He had experienced something like this before, and the memory wasn't a pleasant one. "You're a Charmer?"

Her other hand came to rest over her stomach. "Yes. And now I feel like I might throw up. How did you kick me out like that?"

"I didn't. My kanodrak did."

"Fantastic." She used her fingers to rub her temples, seeming oblivious to the growl of anger in his voice.

"Water's on the..." Jethan trailed off as he came through the curtains, his brow furrowing. "What's going on?"

"She tried to Charm me?" Kasiel snapped.

Jethan looked at Velara, his features twisting into

some conflicted combination of scandalized and delighted. "You didn't?"

She gave him a sour look, her hands sinking to her sides as if the effects of the rejection were fading. "I did. I was just trying to have a little harmless fun."

Kasiel scowled at her. "There are plenty of men in this city who would probably be thrilled to have you playing such tricks on them. Why me?"

A seductive smile eased back across her lips. "Because you're a handsome, heroic figure with a tragic childhood. What woman wouldn't want you?" When she stepped toward him, Kasiel retreated an equal distance from her. She groaned, looking disgusted, and turned to Jethan. "This is your tehnaak, Cousin. I would have expected someone more adventurous."

Jethan's brows pinched together. "I can't tell if that was a compliment or an insult."

She waved a dismissive hand at them and stormed back to her chair. Folding her legs into the seat and her arms across her chest, she stared daggers down at the dancers.

Jethan stepped close to him as many of the lights went out again. "Wait. She's a fairly strong Charmer. Why didn't it work?"

"Niske intervened."

"Huh. That's an unexpected benefit."

"Why didn't you warn me?"

Jethan put a hand on his shoulder and leaned closer. "I honestly didn't expect her to try something like that. I guess that makes me the fool for not realizing what catch you are."

Kasiel breathed a laugh and shoved his hand off. "Calloch."

Velara ignored Kasiel through the remainder of the performance, a choice he supported, though he did his best not to make that offensively obvious. During the final dance, a sensual piece that made him even less comfortable in her company now, Kasiel spotted his unit below amidst the crowd of people flowing with the music. They had worked their way to the front next to the stage.

Jhanik's unit was down there as well. Gratitude swelled in Kasiel as he watched his companions deftly run interference to keep the other Feral away from Nerith, who was by the stage, dancing between Avris and Merrin. After a few minutes, he ignored Jhanik and focused solely on Nerith, watching her sway with the music. The rhythm of the drums moved through him, his heart seeming to pump in time with the irresistible beats. He wanted nothing more than to be down there with her, sliding his hands around her waist, holding her as they danced together.

It was exquisite torture to watch her from afar. He barely noticed the dancers on the stage. That last performance lasted too long and ended too soon. When the music stopped and the sconces were lit again, Velara stood abruptly, drawing his attention to her.

"I'm ready to leave," she announced, not looking at

either of them.

He glanced down to find that Nerith and the rest of the unit had already vanished from the crowd. Frustration refreshed his anger with the khesran. She was the reason he and Jethan didn't get to enjoy this time with their companions. And her attempt to Charm him... There was no excuse for that.

"If you wish, Khesran," he said, earning a raised brow from Jethan for his frosty tone.

Velara winced, a hint of hurt in her eyes before she buried it beneath a glare. "I do."

They walked to the palace in silence. Velara's attendant and two more guards met them inside the main entrance. She gave Jethan a quick hug before striding off with them, refusing to give Kasiel so much as a glance, which suited him fine.

"I'm going to the barracks," he stated when she was gone.

"Ah, you might want to stop by your rooms first." The corner of Jethan's mouth twitched up.

Kasiel gave him a wary look, a flicker of hope taking root in his chest. "Where are you going?"

"I was going to find Keyla, Velara's tehnaak," he clarified, "so I might compliment her on her performance tonight."

A hint of unease stirred in his gut. "You won't Charm her, right?"

"Not with my ability." He cracked a full smile now. "Go to your rooms, Kas. Trust me."

"I do."

"Fool." Jethan put an arm around his shoulders, giving him a half-hug before moving away. "Sleep well, tehnaak. Or don't," he added, a mischievous gleam in his eyes.

Kasiel grinned, eager to get to his rooms now. "You had best not be toying with me."

"I guess you'll find out when you get there."

They split up, and Kasiel walked as fast as he could, breaking into a brief jog to cover the last short stretch of hallway to his rooms. He stepped in to find it dark except for one candle burning on a table next to the chair where Nerith sat. Her head rested back, braids pulled out of her long hair to let it hang loose in a silvery cascade. Kasiel went to stand in front of her. She opened her eyes, looking up at him, but didn't move. Was she still upset with him for the incident with Jhanik? Would she be here if she was?

"I saw you dancing below," he whispered, putting his hands on the arms of the chair, and leaning over her.

"Did you like what you saw?"

"I did." He placed a light kiss on her lips, encouraged when she kissed him in return, though she still didn't move. "I'm sorry."

She clasped her hands behind his neck, a wicked gleam in her eyes that set his blood on fire. "Show me how sorry you are."

He slid his hands around her waist and pulled her to him, claiming her lips in a deep kiss. Then he lifted her into his arms and carried her to the bed.

Later, Nerith lay against him, sweat from their lovemaking drying on their skin in the cool air that crept in through a cracked window. She rested her head on his shoulder, tracing the symbols of his ke'hanoath lazily with one finger.

"I saw you and Jethan in the city with Khesran Velara."

He lay with his eyes closed, content to listen to her voice and feel her touch. "You should have gotten my attention. All day it was you I wanted to be with."

"Jethan sent a messenger to let us know his cousin had commandeered you two. He also sent me a private note detailing how I could get into your rooms tonight."

"Sounds like I owe him."

"We both do." He could hear the smile in her voice.

Kasiel opened his eyes and reached across to brush her hair behind her ear. Any excuse to touch her. "About what happened with Jhanik."

Her finger moved to his lips. "Jhanik can be difficult. I know that, and I know that you're better than him. I just want you to remember that next time he starts to get under your skin."

"I'll do my best." It was a big ask, since he had the urge to punch the other Feral regularly, but he would try for her.

Nerith wrapped her arm around him and pressed her body closer. "I went to visit my family this morning. Then I visited Leysa's family. It was my first chance to talk to them since she..." she trailed off, her voice tightening.

Kasiel hugged her to him and kissed her head. "I'm sorry. I should have been there with you."

"No, it was easier alone. But I was hoping you might come meet my parents tomorrow after the parade." She shifted up onto her elbow to look at him. "Before you decide, you should know they won't like you. You're not Jhanik, so that's one count against you. You're also the dhomvalen's son, which probably equates to two or three counts against you in my father's eyes. I just want them to understand that you are the man I've given my heart to, and nothing they say is going to change that."

He slid his hand into her hair, staring into those warm eyes he adored. "Count me in."

"Good." A playful sparkle lit her eyes as she moved up to straddle him. "Now, tell me more about what you were thinking while you were watching me dance."

He grinned. "Why don't I just show you?"

*

Morning came too soon. Fortunately, preparing for the parade proved relatively simple. They set up Kasiel's unit and tethdraks to ride on one side of the royal family, with Jhanik's mirroring them on the other. Kasiel and Jhanik, given the size of their kanodraks, stayed slightly behind the royal family so as not to obstruct the people's view of their leaders. Arhk and Dhomen Aleren took places ahead of the Khemron and his children in the center, behind a unit of royal guards following a company of musicians and dancers. There was something to be said for not being in charge of anything beyond keeping his beasts in line. It struck him as far easier than meeting Nerith's parents was going to be, considering that they already resented him for who he wasn't and for who he was.

It wasn't until he saw how many people came out to watch them that anxiety kicked in. The entire city appeared to be lining the broad street when the parade started moving, filling him with an intense desire to disappear. Then Niskenya's presence flowed through him, pushing away his anxiety and boosting him with her confidence. Kasiel straightened, sitting tall on the kanodrak's back in the ceremonial black and silver attire they had provided him with that closely matched his father's. After a night spent with Nerith in his arms, he found it easier to ignore Jhanik, trusting Niskenya to keep them in pace with the other kanodrak.

They had gone a few blocks when the column paused to let the dancers perform a number for their audience. Velara maneuvered over next to him, forcing him to increase his calming influence on her horse. A glance at her father's frown made it apparent that she wasn't supposed to be breaking formation, but the crowd cheered when she sidled up beside the kanodrak.

Velara gazed at Niskenya with open fascination. "What is it like to ride such a magnificent creature?"

Niskenya passed a sense of playful encouragement through to him. Fully aware of the rapt attention of the crowd nearest them, Kasiel held a hand down to her. "Find out for yourself."

Velara's face lit, and she hopped off her mount. One of her guards steered his horse over and grabbed the abandoned animal's reins before it could cause more disruption. Niskenya sank to a lower stance while Kasiel leaned down and took Velara's arm below the elbow. She grabbed the back of the saddle to help pull herself up behind him. One hand slid around his waist as she waved with the other. The crowd let out a wild cheer. Niskenya straightened, and the column began moving again.

Velara's hold on him tightened. "Jortan's ass. It's a long way down."

Kasiel chuckled, twisting in the saddle to look over his shoulder at her. "Whose ass?"

She flushed. "Jortan's an old history instructor at the mind-crafter academy here. The students joke that he has a stick so far up his ass it messes with his hearing. Somehow, Jortan's ass has become a common exclamation around the campus." She leaned close to his ear as he faced forward. "Don't tell father I was speaking so crudely."

"I have a strange feeling it wouldn't surprise him."

She giggled and rested her chin on his shoulder. "Does this mean you've forgiven me for last night?"

Kasiel stiffened. "Have you apologized?"

"No."

"You have your answer, then."

She shifted back to wave to the delighted crowd before leaning close again. "Jethan says you have a girlfriend."

"I do." A girlfriend riding behind them, who probably didn't appreciate Velara's current position. Someday he would learn to think his impulses through before he acted on them. "I hope you realize that isn't the only reason you should apologize for what you tried to do last night."

"He also told me about the Charmer who helped some traitors abduct you. While your escape makes for an impressive story, I am truly sorry that happened to you. I'm also sorry I tried to Charm you. However, I will not apologize for trying to kiss you."

Kasiel mustered up a smile for a young girl who was tugging at her mother's sleeve and pointing at Niskenya. She beamed up at him.

Velara waved to the girl, and she bounced excitedly, waving back at them. "So, am I forgiven now?"

"No, but I'm willing to put up with you to please the crowd."

"Ass," she muttered, jabbing him in the ribs with two fingers.

Her impeccable aim went right into the healing bruises from his fight with Jhanik, and he flinched, sucking in a breath.

"I thought soldiers were tougher than that." She turned to wave at more of the crowd, producing another round of exuberant cheers.

"I bruised my ribs on the trip up."

"Really?" Her tone held no sympathy, just enthusiastic curiosity. "An injured cliff cat and bruised ribs. There must be a story behind this."

He opened his mouth to growl a no at her, but stopped when Niskenya sent a wave of patience. "Nothing interesting," he said, keeping an even tone.

She leaned her chin on his shoulder again. "Tell me over lunch, and I'll decide how interesting it is."

"No. I have other obligations after this foolishness is done."

"Oh. Too good for the khemron's parade, are we?"

She straightened. "I can't say I disagree with you. How about after tonight's dinner, then?" Another wave delighted the people they were passing now.

Did that mean they were stuck attending another formal meal? He hoped not. "We'll see."

"We certainly will." Her tone said she believed she had won.

When they got to the end of the route in a blocked off courtyard before the palace, Jethan trotted up to offer Velara a hand down, reaching her ahead of her guards.

She gave Kasiel a quick kiss on the cheek. "Thank you."

He nodded, a glance around bringing his attention to a wide array of reactions from others. The khemron merely shook his head, while Dhomen Aleren looked amused. Arhk wore his signature unreadable expression, though Kasiel thought he caught a barely discernible hint of what looked like satisfaction in his father's eyes. On the other side of the square, Jhanik gave him a disgusted sneer and rode off with his tethdraks behind him. Nerith had suddenly learned how to give that flat expression even better than his father. The only thing he was certain of was that she wasn't amused.

As the group gradually dispersed, the royal family heading into the palace with an escort of guards, Kasiel urged Niskenya over to Nerith, the kanodrak easily clearing a path with her intimidating presence.

He held a hand down, moving his foot out of the stirrup on that side. "Want to help me take Niske and the tethdraks back to the habitats?"

For a tense second, she stared up at him, and he thought she might refuse. Then Niskenya shifted closer to her and sank into a lower stance.

"I..."

Darro came and took her horse's reins from her.

She eyed the kanodrak. "Niske won't mind?"

"I'm pretty sure she'd prefer you to Velara." He got a mental growl from Niskenya in response to that, though he couldn't tell if that meant the opposite was true or that she just didn't like him making assumptions about her preferences.

Nerith reached up and took his hand, letting him help her up. She slid her arms around his waist, and he put a hand over hers, wrapping the other around the grip on the saddle. They moved clear of the crowd, and he encouraged Niskenya up to an easy lope, wanting to give Nerith something more than Velara had gotten. She let out a small gasp and tightened her hold on him, pressing against his back. Kasiel smiled to himself and focused on guiding the tethdraks along with them.

They dropped off the tethdraks first. On their way to the kanodrak enclosure, they spotted Jhanik leaving. The other Feral ignored them. Once he had Niskenya settled in a fenced off section of the habitat, Kasiel returned to Nerith and reached for her hand.

She moved it away, her gaze piercing into him. "Are you attracted to her?"

"Velara?" He shrugged. "She's lovely."

Nerith's lips pressed into a tight line, and she took a step back from him.

He stepped forward. "You want me to lie to you?"

"Yes." She shook her head. "No."

Kasiel chuckled and took another step closer. A light touch on her cheek got her to look at him. "It's not the khesran I'm interested in. I want to gaze into your eyes. I want to kiss..." he leaned in to give her a soft kiss, "... your lips."

She blew out a heavy breath. "I'm sorry. It's just... You're military nobility, Kas. Everyone knows you could do better."

Placing a finger gently under her chin to discourage

her from moving away, he leaned close to her ear and whispered, "I don't see it that way." He grinned when she shivered.

She turned so their lips were almost touching. "Maybe we should skip my parents."

Kasiel kissed her before stepping back and offering her his hand. "How bad can it be?"

Nerith sighed and twined her fingers through his. "You don't know my father."

The stroll to her parents' house was interrupted – deliberately, he suspected – by many stops to point out favorite shops, buildings that had changed since her last visit, or the houses of people she spent time with growing up in Doran. When they finally ended their walk before a modest, single-story home, she gave him an apologetic look.

"You don't have to do this."

He gestured to the door.

Holding his hand like it was a lifeline, she led him into the house. The small entry reminded him of his home in Fernwallow. Simple, but neat. That opened onto a large sitting with a fireplace to one side. The finish of everything was cozy and unpretentious, but of high quality. The home of a family that lived a comfortable life, if not a substantially wealthy one. Jhanik and two older couples sat on well-made, comfortable-looking chairs and a couch around a polished marble table sharing drinks and conversation.

Nerith's brow furrowed, and she dropped Kasiel's hand, stepping forward with her eyes locked on a man with angular features and graying blond hair. He had one leg crossed over the other, an arm resting along the back of the couch behind a woman who looked a lot like an older version of Nerith.

"Father, I don't understand. What are they doing here?" She gestured to Jhanik and the other couple who, given the way they looked at Kasiel like they were being asked to swallow poison, had to be his parents. That would make the woman the mind-crafter Arhk had disgraced and supplanted as dhomvalen.

Her father's haughty smirk made Kasiel instantly dislike him. "Why wouldn't they be here? My tehnaak and his family are always welcome in this house."

"But I told you I was bringing Kas by."

Her father's gaze shifted to Kasiel, a hint of disgust in the curl of his lip. "After that display at the parade, I assumed the young man had moved on to courting a more appropriate match."

Nerith's jaw tightened, and he saw her shoulders rise and fall with a deep breath as she fought to maintain calm. Jhanik's superior gaze made Kasiel yearn to punch him again. There were no beasts to interfere here. He felt the judgmental looks of Jhanik's parents drilling into him.

"Father." Nerith's hard tone spoke volumes.

"This," her father said, gesturing to Jhanik and his parents, "is *our* family. If you are serious about this young man, he should know the people he is getting involved with. He should know what *his* family has done to them."

Nerith's outrage was a storm crashing against her father's calm belligerence. "Kasiel had nothing to do with the conflict between Jhanik's family and his father. He wasn't even in Vanris when all of that happened."

"True." Her father gave Kasiel an icy look. "He was being raised by the people we're at war with. I hope you understand why that doesn't endear me to him as a match for my daughter."

"We're leaving." Nerith spun and grabbed Kasiel's wrist.

"Nerith." Her father stood. "If you walk out that door with him right now, you will not be allowed back in."

She froze. Kasiel was the only one who could see the weight of her father's words crushing her when moisture sprang to her eyes.

Her mother got up. "Andross, I may not approve of her choice any more than you do, but I will not let you ban our daughter from this house."

Jhanik's father stood as well, gesturing for his family to join him. "We should go. This is something the three of you must work out amongst yourselves."

Andross glanced at him and nodded.

Kasiel stepped to the side to let them pass, making a point of keeping his eyes on Nerith, to avoid the temptation to slug Jhanik as he walked by. Nerith was staring down now, avoiding looking at any of them. When they were gone, she met his eyes.

"What can I do?" he whispered.

"I'm sorry. You should go. I'll see if I can salvage this." Her expression hardened. "If it's even worth salvaging."

"You're sure?"

She nodded.

Kasiel cupped her cheek with one hand. "I love you."

"I love you too." She popped up on her toes to kiss him.

"Out," her father demanded.

Nerith gestured to the door, the anger blazing to life in her eyes making him almost glad he was leaving, though he hated feeling like he was abandoning her. She turned her back on him, going to wage her own war. A war she hadn't asked him to fight in. Kasiel went outside. The moment the door shut behind him, he heard her father shouting.

"I will not have my only child flaunting herself around with the earless son of Arhk Cavenos!"

"It's not your decision," Nerith spat back. "The only thing you get to choose right now is whether you want to continue being part of my life!"

Silently wishing her luck, Kasiel began removing the winged ear cuffs and braids he had worn for the parade as he walked away.

Kasiel was to meet Jethan and the others to spar at the barracks later in the afternoon. With how quickly the encounter with Nerith's parents had fallen apart, he had over an hour to find another way to occupy himself. Not wanting to wear his parade finery in the practice ring, he struck out for the palace. Several people greeted him along the way, recognizing him as Ahninveth Kasiel, the dhomvalen's son, or the Feral hero from Etrion. One shopkeeper even gifted him a selection of fruit, saying he looked hungry, which he was. Though he greeted them warmly in return, he couldn't help wondering how many considered him the earless son of Arhk Cavenos.

Would he be the reason Nerith became estranged from her family? Was he worth that?

When he reached the private living quarters in the palace, he discarded the fancier clothes on his bed and put on simpler attire suitable for combat practice. That used up about five minutes. He stepped out into the hall, not sure where to go from there. When he had been standing there for several minutes, a passing female attendant approached.

"My lord, might I be of assistance?" She offered a slight bow.

"Is there someplace quiet I might go to be alone

with my thoughts?"

"I know just the place. Follow me."

He let her lead him upstairs and down another hall to a set of elegant doors made of a dark, red wood with a detailed vine pattern carved around the frame.

She reached for the handle. "The sitting area on this balcony overlooks one of the palace's interior gardens." She opened the door, and he started through. "It's Khesran Velara's favorite place to go when she needs to clear her head."

In fact, Velara currently sat beside a small round table near the far end of the balcony. She glanced over, spotting him before he could make a quick reversal. Drawing in a deep, bracing breath, he turned and started toward her. Velara ran a slender finger around the rim of an almost empty stoneglass goblet while she watched him approach.

The attendant hurried over to her. "Your highness, I didn't realize you were still out here. Can I bring you anything?"

Velara's gaze lingered on Kasiel. She gestured to the chair on the other side of the table. "A decanter of the Night Pearl and another goblet for Ahninveth Kasiel."

"Right away."

The attendant hurried off as Kasiel slid the chair forward and sank into it, resting his boots on the balcony railing.

"You look as if your day took an unpleasant turn."

He shrugged. It felt inappropriate to talk about Nerith with her.

Velara didn't press. Instead, she swallowed the last of her drink and gazed out over the garden.

It was beautiful. A magnificent tree with long, draping branches weighed down with early spring foliage made a grand centerpiece. Few of the wide array of plants between the winding stone walkways were in full bloom, but the shades of green varied from the palest mint to the deepest olive. The shapes of the leaves he was close enough to see varied widely too. Everything from graceful emerald teardrops to some almost rectangular leaves, the corners tipped with spikes. This far from his childhood home, he didn't recognize many of the plants, but the simple peacefulness of the garden and the familiar aroma of vegetation were soothing.

He placed the pieces of fruit he hadn't eaten yet between them on the table along with his ear cuffs, not wanting to crush them in his pockets. They sat together in unexpectedly comfortable silence until after the attendant delivered a dark red wine about the color of Velara's hair. After a few sips of the bold blend she had requested for them, Kasiel dared to speak.

"When you first... crashed into me yesterday, you seemed upset." He could barely believe that had been just yesterday. "Would it be too forward of me to ask why?"

She took a drink before answering and pulled her legs up into her chair in a pose that made her look disturbingly vulnerable. She stared at a few of the elegant rings she wore. "Not too forward, no, but I am not supposed to talk about it."

He nodded and turned his gaze back to the garden.

"The kingdom of Delaphine is offering to ally with Vanris." She threw the words out like rubbish she couldn't wait to dispose of. "They want to seal the agreement with a political marriage."

"Oh." No wonder she appeared distraught. He looked at her. "Just Delaphine?"

"Yes." She set down her wine and picked up one of his ear cuffs, running a finger along the smooth upper edge. It surprised him how intimate the gesture felt, as if it were his actual ear she caressed. He had to suppress the irrational desire to snatch it back from her. "Father thinks they are acting without the knowledge of the other Alliance kingdoms. They share borders with Vanris, Sarket, and Fallend, but Fallend is no threat. Everyone knows they only joined the Alliance because Sarket and Delaphine strong-armed them into it."

Kasiel held his tongue, reluctant to admit that he hadn't known that.

"If Delaphine abandons the Pandrean Alliance to join with Vanris, it is possible Fallend could be persuaded to abandon the Alliance as well, leaving Sarket on their own."

This was big. In fact, it was huge, and clearly privileged information. "But why would Delaphine leave the Alliance? I can't believe they've suddenly developed a fondness for mind-crafters."

"My understanding is that, for a variety of reasons, they have suffered a more substantial share of the losses whenever things turn violent with Vanris. The elixir that made their soldiers immune to our mind-crafters was the first thing in the war that gave them any real advantage. For a short time, they believed they had a chance of winning. However, since your unit brought down the production of that elixir and its creator, we have decisively crushed them on every front."

She gave him a coy smile. "One of several reasons a Vanrian woman might be inclined to kiss you, by the way." The smile faded, and she set his ear cuff back on the table. "The way things are going, my first kiss will be with some earless southerner." She winced at her own words. "No offense."

"You know I'm Vanrian, right?"

"Of course. I wouldn't have tried to kiss you otherwise. But you were raised in the south and..." She gestured vaguely at the side of his head.

"And my ears are cut."

She nodded, a hint of color rising in her cheeks.

Her words brought back what Nerith's father had called him, threatening to break the tentative peace he had found in this lovely spot in spite of, or possibly because of, Velara's company. He pushed the darker thoughts away, pulling on calm from Niskenya, who was basking in the sun out in the habitat. *"You've* never been kissed?"

She picked up her goblet and swirled the drink, frowning at the contents. "Why does it sound as if you find that hard to believe?"

"Because I do find it hard to believe?"

"Why? Because I'm a Charmer or because I'm—"

"A flirt," he filled in bluntly.

She narrowed her eyes at him. "Playful, as my father would say."

"No. Because you're beautiful, and far more intelligent than you let on."

She stared at him long enough that he struggled not to look away, then a slow smile crept across her lips. "Thank you, Ahninveth Kasiel."

"And a flirt," he added with a teasing wink.

"Sheyvyosk."

He arched a brow. "What did you just call me?"

Her cheeks turned a warm shade of pink. "It means stinky... smegma."

He arched a brow. "Stinky what?"

"You know. The um..." Her cheeks brightened. "Like the stuff that collects in a male horse's... Around his..."

Kasiel couldn't hold back his laughter any longer.

"Calloch!" She threw an apple at him. "You already knew what it was."

He surprised himself by catching the apple with his left hand. Maybe there was hope for him. "I did grow up in the country. Though I've never heard sheyvyosk before."

"Shocking, given how it fits you." She shook her head at him and reclined back in her chair. "Maybe you're suited to be Jethan's tehnaak after all."

He grinned and followed her example, relaxing with his drink.

They sat in companionable silence for a short time, both taking sips of wine. He couldn't imagine any of the southern kingdoms allying with Vanris. Then again, he was there for some of the recent battles Velara mentioned, and the south had taken significant losses. If Delaphine was suffering the brunt of those losses, maybe it made sense for them to consider other options. Vanris wasn't the aggressor. They had never pushed beyond the Crimson Break. They had everything they needed in the north. The south just didn't want to share a border with mind-crafters and wasn't content to sit idle with them there.

If he were to be honest, he could see their point. He grew up without knowing there were people who could manipulate the minds of others. Now that he was among them, one of them even, he still found it a little unnerving. Falling victim to his father's Frightener ability early on, and then to the Charmer who tried to sell him off as a prisoner to the south, made it easier for him see the other side of this.

"I can't believe the khevarin would consider marrying you off to a southerner."

She took another sip of wine, eyes narrowing as she glared over the garden. "Believe it. My mother would do anything for this country, and to hold on to her place within it."

"What about your brothers?"

"Nakhul is still too young, at least by Vanrian standards, and Karith is married. That makes me the lucky one." She set the wine down, her gaze sinking to her hands as she folded them in her lap. A stillness fell over her that called on him to listen carefully. "I'm a little scared of what's coming," she said in barely more than a whisper. "When word gets out, there will be plenty of people on both sides willing to do anything to stop this."

Kasiel moved the decanter out of the center of the small table. He held a hand out to her. She glanced at the hand, then met his eyes and placed hers in it.

"Jethan and I will do everything in our power to help you and keep you safe. I promise."

"What if it's not in your power?"

He closed his hand around hers and grinned. "Then we'll let Niske handle it."

A tremulous smile teased at her lips. "Your kano-drak? Must be nice to have such a creature on your side."

He gave her a solemn look. "You tell me. Is it?"

She nodded at him as if coming to some decision. "You're surprisingly tolerable for a soldier."

Leaving her hand in his a little longer, she leaned back and put her feet up on the railing. The black and gold split skirt she'd worn in the parade fell away from her matching, fitted pants with a soft whisper. They stayed there for a time, sipping wine and enjoying the mild, early spring weather. When he finally stood to leave, she sat up as well, poised on the edge of her seat as if intending to rise.

"Relax and enjoy the view," he said, casting an appreciative last glance over the garden. "I'm going to get Irith and head to the barracks for some practice."

"Always working?"

A bee danced past his face to land on an apple he had left on the table, agile and efficient. He flexed his right hand out of habit, feeling the catching in the scar tissue. Not so agile anymore. "I've got an injury to learn to work around."

Her gaze sank to his arm. "Ah, yes. I've heard the

stories of how you used your arm as a shield against the Delaphinian general's mace."

He answered with a dry laugh. "It really doesn't sound smart when you phrase it that way."

"I suppose not." Her silver eyes shone with amusement and something else he tried to ignore. "It sounds much more heroic when they say you sacrificed your sword arm to keep the general from killing a group of Vanrian prisoners."

"It does." He shifted his attention to the bee, uncomfortable with the look she was giving him. "Well, Khesran Velara, it's been a pleasure—"

She stood, pulling a lock of blood-red hair forward over her shoulder and twirling it around her finger. "I'll come with you, if that's all right."

"I'm not sure if I rank high enough to tell you where you can and can't go, Khesran."

"I'm asking for your feelings, not your permission, Ahninveth." She added a sarcastic emphasis to the title. "I was told we'll be leaving tomorrow. It couldn't hurt to meet more of the people I'll be traveling with."

"Tomorrow?" It felt like they had barely arrived, probably because they had.

She nodded.

He hesitated. Arriving with Velara might not sit well with Nerith, if she had even escaped her family yet. Then again, they would all be traveling together to Etrion. The unit needed to get used to Velara being around for a while. As much as he hated to admit it, that wasn't the only reason he was tempted to welcome her company.

"Honestly," he said, rubbing at the back of his neck and staring at the fuzzy little bee busily examining the apple, "if you don't come, I'm not sure I'll be able to find my way to the barracks from the cliff cat enclosure."

Not one to spare his emotions, Velara laughed. "Come on, I'll be your escort this time."

Walking through the city with Velara was a different experience from doing so with Nerith. Where Nerith brought his attention to the city itself and her memories of growing up within it, Velara took him outside the walls, painting him a picture of the surrounding countryside. To the north was Lake Zephanis where she and her brothers often swam when they were younger. To the west, several meadows within the forest provided excellent spots for picnics and collecting wildflowers. She went on for a time about galloping through the fields to the northeast and trying to lose her guards in the forest beyond, two of whom walked silently along with them now, their long-suffering looks confirming her stories.

Was the deviation in focus between the two women a product of their very different social classes and upbringings, or simply a result of the years Nerith had spent away from Doran? How would Velara see this city after she had been away for a time?

That thought opened a hollow in his chest.

Velara's time away from Doran had significant potential to change her. If she returned, it might be as a woman wed to a stranger, forced to take an "earless southerner" as her partner. What would that do to her? In part, it would depend on what kind of man her future husband turned out to be. But no matter his personality, their different origins would make them forever hated by most of each other's people. A fact that could leave them both feeling ostracized and unwelcome wherever they went. He knew how that felt from his own experiences, though it had gotten a little better for him. Would it ever do so for her?

At the habitat, Kasiel found Irith much improved after some good rest and care. He could barely keep the big cat from leaping up on him in his excitement and possibly hurting himself. To avoid that, he knelt, and Irith rubbed against him, nearly knocking him over several times. The big cat caught Kasiel with a head-butt to the face that left his cheek throbbing. The pain was more than worth having his companion at his side again.

When they arrived at the barracks, the entire unit was there preparing for departure, except for Nerith. They kept a respectful manner around Velara, standing outside the practice ring. She was royalty. Technically, Jethan was royalty too, but not the way the khesran was. They'd also had years to get used to working with him. The men were particularly wary around her, something that drew Kasiel's attention to how stunning a woman she was with her refined features, silver eyes, and un-usual hair. How had he gotten comfortable around her so quickly?

His thoughts scattered when Merrin came at him with her sword high and bloodlust in her eyes. By letting himself become fully immersed in Niskenya's presence to the point he barely felt human anymore, he succeeded in holding his own against her. He also let go of his concern for Nerith and the lingering upset from his encounter with her father for a while. Everything became aggression and reaction, avoidance and attack. Their surroundings disappeared, narrowing down to the opponent across from him and the remarkable beast whose instincts guided him.

When they finally stopped, he struggled his way free of the kanodrak's influence, becoming aware of the sweat that dampened his clothing and several sore spots where fresh bruises were forming.

Merrin regarded him with a proud gleam in her eyes. "That was a battle worth fighting."

As the others offered praise and found ways to tease him, Velara watched him shrewdly from where she leaned against the corner of the overhang. Nerith re-mained absent.

"So, what happened with Nerith's family?" Jethan asked as they made their way back to the palace, Velara's guards following behind.

"Nerith?" Velara leaned forward to look at Kasiel from Jethan's other side, a position she had taken to avoid the stink of his sweat. "You don't mean Andross Gaverin's daughter?"

Kasiel nodded, an itch of discomfort between his shoulder blades that he chose to attribute to drying sweat.

Her finely shaped brows rose toward her hairline. "You do know your father has an extremely contentious history with their family, right? They despise him. And not in a passive way. More like an 'I would stab you in the street if I didn't think anyone was looking' kind of way. Couldn't you have picked a less controversial match?"

Kasiel heaved a sigh. "I wasn't exactly aware of that when I met her."

"But she must have been."

That was true, though Nerith admitted she hadn't expected to fall for him. She had merely been following orders. No wonder she had been upset when the khevarin first told her to get close to him. Though it did seem like something she should have brought up earlier in their relationship. "It's a little more complicated."

"Isn't it always?"

Kasiel glanced at Jethan. "Did you know?"

Jethan shrugged. "I knew there was a scandal when Arhk took over as dhomvalen, but honestly, I didn't pay that much attention."

"Too busy pretending to be common?" There was an edge of reprimand behind Velara's teasing smile.

Jethan looked at her. "Why do you know so much about it?"

She averted her gaze. "Perhaps you missed how

intimately my mother was involved in the situation. If she wasn't the khevarin, I believe Andross and his family would be just as hostile toward her over the matter. It's always good to keep track of potential enemies."

Jethan shrugged. "Fair point."

A trio of children ran their way, the one in the lead skidding and landing on his rear in front of them when he saw who was walking there. The other two darted to one side and stood staring, wide-eyed, as if they feared their friend had committed some horrible crime.

Kasiel reached down to him. "Are you all right?"

The boy's mouth hung open as he took the offered hand and let Kasiel lift him. "Thanks, Ahninveth," he said, his voice cracking. He darted over to his friends. "Did you see that? The Hero of Vanris spoke to me and touched my hand!" He held up the appendage in question before them as if it were a glorious trophy.

The three hurried off, chatting excitedly.

Velara covered her mouth as she breathed a laugh, gazing at Kasiel with a gleam of affection in her eyes.

Jethan chuckled. "It seems being royalty makes us second class these days."

Heat rose in Kasiel's cheeks. He resumed walking at a brisk pace.

"Is Keyla coming to Etrion?" Jethan asked as he and Velara fell into step.

"He asks with no ulterior motives," Kasiel added, earning another laugh from Velara.

At the palace, Kasiel took time to bathe and dress for another formal dinner. He had little interest in gossip and social politics. Instead, he let Jethan distract him throughout the meal with embarrassing stories about various lords and ladies seated around them. Their occasional muffled laughter earned them stern looks from Arhk and the khemron, though Velara and Nakhul gazed on appreciatively from their places next to their older brother.

When he finally escaped to his rooms, they were disappointingly empty. He pulled a book about Doran's founding from the shelf and dug Sylaryth's claw out of his bags. Then he reclined on the couch and read, absently rubbing a thumb across the smooth surface of his late companion's lethal talon until his eyes would no longer stay open. It was well after dark when he crawled into his bed, his gut knotted with worry for Nerith.

CHAPTER ELEVEN

Their departure was kept low-key. Kasiel and Jhanik gathered their beasts and joined their units and the rest of the company at the gates. Velara, along with Keyla and a personal attendant, were there in a finely made, but simple carriage with four of her guards positioned around it.

Kasiel caught sight of an unfamiliar man in his unit with the symbol of the healers tattooed next to one eye. Nerith was nowhere to be seen. Jhanik, mounted on his kanodrak, was also looking over Kasiel's unit with his brow furrowed. As much as he wanted to blame the other Feral for Nerith's absence, the man didn't appear to know what was going on, either.

Urging Niskenya over to them, he addressed the strange healer. "Where's Nerith?"

The man, his dark blond hair worked into a series of tight braids against his scalp, couldn't seem to look away from the kanodrak. "I'm Harif. I received orders to fill in as a second healer in your unit. That's all I know, Ahninveth."

"And why am I finding this out now?" Kasiel let anger loose to hide the fear that was feeding it. Niskenya growled. Irith stood up in the back of the cart he had been relegated to, his lip lifting in a snarl.

The man paled.

Arhk rode up alongside him. "There was no time, Ahninveth Kasiel."

"Where's Nerith?" He turned his worried gaze on his father now.

Arhk gestured to the side with a jerk of his head, and Niskenya followed him away from the others.

When they were far enough to speak privately, Arhk faced him, keeping his voice low. "Her father placed a formal dispute against her."

"What kind of dispute?"

Niskenya extended her claws into the dirt.

"I do not have that information."

Kasiel narrowed his eyes. As dhomvalen, he suspected his father could have easily gotten that information if he wanted to. "So, what does that mean?"

"It means that she cannot leave Doran until this is resolved."

Panic burned through him like wildfire. Protective anger absent a target came from Niskenya. She shifted beneath him, digging runnels in the dirt with one front paw. "Then neither can I."

"This is not your fight."

"Maybe it is," he snapped.

Darkness moved at the edges of Arhk's eyes. "You have a job to do. A single healer we can replace with little notice. We cannot do the same with you."

Kasiel found it hard to breathe. "I can't leave her to face this alone."

The darkness retreated. Arhk shook his head, his tone softening. "I am sorry, Kasiel, but you must. There are greater things at stake than your relationship with Nerith. Let her fight her own battles."

He glanced at the carriage. Velara watched them through an open window, one delicate hand gripping the sill. Tath rode into his line of sight, inclining her head to Arhk.

"Forgive me for interrupting, Dhomvalen, but I thought this might be relevant." She held a sealed letter out to Kasiel. "Nerith asked me to give this to you, Ahninveth."

Kasiel stared at the letter. He didn't want to take it. Even without reading it, he knew it would force him to accept this.

"Kas," Tath prompted gently.

With everyone watching, he felt trapped. Niskenya's tail lashed. He leaned down to take the letter, cracking the seal and unfolding it as he straightened.

Beloved Kasiel,

As you may already know, my father has put forth a formal dispute against me. I won't go into the details. Suffice it to say, the whole thing is absurd, and I am certain I will have no difficulty convincing the council of that. Please do not worry about me. I promise I will join you in Etrion as soon as I can.

You carry my love with you,
Nerith.

His hand closed into a fist, crushing the letter. If it was nothing to worry about, why hadn't she come to tell him in person?

"Get in your ranks," Dhomen Sorval shouted. "Ahninveth Jhanik, I want you and your unit in front of the carriage. You will manage the horses pulling it along with your units' mounts. Ahninveth Kasiel, your unit will ride behind. I want you to find an avian scout or two and keep an eye out from above us as well. Keep the tethdraks guarding on either side of the carriage."

Kasiel met his father's eyes. What wasn't he telling him?

Everyone was moving into place.

"We can talk about it later." Arhk turned to head to the front with Dhomen Sorval.

Kasiel gazed back into the city. Was she at her parent's

home? Or somewhere else perhaps, trying to avoid them? How was he supposed to just ride away and leave her to deal with this alone?

Tath had joined the company. In her place, Jethan rode up next to him.

"What's happening?"

Kasiel handed him the crumpled note.

Jethan read through it, then held it up facing Kasiel, his finger above the words 'Please don't worry about me.' "Trust her, Kas. There's not much else you can do in this situation."

Kasiel urged Niskenya into place behind the carriage. Defeat rode heavily on his shoulders. He trusted her, though not in the way Jethan meant it. He trusted her to shield him from her problems, and try to deal with them alone, even if she should ask for help. That didn't make it easier to walk away.

The company tried to maintain a fast pace. It was the cart Irith rode in that slowed them the most. Unlike the carriage, it didn't have the suspension needed to make faster speeds tolerable over long distances. As they got ready to continue after a midday break, Dhomen Sorval and Arhk took Kasiel aside to discuss the problem.

Velara came over uninvited, inserting herself into the conversation. "Why not have Irith ride in the carriage? If the three of us ladies sit on one side, there's room for him to stretch on the other."

"We're not putting a cliff cat in with you, Khesran Velara. It isn't safe," Sorval stated.

She met Kasiel's eyes. "What do you think, Ahninveth Kasiel, would Irith harm us?"

"No."

"It's settled then." She turned and started back toward the carriage.

Kasiel sent Irith with her.

Sorval scowled. "Be advised, Ahninveth. If anything

happens to her, you will be held accountable."

"You chose Ferals to protect her," Kasiel answered, anger at leaving Nerith barely contained behind his dry tone. "You trust us, or you don't, Dhomen."

Arhk was cautiously silent, his expression guarded, though Kasiel got the impression that his father somehow both approved and disapproved of his behavior. For the moment, he couldn't bring himself to care. Niskenya came up behind him, attentive to his intent, and he mounted, moving into position to head out.

After that, it was an ongoing struggle to resist the temptation to distract himself by eavesdropping through Irith on the women in the carriage. An idea Jethan put in his head, mostly because he wanted to know if Velara's tehnaak had anything to say about him. Kasiel looked in on them a few times, just to be sure Irith wasn't taking up too much space in the carriage. Toward the end of the day, when he snuck a peek through Irith's eyes, Velara was sitting with the big cat, and he had his head resting in her lap. It gave Kasiel an odd view of the rise of her breasts and the underside of her chin. He hastily backed out.

After settling his tethdraks at camp that evening, they made a makeshift ring, and he began warming up his arm to spar with Darro. Jhanik stalked out, heading for Kasiel. The other Feral left his tethdrak at the opposite edge of the ring from Irith, who had reluctantly abandoned the comforts of the carriage to join them. The cliff cat stood, his growl too low to hear, but Kasiel felt it in his mind. He sent calm back to him, though it was difficult to do so with Jhanik approaching.

"Is she all right?" Jhanik demanded, accusation in his voice and narrowed eyes.

Kasiel tried not to give attention to an immature flash of annoyance with the man for being a few inches taller. Ignoring Jhanik's question brought him a little satisfaction, though he knew doing so was rather juvenile as well. "The night we fought, you wanted to tell her something. What was it?"

Jhanik's nostrils flared, the only visible indication of his annoyance. "When I was called to Etrion to help on the front, I asked her father's permission to propose to her and bring her back to Doran with me. He gave it."

Hatred uncoiled like a venomous serpent in Kasiel's chest. Irith's growl was loud enough for them to both hear it this time. It drew attention from others around the camp.

Jhanik glanced at the cliff cat, eyes narrowing. "Do you honestly think that has anything to do with her absence?"

"I think it might. Her father placed a formal dispute against her, so she can't leave Doran until it's resolved." Kasiel imagined letting his tethdraks, currently resting at the edge of the camp, tear the man apart. A few raised their heads, looking in their direction.

The side of Jhanik's mouth curved up a fraction. "You know you're making her miserable. This would all go away if you would just leave her alone."

"And let you and her father try to force her into a life she doesn't want? I don't think so. From what I saw in Doran, it isn't me who's making her miserable."

Jhanik leaned in, his hand sinking to his sword hilt. "Earless bastard. You're not good enough for her."

Fury rose in Kasiel, though he was keenly aware of the fact that he held only a wooden practice sword. He had left the rest of his weapons over by Irith. "And what makes you think you are?"

"Give me that, Inveth." Arhk's voice drew their attention. He was taking Darro's practice sword from him. Then he strode out to them, his icy gaze settling on Jhanik. "Your weapons, Ahninveth."

The other Feral hesitated a second, then he removed

his sword belt and the dagger in his boot and passed them to Arhk. The dhomvalen handed the practice sword to Jhanik hilt first, though he didn't let go of the blade when Jhanik accepted it.

"If any of your beasts get physically involved, you will both be demoted. That also means there will be no knockout blows dealt." His gaze shifted from Jhanik to Kasiel, then he released the sword and strode to the edge of the ring to intercept Dhomen Sorval.

Sorval watched Kasiel and Jhanik step back from each other, shifting into combat stances. "Is this wise, Dhomvalen?"

"No," Arhk answered, "but I believe it is necessary."

Kasiel reached out to Niskenya. He didn't need to invite her. She swept in the moment his awareness touched her, bringing her raw power and aggression into him. She made him stronger and faster through her ability to bury his doubts and anger beneath pure reliance on her instincts. He struggled a moment to remember what he was, a man with a weapon, not an apex predator who could bring down prey with teeth and claws. When he found the balance he needed, he nodded to Jhanik.

The other Feral lunged in, going for a quick surprise slash. He was fast, and had years of training Kasiel lacked, especially now that he had to relearn everything with his left arm. But Jhanik's moves were swift and violent, driven by emotion. Niskenya wouldn't allow Kasiel to be controlled by such things. For her, this was a dance between predator and prey. The predator needed to be calm, alert, and efficient.

Kasiel blocked the wooden blade with his own, pushing it toward the center. He brought his other arm in under as he sidestepped to the left and grabbed Jhanik's wrist. His right arm wasn't as good as it used to be, but it was strong enough. Leveraging Jhanik's momentum against him, Kasiel pulled him forward and brought his sword around to strike the other Feral across the ribs before letting go and stepping back out. Jhanik grunted with the force of the blow but righted himself quickly and spun to face Kasiel.

Jhanik charged back in, barely twisting clear of a fast strike meant to hit his collarbone. Moving closer, he attacked with a series of swings and attempted grabs that Kasiel had to fend off with his blade and right forearm in equal effort. He took a hard strike to his upper arm that might have been debilitating, had it been from a real sword, but then his first strike on Jhanik would have been as well. Niskenya's instincts helped him find the speed and dexterity to match his opponent. He finally cleared an opening for a thrust into Jhanik's lower ribs that drove the other man back with another grunt.

Kasiel narrowed his eyes, hiding the increasing pain in his right arm behind a feral snarl. Niskenya soaked up some of that distracting ache, improving his focus. Jhanik didn't hesitate to engage again. They exchanged several blows, blocking each other out. The other Feral started in as if he meant to attack with a thrust, changing direction at the last second to go for a higher swing. Kasiel dodged back and to the right, the tip of Jhanik's blade brushing the side of his neck.

Ignoring the sting of the contact, Kasiel put both hands on his sword hilt and swung a powerful blow into Jhanik's back below the ribs. Jhanik twisted into the sudden pain and Kasiel stepped up, using his forearm to deflect Jhanik's left arm out of the way. With the path clear, he brought his sword pommel down on the back of Jhanik's right hand.

Jhanik cried out. His sword fell to the ground, and he grabbed the wrist of the injured hand. At the edge of the ring, his tethdrak advanced a few steps, snarling. Kasiel came around and struck Jhanik behind one knee, dropping him into a kneeling position. Niskenya pushed him to finish the kill. He could do it, even with a wooden sword. A blow to the right spot on his opponent's head would end it. The stinging on his neck where Jhanik's blade tip scraped across fed the urge for blood.

Kasiel retreated several steps, drawing a shaking breath, and forced distance between himself and Niskenya, calming her with a sense of gratitude. Everyone in the camp stood around the ring now, watching them.

Jhanik glared up at him, clutching his wrist and trembling with pain or rage. Perhaps both. "Bastard," he snarled.

Arhk strode over, beckoning to Jhanik's two healers as he came. "Have that seen to." He gestured to Jhanik's hand.

Jhanik struggled to his feet and went to meet his healers, who led him from the ring. Once he was gone, Arhk faced Kasiel.

"Using your kanodrak does not negate the need to build strength back in your injured arm. I think this demonstrated that." His gaze moved to Kasiel's neck. "You are bleeding. Have one of your healers tend to it." He started walking away.

"Wait, why did you encourage us to fight?"

Arhk turned back and considered him for a moment. "If you introduce two beasts, they will often fight to establish a pecking order. You are both Ferals. Similar rules apply. Besides, an injury like that one," he said, gesturing in the direction Jhanik had gone, "will not affect his ability to run his beasts."

"He didn't use his kanodrak to fight."

"No. Jhanik's ability is not as strong as yours. Nor does he have your empathy for the beasts that allows you to work so closely with them. That empathy also makes fighting in battles harder on you." His gaze moved pointedly to Velara, who stood talking with Darro and casting concerned glances at Kasiel. "You know why we are taking her to Etrion?"

Kasiel wiped his neck. His fingers came away with a light coating of blood. "I'm not sure what you mean."

Arhk's scathing look called his bluff. "Your empathy works on more than just beasts, Kasiel. Given how Velara has taken to you, it would surprise me if she had not told you what this is all about. If this can end the war, you must see why that takes priority over your relationship with Nerith."

Kasiel forced a nod. His father wasn't wrong, but that didn't mean he had to like it. "Does my being with her bother you? Would you rather see me with someone else?"

"It is not something I lose sleep over. I considered intervening when Seylin suggested you as a possible match for Velara. That was before we received the first missive from Delaphine. Now that Velara's fate could help bring an end to this conflict, your choice of lovers is less of a concern." His thoughtful gaze rested on the khesran for a second, then he started walking away again. "Get that wound seen to, Ahninveth."

Him and Velara? He glanced over to where she stood with his unit. She was watching him now, her dark red hair appearing almost black in the fading light.

He shook himself and started toward them, toward Tath in particular, since he wasn't ready to acknowledge the new healer as part of their unit, temporary or otherwise. Irith joined him as he reached Tath, and he placed a hand on the big cat's head. Tath lifted his chin to look at the wound, the interaction taking him back to when they first met, and she tended the injuries he had sustained during his time with the mercenaries.

She glanced up, smiling at whatever she saw in his expression. "Just like old times, huh? This is just a surface scrape. It should clean up easy."

"I can do that much." Velara spoke right behind him, startling Kasiel, though he managed not to react visibly.

"Leave them alone, Cousin." Jethan came up beside her. "I'm pretty sure Tath can handle it."

Velara's brows pinched together in an unfortunately charming show of annoyance. "I want to be useful. Sitting in the carriage all day makes me feel—"

"Like a pampered little khesran?"

She elbowed Jethan in the ribs. "Go pester Keyla. She's got more patience for you than I do."

Jethan brightened. "If you insist. Can I tell her it was your idea?"

Velara gave him a sharp look, to which he responded with a grin before wandering away, leaving Kasiel to fend for himself.

Tath handed Velara a clean cloth, a flask of water, and some of the wound salve. "I'm getting something to eat. Watching that fight made me hungry." She winked at Kasiel before wandering off toward the campfire and the others.

Somehow, he was now standing all alone with Velara and Irith, though her guards weren't far away. She pointed to a log, sitting next to him when he obediently settled on it. He could see more evening insects coming out now. Soon the light would fade enough for bats to hunt. What would it be like to get in the head of a bat? Few flying creatures were as agile, but he suspected it might be nauseating trying to get used to the way they moved.

"Chin up."

He did as ordered. "Do you have enough light?"

"Mm-hmm." She focused on moistening the cloth and wiping away the drying blood, her careful touch causing little pain. Then she set it aside and opened the salve. "Did you use Irith to spy on us today?"

He felt his face grow warm, though he hadn't done

anything of the sort. Not really. "I glanced through his eyes a few times to make sure he wasn't causing trouble."

"Is that all? You didn't listen?" She almost sounded disappointed.

He looked at her. "Did you want me to listen?"

"Chin up," she snapped, waiting until he had done so to resume tending the scrape. "Maybe. I told Keyla all about you. You're quite a remarkable individual, Kasiel Cavenos. I feel I underestimated you when first we met."

"I'm not so sure of that." He lowered his head again when she started closing the salve container.

She met his eyes, a fond smile curving her lips. "I am."

He stared at her for a moment, her silver eyes as extraordinary in their way as Nerith's, glinting in the light from the campfires. How could the khevarin think he might be a suitable match for her? Had Seylin finally seen some value in him beyond his use as a weapon for Vanris? Or did his usefulness as her weapon and his status as Arhk's son gain him enough prestige that she considered him worthy of her only daughter? Maybe there just weren't many eligible options to choose from, not that it mattered now.

Velara's smile faded. "What?"

He shook his head and stood. "Nothing. We should get something to eat before it's gone."

She held out a hand, and he instinctively took it, lifting her from her seat. Then she slid her hand up his arm to rest it in the crook of his elbow.

"As champion of this evening's tournament, you can be my escort to dinner."

He chuckled. "I'm pretty certain they don't bother with escorts out here, but I'm happy to help if it makes you feel more at home."

She squeezed his arm, leaning closer. "And that's why I like you."

CHAPTER TWELVE

The next few days passed uneventfully. Jhanik stayed away from Kasiel, a development he found agreeable. The bleak, empty place within him that Nerith's company normally filled compelled Kasiel to seek out Velara. But, for reasons he didn't entirely understand, knowing the khevarin had considered matching him with her made him more acutely aware of the things he liked about her. As a result, he tried to resist the compulsion, seeking instead to spend more with Jethan and the rest of his unit. As it turned out, given that Jethan was Velara's cousin and one of a few people there she was comfortable around, spending time with him inevitably translated into spending time with her. Kasiel finally settled for maintaining an emotional distance between them if he couldn't keep a physical one.

Travel was faster with Irith riding in the carriage. The big cliff cat enjoyed his leisurely accommodations with Velara and Keyla. Enough so that he alternated between warming their feet and lying next to Kasiel at the evening campfires. After the first two nights, Velara started sitting between Kasiel and Jethan, to make things easier for Irith. While he worried that she could have hidden motivations, he couldn't pretend he didn't enjoy chatting with her. She knew everything about the political history of Vanris and let him pick her brain on the subject. She also had an endless curiosity about him. Not just his exploits since arriving in Vanris, but his journey there and childhood in Fernwallow as well.

Velara's tehnaak, Keyla, was a vivacious woman with long, honey-blond hair and brilliant, sapphire eyes. She had a dancer's poise and musculature, which gave her a degree of body control that any fighter could admire. It was hard not to watch when she moved, simply because her effortless grace was captivating. She also had a sharp wit, more than equal to the task of navigating Jethan's humor. The glimmer in her eyes when she verbally sparred with him made it clear she enjoyed it. Kasiel delighted in seeing how happy Jethan was when they bantered, though it made him miss Nerith more. He felt as if something had been torn from his chest, leaving a gaping hole behind.

They arrived in Etrion on the evening of the fifth day. Kasiel and Jhanik rode around the city to take their beasts and mounts to the habitats. Arhk sent Dhomen Sorval with them for reasons that required no explanation, going to escort Velara to the palace himself along with the rest of their two units. Jethan met them at the top of the lift overlooking the habitats with Jhanik's tehnaak, Keryk, the two chatting companionably when they arrived.

Kasiel hung back, waiting for Sorval, Jhanik, and his tehnaak to leave. Irith, who was well enough now that he had come along, stood by his side, watching the other Feral with his hackles up. Kasiel smiled at the beast and scratched him behind the ears.

"I assume Velara's with her mother now?"

Jethan nodded. "Keyla too, unfortunately. The dhomvalen dismissed our units at the palace entrance and continued with internal guards from there."

Deciding the others had time to get far enough ahead, Kasiel started walking toward the exit. "Do you think they'll let me go back to Doran?"

Jethan's expression closed. "I don't know, Kas. It probably depends on what they have planned. I doubt they brought Vel here just because my aunt missed her."

Kasiel held the front door open, staring at Jethan as he came through behind Irith. "Velara didn't tell you?"

Jethan stopped outside the door and frowned at him. "She told you?"

Kasiel let the door fall shut, using Irith's superior hearing and sense of smell to determine if anyone was near enough to overhear them. Even after deciding it was safe, he took a step closer and lowered his voice. "Delaphine is offering an alliance. They're considering a political marriage to strengthen the union."

Jethan recoiled. "No. They can't marry Vel off to some earless southerner. No offense."

Kasiel suffered the jarring sensation that he'd had this conversation before. Probably because he had. Anger tightened his shoulders and back. "You know, I actually believed you were the one person I could count on most to remember that I am Vanrian."

Jethan turned a bright shade of red. "I didn't mean it like that, it's just—"

"I get it." He started toward the cliff cat enclosure at a brisk pace.

"Kas." Jethan jogged to catch up with him.

He didn't slow. "It's fine. I'm tired. I'm going to put Irith away and turn in early."

"Let me walk with you."

"No." The word came out sharp and angry. Kasiel drew a breath and evened out his tone. "Thank you, but I could use some time alone."

Jethan stopped walking, letting Kasiel go on without him.

After leaving Irith in the habitat, he didn't go back to the palace. Instead, he returned to the tethdrak enclosure and sat on the rock platform where he had often sat with his first companion, Sylaryth. Some of the other tethdraks ventured near to lie around the base of the rock, but none attempted to join him, seeming to sense that a memory occupied that space. Kasiel held Sylaryth's claw in his hand, rubbing his thumb along the smooth surface from base to lethal point.

Despite everything he had accomplished, even now that many lauded him as a hero, they still saw an outsider, a danro. The first thing everyone noticed was that he was different. His cut ears would forever mark him. For a time, he dared to believe it didn't matter so long as he had his unit around him, his new family. But Jethan had proven that wasn't true. His own tehnaak couldn't overlook the obvious differences.

Pushing his thumb against the point of the claw, he drew a drop of blood. The sting of the puncture prompted a sudden query from Niskenya. The kanodrak's protective, almost maternal presence enfolded him, full of concern and affection.

Slipping the claw into the pouch on his belt, Kasiel got up, walking out and around to the kanodrak habitat. Adnar had given him a key again after the battle in Sharith. Not forgiveness for taking Niskenya without permission. More like a second chance to prove they could trust him with it. He suspected another such infraction would get him put to death, hero or not. That was the one reason he wasn't seriously considering riding her back to Doran on his own.

When he stepped through the gate into the kanodrak enclosure, Niskenya lowered her naturally armored head and pressed it to his chest, as if trying to absorb his sorrow.

"It's all right." He ran a hand along her neck, feeling the smooth scaled hide and iron hard muscle beneath his fingertips. It was still difficult to believe this amazing beast had chosen to bond with him. Perhaps she was the only one who didn't see him as an outsider.

Niskenya raised her head, narrowly missing his face with one of her long front fangs, and peered toward the canyon entrance with her milky white eyes. Kasiel turned, following her gaze. A soft click preceded the opening of the door. Jethan strolled into the front section of the habitat, slipping something into his pocket as he approached them.

Niskenya stepped forward to stand beside Kasiel, and he reached up to rest a hand on her shoulder. "How did you get in here?"

Jethan shrugged, stopping at the bars that separated them. "I got very good at picking locks and sneaking into rooms around the palace when I was younger."

"Younger being what, sixteen?"

Jethan couldn't hold back a grin, though it faded fast. "You know, Kas, our people revere that magnificent creature next to you. You are one of five Ferals in all Vanris right now that can ride one. Anytime anyone, your tehnaak included, says something stupid to suggest you're anything other than Vanrian or that your ears make you lesser somehow, Niskenya should be all the proof you need to counter that."

Kasiel passed a wave of affection through his bond with her. "A kanodrak is never wrong," he murmured, quoting something Adnar had said to him once.

Niskenya pulled him in behind her eyes and looked at him, showing him the blue light that stretched from her chest into his. It had grown from a mere thread to a rope in thickness, the bond strengthening with time. Then she faced Jethan, focusing on the brilliant violet light that pulsed between him and Kasiel. After a few seconds, she pushed him out of her mind and wandered away, leaving him with his tehnaak.

Kasiel watched her go, then he stepped out of the habitat.

"In Doran, Nerith's father called me the 'earless son of Arhk Cavenos'," he said, locking the gate behind him. "I found out from Jhanik that, when they summoned him here to fight, he got her father's permission to propose to her. I suppose Andross had no way to know about our relationship before that, but I'm confident that would only have made him more determined to support Jhanik."

Jethan grimaced as they walked to the exit. "So that's what this dispute he raised is about?"

"I'm guessing so."

"The old bastard's an idiot. She'd be marrying up if she married you."

"I don't think he cares."

"He should. You're a better match from a status standpoint, and from a personality standpoint. Jhanik's a calloch." He fell quiet for several strides, waiting until they were through the tunnel to speak again. "I'm sorry, tehnaak. I got so wrapped up in trying to impress Keyla that I failed to consider everything you might be dealing with."

"Is it working?"

"Impressing Keyla?" Jethan's boyish grin was a sufficient answer. "Seems to be. Why don't we investigate getting you back to Doran? I can probably get us an audience with my aunt tomorrow if I make a big enough pest of myself."

"I'd appreciate it."

*

It was a little after noon the next day when Jethan's request for an audience got them called into one of the smaller meeting chambers in the palace. Dhomen Aleren was there, which came as a surprise since she hadn't ridden south with them. She had to have struck out right after their party left Doran to be here now. Arhk was also present. Something Kasiel hadn't expected, though his father's presence no longer inspired the fear or anger in him it once had. Not that the dhomvalen was any less of an imposing or terrifying figure, but they had found a balance that, while not what he would call affectionate, had at least crept into the realm of respectful.

Aside from the khevarin, her tehnaak, and Arhk, a few of the khevarin's personal guards stood at the back of the room. Seylin sat atop a raised dais on a black stone chair carved in the aggressive angles characteristic of most structures in Etrion. Her white-blond hair and shimmering ivory gown stood out bright against the dark throne. Arhk waited to one side with Aleren on the other, a hint of curiosity in her gaze as she watched Kasiel and Jethan approach. They passed a series of portraits along the dark walls. Vanrian men and women in military or noble attire, a few of whom Kasiel recognized from the history texts he had read for classes at the mind-crafter academy.

They both knelt on the swirled black and ivory stone floor at the base of the dais. The khevarin left them there for several seconds before acknowledging them, a small reminder of who was in charge.

"You may rise." When they had done so, she looked them both over, her gaze lingering on Kasiel. "You wished to speak with us?"

"Yes, Majesty." Kasiel bowed his head respectfully, hoping to start the conversation with a favorable impression. "I would like your permission to return to Doran to assist Healer Nerith, as a member of my unit, with the dispute her father has brought against her."

"No. But we are glad you sought us out. It saves us

the trouble of summoning you later."

For a second, the immediacy of her response left Kasiel too stunned to feel anything. Then anger swept in like a flash flood. Only Jethan's touch on his arm stopped him from unleashing his frustration with potentially disastrous results. He took a deep breath, glad now that he hadn't brought Irith with him.

Seylin was watching him, one fine brow arched as if waiting for an explosion. When it didn't come, the corner of her mouth curved up a fraction. "Ahninveth Kasiel, your unit will be part of the company escorting Khesran Velara to Trenath on the eastern coast. Velara is comfortable with both of you, enough so, it seems, that she exposed the purpose of this very delicate mission to one of you."

Her eyes narrowed at Kasiel before she continued. "She will be meeting Prince Kaden of Delaphine to see if they can tolerate one another enough that their union might serve as a symbol for the alliance that is currently under negotiation. A purpose we expect you to be most discreet about. We cannot emphasize enough the danger of letting this become common knowledge too soon. There are many who might resent the idea of this alliance enough to kill to prevent it from becoming a reality."

Her expectant look demanded a response, so Kasiel and Jethan both inclined their heads and said, "Yes, Majesty."

"Good. Jhanik's unit will also accompany you, though there are to be no incidents similar to those we were told occurred on the trips to and from Doran. The two of you, however, will serve as more than just protection for the journey. She has requested you as her personal guards and escorts. This means that you will be called upon to watch over her within the city and castle while there, as well as attend her on various engagements as escorts or guards, depending on what she requires."

She gestured to Aleren. "Our tehnaak, Dhomen Aleren, has graciously agreed to lead this mission. You will answer to her until your return to Etrion."

At least Jhanik wouldn't be heading to Doran while they were away or waiting in Etrion if Nerith came back. It was a minor consolation, but better than nothing. "About Healer Nerith. She is part of my unit."

"Healer Tath has not taken her as tehnaak, so there is no reason the healer assigned to you on your departure from Doran cannot continue to fill that role. We must not let ourselves be distracted by such paltry affairs at a time like this, Ahninveth. Leave her to fight her own battles. Go prepare your unit, but do not disclose the purpose of this mission to them yet. You will depart in two days."

Kasiel was sick of being told to let Nerith deal with this. He was part of the reason she was in this situation. Didn't that make it his battle too? Still, he didn't appear to have much choice.

"Will the Ferals be taking our beasts, Majesty?"

"Yes. We will show Delaphine a glimpse of our might to remind them why they are seeking this alliance. Now go." She flicked the silver-tipped fingers of one hand at them as if she no longer wanted them in her presence.

"Yes, Majesty." He bowed stiffly before striding from the room with Jethan.

They hadn't gone far when the door opened and closed again behind them.

"Kasiel." They stopped and turned to face his father. "While you are away, I will send someone to check on Nerith and see if something can be done to resolve her situation."

A surge of affection shocked Kasiel. If the dhomvalen

couldn't fix this, who could? "Thank you. That means a lot."

"I do not require your gratitude. I simply need you to focus on your mission. If anything goes wrong, it could turn an opportunity to move toward peace into a violent escalation in the war. I would rather find myself with no purpose than find myself with no family again." He spun and strode back to the room without giving Kasiel a chance to respond.

"He's definitely trying to build a relationship," Jethan said when the door shut behind Arhk.

Kasiel wanted to believe that, but what if he was reading too much into it? "Maybe he's just trying to make sure I don't fuck this up?"

Jethan rolled his eyes. "Pessimist. Come on, let's let the others know we're heading out again."

"Do you think they regret bringing me back to Vanris now?" he asked as they resumed walking. "They barely get any time to rest lately."

"True, but they earn a lot of extra pay doing missions like these. I doubt they mind that much. And I don't think we've gotten bored once since you came around."

Kasiel eyed him skeptically. "I have a feeling Tath and Wedro would have preferred to be bored."

Jethan's humor vanished. "They could have lost their tehnaaks in any battle, Kas. It's not as if we weren't at risk before you got here."

That was true, though it didn't ease the weight of guilt Kasiel carried for playing a part in those losses. But maybe it was better to let that go for the moment. "What's Trenath like?"

"I don't know if any of us have been there. Possibly Darro and Kince. It's a coastal town that sits on the northern edge of the Break. It belonged to Delaphine before the war. Vanris took it over to make use of the

port, but no one lives in the castle now. The town main-
tains it largely so people can visit it as a rare opportunity
to experience Pandrean Alliance construction and aes-
thetics."

"So, it's by the ocean."

Perhaps it was the edge of wonder in his tone that
brought a spark of excitement to Jethan's eyes. "Yes. A
sight very few of us have seen. I'm willing to bet the
others will be almost as thrilled about this as they were
about going to Doran."

Kasiel smiled as they walked out into the streets,
recalling drawings and descriptions of the ocean from
books he had read growing up. Then another thought
occurred to him. "Do you think Nerith's ever seen the
ocean?"

Jethan put a hand on his shoulder, his grin full of
encouragement. "If we help bring peace to Vanris, maybe you can take her there yourself someday."

It took six and a half days to get to Trenath on good roads. Along the way, Darro and Merrin kept training with Kasiel, helping him build coordination and skill both with and without Niskenya, per Farren's recommendation, since the kanodrak might not always be within range. The rest of the time they spent on the move or sleeping. Irith continued to heal, though he still spent part of each day in the carriage with Velara, Keyla, and the khesran's personal attendant. How necessary that was versus how much was born of a newfound fondness for traveling in luxury and being fawned over by the three women, Kasiel wasn't sure, but he suspected he might have to intervene on the return trip. For now, Irith needed to finish healing, so he let them spoil the cliff cat.

They saw the unending expanse of blue on the horizon long before the crisp salt smell of the ocean reached them. The lay of the land, dipping low then rising gradually to the cliffs along the coast, hid that view from them as they got closer, bringing them all the way to the gray stone walls of Trenath with no further sight of the water. The city, when they rode through, presented the strange dichotomy of a Vanrian populace living in homes and shops with a southern aesthetic. Wattle and daub construction was mixed with pale brick and stone. Driftwood sculptures, often incorporating seashells in their design, were popular decoration around the fronts of homes and shops. Many depicted the revered kanodraks and tethdraks of Vanris, making it clear some were added after the city changed hands.

When they reached the towering gray stone castle, Kasiel and Jhanik settled their tethdraks and kanodraks in specially built enclosures added to the city after Vanris claimed it. Aleren exhaustively questioned guards from the company who had ridden ahead to ensure the castle was secure and fit for royal occupation. Then she took several soldiers in to review the premises herself before allowing their retinue to enter.

Kasiel, Irith, and Jethan stayed close to Velara and Keyla as their assignment required, following her into a towering white stone entry hall. Velara stopped and peered around at pale stone walls decorated with paintings of landscapes from the Vanrian homeland as if searching for something. Her gaze came to rest on an open doorway beneath a curved staircase in one corner of the room.

"Aleren, is the contingent from Delaphine here yet?" she asked.

The dhomen gave her a shrewd look, as if expecting a trap. "Not yet, Khesran."

A delighted grin broke across Velara's face, lighting up her silver eyes. "Perfect. Come, darlings, I have something to show you."

She took Kasiel and Jethan each by the hand and led them through the doorway. After several turns, she let go and broke into a jog, navigating a series of corridors and cutting across a couple of lavish rooms as if she had grown up there. They had to jog to keep up.

She took one last turn and threw open a large wooden door with a storm-tossed ocean carved into its surface. The sound of rushing water washing on the shore met them. The salty, crisp scent of the ocean wafted in on a breeze that blew Velara's blood-red hair back. She went through and walked to the railing of a stone terrace that looked out over the beach below. Smiling, she threw out her arms as if to embrace the spectacular view.

Kasiel and the others joined her. Irith tensed, making a soft chittering sound as he watched birds on the beach below hunting for something in the sand. Small waves rolled onto the shore, sweeping up with an odd hissing sound. The undulating blue expanse stretched as far as Kasiel could see.

"Given how quickly you navigated the castle, I'm guessing you've been here before," Jethan said.

Velara's smile widened. "You would be wrong. I found a layout of the castle in a book in the Etrion palace library." She turned toward a set of stairs that switched back and forth down the cliff face to the beach. "Shall we?"

When they reached the bottom, Velara strolled out on the sand, angling gradually toward the water. Kasiel started after her, stopping when Jethan and Keyla didn't follow. He glanced back at them.

"You two go ahead." Keyla watched Jethan, fiddling with one sleeve of her dress, a pale blue and ivory garment that shared the same split front skirt design Velara favored.

Kasiel nodded, noticing Velara's guarded glance back at them. He increased his stride to catch up with her, letting Irith sprint ahead. They were almost at the edge of the water before either of them spoke.

"Do you love Nerith?" she asked.

Unease crept across his shoulders and up the back of his neck. He was attempting to put Nerith from his mind and focus on the task at hand, trusting his father to handle things. It wasn't easy to give that trust after their tumultuous beginnings. Nerith worked her way into his thoughts often, but he tried, with marginal success, not to fret over things he couldn't currently control.

"Why do you ask?"

"Just making conversation." She shrugged and lifted her deep blue skirt, kicking off her shoes to make walking easier.

Kasiel picked them up for her. "Yes, I do."

Velara walked out far enough for the edge of the surf to wash over her feet, jumping when it did so. "Oh. It's colder than I expected." She gave his boots a meaningful glance and took her shoes from him, tossing them up the beach to the dry sand.

Taking the hint, he pulled his boots and socks off, throwing them after her shoes, and walked down to let the reaching waves hit his feet. He grinned, resisting the urge to move when the sand shifted underfoot as the water retreated.

"How did you meet her?"

"Your mother tasked her with getting close to me and reporting back on my activities. I guess she wanted to be sure I wasn't loyal to the south."

Velara let out a laugh. "Seriously? My mother sent her to spy on you?"

Kasiel nodded. He started strolling along the beach, staying within reach of the surf. Velara joined him, holding up her skirt and stopping every few steps to poke at a piece of shell or a pebble with her toes.

"You mean that's not how everyone meets their partners?" Kasiel joked, catching sight of a larger wave rolling in when he glanced over at her.

"No." She laughed again, and the smile she gave him was starlight on a lonely night.

The Delaphinian prince was a lucky man.

He watched the water rush in.

Her expression sobered when she met his eyes. "What?"

Kasiel jumped back as the wave hit, laughing at her

squeal of surprise when cold water splashed halfway up the calves of her fitted pants. Anger and amusement warred across her features when she faced him.

"You saw that coming," she accused.

He laughed harder. "I'm sorry. I couldn't help it."

Velara grabbed a handful of wet sand and threw it at him. He twisted, letting it splatter across the side of his travel jacket. Irith sprinted between them then, sending a spray of watery sand over them both. Velara started laughing hard enough that she stumbled, and Kasiel caught her arm, steadying her. While she regained her balance, he noticed how riding in the carriage had allowed her to avoid the dust and sweat of the beasts on the road. The smell of her delicate perfume flitted about like an elusive whisper in the salty breeze. He breathed it in, his pulse quickening.

She reached up to brush a bit of sand from his cheek. "You and your beast are troublemakers," she said, her voice as warm and inviting in that moment as her smile.

Kasiel broke eye contact and let go of her arm. His gaze moved back along the beach to where the other two were. Keyla stood against the post at the foot of the stairs, her eyes locked with Jethan's while he leaned in closer. Kasiel's breath caught in his throat, an ache of loneliness spreading through him. He watched their lips touch in a soft, tentative kiss of discovery.

A distressed sound drew his attention back to Velara standing beside him, her lips slightly parted, the shine of unshed tears rising in her eyes. For a second, she simply stared at her tehnaak and cousin, then, as if breaking from a trance, she sprinted back along the beach as fast as the sand would let her go. Kasiel jogged up to grab their shoes and hurried after her. He heard Keyla asking if something was wrong, but Velara raced past her and up the stairs barefoot.

Jethan looked at him as he came up beside them. "Is

she all right?"

"As all right as she can be." He watched Velara rushing up the steps. "I think she just remembered why we're here."

Keyla's expression sobered, though a faint flush remained in her cheeks. She took Velara's shoes from him. "I'll take care of her." She touched Jethan's hand in an absent gesture of affection before hurrying after her tehnaak.

Kasiel watched the two women for a moment. Velara was a third of the way up without showing signs of slowing. Either she was that upset, or she was a lot more fit than he would have expected a princess to be. Perhaps both. She wasn't the kind of princess he had read about in Edmund's collection of books. She was a khesran of Vanris. If he had learned anything, it was that Vanris discouraged vulnerability and weakness in all its people.

"Does Velara know how to fight?"

Jethan arched a brow at him. "Of course. She's had combat training like anyone else. She's quite adept with a sword and dagger."

Interesting. He glanced at his tehnaak. "Was that your first kiss?"

"Mine? No." He winked and offered his best scoundrel grin. "I've kissed many a lady."

"I meant with her, calloch."

Jethan nodded. "It was." He started up the stairs. "I suppose, as Vel's personal guards, we should get up there before we lose her entirely."

Kasiel joined him on the stairs, carrying his boots.

Once they entered the castle, Velara hurried through the halls, staying ahead of them. She found someone to show her to her assigned rooms and vanished into them with Keyla on her heels, not coming out again for the rest of the afternoon. Kasiel, Jethan, and Irith stood watch outside her door until Aleren swapped them out with two other guards, advising them to change their attire. They were to act as Velara's escorts for an introductory dinner with the Delaphinian prince. To put the visiting retinue at ease, Irith would go into an enclosure for the evening, rather than accompany Kasiel.

When Velara emerged from her room, she wore a flowing gown of dark blue, generously embroidered with silver thread down the front where it split, and around the hemline and cuffs. Elegant feather patterns, also done in silver, decorated the skirt, adding a shimmer to every movement she made. The attendant had woven a fine web-work of braids through her hair, pinned in place with gleaming gems that helped hold the rest back from pointed ears decorated with silver earrings and cuffs. Her eyelids were colored with a light shading of silver and blue. The silver accents through the outfit enhanced her eyes and the faint silver outlines around the symbols of the ke'hanoath tiara tattooed upon her brow.

Jethan offered her his arm. As her cousin, he would walk with her. Keyla took Kasiel's arm. Lovely as she was, he barely noticed her. From the moment Velara emerged, he had hardly drawn a breath.

An attendant announced their arrival as they entered the dining room. A long, curved table sat on a raised platform, one half occupied by the retinue from Delaphine, all of whom stood respectfully for them. Prince Kaden of Delaphine waited at the center of the table next to an empty seat to which Jethan would escort Velara. Dense locs of jet-black hair a few inches long added to his notable height, and he had skin as dark as Danica's. He wore ivory formal breeches and a matching jacket trimmed in lavish gold. A hint of lingering youthful lankiness detracted little from a man who showed promise of becoming an imposing figure.

Velara leaned close to Jethan. "His skin is rather beautiful, but why is his hair so short?"

"Cutting it short is common in the southern kingdoms," Kasiel offered.

Velara gave him an appraising look over one shoulder. "Thankfully, you didn't adopt that practice."

He dredged up a tight smile. Truthfully, he would have happily adopted a shorter style growing up if not for the need to keep his cut ears hidden. Now, he wouldn't dream of it.

They walked around the table to the chairs nearest the Delaphine prince. He greeted Velara with a strained smile, though no more so than hers when she returned the greeting. When the full Vanrian retinue, consisting mostly of soldiers ranking inveth and above, had entered, Velara and the prince sat, giving the rest silent permission to take their seats. Looking over the assembly of mostly dark-skinned men across from them with their shorter hair and round ears, Kasiel got the impression they were also primarily military. This was a clandestine meeting. An opportunity for the khesran and prince to consider one another before making commitments and grander plans.

Once everyone sat, attendants brought out a parade of dishes representing Delaphine and Vanris in equal measure. When the presentation finished, Kasiel feared the tables would collapse beneath the weight of it all. Entertainment ran through the evening, in the form of music, dances, and brief skits representative of both countries.

Kasiel sat two chairs down from Velara, with Jethan and Keyla between them. Aleren sat on his other side, managing to appear engaged in conversation, the meal, or the entertainment while her watchful gaze kept a careful accounting of every person in the room. Without a beast there to aid him, Kasiel took his cues from her, listening attentively to catch moments of conversation between Velara and Kaden while he kept watch for anything amiss.

As the meal wound down, the entertainment changed to a selection of quiet songs to allow for conversation. Tonight, there would be no dancing or other revelry. Prince Kaden and Khesran Velara would merely dine together without the expectation of any performance on their parts.

A pair of individuals wearing the simple garb of Delaphine's serving staff emerged from a hidden door to one side of the room. The curve of the table let Kasiel see how Velara watched them a moment before turning to the prince.

"I was wondering about the concealed passages in the walls. Is that common in Delaphine?" she asked.

Kaden nodded, a stiffness to the gesture that had plagued all his interactions with her so far. "Yes. For servants."

Velara used her fork to nudge a bit of a Delaphinian pastry she had barely touched to one side of her plate. "In Vanris, we have attendants, not servants, and we certainly don't hide them away in dark little passageways like criminals."

There was a slight tightening of Kaden's jaw in response to the judgement in her tone. "Your *attendants* walk the halls among you?"

"Naturally."

"You don't worry about assassination attempts?"

"Of course not." Velara's tone suggested that the mere thought was absurd. "Our attendants go through screening with a Charmer and an Evoker before being brought into the palace. They repeat that process twice a year for as long as they work there."

Kaden's brows pinched, and he turned in his chair to face her more. "So, you interrogate them, like criminals?"

Velara lifted her napkin from her lap, folding it with quick, angry motions. Next to Kasiel, Keyla picked up her own napkin, setting it on the table beside her plate.

"Not like criminals, I assure you," Velara countered sharply.

"What is the difference, exactly?"

She faced him, denying Kasiel the input of her expression, though her tone was enough to confirm her irritation. "If they were criminals, there would be a Frightener in the room."

Kasiel sighed inwardly. Reminding the prince of mind-crafters during dinner was bad enough without bringing up one of the most feared and hated abilities. Not that he disagreed with Velara's feelings on hiding one's servants or attendants away, as if they were unworthy to walk the same halls.

"You see, Khesran Velara, we do not have mind-violators where I come from."

Velara dropped her napkin on the table and shoved back her chair, getting up so abruptly that the rest of them, Prince Kaden included, scrambled to follow suit. "Excuse me, I am feeling rather weary from all the travel. I think I will retire. Please," she said, casting her gaze over the two sides of the table, "continue to enjoy your evening." Turning to Kaden, she offered a brief curtsy. "My lord."

Keyla, Jethan, and Kasiel, as her tehnaak and escorts, followed Velara. She exited the room quickly, not slowing until she reached her rooms. Without a word, she vanished inside. Kasiel walked a short distance down the hall to give Jethan a moment of privacy with Keyla before she followed Velara. Four guards arrived a few minutes later, sent by Dhomen Aleren to give them the night off. They were to rest and resume their duties in the morning.

"Dinner could have gone better," Kasiel remarked,

stepping out of the way of the new shift of guards.

"Hm?" Jethan glanced over at him, a giddy grin plastered across his face.

"Nothing." Kasiel chuckled at his tehnaak's joyful distraction. "Goodnight, tehnaak."

"Goodnight," Jethan said as he wandered into his room next to Velara's.

The good humor lasted until he was alone in his assigned room next to Jethan's. Loneliness and a poignant longing for Nerith crept in. He wanted to hold her in his arms and tell her all about the events of the day. She would talk about her day, then they would let it all fade away and lose themselves in each other.

He removed the decorative ear cuffs and hung up his formal attire. After changing into comfortable evening clothes, he pulled out Sylaryth's claw and one of several stoneglass bottles of Vanrian Black Mead tucked in a side cabinet and poured himself a mug. He settled in front of the fire someone had prepared to warm the room and sipped at the mead, running his thumb along the edge of the claw.

The mug was half empty when a hidden door in the back wall of his room clicked open. Gripping the claw like a weapon, Kasiel crept around beside the door as it swung in. When a figure stepped through, he grabbed them from behind, bringing the claw to their throat.

It was Velara's scent and squeak of alarm that made him let go. She spun away, one hand going to her chest as she tried to catch her breath, drawing his attention to the clinging fabric of the long beige and gold dressing gown she wore.

Her gaze locked on the claw he was brandishing. "Were you going to kill me?"

He lowered his hand. "Not before I found out what you were after."

She drew a shaky breath. "Your company."

"You shouldn't be here." He strode past her, set the claw on the table, and picked up the mead, taking a swallow.

Velara came up behind him. "Those passages are more useful than I expected. I almost wish we had some back home. Not for hiding our attendants, though," she added, bitterness hardening her voice. She caught his hand and took the mug from him, sniffing at it as he faced her. "Vanrian Black Mead. Excellent choice."

"What are you doing here, Vel?"

She took a drink of the mead then set the mug next to Sylaryth's claw. When she looked up, he noticed a rim of red around her eyes. She had been crying. He resisted the urge to comfort her. Jethan could do that, or Keyla. Not him. That wasn't his place.

She stepped closer, desperation in her eyes. "I don't know if I can do this, Kas. Did you hear him at dinner? So judgmental about our people. So cold."

"I heard two people who were raised to hate each other trying to make the best of an uncomfortable situation."

She slammed a fist into his chest. "To the Break with you! I don't want your sensibility. I want your sympathy and understanding."

She tried to hit him with the other fist, but he caught her wrist. "You have those things. This was never going to be easy, but think of the countless lives you two could save if you help bring an end to this war. That's worth trying for, isn't it?"

A few tears welled up and spilled over, running down her cheeks. "What, so everyone else... so you and Nerith can live out your happy lives while I..." Her voice cracked, and the tears came in earnest.

Kasiel let go of her wrist and wrapped his arms around her. "I'm sorry, Vel," he murmured, pressing his lips to her head as he held her. Noticing how thin the fabric of their nightclothes was between them made it hard to focus on comforting her. He wasn't supposed to end up in this position.

When she got her tears under control, she pulled away, going to the washbasin to splash water on her face. She patted it dry and glanced in the mirror. "I look awful."

"You could never look awful," he countered.

Setting the cloth by the basin, she walked to him, coming closer than he was comfortable with. She looked up at him, a tempest of emotion in her silver eyes. "Kiss me."

He moved to step back, but she grabbed his arm.

"Please. Just once so that man won't be the only one whose lips ever touch mine. It doesn't have to mean anything."

Longing surged in him. It was one thing to kiss her only for the reason she gave, but he wanted to kiss her like he had wanted very few other things in his life, and he couldn't blame her for it. She wasn't Charming him. Niskenya would have intervened.

Would it matter if no one else ever knew? A single kiss that meant nothing. What harm could there be in giving her that?

He leaned in, gazing into those silver eyes. She tilted her head back to meet him, her eyelids sliding closed an instant before their lips touched. How he missed the feeling of someone's lips, soft and warm against his own. He yearned for that sense of connection – of welcome and wanting – so much it hurt.

He sank into the contact, prolonging it. His heart pounded in his chest. The urge to pull her closer and kiss her more deeply, to do more than just kiss her, raged like a wild beast within him. In his mind, Niskenya encouraged him to take what he wanted, not understanding why he would resist. Ending the kiss, he drew back a fraction, still close enough that their breath mingled. All he had to do was move in again. The tremble in her breathing and the way she held onto his arm, as if seeking some way to maintain the contact, told him she didn't want it to end either.

Nerith.

Feeling as if he had stepped into a trap of his own making, he forced himself to move away from her.

"You should go." His voice sounded strained, even to his own ears.

"Kas."

"Please."

Fingers still touching his arm, she whispered, "Thank you." Then she slipped out through the servants' door, leaving him alone again.

A thousand reasons he should never have kissed her raced through his head, none of them as insistent as the voice screaming for him to go after her. He threw himself on the bed and reached out to Niskenya. Riding along in her mind, they easily cleared the fence of her enclosure – a construction designed more to comfort the southerners than to keep such a creature in – then leapt the low outer wall and went to hunt.

espite a restless night, Kasiel was wide awake before the sun came up. After making himself crazy trying to fall back asleep for an hour or two, he got up and dressed, letting Velara's current round of guards know where they could find him on the way out. He didn't want to dwell on her late-night visit, and there was one way he could think of to get it out of his head for a while.

After retrieving Irith, he went to the barracks near the castle, not at all surprised to find Merrin and Wedro out training in one of the two big sparring rings. The early morning air was crisp and cool, the gradually brightening sky overcast. It was the perfect time for strenuous exercise. He went inside and donned a set of training armor, careful not to wake the rest of the unit, then waited by the fence that surrounded the ring, watching the aggressive dance the two were engaged in.

Before long, Wedro called for a break and turned to Kasiel. He pointed to Merrin with his practice sword. "Care to have a go at her so I can catch my breath?"

Kasiel nodded and ducked through the fence while Irith paced over to lie down next to a bench on one side. Wedro handed Kasiel his sword and went to join the cliff cat.

Merrin sized Kasiel up with her shrewd gaze.

"Kanodrak or no?"

"Does it matter?"

"I just want to know how hard I should try to kill you, Ahninveth." Her eyes sparked with a wildness that any Feral could appreciate.

Kasiel invited Niskenya in, letting her untamable energy run rampant through him for a moment before he attempted to focus them on the task, their wild nocturnal run still fresh in his mind. "Kanodrak."

Merrin nodded and slipped into a fighting stance. Kasiel did the same. They dove into combat as if it were a meal they were both starving for, exchanging fierce blows that, when they made contact, left stinging bruises through the practice armor. Merrin was easily the fastest fighter he had faced outside of his father. With Niskenya's help, he could keep up with her, blocking and landing as many strikes as she did.

They had been going for several minutes when a flicker of unease from Irith caught his attention. He split his sight, getting a quick glimpse of the person now standing at the edge of the ring opposite Wedro and Irith through the cliff cat's eyes. His stomach turned, throat constricting with the memory of her mace crashing down on his arm.

"Hold," he called, narrowly dodging a swing before turning his attention to the new arrival.

General Itana had her long black hair woven into tiny braids and bound back the way it had been when he fought her in Sharith, her gaze hard and calculating. Irith trotted up beside him as he lowered his sword and approached her.

Itana smiled, her teeth bright against dark skin. "You appear to fight better with your left arm than you did with the other, Ahninveth Kasiel."

It took him a moment to adjust to the idea of speaking Pandrean Common. He had listened to it throughout the dinner last night but hadn't needed to make the words himself yet. A year ago, the idea of being surrounded by people who spoke primarily Vanrian had terrified him. How quickly things changed.

"General Itana." He offered a respectful nod, pleased that unpleasant memories of their last encounter didn't undermine the confidence in his voice. "You could have killed me that night. What made you hold back?"

"I could have." She gave him a more predatory grin this time. "Combat isn't all about killing. Sometimes you need to know when it is prudent to withdraw. Had I taken the extra minute to end you, I might not have escaped before your father could get to me. His ability as a Frightener is not the only reason people are terrified of him."

"We appreciate your prudence, General," Merrin said, walking up to take a protective stance next to Kasiel.

As she spoke, a Delaphinian man in the attire of a royal servant came to stand near Itana's left flank. He folded his hands politely in front of him.

Itana considered Merrin for a second before responding. "Had I known he would adapt so well, I might have risked it, but I did not come down here to reminisce about old times." Her gaze returned to Kasiel. "Prince Kaden would like to speak with you, Ahninveth." She gestured toward an upper terrace alongside the castle.

Kasiel looked up, spotting two Delaphinian guards watching them from the front corners of the terrace. They were above the beach level at the barracks, but a couple of floors below the ground floor of the castle and the terrace. A stone staircase climbed the side of the cliff leading up to it.

"I'll be back." Kasiel ducked between the fence rails before Merrin or Wedro could object. Irith leapt over to come with him.

"Stop," Itana ordered. "You cannot take that beast in the prince's presence."

Kasiel's eyebrows went up. "You expect me to go up there with no protection?"

"From what I saw out there, you are your own protection."

"Not good enough," Merrin objected, stepping forward as if she meant to join them.

Kasiel held up a hand to stay her. Irith would accompany him or he wouldn't go. Before he could say as much, the Delaphinian servant cleared his throat.

"If I may, General Itana, Prince Kaden requested that Ahninveth Kasiel bring his companion creature."

Itana stared at the servant, looking as if she wanted to throw something deadly at him. "You are serious?"

"Yes, General."

Her lips pressed together. "Idiot," she muttered under her breath.

Kasiel stripped off the practice armor and left it and the sword with his companions. He glanced at Itana as they started walking, the servant falling into step behind them. "Do you often act as a messenger for the prince?"

She grinned. "Only when I have an interest in who the message is being sent to. I wanted to watch you fight from up close."

Kasiel nodded and set a hand on Irith's shoulders as he followed her up to the terrace.

There were six more guards positioned around the large space at the top, besides the two he had seen from below. Prince Kaden sat at a table laden with an elaborate platter of fruits, cheeses, and bread, similar to what Kasiel had grown used to at the palace in Etrion. Once again, there appeared to be a judicious blend of Vanrian and southern foods in the selection.

Kaden stood when he approached, and Kasiel offered

a slight bow, keeping one hand on Irith's shoulders as he did so. The prince wore more casual attire, though the fine fabrics that made up his clothing were enough to reveal his elite status. Something Kasiel himself had grown more aware as a member of Vanrian nobility. Even what he wore now, rumpled as the garments were by the practice armor, was a far cry above average in quality and craftsmanship.

"Ahninveth Kasiel, you are the Warden's son, yes?"

"Dhomvalen Arhk Cavenos is my father."

Kaden looked him over in thoughtful silence, his gaze lingering on Irith for a second. Then he gestured to a chair on the end of the table, sinking back into his seat with a practiced grace. "Join me a moment if you would." He was silent while Kasiel took the offered seat, his fingers steepled before him. Once they were both settled, his gaze shifted to the blue horizon. "It seems that most of your company speaks Pandrean Common."

"Everyone in Vanris does," Kasiel answered.

"Surely you don't waste such education on the servants... ah, attendants and common soldiers." Kaden picked up a dense wedge of a savory pastry and took a small nibble.

His tone and choice of words put Kasiel's mental hackles up, but he made himself relax. He needed to avoid riling Irith up and remain diplomatic. After all, no one had forced him to accept the prince's summons. "We educate *all* our people."

The prince's brow furrowed. "But... Never mind. That is not why I wished to speak with you." He eyed the pastry a moment before setting it back on the platter.

"That's an acquired taste," Kasiel offered.

Kaden eyed him curiously. "You grew up in Fallend. Have you acquired the taste?"

Kasiel got the sense that they were discussing more than just the pastries. "I have, my lord."

The prince pushed a black Vanrian evalis fruit a little farther away on the platter. "How strange it must be to go from living in a small village at the far reaches of the Pandrean Alliance most of your life to becoming one of the more notorious mind-crafters and soldiers in Vanris."

The prince was unlikely to have an inkling how strange it actually was, and Kasiel wasn't in the mood to tell him. "I don't imagine you called me up here for my life story."

"No, of course not. You are one of Khesran Velara's personal escorts, are you not?"

For an instant, he could smell her perfume and feel her lips against his. He aggressively pushed those memories away. "I am."

"I understand why we are here, and that our purpose is greater than either of us. Unfortunately, I let ingrained prejudices get in the way last night. I do not believe I made a great first impression. I was hoping you might help me find common ground with her. Tell me what her interests are, perhaps."

He didn't want to. Helping Kaden earn Velara's affection was the last thing he wanted to do at the moment, but that inclination was misguided and inappropriate at best. Jealousy around Nerith might be understandable, but here it had no place. Reining it in, he considered what he knew about her that might help the prince. He barely caught a surge of fondness before it could manifest as a smile upon his lips.

"Khesran Velara has a remarkable head for politics."

"You mean court gossip?"

Kasiel drew a quiet, calming breath, immersing himself more in Irith's comforting presence, hoping it would help him avoid making any costly mistakes. He didn't have the experience to be navigating a conversation with foreign royalty. "I mean politics and history as well." Kaden looked instantly intrigued, and Kasiel wondered if they had warned the prince that his prospective bride was a mind-crafter. It was probably best to err on the side of caution and not mention that. "She also has an eye for beauty," he said, recalling that the garden balcony at the palace in Doran was one of her favorite spots. "And an affinity for animals." A relatively safe assumption given that she had gone for Irith right away when they first met. "I've been told that she's quite skilled in combat with a sword and dagger, though I haven't tested that for myself."

Kaden's eyes widened in response to those last words and his relaxed posture became slightly less so. Kasiel caught a faint smirk from Itana before she glanced out over the stone balustrade toward the practice ring.

"Not many of our women train in combat. Particularly those of noble birth," the prince added with a meaningful glance in Itana's direction. "It's not considered an appropriate part of a genteel woman's education."

"Perhaps it would help to show an interest in her views on such subjects," Kasiel suggested, barely keeping the irritation from his tone.

Kaden gave a slow nod. "Perhaps."

Kasiel reached over to scratch behind Irith's ears. The big cat's rumbling purr startled a few of the guards who had been staring at the beast since they arrived.

The prince watched the cliff cat for a second, curiosity rising in his dark eyes. "I understand you are what they call a Feral. What is it like to be in the mind of a beast?"

Kasiel looked into the big cat's bright blue eyes and smiled, sending affection across to him. Irith stood, the volume of his purr rising, and head-butted him in the arm, bumping his entire chair a few inches to the side. Kasiel chuckled and pushed the cat's head away. "There is nothing else like it."

"Prince Kaden." Itana glanced back at them. "Khesran Velara has entered the grounds below."

Kasiel stood, hoping they hadn't noticed the heat rising in his face at the thought of seeing her after last night. "I should get back to my duties."

Kaden stood as well. "Excellent. I will accompany you. I would like to speak with her."

So would I.

On the spot, Kasiel could come up with no valid reason to discourage him. He gave a brief bow before starting down the stairs with Irith. Itana and the prince came after, the prince's guards trailing behind them.

Velara caught sight of them immediately and walked over near the foot of the stairs to wait, with Jethan, Keyla, and two other guards accompanying her. Merrin and Wedro also joined Velara's retinue, perhaps trying to balance her numbers with the prince's larger group.

The khesran wore a dark green dress today, trimmed with gold. The split skirt hung open in the front, exposing tan fitted pants beneath that were embroidered in gold and a dark green that matched the outer dress. It was far simpler than what she had worn to dinner, though no less flattering, and her hair had only two braids worked into it along one side, arranged to expose one pointed ear. Behind Kasiel, Kaden commented to Itana how beautiful the khesran looked. Kasiel silently agreed.

Her eyes met his for an instant, but her expression remained diplomatically neutral, her composure perfect.

For his part, his unruly gaze sank to her lips as he approached. He inclined his head in a respectful nod to hide its straying. "Khesran Velara."

"Ahninveth Kasiel. A good morning to you."

"And to you." He moved to the side as her attention shifted to the approaching prince.

"Prince Kaden." She offered the barest curtsy.

"Khesran Velara." His bow was deeper, more gracious.

"I understand you summoned Ahninveth Kasiel up to speak with you." The slightest edge of irritation that Kasiel suspected the prince would miss undermined her calm tone.

"Yes, my lady. I had hoped he might offer some insight into how I could avoid offending you, as I did last evening."

Kasiel had to give him points for honesty, though Velara's expression said she remained unimpressed.

"Why him?"

Kaden's gaze flickered to Kasiel. He appeared to sense that the conversation was going wrong, but he didn't seem to understand why or how to avoid making it worse. "Ahninveth Kasiel was raised in the south. I thought he might be in a unique position to navigate the differences between our cultures."

"If you wish to avoid offending me, you can start by recognizing that Ahninveth Kasiel is, and always has been, entirely Vanrian. I expect him to be treated as such. Going forward, if you wish to learn more about me, I advise you to come directly to the source."

Kasiel struggled to hide his grin. Wedro looked away, fighting a similar internal battle. Keyla covered her mouth, pretending to cough. Jethan, in his charming fashion, didn't bother to hide anything, letting his amusement show in a wide smile. Among them, Merrin was the only one whose professional demeanor didn't falter.

Kaden also smiled and Velara drew back from him a fraction, apparently not expecting that response.

"As I have clearly run afoul of your wishes this morning already, perhaps you would you honor me with a walk along the beach so that I might have an opportunity to learn who you are from you."

The brief flicker of confusion in her eyes vanished as

she found her composure again. "A reasonable request, my lord."

They descended a staircase to the beach amidst their individual retinues. Once they were there, Velara asked most of them to wait by the stairs, keeping only one guard and Keyla with her. Following her lead, Kaden did the same for his group, letting Itana and a young retainer accompany him.

Velara removed her shoes and set them near the stairs, then arched a brow at the prince.

Kaden hesitated a moment, then bent over to take off his shoes and socks. "I was told you have a remarkable head for politics and history, my lady."

"Oh?" She cast a quick glance at Kasiel, a pleased smile tugging at the corners of her mouth. "What else were you told?"

Kasiel watched them walk away, unsettled by the jealous longing that welled up in him. What had he done? The kiss was supposed to have meant nothing. Why couldn't he make himself let it go at that?

For the remainder of that day, the prince and Velara engaged in various activities together, from their walk on the beach to a long afternoon tea and a somewhat more private dinner. Between diversions, Velara retired to her rooms, taking Keyla with her so that Jethan had few opportunities to engage with her. If Kasiel's kiss with Velara meant anything to her, she hid it well. He did his best to follow her example, stamping down moments of envy for the prince and struggling not to let his gaze linger upon her longer than appropriate. He considered telling Jethan what had happened, but there wasn't anything to say. It had been a mistake, and he needed to put it behind him.

That night, sitting before the fire in his room searching for the calm that would let him sleep, the hidden servants' passage door clicked open again, and Velara stepped in.

"Those passages really are rather fun, if a bit musty." She cast a glance back into the darkness behind her before shutting the door.

Kasiel stood. "You can't be here. If we're caught alone like this, it would be unpleasant for both of us."

"I only want to talk." She held up a stoneglass bottle. "I promise."

"You can't talk to your tehnaak?"

"Given that it's your tehnaak she's obsessed with, I expect you can understand better than anyone why that isn't especially productive right now."

He understood completely. "Does she know you're here?"

"No. I encouraged her to sneak off and have an evening visit with Jethan. I'll be surprised to see her again before morning."

He considered pointing out that it was hypocritical to tell her tehnaak to spend time with Jethan, then complain about her being obsessed with him. But he had encouraged Jethan to pursue the growing relationship with Keyla as well, so would be a hypocrite himself to bring it up.

She took a few more steps into the room. "Please, Kas. Just to talk."

With strong misgivings, he gestured to the empty chair before the fire and grabbed two mugs, setting them on the table. He returned to his seat as she filled them.

She sat down and took a drink, then set her mug down and ran a finger over Sylaryth's claw. "You had this out last night too. It's a tethdrak claw, isn't it?"

"Yes." He picked it up, recalling Sylaryth's pain and fear as he had tried to comfort the dying tethdrak on the battlefield. For a second, he couldn't find his breath. How could the memory still hurt this much? "It belonged to Sylaryth, my first companion beast."

She curled her legs into the chair and settled back with her mug, firelight glinting in her silver eyes as she watched him. "Tell me about Sylaryth. Bring your former companion back to life for me."

A wistful smile crept across his lips. He ran his thumb along the length of the claw. "I met him as a juvenile the day after I arrived in Etrion." He leaned back in the chair. "Almost a week before I was supposed to encounter my first tethdrak, thanks to Jeth."

He told her all about Sylaryth then, surprised by how good it felt to speak of him, even if it did break his heart again by the end. They spoke well into the night, Velara confiding some of her loneliness and fear around what the future would hold. Feelings that reminded him of how he felt first coming to Vanris after learning his entire childhood had been a lie. Eventually, she snuck back to her room, keeping to her promise that she would ask for nothing more than conversation.

The next three days went much the same. Jethan joined him on his morning visits to the sparring ring, helping him get practice in without Niskenya's influence. After that, they followed Velara through social visits with the prince intermixed with periods spent standing guard outside her door while she hid away in her rooms with Keyla.

At night, he stayed up late to wait for Velara's visit. Together they sat before the fire, drinking mead and talking. They didn't speak of Nerith, Prince Kaden, or the war after that first night. Instead, they shared childhood memories, favorite places, and the things that interested them. She spoke to him of her life growing up in the palace and made him laugh with humorous tales of many misadventures she and her younger brother Nakhul embarked upon, such as climbing on the palace rooftops. An adventure that had gotten them both restricted to their rooms for a month.

He told her about learning to identify plants and animals in the forests and swamps around Fernwallow, and shared the experiences of his journey to Vanris and many of the things he found most challenging about adapting to his new life in Etrion.

For an hour or two each night, they let the difficulties that troubled their current situations fade away and drift into slumber along with the people shut outside of that room. Their time alone, risky though it was, quickly became Kasiel's favorite part of those few days. He never would have guessed he would have this much to talk about with someone so high above his station, but with expectations cast aside, she became almost as easy and enjoyable to spend time with as Danica had once been. The hollow left by Nerith's absence and Jethan's distraction got a little smaller each night.

On their fifth day in Trenath, Prince Kaden and his retinue were to depart for Delaphine. Velara convinced Dhomen Aleren to let the Vanrian company stay in the coastal city for one more night, sending a messenger ahead to tell her mother they would be returning to Etrion a day later than expected. When Kasiel and Jethan arrived at the barracks that morning, Velara and Keyla were there with her night shift guards. Velara accompanied them inside and removed the split skirt over her pants to put on training armor, something Kasiel hadn't realized was an option.

When they went back outside, she claimed a practice sword and dagger from the rack alongside the building, leveling the longer blade to point at him. "I was hoping we might spar, Ahninveth."

Beside her, Jethan's brows went up. He shook his head. "I don't think that's—"

"Oh, let her have a little fun," Keyla interrupted, taking his arm.

Smiling at her, he shrugged and gestured to the ring. "All right. Try not to damage the khesran, tehnaak."

Velara ducked through the rails into the ring. Kasiel followed her, trying not to appreciate the way the fitted black pants accentuated her shape too obviously. Not at all might have been better, but how was he supposed to not notice that?

He stepped closer to her. "You're sure about this?"

She smiled. "Afraid I might hurt you? You do look a little tired today."

Kasiel breathed a laugh and whispered, "Only because someone kept me up half the night chatting." It really was inappropriate that she had this much energy.

Velara winked at him and moved to the center of the ring. He considered her fighting stance, wary of the dagger. Without a shield or second weapon, he would have to be extra attentive to the smaller blade that could sneak into any opening he left while dealing with her sword. It wasn't his first time facing a duel-wielding opponent, though. Farren had taught him a few tricks for handling that particular challenge. The best option, of course, was to relieve them of one of their weapons quickly.

Drawing in Niskenya to give himself more time to analyze Velara's style and lessen the risk of injuring her, Kasiel lunged. She shifted back, choosing to block with the dagger and swing with the sword. Kasiel leapt to one side, grinning when the tip of her practice blade skimmed across the chest of his armor. She responded with a fierce, hungry look, rushing in to keep him on the defensive.

It became a dance of strike and evade, Kasiel letting Niskenya's instincts move him clear of her off-hand attacks. Velara's speed and technique were exceptional, though she left a few openings that suggested a lack of recent practice. Those small mistakes were all he needed to first rid her of her dagger and, a few exchanges later, her sword as well. As her blade flew through the air, he stepped in close, bringing her to a stop with his sword resting against her neck. He could see her pulse racing beneath the soft skin there, the unexpected desire to touch her sending a flush of warmth through him.

The challenge that flashed in her eyes was his only warning before she twisted in, grabbing his wrist to pull him off balance. She kicked the side of his foot and ankle, knocking that leg out from under him as she followed her momentum through, slamming her shoulder into his chest to knock him over. He twisted before he hit the ground, catching himself with his hands, and swung a leg out to sweep her feet out from under her. She hit the dirt on her back with a gasp.

Kasiel hopped to his feet and hurried to offer her a hand up. "Apologies, Khesran."

She let him lift her, taking a moment to brush the dust from her pants when she was on her feet. Then she scowled at him. "You went easy on me."

Her silver eyes drew him in, making it impossible for him to lie. He smiled and brushed a lock of hair away from her mouth. "I didn't want to hurt you."

"I'll remember that," she whispered. Her fond smile made his chest ache. Raising her voice as she turned away, she said, "I expect you not to hold back so much next time we spar."

"Are you all right, Khesran Velara?"

They stepped apart as the prince's voice reached them. Kaden was approaching one side of the ring with Itana, a retainer, and four guards.

Velara offered him a polite smile, far more reserved than the one she had given Kasiel. "I am quite fine, my lord, but I thank you for your concern. It is far from the first time I have been defeated in a practice ring."

Kaden's brows pinched together, and he looked at Kasiel as if he were seeing him for the first time. Whatever path his thoughts had gone down, he didn't share it. "I had hoped you might breakfast with me and enjoy a last walk on the beach before my entourage departs."

"Of course, my lord. Give me a moment to tidy up." She caught Keyla's eye and her tehnaak hurried to the barracks with her.

"You were right, Ahninveth Kasiel," the prince said, catching Kasiel before he could follow them inside. "She does fight well."

"She does, my lord." His bruised ass would remind him of that later. Kasiel picked up her practice sword and held it out to Jethan, who quickly ducked through the fence. Before they had time to do more than select their starting stances, Velara was coming back out, her overskirt restored, and the bit of unruly hair tucked into place. They both lowered their weapons.

Velara beckoned to the guards who had accompanied her out. "Jethan, you and Ahninveth Kasiel can stay and practice or get some breakfast for yourselves. I have plenty of guards who can stand around and watch me eat."

"You're certain? I feel as though we've gotten quite accomplished at watching you dine. Every little nibble. Every little dribble," Jethan teased.

She sighed and shook her head at him. "Thank you, Cousin. If I need further analysis of my dining habits, I will seek you out." She looked at Kasiel, lips parting as if she meant to say something. Her attention lingered on him perhaps a moment longer than it should before a slight flush warmed her cheeks, and she turned away, going to join Kaden.

Kasiel watched the two chatting politely as they strode toward the steps to the terrace, an array of guards, attendants, and Keyla walking with them. He grunted with an unexpected burst of pain when Jethan's sword struck him solidly in the ribs.

"You Break-blasted idiot," Jethan snapped.

Pressing a hand to his side, Kasiel glowered at his tehnaak. "What was that for?"

Jethan brought the blade up as if considering another blow, then he snapped it out instead, pointing after the departing group. "What are you doing?"

"What do you mean?" It wasn't as if he didn't suspect what Jethan was getting at, but he needed to be wrong. He needed his tehnaak to be mad about something that had nothing to do with Velara.

"I saw the looks passing between you and my cousin. It's not you she's here to fall in love with, Kas. I don't know what is going on between you two, but it needs to end now."

"It's nothing."

"It's not nothing." Jethan made his voice an exaggerated imitation of Kasiel's, bringing a hand toward Kasiel's face. "Here, let me brush your hair gently aside while we make doe eyes at each other." He shook his head. "Get your thoughts back on Nerith, where they belong."

Kasiel jerked away from his hand, giving him a glare of warning. "Nerith isn't part of this."

Jethan stared at him, his flat look making clear he thought it a waste of time to repeat his argument. "I get it, Kas. I like Nerith, but with how dramatically your life has changed over the past year and how much you've had to change to keep up with that, I think it's reasonable to explore your options. Vel isn't one of those. She's a khesran of Vanris on track to be married as part of a political alliance. Explore somewhere else. Someone else."

That was the problem. It wasn't about exploring. Pretending it was wouldn't change the reality of the situation. And the twist of guilt in his chest belied the claim that it didn't involve Nerith. The more he got to know Velara and enjoy her company, the harder it became to ignore his growing attraction to her. "I'll deal with it," he muttered under his breath.

"I can talk to her if you like," Jethan offered. "Once I'm sure I've gotten through to you, that is. You realize what's at stake, right?"

Glancing up at the terrace, Kasiel ran a hand through his hair and considered the merits of kicking something. Given that Jethan was the only close option, he reached out to Niskenya instead, seeking comfort she was quick to provide. "Yes. I'll take care of it."

"Hey kids, what are we fighting about?" Avris, who had emerged from the barracks at some point, hopped the fence and placed a hand on each of their shoulders.

Jethan's gaze moved to the terrace. "Nothing."

"Fantastic. Who wants to spar, then?" She grinned at Jethan. "You and I could team up against Kas."

Jethan sized him up, the hint of hostility in his regard disconcerting. "I like that idea."

*

When it came time for the Delaphinian contingent to depart, a portion of the Vanrian company escorted them from the city. Velara rode alongside the prince, Keyla, Aleren, and a few guards close behind her. Kasiel, sporting a plethora of new bruises from earlier sparring sessions, and Jhanik came out on their kanodraks. Along with Kasiel's cliff cat and Jhanik's tethdrak, the impressive beasts provided a not-so-subtle reminder of Vanris's might. Both of their tehnaaks rode near them as well, and the ranking officers from each unit. In Kasiel's case, that meant Kince and Darro also accompanied him.

The company stopped outside the edge of the city, and Velara rode to Kasiel with Kaden at her side. Several of the prince's guards followed close behind, warily eyeing the kanodrak.

"I had to get a better look at this amazing beast." Awe deepened Kaden's voice as he stared at Niskenya in wide-eyed wonder. "Not a creature I would want to face in battle, but like this... truly magnificent."

Kasiel place a hand on her shoulder. "I believe we came here to help make certain that never happens."

"Indeed." Kaden smiled at Velara as though she were a prize he had won.

Niskenya growled softly in response to the spark of protective anger that flashed through Kasiel. The prince startled, moving his mount back a step.

Quickly passing calmness to the kanodrak, Kasiel offered Kaden a deferential smile. "Apologies, my lord, she sometimes gets irritated with my cliff cat." Niskenya did get annoyed with Irith at times, though not at that moment, but the misdirection would appease his audience.

Kaden gave a tense nod. "I am surprised the horses are so calm around it?"

"Her," Kasiel corrected. "They're calm because I'm keeping them calm."

Some of the prince's guards eased their hands closer to their weapons, apparently disturbed by the thought of him controlling their mounts with no obvious effort.

Kaden swallowed hard, tightening his grip on the reins. "I see. Well, it has been most interesting making your acquaintance, Ahninveth Kasiel."

"Likewise, Prince Kaden."

Niskenya's claws dug deep in the sandy soil.

The prince and his group rode back into their company. Velara followed, casting a discreet smile at Kasiel before she turned away. He wasn't close enough to hear what passed between her and the prince as they said their goodbyes. For a second, he considered eavesdropping through someone's horse, but decided against it. Niskenya already had her hackles up because he couldn't keep his emotions in check. It would be foolish to risk making that worse.

Velara came back to him as the Delaphinian company moved out. Dismounting, she handed her reins to

one of her guards and walked up beside Niskenya, looking expectantly up at him.

"Might Niske consent to a second rider, Ahninveth?"

Trying to pretend he didn't see Jethan's frown, he
moved his foot out of the stirrup and held a hand down
to her, helping her up behind him. She was the khesran. Was he supposed to refuse her? When they turned
to head back to the castle, he spotted Jhanik watching
them, a calculating look in his eyes.

For the noon meal, Velara joined the soldiers in the
barracks, seeming pleased to enjoy simpler fare and companionship after several days of lavish meals with Prince
Kaden. Afterwards, she put the units to work scouting
the area for materials to build a bonfire on the beach.
The process kept them busy throughout the afternoon.

As evening fell, she invited them into the castle
for an extravagant meal to use up some of the leftover
perishables and wine brought in special for her and the
prince. The large dining hall took on a celebratory feel
with just the Vanrian company there. Relaxed laughter
and conversation filled the space, vying for dominance
with lively music. As people finished eating, Velara began pulling them out onto the floor to dance.

Despite how much he enjoyed his opportunities to
dance with her, Kasiel made a point of sharing at least
as many forays onto the floor with others in the group.
Velara did the same. He hoped, by the time the evening
was over, that Jethan would no longer be concerned
about his interactions with her. Particularly given that
his tehnaak had danced nearly every song with Keyla.

When the current musical number ended, Velara
spun away from her partner and placed herself in front
of Kasiel. The playful light in her eyes captivated him,
her bright smile leaving him speechless for an instant.
The next song began.

He listened to the melody for a moment and shook

his head. "I don't believe I know this one."

"I'll teach you." She took his hand to lead him out to the floor. When he didn't move, she looked back at him. "This one isn't as fast. You'll be fine."

A quick glance around the room assured him that Jethan was with his lady love. Relenting, he stepped out with Velara. Picking a spot, she faced him and took his wrist, bringing his hand up between them and placing her palm against it. Then she held up the other, and he did the same. Keeping her voice low enough that he could barely hear it through the music, she explained the steps. Her soft words, the movement of her lips, and a few too many mugs of mead put him in her thrall. Giving her control of the moment, he let her guide him through the dance, forgetting the rest of the room and the people in it.

When the music stopped, their eyes stayed locked for what felt like an eternity before she turned away, letting him breathe again.

"Grab your mugs, my friends," she called to the room. "The bonfire awaits."

The musicians led the way to the beach, where the enormous fire blazed. Velara and Keyla danced behind them, leading the rest of the procession. A few people carried wine or mead down with them. A crate full of stoneglass bottles of Black Mead also awaited them at the foot of the stairs.

The music picked up a heavier drumbeat and Keyla led them into a wilder improvised dance. Kince walked past, filling Kasiel's mug from the bottle he carried. Back away from the fire, Darro snuck up behind Tath and lifted her in the air. Then he set her down and spun her to face him, capturing her lips in a passionate kiss as though no one else were there to see them.

Loneliness twisted in Kasiel. He downed most of his mead in a few large swallows and turned away, his gaze landing upon Velara where she and Keyla danced, her lithe form undulating with the music. She ran her hands up through her blood-red hair, letting it cascade unbound over her shoulders. His pulse beat in time with the drums. In his mind, he deliberately thought of kissing Nerith, but the image quickly transformed, and it was Velara whose lips he kissed with passion equal to that of Darro and Tath behind him.

Jhanik stepped up beside him, breaking the moment. "Lucky for you, Nerith isn't here to get in the way of your blossoming romance with the khesran. Though, I wonder how the Delaphinian prince is going to feel about it when he finds out. Or the khevarin, for that matter."

Kasiel averted his gaze, guilt punching a hole in his chest. He tossed his mug into the sand near the crate so no one else could fill it, not that it was going to change things much at this point.

The music switched to a festive tune. Before he could think of a response for Jhanik, Avris danced past with Merrin, grabbing his hand and pulling him with them.

"We're much better dancers than he is," she said, laughing.

The three of them danced together for some time. Jethan, Kince, Darro, and Tath wandered over to join them. Etris coaxed Wedro and the new healer, Harif, out. For a seemingly endless string of songs, they danced, one or more of them dropping off occasionally to grab a drink before stepping back in. Somewhere in there, Keyla and Velara entered their group.

Kasiel wasn't sure how long they had been out there, though the bonfire had burned down considerably. He and Jethan had their elbows locked, dancing to a spirited piece that was almost more combative in style, when he ran into someone else and found himself flat on his back in the sand with them on top of him.

Laughing and breathless enough that she could barely get her arms under, Velara struggled to lift herself off his chest. Kasiel tried to help her up, his own laughter making it nigh impossible. Giving up, she rolled off and lay in the sand next to him, staring up at Jethan and Keyla, who were grinning down at them.

"I think I'm done," Velara gasped. "Take me to my rooms, my guardians." She held out her arms.

Jethan took one arm and Kasiel got to his feet to take the other, helping his tehnaak pull her up.

Velara looked at the people still around the bonfire, some dancing, others now settled in the sand, relaxing. "Enjoy the fire, my revelers. I must retire."

She received a chorus of cheers and raised mugs as she bowed inelegantly, then stumbled to the stairs. Jethan, Keyla, and Kasiel followed with similar levels of gracelessness.

She stopped at the foot of the climb and frowned at her sandy feet. "Does anyone recall where I left my shoes?"

Kasiel spotted a large depository of footwear off to one side of the stairs. A quick rummage found hers along with his boots, though he only distantly recalled taking them off. He helped Jethan locate his and Keyla's before they began the climb up. Halfway to the top, Velara stopped and rested against the stone railing, her gaze picking him out of their small group.

"Was it this long a climb yesterday?"

Jethan chuckled. "No. I saw them adding to it just this morning."

She rolled her eyes at him. "Calloch." Then she held a hand out to Kasiel. "Come, brave soldier, you shall escort me to the top so that I have someone to pull down with me when I fall."

Kasiel grinned. "Such an irresistible offer."

She arched a brow at him. "That was no offer, darling. It was an order."

"In that case..."

He tucked their shoes under one arm and offered her the other. She wrapped hers through it, and they continued the ascent with her leaning against him. When they finally reached their rooms, Velara slipped inside past a pair of guards who had been waiting for them. Kasiel left Jethan and Keyla in the throes of a kiss that it appeared might never end, and ducked into his own room. He sank into a chair for a few minutes, closing his eyes while he checked in with Niskenya, Irith, and the tethdraks. When he drew back from them, Velara pushed into his thoughts again. Her laughter, her smile, the way she danced.

Releasing a heavy exhale, he got up and removed his shirt, tossing it over the back of a chair. He had begun unfastening his trousers when the servants' door clicked open. His heart skipped a beat as Velara entered. Her eyes widened a fraction when she saw him standing half-naked in the flickering light of a low fire. He hadn't bothered to light any of the sconces or candles.

"I wasn't expecting you." Thinking and forming words had gotten more difficult after all the dancing and drinking of the evening. All he felt capable of now was staring at her as she advanced, absorbing every detail.

Her gaze roamed over him unabashedly, the long ivory and silver dressing gown she wore whispering across the floor. When she reached him, she brought one hand up, running her fingers along one side of the ke'hanoath chain tattooed around his neck and down onto his breastbone. He knew he should send her away, but her light caress broke what little resolve he had. If he touched her now, it wouldn't be to stop her.

He watched her gaze pick out the various scars he had gained over the last year and the recent bruises from sparring. Then she looked up at him and took a step closer. He drew in a breath when the thin fabric of her gown brushed against his chest.

"Kiss me," she whispered.

He did, but this time, it didn't stop at that. One hand slid to the small of her back, pulling her against him. She opened her mouth to him, inviting a deeper union. Her arms slid over his shoulders, the fingers of one hand twining into his hair as she pressed herself closer still. Blood pounded in his ears, a desperate hunger burning through him. She broke the kiss and leaned her head back, letting him support her as she opened her neck to him. Kasiel accepted the invitation, trailing kisses along her soft skin, eliciting a breathless gasp from her. One hand slid over her hip and down the smooth fabric of her dressing gown.

In such a moment, he would have expected the world around them to disappear, but the barely audible click of the servants' door opening again was a scream in his ears. It felt as if something burst in his chest, sending ripples of fire out to his extremities, demanding a reaction. He grabbed Velara and spun her behind him, so he stood between her and the hidden entry. A crossbow bolt flew past, clattering against the fireplace.

The cloaked figure in the shadows of the passage yanked the door shut. He could hear their footfalls as they ran.

He turned to Velara. "Are you all right?"

She stared at him, the color drained from her features. "I think so."

Kasiel ran to the servants' door, trying to get his fingers into the flush, barely visible edge to pry it back open. He let out a snarl of frustration when he couldn't get purchase. Every second, the attacker was getting further away. He turned and spotted his dagger lying on a chair in the corner.

"Kas."

The terror in Velara's voice pulled his attention to her.

She gripped her arm below a thin line of red staining one sleeve where the bolt had grazed her. "Something... wrong." She slurred the words. When she took a step toward him, her eyelids fluttered closed, and she collapsed.

Velara!" Kasiel got there just in time to catch her before she hit the floor.

Lifting her, he rushed out into the hall and across to the room Dhomen Aleren was staying in. The door shook when he kicked it. He shouted for help, not caring who came running as long as someone did. The two guards outside Velara's room hurried over, hands moving toward their weapons. Aleren answered right before they reached him. Down the hall, the door next to Velara's rooms flew open and Jethan and Keyla emerged together. Aleren looked at Velara lying unconscious in his arms and stepped aside.

"Bring her in," she ordered. "What happened?"

"A cloaked figure came in through the servants' passage and tried to shoot her. The bolt only grazed her, but it must have been poisoned." He laid Velara on the bed. Her breathing was shallow, almost undetectable. Kasiel could barely breathe himself. His ribs felt like they were collapsing inward.

"Is the bolt still there?"

He nodded. "By the fireplace."

"In *your* room?" Aleren's look was glacial.

Kasiel nodded. They could deal with the fallout of that later. Right now, Velara's life was all that mattered.

"Jethan, go find it and bring it here." Aleren gestured

to his tehnaak who had stepped into the doorway, his shirt hanging askew as if hastily thrown on. "Be careful not to touch the head. We need to find out what was on it."

Jethan sprinted out past Keyla, who stood staring at Velara with her hands over her mouth, quiet tears running down her cheeks.

Aleren pointed to one of the two guards. "Activate everyone to search the castle and grounds. Especially the servants' passages. Tell them only that someone tried to kill the khesran. The individual may be wearing a cloak and carrying a crossbow if they haven't disposed of those items."

Kasiel was working on that already, reaching out to rodents throughout the castle and grounds in search of the cloaked assailant.

"Yes, Dhomen."

After the first guard nodded and ran from the room, she looked at the second. "Get Inren Merrin and a healer from the barracks. Set the rest of the soldiers to searching. Run!"

Merrin?

The guard nodded and sprinted from the room, nearly slamming into Jethan, who was rushing in with the offending crossbow bolt. He was also carrying Kasiel's shirt. After handing the bolt to Aleren, he balled up the shirt and threw it at Kasiel in a less-than-friendly way, jaw tight with anger. Holding his silence and continuing his search, Kasiel put the shirt on.

"Keyla, bring me water and a clean cloth." Aleren met his eyes as Keyla jumped to do her bidding. She put a hand to Velara's neck, feeling for her pulse. "Why did they come to your room, Ahninveth?"

With all the reasons she might ask that, he wasn't sure how best to answer. He settled for the most obvious. "Because she wasn't in her room."

She tore open the sleeve of the dressing gown from the hole the bolt had made, then took the cloth Keyla brought and soaked it, using it to rinse the wound. "Obviously, but why *your* room?"

"Could they have been after him too?" Jethan asked.

Aleren nodded. "That's one possibility. His status and abilities make him a prime target. Or perhaps they expected her to be there." Her shrewd gaze laid Kasiel bare.

He looked down at Velara. She was so still. Was she even breathing now? "She's used the passages to come to my room every night since we arrived here. We sit and talk. That's all."

"You often talk with ladies half-dressed?"

When he tried to draw a breath, his throat constricted. The full truth about tonight was something he couldn't share, for Velara's sake and his own. Though he could give part of it. "I wasn't expecting her tonight. I thought she would be tired after all the festivities. She arrived minutes before the attack. I tried to protect her, but I wasn't fast enough." He had failed. Clenching his teeth, he struggled against the desperate ache in his chest.

"It would have to be someone who was in a position to watch them rather closely for them to have expected her to be there." Jethan straightened his own shirt as he spoke, not looking at Kasiel. "Or they could have gotten lucky and spotted her in the passage when she snuck into Kasiel's room."

Keyla brushed trembling fingers through her mussed hair.

The motion drew Aleren's gaze to her. "You weren't in the room the two of you shared either, I take it?"

Keyla shook her head. Tears spilled down her cheeks in a sudden flood and Jethan put his arms around her, pulling her into his embrace as she began sobbing.

"Will she live?" Kasiel asked.

"Her pulse is very weak. It depends on what was on that bolt and how much got into her system." She paused, staring at the shallow wound. "As much as I hate to admit it, had she been in her room alone, I suspect she would be dead now. I don't condone your behavior, but it may have given her a chance. If she survives this, we'll need to keep the circumstances quiet to avoid an explosion of additional problems."

Merrin rushed into the room then. Her gaze took in the scene, quickly assessing the situation. "Is this the weapon?" She reached for the bolt sitting on the bedside table.

Tath came in close behind her with a satchel over one shoulder.

"Yes." Aleren moved out of the way to let Tath examine Velara.

Merrin held the bolt in the light of a sconce and peered at it. She sniffed the tip and recoiled. Without a word, she held it in front of Tath, who inhaled and reacted much the same.

"I know this poison. It's got kenis seed and melinar in it." Merrin set the bolt down. "The kenis seed is a useful sedative properly diluted. Melinar has a similar effect but is too strong for safe use on humans, even heavily diluted. At this potency, a small dose could shut the body down completely. It was definitely intended to kill."

"She's barely breathing, and her pulse is weak, but she doesn't appear to be declining." Tath pulled the satchel off her shoulder and began rummaging in it. "With how shallow the wound is, I think there's a good chance not enough of the poison got in to be lethal. I have something we give people if we need to wake them up early from sedation. It's not as effective against melinar, but it may help some. If I can keep her stable for the next few hours, she should recover. I'll have Harif brew something for headaches and nausea. She's going to feel awful when she wakes up."

When.

If Tath thought she would recover, Kasiel would try to trust in that. "The ingredients were Vanrian then?"

Merrin met his eyes and nodded. "If word has gotten out about this proposed union, there are plenty of people on both sides who would find the idea of such an alliance offensive."

Kasiel focused outward, abandoning the conversation within the room completely. He called on Niskenya, bringing her toward the castle. Then he started jumping between rodents and a few cats he found in and around the structure, following sounds and scents. He finally spotted the figure hurrying along a dark, narrow passage from behind the eyes of a mouse. Slipping through a crack in the wall, he came into the kitchens. That told him which direction they had been heading. Making a guess at where they might be going, he jumped ahead, bouncing about until he spotted them again. His suspicion confirmed, he reached out farther, finding a family of sand mice near a terrace on the far back corner of the castle that appeared to be the assailant's destination. He sent Niskenya there.

"Kas?"

He became aware of Aleren and Jethan watching him. "I think I've found the person who attacked Velara."

Aleren stepped closer, one hand reaching habitually for the sword she wasn't currently wearing. "Where?"

Kasiel stayed her with one hand.

Letting his focus turn to Niskenya, he slipped behind her eyes, grateful that she allowed it, and lunged up the rocks alongside the castle with her. In a matter of seconds, she was leaping onto the terrace. The cloaked figure was sprinting toward the back corner when

Niskenya landed. The kanodrak swept out, catching their cloak with her claws and pulling back hard enough they hit the ground with a distinctly feminine gasp. Kasiel could see a rope now, tucked in the corner next to a planter and tied to the balustrade.

There was a thump behind the kanodrak. She turned to see Kince drop from a balcony above the terrace. He landed with his crossbow ready and aimed past her at the figure now struggling out of the pinned cloak. The moment the woman was free, she bolted for the back corner, grabbing the rope.

Niskenya's snarl stopped her in her tracks.

"How far do you think you'll get with a kanodrak hunting you?" Kince asked, a menacing darkness in his voice.

The woman turned, the backs of her legs pressed against the stone balustrade. She was petite, perfect for moving through the servants' passages, her blond hair pulled back into a single braid, revealing pointed Vanrian ears. Her trembling hands came up in a gesture of surrender, her gaze jumping between Kince and the kanodrak as if she couldn't decide which was the greater threat. "Please, don't shoot."

Kince strode up next to Niskenya, his crossbow still trained on the woman. "Then talk. Why did you try to kill Khesran Velara?"

"I was hired to."

"By whom?"

She started shaking her head, and Niskenya growled. After a quick glance over one shoulder at the drop behind her, she drew a shaky breath and met his eyes. "I don't know. I never saw the face of the man I spoke to, but I got the impression he was working for someone else. He spoke in Vanrian and the jacket beneath his cloak had a Vanrian cut to it. That's all I know."

Kince moved closer, advancing past Niskenya now.

"Where did you meet him?"

"The market in Doran."

"You came all the way here from Doran to kill her? Why?"

"To prevent the alliance." Her tone called him an idiot for asking. "It's irrelevant now, regardless."

Kince took the bait. "Why is it irrelevant?"

"Even if the poison doesn't kill her, she's no longer fit to wed the prince. I saw her with the dhomvalen's son. They were quite intimate," she said, her eyes widening for emphasis.

Kasiel's stomach turned. Of course she had seen, and now she would flaunt that information before anyone who questioned her.

Kince cursed under his breath, lowering the crossbow. The woman's smile was victorious. The assassination might not have gone as planned, but this would destroy Velara's reputation and suitability as a pawn in the alliance.

Apparently trusting Niskenya's presence to discourage any attempt at escape, Kince paced back and forth between the kanodrak and the woman a couple of times, scanning the area as if searching for something. Then he stopped directly in front of her, slowly shaking his head, and let out a heavy exhale. Kasiel's breath caught when Kince reached out and shoved the woman over the side. She didn't scream, but the thud of her hitting the cliff partway down sent bile rushing to the back of Kasiel's throat. Kince leaned over the edge. After several seconds, he nodded and turned to look Niskenya in the eye.

"If you're paying attention, Kas, tell them the woman jumped. When I get back in there, we need to have a talk."

Kasiel directed Niskenya to return to the enclosure. When he looked out through his own eyes, he found everyone watching him except Tath, who was busy monitoring Velara.

"Did you find the assassin?" Jethan asked, meeting his eyes for the first time since entering Aleren's room.

He nodded and told them what had happened, skipping the part about her seeing him and Velara and ending it the way Kince had instructed him to, with the woman throwing herself off the cliff.

"Blast it!" Aleren snapped. "She knew we would put her to death for what she had done. I don't imagine Kince could have prevented it, but I would have liked a chance to question her more. I'm a little surprised she told him anything, considering."

Kasiel said nothing. He'd had enough of partial truths and lies of omission tonight to last him a while. Silence seemed the most prudent way to avoid piling any more on.

When Kince arrived, Aleren questioned him for several minutes, asking for information about the woman. He gave her the same accounting Kasiel had given, filling in a few details regarding her attire, appearance, and weaponry in case they offered any clues. When she was satisfied, she dismissed him.

Kince bowed to her but didn't leave. "If I may, I would like to speak with Ahninveth Kasiel a moment."

Aleren glanced at Kasiel and nodded. "He's free to go." She looked at Jethan and Merrin. "You two may also leave if you wish. You and the rest of the unit should try to get some rest. The castle guards can finish scouring the area as a precaution now that we've neutralized the known threat. Just be sure to block the servant's entrances in your rooms and don't stray far in case you're needed."

Jethan lingered, one arm still around Keyla. Merrin left, wandering off down the hall. Kince and Kasiel walked back to his room. Someone had moved a heavy dresser in front of the hidden passage to keep more unwanted visitors from entering.

Kince shut the door and faced him, his intensity particularly unsettling after Kasiel had just watched him push a woman off a cliff. "Tell me you didn't have sex with Khesran Velara."

"I didn't."

Kince narrowed his eyes. "What *did* you do?"

Kasiel walked over by the fire, his gaze lingering on the chair Velara usually sat in. "We kissed."

"Anything else?" He held his hands up. "Forget it. I don't need to know. Have you talked to Jethan about this?"

Kasiel gripped the back of the chair. If only he could undo what he had done. But then, even Aleren admitted that if Velara hadn't been with him, she would almost certainly be dead now. Because they had broken the rules, because the killer hadn't found her alone, she might survive. What moral lesson was he supposed to get from that?

"He has his suspicions."

"The others don't need to know about this, but if you don't tell Jethan, I will. He's your tehnaak." Kince walked to the door. "I'll let the others know we can quit searching."

Kasiel nodded. "I'm sorry you had to—"

"She jumped. It's unfortunate. That's all that needs to be said. I'm counting on you to remember that if they choose to have us talk to an Evoker when we get back to Etrion."

"How did you get there so fast?" Kasiel asked.

"They came for Merrin and Tath and set the rest of us to searching. I considered how I would make my escape if I had just tried to kill the khesran." He opened the door. "I'll send Jethan in."

"You don't have to—"

Kince strode out and slammed the door, cutting him off. Kasiel ran a hand through his hair and walked around in front of the chair, sinking down into it. He had barely settled when Jethan stormed in, shutting the door firmly behind him. His look shot daggers through Kasiel.

"Just talking?"

Kasiel gestured to the other chair. "Sit." When Jethan had done so, he told him everything except what happened with Kince on the terrace. He would let Kince choose whether to share that.

*

A firm knock startled Kasiel awake. He had lain down on his bed after Jethan left, not expecting to be able to sleep. Clearly, he had been wrong about that. Without waiting for his answer, Aleren entered, closing the door behind her.

He bolted to his feet. "Velara? Is she..." Fear strangled his words.

"She's awake and violently throwing up in my room right now. Tath is doing what she can for her."

With a relieved exhalation, Kasiel sank back to sit on the bed.

Aleren glanced at the hidden door with the dresser shoved in front of it. "Between bouts of throwing up, she told me you pushed her behind you last night to protect her. Is that true?"

"I tried to protect her, but I failed."

"She's alive. Had you failed, she wouldn't be." Aleren took a deep breath, as if her next words were going to require some effort. "She's afraid after what happened last night, but she trusts you, Ahninveth, and you seem to care for her. She wants you and Jethan to continue as her personal guards. You especially. I have misgivings about this, but you have proven that you will risk your own life to protect her.

"If you are to remain in this role, there will be no more quiet evening chats with just the two of you. There will be no lingering looks or touches. It must be entirely professional. Do you understand?"

"I do."

"Good. Ahninveth Kasiel Cavenos, do you accept assignment as a personal guard and protector to Khesran Velara Markanis until such time as you are relieved of that responsibility?"

He hesitated, thinking of the family he had made here. "My unit?"

"Will still be your unit, though you may find it necessary to pass command duties to Inveth Darro more often. You will still get off-duty time and, because you are a Feral, it may be necessary to deploy you and your unit for various assignments during which her other guards will have to fill in for your absence. Do you wish to accept?"

He could still see the terror in Velara's eyes the instant before she fell. If he could do anything to keep her from experiencing that again, he was willing to try. "I do."

Something that might have been approval flashed briefly in Aleren's eyes. "Get yourself and your unit ready. Despite my counsel against it, she wishes to depart today, as soon as she has nothing left to throw up. You and Jethan will escort her to her carriage when she is ready."

"Wait. Did Jethan accept the assignment?"

Aleren gave him a long, scrutinizing look. "Lord Jethan said he trusted you and would follow your lead."

After everything he confessed to Jethan last night, that surprised him a little. "We'll be ready."

When the time came to leave, they escorted Velara

from Aleren's room. Someone had helped her clean up and change. She kept the hood of her pale gray cloak pulled up to hide her face and barely spoke to any of them. Each step seemed to require great effort, and she paused often along the way to catch her breath. Kasiel and Jethan walked on either side of her. Whenever she wavered, it was Kasiel's arm she grabbed hold of to steady herself. There was a tremor in her touch. As they walked into the large entrance hall, she stopped and stared across it at the front doors.

"I can't," she breathed, a harsh edge of despair in her voice.

Kasiel put an arm around her back and brought the other up behind her knees, lifting her. "You don't have to," he whispered.

Velara draped her arms around his neck and closed her eyes, resting her head against his shoulder as he carried her out. Ignoring the looks of everyone watching, he walked to the waiting carriage and placed her inside.

For the duration of the return trip, Velara kept to herself, remaining in the carriage during the day and coming out to take meals in silence once she felt well enough to eat at all. Kasiel and Jethan stayed close, not pushing her to engage. Irith rode with Velara and Keyla most of the time, though he didn't need to now. Kasiel allowed it, hoping the big cliff cat's presence might help her feel less vulnerable.

Kasiel pulled in a couple of sandhawks, using them to scout out around the company and watch for danger. By the evening they arrived back in Etrion, the birds no longer tried to leave when he pulled away from them. Working with them for so many days and luring out food for them to spare them the effort of hunting after long hours spent scouting had bonded them with him. Kasiel released them when he joined the small group that rode up the secure passage inside the wall to escort Velara back to the palace. The raptors would be nearby if he needed them again.

They marched through the palace with Aleren in the lead. Jethan walked on one side of Velara with Kasiel and Irith on the other, and an array of guards behind. All he cared about right then was getting through the formalities so he could find out if Nerith was back. He wanted to tell her everything that had happened and ask her forgiveness. Then maybe he could make himself believe the connection between him and Velara was a mistake. One they needed to leave in the past.

The room they entered was one of the smaller meeting chambers. Kasiel thought he had been in this one at least once, though they were all starting to look the same. Just another place to go to find out his next mission. The khevarin and Arhk were in the room, along with the usual selection of guards. The moment they walked in, Seylin looked at Velara and hurried to her, Arhk following at a respectful distance.

Velara ran to her mother, throwing her arms around her and breaking into sobs that made Kasiel feel marginally less guilty about Kince's handling of the assassin. The woman may have failed at killing Velara, but her actions continued to haunt the khesran in unforgivable ways.

The khevarin folded Velara into her embrace, eyes blazing when she looked around at them, her gaze settling on her tehnaak. "Dhomen Aleren, would you care to explain why my daughter is so distraught?"

Aleren inclined her head. "An assassin attempted to kill her on our last night in Trenath, Majesty."

Kasiel had never seen the khevarin show as much emotion as she did then. Pure rage twisted her fine features. A hint of pressure filled the room, and he glanced back at his father, catching the faint swirl of darkness at the edges of his eyes.

Seylin schooled her expression closer to her usual cool composure and took Velara's shoulders in her hands, moving her back. Her voice was uncommonly gentle when she spoke. "Vel, my darling, go to your rooms and rest. I will speak with Aleren now. You and I can talk in the morning after you have gotten some sleep."

Velara's hand came up as if she might try to hold

on to her mother. The vulnerability in the gesture cut into Kasiel. If only he could give her the reassurance and solace Seylin was denying her. It still wasn't his place, though. It never had been, and it never would be.

Seylin turned her daughter to them, gesturing to two of the guards in the room. "Please, escort her to her rooms. My guards can stand watch once she is safe within, so you can leave her and get some rest yourselves. I will call upon you all tomorrow."

Kasiel didn't join the others as they turned away. His gaze moved to Arhk. "I hoped to speak to the dhomvalen a moment, Majesty."

Arhk stepped forward. "I will seek you out after we finish here."

Kasiel inclined his head. "Thank you."

When they reached the rooms that were set up for Velara, she stopped in the doorway between the palace guards, staring into the chambers beyond.

Keyla placed a hand on her shoulder. "Are you all right, Vel?"

Velara glanced back at Jethan, then at him. She looked as though she wanted to say something. Or perhaps she wanted him to say something.

Kasiel longed to go to her, but it was Nerith he loved. Nerith he was permitted to love. He pulled her up in his mind, her silvery hair and lavender eyes. Her playful smile. Then her features changed, her hair turning a deep blood-red.

What had Aleren said about lingering looks? He lowered his gaze, staring at the seam between the wall and floor.

Velara went inside without a word.

They took Irith out to the enclosure, then he and Jethan retreated to his rooms to share a meal. After all the exotic foods and constant activity in Trenath, sitting in a familiar room, eating the usual fare with his tehnaak made it possible to release some of the tension keeping every muscle taut.

Kasiel laid his head back on the couch and let out a long breath, loosening the knot of stress in his gut a little.

"The more I watch you fight with yourself, the more I wonder why you accepted this assignment." Jethan popped a slice of fruit into his mouth.

Kasiel dragged his head up, surprised by how hard that simple effort was. He was exhausted. "She's afraid, and we're the people she trusts. The ones she wants watching over her. Was I supposed to disregard that just because the situation makes me a little uncomfortable?"

Jethan arched a brow at him. "She more than trusts you, Kas, though I honestly don't see the appeal."

Kasiel chucked a piece of bread at him. It bounced off his shoulder and hit the floor. Jethan chuckled and picked it up, setting it on the side of the tray.

Someone knocked at the door.

"Come in," Kasiel called, a spark of hope igniting in his chest that it might be Nerith. As much as he dreaded telling her the truth, the sooner he got it over with, the sooner he could start working on trying to repair the damage his actions were certain to cause.

The door opened and two guards walked in ahead of Velara and Keyla. Velara's eyes met his and she hesitated, seeming to forget what she was doing.

Keyla set a hand on her arm. "Would you mind if we joined you for a bit?"

The knot in Kasiel's gut pulled tight again. He minded. "Not at all. Have a seat." He moved to the chair at one end of the table across from Jethan, leaving the couch for the two women.

Once the guards had checked his rooms for threats, Velara sent them to stand outside. Her light perfume drifted over when she sat on the end closest to him.

That simple scent evoked intense memories. The taste of her lips. The curves of her body pressed against him. Passion broken by fear. Kasiel avoided her gaze, getting up again to retrieve two more goblets from a cabinet. He sat down and poured them each some wine, setting it on the table in front of them to avoid any incidental contact that might result from handing it to Velara.

He practiced not staring at her while Jethan engaged the two women in a casual discussion of the differences between Etrion and Doran. Military population versus trade oriented. Dark construction materials versus light. They had been chatting for less than ten minutes when another knock came at the door.

Eager for any excuse to disengage, Kasiel walked over to answer it.

An attendant stood between Velara's frowning guards. "The dhomvalen requests your presence, Ahninveth Kasiel."

"I'll be right back," he said, not looking at the others before he stepped out to follow the attendant.

Arhk was waiting on the couch in his sitting room wearing casual trousers and a comfortable, loose-fitting shirt. He gestured for Kasiel to sit and took a sip of the wine he was drinking. Kasiel sat on the edge of one chair, not quite at ease with his father looking this relaxed. It felt like a trap.

Arhk looked at the way he was sitting, a faint smirk curving his lips. "It sounds as if you did well watching out for Velara in Trenath. You protected her from a would-be assassin."

Kasiel shrugged. "I did what I was supposed to do."

"Did you?" Arhk sat up and placed his wine on the table. "Something about Aleren's recounting of events rang untrue to me. Perhaps you could enlighten me. What was she not telling us?"

"Is Nerith here?"

Arhk's eyes narrowed. "If you choose not to tell me, I could bring an Evoker in or simply draw my own conclusions from the way you were looking at the khesran earlier."

"You'll do that anyway. Is Nerith here?"

Arhk relaxed into the chair. "No. She is still in Doran. Her situation is delicate. Andross has a say in her future, and he accepted Ahninveth Jhanik's proposal."

Anger flashed through Kasiel, the heat of it distracting from his effort to match his father's composure. Niskenya answered that anger with comfort, enfolding him in her protective presence. He took a deep breath, letting her influence calm him. "Nerith doesn't want to marry Jhanik."

"He is a Feral ahninveth, and they have known each other for a long time. In the eyes of the council, he is an excellent match for her. Since he has not yet formally presented his proposal to her and had it rejected, the council considers her father's acceptance valid, especially in the absence of a better offer."

Even Niskenya's influence couldn't counter the burst of frustration. Kasiel snapped to his feet. "Then I'll go to Doran and give her a better offer."

"You will not." Arhk's calm demeanor made Kasiel's temper flare hotter. "You formally accepted assignment as Khesran Velara's guard from Dhomen Aleren. In two days, you and your unit will accompany her to Norvask in Delaphine."

They were making Velara travel again so soon? "Is that safe after what happened in Trenath?"

"Are you worried about her?" A faint, knowing smile curved Arhk's lips. "Given that all evidence points to the individual or individuals behind the assassin being Vanrian, no place is truly safe. It gains us nothing to allow such tactics to delay the alliance, but it is good to see that you, as her devoted guard, are so concerned for her well-being."

Kasiel ignored the suggestion in his tone. "If we're traveling again, then Nerith should be here. She's part of my unit."

"Nerith has no tehnaak. Her only role in your unit is as a healer to take Ahrin's place. Until Tath takes a new tehnaak, any healer can fill that role."

Kasiel's hands curled into fists. "I can't just let this happen to her. I love her."

"And Khesran Velara, do you love her too?"

"I don't..." The hint of darkness at the edge of his father's eyes dared him to lie. Kasiel clenched his teeth. Somehow, Arhk knew there were feelings there, but that didn't mean he had to admit it out loud. "It doesn't matter how I feel about Velara. She's going to marry the Delaphinian prince."

"And yet you do have feelings for her." Arhk picked up his wine and tapped a finger on the glass, eliciting a soft, hollow ring. "I will not allow you to make a commitment of marriage to Nerith while your heart remains unsure. You are young, Kasiel, and you have not been in Vanris a full year yet. Give yourself time."

"Nerith doesn't have time!"

Arhk took a leisurely sip of his wine.

The room closed in around him, suffocating. "So, even if I proposed—"

"I would object."

Kasiel yearned to punch the tranquil expression from his father's face. Rage brought bile to the back of his throat. He couldn't think clearly enough to make an argument that didn't involve his fists, so he turned and stormed from the room. When he got close to his own chambers, he took a deep breath, doing his best to appear calm as he passed the guards and stepped through the door.

"What if our children came out earless like the

prince?" Velara was asking, a shudder in her voice.

Earless southerners. No offense.

They looked at him as he walked in. Kasiel couldn't focus past the white noise screaming in his head. He stalked across into his bedroom and yanked the door shut, locking it behind him. Then he went and closed the panel to block off the pass-through fireplace.

"Kas?" Velara's voice accompanied a tentative knock.

"You should probably go," Jethan said. "I'll check on him."

Kasiel glanced at his reflection in the mirror. The man looking back at him was stronger and more capable than he had ever been. A soldier of Vanris. Ahninveth. Feral. Kanodrak rider. A personal guard to the khevarin's daughter.

He glanced down at the tattoos on his hand.

Honored. A hero.

Powerless.

His hand clenched into a fist, ready to lash out at the reflection when the door to his room opened. Surprise derailed his flare of rage. He turned to stare at Jethan, who stood in the doorway looking pleased with himself.

"By the Break, Jeth, do you have any skills that aren't ethically questionable?"

Jethan grinned. "Not really. Vel and Keyla are gone. Come talk to me. Let me help you decide if whatever is going on is worth the life of another mirror. I've heard they think it's bad luck to break a mirror in the south."

Kasiel glanced at the reflection, then followed him back to the sitting room. "They don't think that here?"

"No. Here they just think it's wasteful and expensive. What did you find out about Nerith? Nothing good, I'm guessing."

Kasiel flopped on the couch, the lingering scent of Velara doing little to help his mood. "The council thinks Jhanik is a good match for her. It sounds like they intend to hold her hostage to her father's dispute, at least until he returns to make a formal proposal. Unless someone comes with a better offer."

"Which you can't do because you're committed to serving Velara."

"Exactly. And my father thinks I'm not ready to make that kind of commitment. He said he would object if I proposed. What's the point of having all these skills and recognitions if I can't even help the people I care about?"

Jethan filled Kasiel's goblet and handed it to him before topping off his own. "Let's put aside the question of readiness right now, since it's irrelevant. It seems to me that you are helping people you care about. You just can't help all of them at the same time."

"Not helpful." Kasiel growled the words under his breath, the peculiar urge to bite someone telling him how closely Niskenya was riding along with his emotions.

Jethan took a swig of the wine, grimacing as he swallowed. "Hold on, my savage Feral. What if there was something we could do?"

Kasiel took a drink of the wine as he sat up. "Tell me."

"There is one thing the council would prioritize over a marriage proposal. I don't know if Tath is interested or not, but if she proposed a tehnaak bonding, they would not only set aside the marriage proposal in favor of that, they would also likely send Nerith back out with our unit to keep the pairing together once the bond was made."

For a second, Kasiel felt the charge of excitement rushing through him, then he remembered another part of his conversation with his father. "We're leaving for Norvask in two days. We don't have time."

Jethan sat back. "Norvask? That should be...

interesting." He stared through the table for a moment, lost in thought. Then his gaze shifted to Kasiel. "We can still get the proposal sent. It would be enough to get Andross's dispute set aside for the time being, and if she accepts, they should allow her to return to Etrion."

"Do you think Tath wants that?"

Jethan smiled. "Only one way to find out." He slammed the rest of his wine, grimacing as it went down, and got to his feet. "Come on. Let's see if we can find her before it gets much later."

Kasiel followed his example, taking the rest of his wine in one large swallow that left him choking. Jethan stood laughing at him while he hurriedly washed it down with water.

"That was awful. Why would you do that?"

Jethan chuckled. "Because I wanted to see if you'd do it."

"You're a calloch."

He patted Kasiel firmly on the back. "Yes, I am. Let's go. I imagine she'll be home at this hour."

They went straight to Darro and Kince's place. The two officers they shared the house with had moved out about a month ago and Tath, eager to escape reminders of Ahrin, had moved in. Initially, Kasiel found it strange to think of them living together, but the more he considered the fact that Kince and Darro were both in their thirties, the more it felt stranger that neither of them had a serious partner there before this. Then again, maybe long-term relationships were less common in a military city where most of the population lived with the constant risk of dying in battle hanging over their heads.

It was Kince who answered the door. He left it standing open for them to follow him in and walked down the hall to knock on a bedroom door.

"Put your clothes on," he shouted. "Kas and Jeth are here to talk to Tath."

"Be right there," Darro called from within.

Jethan put his face in his hands and shook his head. "Kince, we could have come back tomorrow. You didn't have to interrupt them."

Kince smirked. "I didn't have to, but I wanted to." He gestured to the table. "Have a seat."

Tath and Darro emerged a few minutes later. When they had settled, Jethan explained Nerith's ongoing situation and their idea for subverting her father's efforts.

Tath chewed at her lip, turning the mug of water she was drinking between her hands. "I have been thinking about it. Nerith is a good fit. I just..." She trailed off, staring at the mug, her brows pinched.

Darro slid an arm around her shoulders. "Can she think about it for a few days?"

Kasiel opened his mouth, intending to tell her they would find another way. Taking a new tehnaak couldn't be a rushed decision.

Jethan jumped in ahead of him. "We're escorting Velara to Norvask in two days."

Kince sneered. "Babysitting the Khesran again?"

"I wouldn't call it babysitting," Kasiel snapped. "Someone's already tried to kill her once. She needs us."

"Is it *us* she needs?" Kince narrowed his eyes at him.

The others stared at them both for a second before Jethan moved them on. "This would get Nerith back in the unit and out of her father's hands," he pressed.

"You're sure you want Nerith back in the unit?" Kince met Kasiel's eyes, the same coldness in his gaze that Kasiel had seen after he pushed the assassin from the terrace.

"What kind of question is that?" The puzzled look Darro gave his tehnaak then made it clear Kince hadn't shared what happened on that terrace with him. Which meant he most likely also hadn't told him why it had been necessary.

"It doesn't matter," Tath said, resolve hardening her features. "Nerith shouldn't have to put up with this from her father. I'll send the proposal tomorrow. She might not accept it. It feels a little too soon for me, and it hasn't been nearly as long since she lost Leysa. Regardless, it will offer her a way to put off this other nonsense."

Kince left the room. The rest of them talked for a while longer before Kasiel and Jethan slipped out into the dark streets to head back to the palace.

As soon as they were away from the house, Jethan turned to him. "What's up with you and Kince? I know he's aware of what happened between you and Velara, but isn't he taking it rather personally?"

Kasiel held his silence for several strides. Kince hadn't revealed his indiscretions with Velara to the rest of the unit. He had kept his confidence. It seemed wrong to expose the other man's secret, given that, but this was Jethan.

He drew in a breath of cool night air to clear his head. "The assassin didn't jump. Kince pushed her because she had seen Velara and I together."

"Oh, shit." Jethan was silent for several strides. "So, he killed her to protect you. No wonder he's a little tense about this whole thing."

They went another block in silence before Jethan looked over at him. "Are you sure you want Nerith back in the unit?"

"Jeth!"

He held up his hands in a gesture of surrender. "Just checking."

Kasiel chewed at the inside of his lip. They were doing the only thing they could for Nerith under the circumstances. If it worked, she would have a tehnaak again, and a chance to make her own choices about who she would marry. He felt good about that, mostly. If only he could get Kince's question out of his head. And that look, the one that reminded him of the secret Kince had killed someone to keep for him.

The company that departed for Norvask consisted of only sixty soldiers – one regular unit and two Feral units led by Dhomen Aleren. Kasiel brought a full team of twenty tethdraks. Jhanik didn't have any beasts of his own. He would be responsible for those same tethdraks and for keeping an eye on the two kanodraks part of the time in Norvask, since Kasiel would have other duties to fulfill and the town didn't have proper enclosures for such creatures. In essence, he was Kasiel's second for this journey, which, judging from the barely contained fury knotting his features, didn't sit especially well with him.

Velara, Keyla, and the khevarin rode within one of three gleaming black carriages. Irith had to travel on foot, an injustice that made his hackles go up whenever Kasiel refused to let him follow the khesran to her carriage. Arhk also accompanied them this time, his three elite guards with him as always.

When the small company reached the border of Vanris, they were joined by two more unions led by Dhomen Sorval that had been called in from various bases in the region to avoid significantly depleting the number of troops in any one area. That brought their force up to three hundred soldiers and twenty tethdraks.

Kasiel brought the two sandhawks with them,

keeping them on rotating patrols around the area to watch for threats. When one raptor was in the air, the other perched on top of a carriage to rest or on Kasiel's arm to request one of the freshly caught desert mice he had Irith collecting for him periodically along the way.

They were almost to the Delaphine side of the Break, where the southern watchtowers were expecting them, before Kasiel spotted anything of note. He sent the other bird up to search the rest of the area, keeping the first circling the problem. Then he beckoned Etris with a quick gesture.

She trotted over, the haft of a battleaxe rising above one shoulder. "Ahninveth?"

"Tell the dhomvalen's Speaker I'm coming up there."

As soon as she nodded and her focus turned inward, Kasiel encouraged Niskenya into an easy lope up the side of the column, past the carriages to where Arhk rode near the front. His guards were moving out of the way to make room for the kanodrak by the time he reached them.

"Is there a problem, Ahninveth?" Arhk asked as Niskenya moved in close and slowed her pace to match his stallion.

"The Delaphinian watchtower to the southwest of us is under attack."

"By whom?"

Kasiel focused through the sandhawk's eyes for a second. "They're wearing Pandrean Alliance and Sarket colors. Looks like a single unit. Only about thirty to forty soldiers."

Arhk's eyes narrowed. "What does that tell you?"

"Sarket is aware of the proposed alliance between Delaphine and Vanris."

Arhk nodded. "At the very least, enough rumors have gotten out to provoke aggression. Anything else?"

Kasiel moved his attention to the other sandhawk for a few seconds. "There's a Delaphinian force heading their way from the southeast. Looks like fewer than a hundred soldiers."

Arhk was looking at him when he dropped back from the hawk. "What would you suggest we do with this information?"

Never in his life had Kasiel truly wanted to engage in a fight. Several days spent sitting in his thoughts, trying to sort through his feelings for Nerith and bury his feelings for Velara, all while giving the khesran most of his attention as her guard, left him itching for a distraction.

He met his father's eyes. "We can get there faster than the Delaphinian force if we take a small group. My unit would be enough with the tethdraks."

Arhk motioned to his Speaker, inviting the man up on his other side. "Let the dhomens and the khevarin know I will be accompanying Ahninveth Kasiel and his unit to deal with a minor problem at the watchtower southwest of here. We will rejoin them at the border."

The Speaker nodded, his focus changing.

Kasiel and Arhk moved out from the column with Arhk's three guards close behind them. As they did so, Kasiel signaled his unit and sent Irith to stick by the carriage. He pulled ten of the twenty tethdraks out, and nudged Jhanik through his kanodrak to take charge of the remaining ten, relieved when the other Feral did so. They broke into a gallop. Kasiel bounced between the sandhawk watching the approaching Delaphinian force and the one keeping watch over the tower currently under attack, all while managing the tethdraks and trying to discourage Niskenya from racing ahead. Holding the kanodrak back was harder than it needed to be, since she was privy to his reckless desire to charge in.

Arhk kept close, calling instructions to him as they wove their way through some rock formations. "Your beasts have the advantage in speed. I will target Sarketi soldiers and drive them away from our new allies. Then you can let the tethdraks run them down. We cannot risk injury to any of the Delaphinian soldiers. The rest of your unit can help deal with anyone I miss."

That hunger for conflict and distraction, an urge exaggerated by his connection to his beasts, compelled him to spill blood with his own claws. Clinging to the fact that he had no actual claws – that some of that increased aggression was not his own – he managed a nod of agreement. A mistake here could be disastrous. If he wanted Arhk to have confidence in him going forward, he couldn't let that happen.

Kasiel gestured for Etris to ride up beside him, appreciating that Jethan was paying enough attention to move out of her way. He relayed Arhk's plan to her so that she could send it to the rest of their unit.

The signal fire on top of the tower burst to life, someone only now managing to get it lit. The moment it started burning, the approaching Delaphinian force sped up, but the Vanrian unit was still going to arrive first. They came up a rise and around the side of a plateau, the gray stone tower reaching toward the sky ahead. When they were close enough to hear the clashing of blades and armor, he felt the hint of pressure in the air and glanced over to see darkness moving in at the edges of Arhk's eyes, gradually turning them black.

The tower guards had discarded their Pandrean Alliance tabards, likely in expectation of the coming of the Vanrian company. Instead of red and gold, they wore Delaphine's dark and light blue with gold accents. It made it easier to pick out their enemies even with them engaged in combat.

A few soldiers at the tower called out warnings when they noticed the Vanrians charging in. Moments later, screams of terror replaced those cries when the pressure escalated and Arhk began selecting targets. A few Delaphinian soldiers caught on and jumped in to strike down their opponents as they started fleeing. Others ran for the tower, ingrained fear of Vanrian mind-crafters, Frighteners and Ferals in particular, sending them into panic.

Kasiel sent his tethdraks sprinting past the fighting around the tower, directing them after fleeing Sarketi soldiers and a group toward the back who had been preparing a battering ram to force entry once they got through the resistance outside. He hoped the archers in the tower would have the sense not to fire on them. The rest of his unit and Arhk's guards rode into the fray. They made quick work of the few Arhk missed with his ability. Kasiel yearned to charge in with them, but he held back. When the tethdrak he was using as his eyes took off the shield arm of a soldier with a single swipe, he swallowed bile and pulled away, guiding them through the sandhawk instead. Despite his initial inclination to fight, he had little interest in watching the beasts wreak carnage up close.

In a matter of minutes, he was calling them back, their claws, teeth, and dusty red scales spattered with blood. It was a disturbingly efficient and bloody victory. Recognizing fear in the wide eyes of the surviving Delaphinian soldiers, he moved his beasts out a good thirty feet and had them lie down. A couple of men walked away to throw up after looking more closely at their fallen former allies. The damage tethdraks could inflict on a human body, even an armored one, could have that effect.

A dark-haired man wearing the banding of an officer on his right shoulder stepped forward and bowed to Arhk, gripping the hilt of his sheathed sword. "I'm Watch Captain Erikson. We thank you for your assistance."

Before Arhk could respond, the sound of the approaching Delaphinian riders reached them, causing a rumbling vibration in the ground that made the tethdraks restless. The new arrivals swept out around the near side of the tower, some moving their hands to their weapons when they saw the Vanrians.

The watch captain jogged out with his hands up to stay them. "Soldiers from Sarket attacked us. The dhomvalen and his unit came to our aid," he shouted to clarify the situation.

The man at the head of the column signaled his company to stop and advanced toward Arhk. Kasiel urged Niskenya closer, adding himself to his father's guards, and stopped the man's horse a few feet back to keep him from getting too bold. The rest of the horses in the company snorted and shifted, some pawing the ground nervously, uneasy with the proximity of the massive predators.

"Captain Jorgan Birk," the man said, inclining his head. The way he gripped his reins suggested he was as uneasy as the watch captain. "It is an honor to meet you, Dhomvalen Cavenos. Your reputation precedes you."

Arhk inclined his head, ignoring the incorrect use of his rank and surname. That was how they did it in the southern kingdoms. The black faded from the edges of his eyes. "When did your watchtowers start coming under attack by Sarket's forces, Captain Birk?"

"The first attack was two days ago." He raised his voice to be heard over the restless shifting of the horses. "That's why we're here. We were coming to reinforce the towers. How did you happen to be in a position to come to their aid?" A slight edge of suspicion tightened his eyes.

Kasiel put his arm out, calling the nearest sandhawk down. "Our company is west of here. One of our scouts noticed the situation at this tower," he said when it landed, smoothing the feathers on the raptor's head. Annoyed with having to shout above the noise, he calmed the horses. Sudden stillness and silence fell over the group.

The barest hint of a smirk tugged at Arhk's lips as several Delaphinian soldiers paled. "Ahninveth Kasiel has a way with animals."

The captain swallowed. "Yes, his reputation also precedes him. We appreciate your coming to our aid."

"If you need additional troops, I can request reinforcements from Vanris," Arhk offered.

The captain glanced around at the dead, most of whom wore Alliance or Sarketi colors, though a few were Delaphinian. "I will take that under consideration as I make my rounds. Many of our soldiers find themselves in the position of fighting against people they recently fought alongside. There might be value in having some fighters who don't share that experience."

"You have but to let us know. I will send word back that the offer was made. We should return to our company."

Kasiel sent the sandhawk up and made the tethdraks stand. A ripple of tension moved through Delaphine's troops, hands shifting toward weapons and tightening on reins.

Captain Birk inclined his head, signaling his company to move aside and clear the road for them. Arhk offered a nod of appreciation before deliberately taking the path they provided.

When they were out of earshot of the Delaphinians, he glanced at Kasiel, amusement lighting his eyes. "The goal was to help them, not terrify them."

"Horse shit," Kasiel countered, earning a sharp laugh from Jethan on his other side that turned into a fake cough. "If you hadn't wanted to intimidate them, you wouldn't have gone in with your Frightener ability and your Feral son on display."

Arhk smiled, seeming to appreciate Kasiel's defiance and assessment of the situation. "We tried playing nice. It was never Vanris's goal to conquer the southern kingdoms. After things turned ugly, we retreated to our side of the Break, hoping to be left in peace, but the Pandrean Alliance continued coming after our mind-crafters. We put in the minimum investment required to keep them out and periodically warn them off without suffering or inflicting excessive losses."

Kasiel watched him for a second, Arhk's words leaving a bitter taste in his mouth. "You're saying Vanris was never in danger of losing the war?"

Arhk gave him a long, thoughtful look. "You saw what you and I accomplished there without employing my Dampener. If we called upon all the mind-crafters and soldiers we have throughout Vanris, we could have destroyed them from without, or we could have used Charmers, Evokers, and Enkindlers to dismantle them from within had we wanted to. We have suffered considerable losses at times, but nothing compared to the devastation we could have inflicted on them. Until they developed that elixir, we were never at significant risk of being defeated, and you solved that problem for us."

He turned to the road. "There may be value now in letting them see the destruction we could have caused had we wanted to. You were perhaps a bit too eager to play along, however. There must be balance. We can allow them glimpses of our power, but only in combination with the message that we wish to move forward as allies. In other words, do not intimidate them with your power simply to amuse yourself."

"Or my father," Kasiel added.

"Precisely." Arhk smirked and urged his mount faster, ending the conversation by leading their group into a gallop back toward the rest of the company.

When they reached the others at the watchtower to

the west, Dhomen Sorval and Dhomen Aleren were at the front conversing with the watch captain in charge of that tower. Kasiel glimpsed Velara peering out of the carriage window. Their eyes met for an instant, then she slid the curtain closed. The urge for conflict stirred in him again as he returned to his place in the company with his unit.

They had an option that night to veer off course and stop in a larger town that could offer comfortable accommodation to some of their numbers, though it would mean adding a day to the trip. Or they could skip the town and spend a few more nights in the wilderness, putting themselves in a position to arrive in Norvask faster. The khevarin chose to push on and camp, the increased risk of stopping in a busy, unfamiliar town enough to discourage her from taking that option.

Kasiel and Jethan joined their unit around a fire in the midst of the camp once they were relieved from their shifts as Velara's guards. His quick-thinking companions had seized three logs from around the area to set by the fire, giving them something to sit on.

"Seeing you and your father work together is terrifying," Harif commented, gesturing to Kasiel with his fork.

"I second that," Merrin said. "I feel as though we could've won the war some time ago just by sending you two out together."

Kasiel scratched behind Irith's ears, trying to hide how much it pleased him to have coordinated with his father in the intervention at the watchtower. He was still upset with the man for refusing him the opportunity to help Nerith, but they had found a way around that, with Tath's help. It felt as though his father was coming to see him as someone worthy of his name. No matter their differences or how tumultuous their start had been, the progress in their relationship improved his mood. If only he could get his romantic entanglements similarly sorted.

Speaking of which... He spotted Velara walking their way with Keyla at her side and four guards around them. Keyla held a bundle of what looked like small tarts. Jethan was discussing Arhk's comments regarding balancing shows of power and demonstrations of support with the others when the two women reached them. Irith stood to greet Velara, and she scratched under his chin before meeting Kasiel's eyes.

"I'm weary of the adult fire." She gestured to where Arhk, Seylin, and the two dhomens were sitting on cushions brought in one of the carriages. "Mother said we could join your unit so long as I keep my on-duty guards close. We brought fancy treats to buy our way into your circle."

"Bribe accepted." Jethan moved down the log to make space for Velara and Keyla between them. "Have a seat, ladies."

They sat and began passing tarts around, her four guards moving to stand behind them. Having Velara next to him was distracting enough without the guards listening to their conversation. A quick mental tug at Niskenya solved the problem. The kanodrak trotted over, easily driving the guards out of her way, and stretched out behind the log Kasiel and the others sat on. With her there, the four guards backed off and took up posts farther from the fire, watching out into the night.

Kasiel caught Jethan looking at him, a crooked smile on his lips. "Nicely done, tehnaak."

Velara and Keyla shared a quick smile. It appeared they also hadn't wanted the guards there. Perhaps they simply appreciated an opportunity to feel freer.

Kasiel caught a whiff of Velara's perfume and stared intently into the fire, trying to keep his thoughts from straying. He hadn't been this close to her since their brief visit to his room before they left Etrion. It felt nice having her there. Too nice, perhaps. Her presence stirred desires he had foolishly believed he was getting under control.

"You seem a bit tightly wound, Kas," Avris said. "I could help with that." She gave him a suggestive wink and smile.

"How's that supposed to help?" Jethan asked.

Avris frowned at him. "The same way it did before. Who do you think distracted him after that bastard professor took you?"

Darro turned away, fighting a grin.

Jethan glanced between Avris and Kasiel, his expression gone slack. A quick look at Darro seemed to convince him. "How did I not know about this?"

Kasiel sighed. Now that dalliance was public information. He became more acutely aware of Velara's nearness. "You were absent at the time, Jeth."

Darro bumped Avris with his shoulder. "For a while there, I thought she was going to break her no serious relationships rule for him."

"No serious relationships rule. Is that a real thing?" Keyla asked.

Merrin smiled affectionately at her tehnaak. "For Avris it is. She believes she has bad luck in love."

"Due to bad taste in men," Darro added, earning himself an elbow in the side from Avris. He laughed and looked at Kasiel. "Present company excluded, of course."

Avris rolled her eyes. "Anyway, Kas, the offer stands."

They continued teasing one another, but Kasiel lost track of the conversation when Velara leaned closer.

"When Avris said she distracted you, she didn't mean..." she trailed off as if hesitant to speak the words.

Kasiel felt heat warming his face that wasn't from the fire. "She did."

"So, you two…" She made a closing gesture with her hands. "Just casually? The way you might spar with someone to burn off excess energy?"

"Vel." He hoped his flat tone would discourage her.

"Sorry. I just feel as if I'm learning new things about you."

"You're not." He glanced at her, noticing the delight in her smile. She was enjoying his discomfort far too much.

"I think I am."

It was nice to see her acting more like herself, if only she would find a different subject to play with, especially given the way Kince was now watching them as if he wanted to see them both thrown in the deeps for a while. Kasiel glanced away only to meet his father's eyes at the next campfire over. The knowing look Arhk gave him before responding to something Sorval was saying did nothing to ease the feeling that he was stumbling into trouble again. He turned his attention to the cliff cat resting at his side. That, at least, was an uncomplicated relationship.

Irith jumped up suddenly.

Velara let out a small cry, her hand going to her arm where the poisoned crossbow had grazed it. "What was that?"

"A lizard ran over his foot. It just startled him." Kasiel touched the hand on her arm. She was trembling. "Are you all right?" he asked softly.

She nodded, but fear brought moisture to her silver eyes now, the lighter mood gone. "I'm tired. I should go to the tent."

Kasiel stood with her and signaled the four guards. As they came over, her eyes met his, holding his gaze for a long moment, as if she wanted to say something before she quietly turned away. Keyla squeezed Jethan's hand, a hint of frustration in the look of longing she shared with him before she joined Velara. Kasiel sank back on the log, watching the khesran retreat to the large tent she shared with her mother.

Jethan moved back beside him and said something. Kasiel wasn't quite paying attention.

"Mm-hmm," he murmured, hoping the response was sufficient.

CHAPTER NINETEEN

Norvask was beautiful. The town itself was lovely and remarkably quaint, with wattle and daub, thatch-roofed buildings fronted by planters full of bright spring flowers along every cobbled street. Their destination, the Delaphine Summer Palace, situated on a gently sloping hillside beyond the south end of the town, was breathtaking. The grounds themselves were replete with decorative gardens, many of which exploded with a brilliant array of colorful blooms. Wide expanses of groomed lawns stretched between the gardens and around the sprawling three-story palace with its numerous peaked rooftops.

The exterior of the structure was painted a pale blue with white trim and gold embellishments around the windows and edging the rooflines. The colors of Delaphine on tasteful display. Delaphinian flags soared from the highest peaks, a white stylized raptor with wings outstretched on a background of light and dark blue panels set in an X pattern. Delaphine's banners hung around the large arched doorway with Vanris's black and purple ones arranged beside them, a silver kanodrak rearing up in the center of each. A bold gesture of welcome and unity.

Tournament grounds along one side of the palace had been prepared with tents, a blacksmith, and other amenities to accommodate the bulk of the Vanrian force. Delaphine's extra troops also camped on one section of the grounds.

A general and his unit met them as they entered the property. Dhomen Sorval broke off with most of their company to follow him to the tournament grounds. Jhanik took the tethdraks with them. Arhk, Aleren, Kasiel, and Jethan continued with the carriages and a small collection of dedicated guards into the circular courtyard before the palace.

An array of Delaphinian guards and royal staff turned out to greet them, standing along the entry with expressions ranging from concern to curiosity. Some averted their eyes, perhaps to hide less charitable looks. Prince Kaden waited at the center with the king on his right. An older version of him, thicker through the shoulders and jaw, sporting close-cropped black hair and a beard sprinkled with gray. On his other side stood a dignified woman who looked nearer to Kaden in age than to the king, though her regal attire and the crown she wore marked her as queen.

Arhk and Aleren came forward to escort the khevarin and khesran from their carriage. Seylin, despite days of travel, looked every bit the ruler she was, the strength and confidence in her manner easily rivaling that of the king, and her elegance the equal of her Delaphinian counterpart. Velara presented herself with the royal bearing fitting her station, though Kasiel noticed the quick darting of her gaze over the gathering when she emerged and the way she briefly clenched the fabric of her dress before stepping down.

When those introductions were complete, Arhk accompanied the royal family over to where Kasiel and Jethan waited. As they approached, Kasiel sent Irith around the back of the carriage to Velara, pleased to see some of the tension ease from her posture when the cliff cat came up beside her. Noticing apprehension in the faces of the king and queen and their guards as they approached, Kasiel dismounted, walking up beside Niskenya's head, and placing a hand on her neck. Jethan dismounted and came to stand on his other side.

Kaden's composure faltered before a moment of almost boyish enthusiasm, his eyes lighting up as he gestured to the kanodrak. "This is the beast I was telling you about. Magnificent, isn't she?"

At least he remembered Niskenya was female.

"I believe you've overlooked something." The queen's tone held a mother's patience.

If Kaden's skin didn't have such a warm, dark tone to it, Kasiel suspected he might appear more obviously embarrassed in that moment.

The prince looked at Kasiel and Jethan. "Apologies. Ahninveth Kasiel Cavenos and Lord Jethan Markanis, this my father, honorable King Mahlik Durmond and my lovely mother, Queen Ceanna Durmond." He gestured to each.

After a brief exchange of bows and greetings, the king's attention shifted to Niskenya. "Is it blind?"

Kasiel looked into one milky white eye, a fond smile tugging at his lips. "Not at all, Your Majesty, though she does see somewhat differently than we do."

"Pity. I felt less uncomfortable around it when I thought it might have some disadvantage. Impressive creature. I imagine it makes you feel quite powerful to ride on the back of such a beast."

Kasiel became aware of his rising irritation with the king's insistence on referring to her as it when his temper was reflected back at him by Niskenya. He hastily sent calm across to her. It might not go over well if she growled at the king.

"I feel honored that she allows it, Majesty."

"She seems practically invulnerable," Kaden remarked.

The queen intervened before Kasiel could come up with a way to respond to that leading comment. "Perhaps we should give our guests a chance to freshen up," she said, placing a hand on her husband's arm.

"Of course." King Durmond nodded to Arhk. "You have all been on the road for some time. Please, come inside."

As the royal family started back toward where Seylin, Keyla and Velara waited, Kasiel encouraged Niskenya to join the other Vanrian beasts, offering her reassurance when she hesitated to leave him. Later, he would find out if they could let their companions hunt somewhere nearby or if he would need to lure in meals. For now, he had other duties to see to.

Jethan and Kasiel took up their places behind and to either side of Velara. He brought Irith along at the encouragement of Kaden, though the expressions of the king and queen said it was being allowed only for the indulgence of their son. The prince insisted the cliff cat was no greater threat than any palace hunting hound, making it obvious he had never seen what one could do in battle. All the same, Kasiel wasn't about to object. It resulted in another layer of protection he could provide for Velara.

"This palace is more extravagant than the one in Dekingham," the queen was saying. "We stopped using it once the war started because of its proximity to the border, but it has been meticulously maintained. A wedding unifying Vanris and Delaphine seems the perfect occasion to reinstate it." She glanced at Seylin. "I had hoped to get your opinion on which of the gardens we should use, Khevarin Seylin. Perhaps you and your lovely daughter would join me for a tour of them before dinner."

Seylin inclined her head. "We would be quite pleased to see the grounds once we have had an opportunity to freshen up. Thank you."

They continued their polite conversation as they walked, but Kasiel had stopped paying attention. Were they planning the wedding already? They couldn't mean to marry the two on this visit, could they? Someone would have said something before now. Unless they had been trying to keep it quiet.

He glanced at Jethan, who caught his look and answered it with an unsatisfying shrug, though there was a hint of distress in his eyes. Keyla would follow where Velara went, which could complicate his relationship with her once the khesran married.

They walked into the palace and through a towering entrance lined with columns. The walls and ceilings of the vast rooms they passed were colorful and replete with artwork and ornamentation, much of it gilded. Heavy gold candelabras hung from the ceilings. The floors were as varied as the walls, with complicated parquet patterns or polished stone designs, some with elegant carpets laid over them. The visual excess made Kasiel feel like his eyes were becoming nauseous. It would take hours just to see all the details of one room.

The royal family promised them a more extensive tour later, which he wasn't at all sure he could stomach, before leaving them in their assigned quarters in the east wing. Seylin and Velara received the most opulent rooms, both of which had interior doors connecting them to the slightly less lavish rooms their tehnaaks would stay in. Arhk took the room on the other side of Seylin's. They gave Kasiel a room next to Velara's, with Jethan on the far side of Keyla's room. Other elite guards took quarters further out in the wing for use during off-duty hours. At the dhomvalen's insistence, all the servants' passages into their rooms were locked and had heavy furniture blocking them.

Kaden made a point of showing Kasiel that he had

direct access to a garden patio from his room, which offered an easy way out to where the beasts were being kept from there. It also gave him a way to take Irith outside without disturbing anyone. They provided a large carpet like those they apparently used for their hunting hounds inside the palaces for Irith to sleep on. It remained to be seen if Kasiel could keep the big cat off the bed or the long couch near the fireplace. None of the blue and gold furniture looked up to resisting his claws.

After an hour given to resting and cleaning up from the road, the remainder of the afternoon was spent touring the palace and grounds. Kasiel watched for vulnerabilities, such as servants' passage entrances hidden within most of the rooms, as much because it was his job to protect Velara as because it helped him avoid those lingering looks Aleren had warned him about.

Aleren, Arhk, Kaden, and the king split off after the palace tour to go review the arrangement of the troops on the tournament grounds. Kasiel and Jethan, as Velara's guards, remained with the other group consisting of Velara, Seylin, Ceanna, several personal guards and, of course, Keyla.

They were wandering the pathways within the third, or maybe this was the fourth, garden now. Kasiel had lost track. He felt like his eyes were still looking at the world through a filter of gold from all the gilding in the palace. He recognized several of the plants here from those he studied in Edmund's books back in his quieter days in Fernwallow.

Ceanna glanced back at Keyla where she walked with Velara. "You mean to say that Lady Keyla and Dhomen Aleren gain royal privileges merely by being connected to you and your daughter as these spirit siblings?"

"In many ways, yes." Seylin answered.

"But they are not royal by birth. This idea of a sibling who is not of shared blood intrigues me."

"It is something the Vanrian people have practiced since long before coming to Pandrea." Seylin stopped, the rest of the group halting around her, and reached for a deep red rose at the side of the path. She propped it up delicately with her fingers and glanced back at her daughter. "This is lovely, Velara. Almost the color of your hair."

Velara took a step back, nearly running into Kasiel. Her hand brushed his when she turned to reach for a hanging pink bloom shaped like a heart.

"I prefer this one." She met his eyes. "Some of these would look nice in my room, would you not agree, Ahninveth?"

"I think you'll find those too delicate, Khesran. They begin wilting the moment you pluck them." He held her gaze for a second, that wild aggression that was always waiting to consume him of late nudging him a step closer. Tearing his eyes away from hers, he reached over her head to pick a brilliant violet flower dangling from the drooping branches of an ornamental tree. He held it up between them. "I think you'll find these last longer and have a better scent. They're often used in incense for their soothing aroma."

"Thank you for your recommendation, Ahninveth." Velara took it from him, her fingers brushing his. She placed it under her nose, the bloom partially hiding her smile as she turned away.

"Not an answer one might expect from a soldier," Ceanna observed. "Do you often teach your soldiers botany?"

"No." The khevarin gave Velara a cool stare before turning her attention to Kasiel. "Young Cavenos's upbringing was unusual."

"Ah, yes." A light of recognition sparked in the queen's rich brown eyes. "I have heard tales of you. You are the Warden's son, raised in a small village in Fallend, if I recall correctly."

Kasiel forced his attention away from Velara. "Yes, Majesty."

"I understand you have been instrumental in turning the tides against the Pandrean Alliance over the last year. Such a powerful weapon hidden right under our allies' noses all that time."

"He has proven himself to be quite useful." Seylin gestured the direction they had been walking. "I would love to see the meditation garden you mentioned earlier."

The queen let Seylin divert her, leading them off along the path again.

As they started walking, Jethan stepped firmly on Kasiel's foot. "You two are acting like reckless teenagers," he hissed under his breath.

"Appropriate, given that we are teenagers," Kasiel answered in a low voice.

"It's not appropriate with the khevarin's daughter in front of her mother and the mother of her betrothed."

Kasiel fought the urge to growl at his tehnaak. Jethan was right. They were acting irresponsibly, but he couldn't seem to keep his impulses in check. Being around Velara made him act like a fool more often than not. In hindsight, he should have rejected the position as her guard, not that he could do much about it now.

For the rest of the tour, he tried to put more distance between them without being too obvious about it. His frustration with the situation flared when Jethan picked a flower for Keyla and tucked it behind her ear, flaunting his freedom to express an interest in her. He needed to get away from everyone for a time and cool his head, but the opportunity was slow to come.

After a grand supper that leaned heavily into regional fare of venison and boar with generous amounts of root vegetables and mushrooms in various preparations, Kasiel finally got his chance to slip away. Instead of joining Velara, Jethan, and Keyla in the aptly named Emerald Drawing Room near their bedchambers, he excused himself to check on his beasts, disregarding their puzzled looks. They all knew he could check in on them from afar with his ability, but he needed to breathe air that didn't smell of Velara's perfume for a time.

Niskenya greeted him when he approached the area of the tournament grounds where the beasts were being kept. She lowered her head and Kasiel pressed his forehead to hers, placing a hand against her smooth-scaled hide and closing his eyes. She brought one paw up to his arm as she had done many times before, wrapping her lethal claws around it. Kasiel sank into her presence, letting her enfold him with protective warmth and affection. They stayed that way for several minutes, until Niskenya drew back, a low growl rising from deep in her chest.

Kasiel glanced around, sharing her irritation when he spotted Jhanik approaching. Irith's hackles went up, and Kasiel tried to pass calm to the cliff cat. They couldn't afford any incidents here.

"Ahninveth Kasiel," Jhanik gave a curt nod. "The tethdraks are doing well. I made sure they ate."

"Good. Can they hunt here?"

"There are deer in the woods, but I had some of my soldiers do the hunting just to be safe." Jhanik's gaze shifted to Niskenya. "Careful, Cavenos, you may be allowing her too much influence."

Niskenya bared her teeth and Kasiel pushed additional calm her way. "What do you mean?"

"As intelligent as they are, kanodraks are still wild animals. The ultimate predators, no less. They don't understand the nuances of human society that might require us to deny ourselves the things we want. Give them too much influence over you, and you'll find yourself behaving recklessly. Trust me. It's gotten me into trouble plenty of times, and your bond with her is much stronger than the one I have with Arkos. I pity you the intensity of that bond almost as much as I envy you for it."

Kasiel slid a hand down to Niskenya's shoulder, stealing comfort from her strength. "You're suggesting she could push me to do things I know I shouldn't?"

"Yes." There was a hint of what might be sympathy in the other Feral's eyes when he met Kasiel's. "You are her bonded. Your needs are her priority now. If you want something badly enough, she will urge you to take it, and help you do so when she can."

Defensive anger swelled in the kanodrak, but Kasiel pushed back against it. As much as he didn't want to admit it, he suspected there was truth in Jhanik's words.

"Thank you, Ahninveth."

Jhanik inclined his head, then walked away.

Kasiel lingered with Niskenya and Irith a little longer. He allowed the cliff cat a chance to run while the kanodrak rested in the grass. He leaned against her and looked at the sky, wondering what the sky Nerith was under tonight looked like. When he finally returned to the palace, the others had gone off to bed. Kasiel nodded to the guards in the hall and slipped into his own rooms. After discarding his shirt and putting on some softer pants, he lay back on top of the bedcovers and closed his eyes, listening to Irith's breathing. He allowed himself to bask in Niskenya's fierce confidence, despite Jhanik's warning.

A sound woke him sometime later. Irith hadn't moved from his spot, but he was watching a hidden door push open in the side of Kasiel's room. Velara stepped into the faint moonlight that shone through the high windows above the patio entrance. He sat up on the edge of the bed, trying to shake off the fog of sleep. It seemed reluctant to release him. He wasn't ready for this encounter.

"There's a hidden door between our rooms," she said. "They had a chair in front of it on my side, as if that were anything less than an invitation to explore."

"Isn't there a guard in your room?"

Velara nodded. "There is. I Charmed her. She's sleeping and should be for some time. When she wakes, I'll make her believe it was an uneventful night." She strode boldly over and placed a soft kiss on his lips.

The fire that contact set off in his blood and the lingering disorientation of sleep left him struggling to gather his thoughts. Niskenya's presence moved through his mind, encouraging him. "We can't do this," he whispered.

"I'm not imprisoned in this marriage yet. Until I am, I want whatever I can have of you. Please, Kas." A tremble entered her voice then. "Don't turn me away."

He was supposed to be with Nerith. Velara's body wasn't hers to give. "They'll know if we—"

She cut him off with another kiss, sliding her dressing gown off her shoulders and letting it pool on the floor. Lingering close, so that her lips brushed his when she spoke, she whispered, "There are ways we can enjoy one another without doing that."

Had he ever wanted anything this much? That wild recklessness surged through him, breaking down his resolve. He slid his arms around her naked form and pulled her over him onto the bed, claiming her mouth with his.

Wedding planning took up most of the waking hours for the next few days. Discussions of food, flowers, locations, and differing customs absorbed Velara's time. After dark, when everyone went to sleep, she came to Kasiel, and they lost themselves in each other, always careful not to take it too far, no matter how intense the longing or compelling the encouragement from Niskenya. Then they would lay together and talk for a time, about anything except the current situation, allowing Velara to put it from her mind for those few precious hours. Whenever Kasiel met her eyes during the day, she would look away, her lips curving in a faint smile that reminded him of every kiss and intimate caress they shared in the night. He knew he should feel guilty for risking everything just to be with her. All he really regretted was that they had to hide it.

And Nerith.

He never intended to be untrue to her, yet here he was doing exactly that with a pointless liaison. There couldn't be any future for him with Velara in it. He wasn't even sure if he wanted there to be. Given that it wasn't an option, he didn't let himself dwell on it. He simply gave her what she wanted from him.

The days were boring for him and Jethan. Arhk took

pity on them in the afternoons, swapping them out with other guards to let them wander the grounds and visit with the rest of their unit. Escaping Velara's presence for part of each day was a relief, since Kasiel wasn't sure how good he was at hiding his visceral reaction to her smiles.

Today, Jethan diverted them through a garden on the way to the tournament grounds. Kasiel felt the weight of unspoken concern hanging over his tehnaak. Concern he suspected he knew the source of. He debated ignoring it in the hope Jethan would do the same, but that would only encourage distance between them.

"Out with it. Something's bothering you."

Jethan glanced at him, a sigh easing past his lips. "I'd really like to believe you've been thinking of Nerith every time I've seen you smile lately, but I know that's not true. There's something going on between you and Vel again, isn't there?"

The temptation to lie tugged at him, but this was his tehnaak. If he couldn't be honest with Jethan, could he be honest with anyone? "There is, but we're being careful."

Jethan shook his head. "I'm sure telling yourself that helps you sleep better, but if you get caught, you could destroy the alliance, among other things. Is that worth whatever you're getting out of this? You know it has to end when she's married. It shouldn't be happening now."

"I know." Kasiel kicked a pebble that had worked its way up between the cobblestones. "I just love making her happy."

"Do you think she'll be happy if she disgraces her country and ruins the alliance?"

Kasiel grimaced, wishing he had something to take his frustration out on other than a garden full of beautiful flowers. Maybe Merrin would be up for sparring. "No. She just wants to feel wanted before she's doomed to a life without love."

Irith growled and bit a fat, pink bloom off a plant they were walking past. They chuckled as the cliff cat curled his lips and slid his tongue across his upper teeth repeatedly, snorting as he tried to scrape the petals off.

Seriousness returned to Jethan's demeanor when he spoke. "I feel bad for her too, Kas, but you have to stop. As your tehnaak, I worry about seeing you hurt even more than I worry about my cousin. End it."

Defiance tightened the muscles through his shoulders and back. He didn't want to end it. Still, it would end with the wedding, regardless of what they both wanted. He should listen to Jethan. "Why do they even have hidden doors between all the rooms?"

"They say it's for attendants and ladies-in-waiting to have easy access to the nobles and royals they serve. Rumors about the southern courts suggest that they're also very popular for enabling liaisons with lovers at court events."

"At least we're using it right."

Jethan gave him a good-natured shove. "You're awful, you know that?"

"I do." Kasiel turned to smile at his tehnaak, his lighter mood vanishing when he spotted Prince Kaden coming their way. He put a hand on Jethan's arm, stopping him to await the prince.

"At least he's smiling," Jethan whispered.

After an exchange of cordial greetings, the prince's gaze settled on Kasiel. "Lord Jethan, might I borrow your tehnaak for a moment?"

They shared a glance, and Kasiel nodded.

"Certainly. I'll see you at the tournament grounds, Kas." Jethan gave him a wary look before walking away, warning him to caution.

Prince Kaden turned to the two guards who had followed him out. "Off with you. I'm in no danger here."

They hesitated, and he gave them a fierce glare. "Go." When Jethan and the guards were all out of earshot, he faced Kasiel. "Once again, I find myself turning to you for advice regarding Khesran Velara. It seems that, if I am to make this marriage something more than an act of sacrifice for each of us, it might help to understand more of who she is."

Kasiel pushed hard against a surge of defensive anger. "Should I take that to mean that you aren't attracted to her?"

Kaden started walking, obviously expecting Kasiel to fall in to step with him, which he did, if only to get an answer to his question. "I must ask you not to take this wrong, but, as lovely and intelligent as she is, she is still Vanrian."

Kasiel narrowed his eyes, Irith letting out a low growl next to him. "I'm not sure there's a right way I can take that."

Kaden glanced over at the cliff cat. "He is very responsive to your moods, isn't he? How did you become so Vanrian in such a short time? You have their tattoos, you fight in their army, you use their powers. It is as if twelve years in the south melted away overnight."

"Perhaps because I am Vanrian. The man who raised me in Fallend lied to me about everything. Any devotion I might have had to the things he taught me died when I learned that. My life was ready to be remade." Not that he ever wanted to be a soldier, but Kaden didn't need to know that.

The prince turned them down another path, letting his fingers brush the tops of a row of white and yellow flowers. "You must have had people you cared about in Fallend. Maybe a first love, even?"

Danica.

Kasiel lowered his gaze, not wanting the prince to see the pain those memories caused. "There was someone, but she's in the past and the future is being made here, between our two countries."

Kaden glanced away now. "We were raised to hate one another. That conditioning will not disappear over-night."

"Why are you asking me about her again?"

Kaden looked at him, a certain gravity in his gaze that suggested he knew more than he should. "Because she cares deeply for you, and you for her. It is in every brief look that passes between you and every word she says or does not say when she speaks of you. I recognize it because I have someone like that in my life as well. Neither Khesran Velara nor I are firstborn, bound for the throne. That duty falls to older siblings for both of us. If not for this alliance, we each might have had a chance to choose our own matches, within reason. It seems we both may know who that match would have been."

Kasiel found himself not disliking the prince as much in that moment. The man likely didn't suspect he and Velara had been intimate, or he wouldn't be this casual about it. Or maybe he would. At least he wasn't hypocritical enough to be angry that his future bride cared for another when he himself did the same.

They spoke for a few minutes longer. Kasiel felt as if he were dodging arrows, trying to avoid saying any-thing that might reveal the level of intimacy he shared with Velara or how recently most of it had occurred. When the prince finally set him free, he hurried out to join his unit. Jethan and Kince were sparring when he got there. He exchanged a brief look with his tehnaak, giving a nod to let him know everything was all right. When Merrin suggested they spar, he eagerly agreed.

At the end of the evening, Jethan caught Kasiel's arm before he retired to his room, giving him a hard look. "End it."

Kasiel spotted Arhk watching them from down the hall. Did his father suspect something? "I'll talk to her," he whispered, then ducked through the door.

Velara didn't wait a full hour before coming to his room. The more time they spent together, the less patient she seemed to spend more. Perhaps it was the looming wedding that drove her. He was still wearing his daytime clothes when she entered. Rather than allow her to meet him by the bed, he walked over to intercept her. She moved in to kiss him, and he caught her arms, gently stopping her. He had to be the voice of reason, as much as he hated it.

"We have to end this."

She met his eyes, her silver ones narrowing. "No. Not tonight."

"Vel, we're risking too much."

Anger tightened her lips. The flickering light of a candle glinted upon the faint silver outline of the ke'hanoath across her forehead. The tiara she would always wear. "Do you believe he will ever want me the way you do? Do you think he'll show the same caring and tenderness when he touches me? I'm Varian, Kas. Part of him will always be disgusted by me."

He shook his head, determined to deny her, but struggled to find the words to tell her she could be wrong when he knew from his earlier conversation with Kaden that she wasn't. "It's not—"

She placed a finger over his lips. "Worth it? The man I am to marry will never love me. Maybe you don't either, but whatever you feel for me, it's as close as I'm going to get. Please. Let me feel that again." Her voice dropped to a sensual whisper. "One more night, Kas, let me be yours."

When she took her finger away, she replaced it with her mouth, her tongue brushing his lower lip. Her hands moved up his shirt, sliding along the bare skin of his back as she pressed herself against him. Kasiel's hands, as if possessed of their own will, undid the ties of her dressing gown, and slid it off her shoulders. One more night. Just one.

*

Kasiel lay half-asleep with Velara pressed naked against him beneath the sheets when the door to his room opened and Arhk strode in. They had left a single candle burning, providing more than enough light for his father to see that he wasn't alone and who he had for company. The dhomvalen didn't appear at all shocked to find them together. Kasiel sat up quickly, careful not to pull the sheets off Velara as he did so.

Arhk shut the door behind him, his face as expressionless as stone. "Put on your clothes, Ahninveth."

Kasiel did as he was told. There was little point in arguing. He knew he had done wrong. No attempt at defending his behavior was going to change the fact that he had the khevarin's daughter in his bed.

When he finished dressing, Arhk gestured to the patio doors. "We will speak outside." He glanced at Velara. "Return to your room."

Kasiel caught her apologetic look and the hint of moisture in her eyes before he walked out to the patio.

Arhk followed him out, providing Velara privacy in which to dress. "You might find yourself in trouble less often if you learned to listen to your instincts rather than giving in to the desires of the females in your life."

Kasiel cringed inwardly, all too aware that Arhk was referring, among other things, to his theft of Niskenya when he went to rescue Jethan, something the kanodrak herself had insisted upon. An act that might have cost him his life if they hadn't turned the war back in Vanris's favor by stopping Edmund. In fact, Niskenya had encouraged his dalliance with Velara too, not that he couldn't have ignored her. He just hadn't wanted to.

"There was no—"

"Intercourse?" Arhk's brows went up. "I do hope you are not under the illusion that penetration is all that matters here."

He wasn't, though he had tried to convince himself of that a few times. "This isn't Velara's fault."

"She is a Charmer." His father gave him a long look that offered him a way out.

"No. She tried that on me once. Niske wouldn't allow it."

"You are certain?"

"Yes."

Unease came at him from Niskenya and Irith at the same instant, which struck him as particularly strange given that one was in his room and the other on the tournament grounds. He turned his attention to the two beasts.

Arhk's brows pinched. "Is something wrong?"

"I'm not—"

Explosions shook the night. A blast threw Kasiel away from the building. Collision with a stone bench on the edge of the patio knocked the wind out of him. He tasted blood in his mouth, memories of the night Sylaryth died sweeping in on him. Burning debris rained down around him. Pressure in the air increased, pulling his attention to where his father was getting to his feet, one shirtsleeve torn and damp with blood, a minor cut across his nose bleeding as well.

The windows and one door to Kasiel's bedchamber had blown out. The second door hung askew, fire dancing within the room beyond. Other windows and doors along the side of the building shared the same fate. More flames licked out through those openings.

Panic drove Kasiel to his feet. Irith and Velara had

been in that room. Arhk caught his arm when he went to run inside. Kasiel turned on him, ready to fight his way free, but his father wasn't trying to stop him.

"See if you can find Velara. I must get to Seylin."

His anger deflected, Kasiel nodded and sprinted into the burning room. Arhk followed, continuing past him through to the hall where shouting could be heard. Something shifted within the dust and smoke near the door and Irith stumbled to his feet, shaking off the debris that had landed on him. Kasiel could feel pain from him, but nothing severe.

"Velara!" He shoved the hidden door that now hung on one twisted hinge, forcing his way into the adjacent bedchamber.

Velara's room was also a chaos of debris and fire. She lay face down on the floor under several pieces of broken wood and fabric from the canopy that had once been part of her bed. Her guard lay dead near the door, lips painted with blood, a large fragment of twisted metal from something buried in her chest.

Sending Irith to look for Jethan, Kasiel rushed in and threw the debris off Velara. He knelt and carefully turned her over. Blood dampened her hair and streamed from wounds on her face and neck. Tears in her clothing and more blood suggested injuries elsewhere, as if the explosion had sent the shattered pieces of the bed at her in a violent barrage.

A bit of ceiling fell, hitting the floor next to them. Fire crawled up the furniture. He had to get her out of there. Sliding his arms under her, he lifted her limp form. A guard crashed through the busted main door, hurrying out of the way to let him into the hall.

"Vel!" Keyla came running up, staring in horror at her bloodied, unconscious tehnaak.

It became measurably easier to breathe when he saw Irith and Jethan hurrying up behind her, the same relief reflected in his tehnaak's eyes. Both Jethan and Keyla were dirty and scratched up as if caught in the blast of some debris. Wherever they were when the bombs went off, it looked as if they had escaped the worst of the explosions.

Rubble littered the hallway and several of the rooms on both sides had their doors blown fully or partially off. People, dark-skinned and light, worked together regardless of the shape of their ears, searching rooms for victims or putting out fires.

"Is she alive?" Keyla asked.

Kasiel met Jethan's eyes. "I'm not sure."

"Move the injured to the Emerald Drawing Room patio," someone yelled.

More shouts rang out for help to put out fires and search for survivors.

"Take her there," Jethan said.

He spotted Arhk heading that direction with Seylin and Aleren when he glanced that way. "Come with me, Jeth. There are already too many people crowding the hall trying to help. You'll only be in the way, and I may have need of you."

Jethan nodded and lead their small group toward the drawing room. While they hurried along, Kasiel reached out with his ability and began searching with rodents around the palace. There were fewer in these immaculately maintained halls than there had been in the castle in Trenath, but the servants' passages still provided dark spaces for them to move around and build nests.

When they entered the garden, they saw the khevarin's healer tending a deep cut on her arm. Healers from the other units had plenty of injuries to occupy them. Harif rushed over, and Kasiel let the man guide them to an open spot where he could lay Velara down. He stayed crouched next to her until the healer checked her pulse and nodded, calling for Tath or another healer to help. As Tath rushed over, Kasiel stood and stepped out of the way, reaching out to seize control of some tethdraks from Jhanik. He started them hunting along with Niskenya. Not for a particular person, but for individuals trying to leave the grounds or anyone within them bearing the stink of fear and guilt.

With that done, he refocused on his search inside the palace, bouncing between rats and mice, lingering with each only long enough to look and listen. As he moved along, he landed in a mouse sneaking through one corner of a formal sitting room. The king and queen were there, along with several guards, one of whom knelt before them, offering a folded parchment. Kasiel stopped to listen.

"What is this?" Ceanna asked, one hand extended as though she meant to take the parchment herself.

"We found it in Prince Kaden's rooms, Your Majesties." The guard kept his head bowed until the king claimed the parchment from his outstretched hands.

While he read it, his expression twisting with rage, the queen stood wringing her hands.

King Mahlik stared at the parchment as if he might set it on fire with his gaze alone. "They demand that we call off the alliance with Vanris if we want to see our son alive again."

Ceanna let out a cry, covering her mouth with her hands.

The king frowned at her. "That is not all. It says they will await a demonstration of our commitment to this course of action."

She lowered her hands. "What kind of demonstration?"

"Should any of the Vanrian royalty or nobility survive this night's attack, we are to put them to death ourselves."

"Havaad have mercy," she breathed. "How can we

do such a thing? They still have their beasts to defend them."

A growl rose in Kasiel's throat that she would even consider it if they didn't have the Ferals and their creatures to protect them. Before he could do more with this new information, a sense of satisfaction came to him from one of the tethdraks. Jumping behind the beast's eyes, he looked out into a wooded gully near the edge of the palace grounds where two Delaphinian soldiers were casting off their armor in exchange for civilian attire. When the tethdrak snarled, they cowered and scrambled back, one man with his pants around his knees.

Kasiel sent Niskenya to help the tethdrak before reaching out to Jhanik's kanodrak. He needed to get the other Feral involved. Passing information as best he could to Arkos, he hoped the beast could share it with his bonded rider in a manner that made some sense. When he pulled back, he sent Irith out to join them, so he could use the cliff cat to help guide Jhanik.

Back behind his own eyes, he took a second to re-orient, spotting Jethan crouched beside Velara, holding pressure on a set of deep cuts on her neck.

He met his tehnaak's eyes. "I need your help."

Jethan nodded, handing his position off to Keyla. He followed Kasiel to where Arhk was giving orders to a group of Vanrian and Delaphinian soldiers.

"Dhomvalen, I need your Evoker."

Arhk didn't ask questions, he just beckoned the woman over. "Go with Ahninveth Kasiel. Follow his orders as if they were mine."

The woman nodded, turning her attention to Kasiel.

CHAPTER TWENTY ONE

With Jethan and the Evoker, Kasiel strode into the palace. "What do I call you?" he asked the Evoker as they hurried along, following his awareness of the mouse in the sitting room.

"Ahnvaris Zafyr." Her tone was abrupt, as though she had no time for trivial things like names.

"Ahnvaris?" He glanced at Jethan, hesitant to speak to her again.

"It's a special rank," Jethan answered. "An ahnvaris operates outside the usual military structure. Their sole purpose is to protect and serve the elite personage they are assigned to."

Kasiel felt entirely unqualified to have someone like that under his command, even temporarily, but this wasn't the time for self-doubt. "I'm going to need you two to question the prisoners together. We must have answers as fast as we can get them. I might also need your help getting us past a couple of guards, Jeth."

"We have prisoners?"

A fleeting flicker of amusement moved through Kasiel at Jethan's lack of concern around Charming guards. "We will shortly."

When they reached the sitting room deep in the opposite wing of the palace, the two guards there lowered halberds across the door to block their path.

Kasiel stopped. "Jethan."

Without hesitation, Jethan stepped forward, catching the immediate attention of one guard. The other put both hands on the haft of the halberd he carried, his uneasy gaze jumping between Jethan and the rest of them. Jethan didn't hold back. The powerful soothing sensation that infused his voice when he spoke, pulled the second guard's attention fully to him.

"You can let us in. They're expecting us. Remember?"

The guard staring into his eyes started nodding. The other, getting some of the overflow, eased his grip on the weapon. Jethan turned to meet his eyes, offering a congenial smile as he worked his ability there too. After a brief exchange with each of them, the two guards pulled open the doors for them, bowing their heads respectfully as they let the group pass.

The room they entered was dark blue, its walls generously adorned with ornamental stucco vine work around windows, wall panels, and the rounded corners of the ceilings. The five guards inside put hands to their weapons. Kasiel ignored them, walking forward with his attention on the king. He stopped and offered a bow, unwilling to kneel as he might before the khevarin. King Mahlik held out a hand to stay his men. A flicker of fear lit his eyes when his gaze shifted to the guards standing at the still open doors, recognizing that they had somehow overturned his orders. Despite that, his regal bearing did not falter when he faced them.

"Ahninveth Kasiel, it is a relief to see that you are..." he hesitated, something giving him pause as he looked Kasiel over, "not among those most gravely wounded. I assure you we are focusing all our resources on dealing with this heinous attack against your people. Is the kheva—"

"Not all your resources," Kasiel interrupted. They

had their priorities. Plenty of Delaphinian troops would be searching for Kaden. "I'm not here to ask for more help or make accusations, Your Majesty." He glanced over his shoulder as the khevarin walked in with Arhk at her side. Even bloodied and disheveled, she was every bit the image of fierce royalty. Before she could interfere, he forged ahead. "I will get your son back for you."

"How do you know about that?" the king demanded, one hand balling into a fist as he stepped forward.

Guards drew their weapons, and the pressure in the room jumped. The king glanced at Arhk, retracting his forward step. Kasiel didn't have to look to know his father's eyes were turning black. He could feel it.

He held his hands in a gesture intended to calm the two sides. "We were not involved in the prince's abduction. I only know of it because I was searching for the people responsible for the attack on the east wing. There are eyes and ears everywhere when you can share the minds of beasts. I unintentionally overheard your conversation during my search, and I want to help."

Ceanna stepped forward, her eyes brightening with hope, already seeming to forget what she had said when he was eavesdropping. Knowing he could so easily listen in on them didn't seem to concern her at the moment. "Sheath your weapons. I want to hear what he has to say."

"I will get your son back," Kasiel repeated. "In exchange, you will stand behind the alliance with Vanris." He glanced at the khevarin. "And, assuming Khesran Velara survives her injuries, when we recover Prince Kaden, consider removing their marriage from the alliance agreement. Neither of them wants it."

The queen was nodding, her love for her son apparent in how quickly she wished to accept his offer. "As best we can tell, Kaden's guards were dead an hour or more before the explosions went off in the east wing.

That means his captors have a strong lead on you. How do you expect to find him?"

Kasiel turned to the side, gesturing toward the door as Irith came through with two prisoners behind him, the disheveled men followed by Jhanik and his tethdrak. Kasiel passed gratitude to the tethdrak, knowing the other Feral would feel it. Jhanik met his eyes and offered a slight nod in response.

Kasiel looked at the king and queen again. "First, by seeing what we can learn from these two. Ahnvaris Zafyr and Lord Jethan will question them. The kanodraks are searching for leads now. Everyone on the grounds will undergo a brief interrogation. Our tethdraks won't let anyone leave here until we clear them to do so."

Mahlik's expression clouded over. "You're going to hold everyone hostage here?"

Seylin stepped up alongside Kasiel. "We do not feel that this is unreasonable. Our people came under attack in your palace, King Mahlik. Some are dead, and others, including my daughter, are being tended by our healers for injuries that could yet prove fatal. I think you can agree that extreme measures are called for."

Ceanna's hand went to her chest in what appeared to be genuine distress. "Oh, poor Velara. All our resources are at your disposal to help her, and the others, of course."

"Our healers have the necessary skills and supplies to care for her," Jethan said. "What we could use is a more comfortable space with better lighting in which to tend our injured away from the smoke and fire."

"Consider it done." Ceanna turned to one guard, directing him to show the healers to another section of the palace and gather men to help move the injured.

Behind them, Jhanik had forced the two prisoners to their knees and Zafyr was staring them down, no doubt already picking through surface thoughts.

The king eyed Kasiel shrewdly. "I had planned to send a unit in pursuit. If you are willing to use your considerable skills to bring back my son, you can accompany them. Our soldiers will ensure that you are allowed to move freely throughout the region. As for the alliance, I will stand behind it and discuss a renegotiation of terms with you, Khevarin Seylin. Our adversaries made the apparent assumption your people would be far easier to kill than you have proven to be. I am coming to appreciate the might and skills Vanris has shown they can offer as our allies."

"It pleases us to hear you say so." Khevarin Seylin's icy gaze made Kasiel almost feel sorry for the king. With her daughter in dire condition, she would be unyielding in her demands.

Kasiel faced her and gave a slight bow. "If you have no need of me, Majesty, I'll help move the injured and leave the negotiations and questioning of prisoners to those more suited to such things."

She arched a brow at him. "We are most oft surprised by our need for you after you have already executed upon it, Ahninveth. We shall trust in fate to bring you to us when that need arises again. Dhomen Aleren will find you and discuss this mission you have assigned yourself after we speak with her. For now, you may go."

He exchanged a brief glance with Jethan, wishing he could bring his tehnaak with him, but he had given him another job. Jhanik would stay as well to manage the prisoners. Claiming Irith on his way past, Kasiel strode swiftly from the room. He hurried to the patio, where they had already started moving people inside. Several dead lay at the back edge of the paved area, including two of Velara's personal guards, Dhomen Sorval, and Arhk's Dampener. Velara wasn't there, at least.

Kasiel helped support an injured guard into another large drawing room in the palace where several beds, probably taken from servants' quarters, were being set up for the more seriously injured. Velara wasn't there either. He asked around until someone directed him to a nearby bedroom where he found her laying on the bed, pale as death. The khevarin's healer was meticulously stitching one of a set of deep cuts on the side of her face that started above and below her ear. They came together in a point below her cheekbone with the lower cut continuing up near her eye and across the bridge of her nose. Tath was there too, holding a cloth over the cuts on the side of Velara's neck with one hand while she wiped salve on some wounds she could reach that didn't require stitching.

"How is she?"

Tath met his eyes. "She's lost a lot of blood. She also has some cracked ribs and broken bones in one hand, but her heart's still beating, for now."

Harif walked in to check on them, his gaze settling on Kasiel. "Why don't you sit and let me clean up that cut?"

Using the direction of the other man's gaze as a guide, Kasiel touched his fingers to the side of his head. They came away tacky with drying blood. He nodded to Harif. "Thanks."

"Is any of the rest of that blood yours?" Tath asked.

He glanced down at the red staining the chest and arms of his shirt. No wonder the king had hesitated to call him all right. "I think it's mostly hers."

She scowled at him. "Take the shirt off and let Harif check you over."

Kasiel did as he was told, peeling the bloodied garment off as he went to sit in a nearby chair. Keyla sat on another chair next to it, legs pulled in to her chest, staring at Velara through red, puffy eyes. Kasiel touched her arm as Harif brought over some clean rags and water.

"She'll be all right," he said, trying to keep his

voice low enough that the healers wouldn't hear and be tempted to correct him if he was wrong. He hoped he wasn't lying. If Velara survived, she would have substantial scars, though Seylin's healer's precise stitches would minimize them as much as possible.

Keyla didn't take her eyes from her tehnaak. "Where's Jethan?"

"He's helping Ahnvaris Zafyr question some prisoners. I'm afraid he'll be busy for a while." Kasiel winced as Harif went to work cleaning the wound on the side of his head.

"Apologies, Ahninveth. A little lower and whatever did this would have hit your temple. You got lucky."

Had the bombs gone off a minute earlier, he would have been in the room when it happened. He had gotten very lucky. Not a thought he expected to have after being caught naked in bed with the khevarin's daughter.

Wedro peered into the room. His gaze lit upon Kasiel, and he hurried over. "A few of the tethdraks found more people trying to sneak off the grounds. We've taken them to Dhomen Aleren. The rest are still patrolling. Is it you or Jhanik running them?"

"Both. How many rooms did they hit?"

Wedro glanced at Velara. When he looked back, his pitying gaze landed on Keyla for a second. "Every occupied room in the wing. Most of the bombs were dropped in from rooms above through hidden holes in the ceilings, likely prepared before we got here. The fact that they went off at almost the same time suggests there had to be at least twenty people involved."

Kasiel ground his teeth. That many? All willing to coordinate such a precise attack on the Vanrian company. That didn't make him any more comfortable leaving to go after the prince, knowing he would reduce the number of people Seylin and Velara had to protect them here. The alternative was to risk the king and queen trying something foolish to get their son back. A possibility that could lead to more chaos and bloodshed for both sides.

His gaze shifted to Velara again, watching the healer make those quick, precise stitches to close the wounds. "How did the khevarin get away with so few injuries?"

"Our Speaker, Etris." Tath said, her attention staying focused on Velara. "She noticed a group of soldiers missing from one corner of the Delaphinian camp. It made her uneasy, so she reached out to the dhomvalen's Speaker here in the palace, who also thought it sounded suspicious. Arhk's three guards went to alert him and the khevarin. He had been up late talking with Seylin and Aleren, so they were all awake and dressed. Arhk had apparently left a little before it happened. The bombs went off while Seylin and Aleren were leaving the room. Arhk's Dampener got killed shielding the khevarin."

They had been up talking. About what? At least that explained why Arhk came to check on him so late, though not necessarily why he had felt inclined to do so. Would his father tell the khevarin where he had found Velara? It seemed such a trivial thing now.

Tath looked up, focusing on Kasiel, though not on his face. Her brow furrowed. "That one might need stitches."

"What—" Kasiel sucked in a sharp breath when Harif started cleaning a spot next to his collarbone. He hadn't noticed the wound until that moment. With the sudden intense pain, Niskenya's mental attention swung his way, offering to take some of it from him. Kasiel turned her away gently. The injury hurt, but it was pain he could handle. "It's fine."

"It's not," Harif countered. "There's a splinter of wood deep in there I'm going to need to dig out. I can knock you out for it."

"No." Kasiel's gaze moved to Wedro, focusing on

the long scar on his face from the fight in Edmund's castle. They all had so much suffering being written upon their flesh. This alliance had to be salvaged if there was ever going to be an end to the war. "Wedro, bring the unit in. I need to talk to all of you. Find an empty room along this hall where we can meet privately."

"Ahninveth." Wedro inclined his head and hurried out.

"Let's move you somewhere you can lie down." Harif gestured to the couch. "I'll pour something in the wound to numb it. It'll sting like a crag fly bite for a few seconds, but it will help."

Kasiel did as directed.

Harif poised a small bottle over the injury and met his eyes. "Ready?"

He nodded.

Harif poured and Kasiel let out a string of expletives as cutting pain burst through the shoulder. If this was what being bitten by a crag fly felt like, he never wanted to meet one. "By the Break," he gasped when the pain died away and sensation faded from the wound, "what is that?"

"Useful," Harif answered.

The healer went to work on the wound. Even with the numbness, it hurt as he dug deeper in to pull out the fat, inch-long splinter of wood. Enough so that Kasiel accepted Niskenya's second attempt to soak up some of his pain. By the time the digging part was done, Wedro had returned. Kasiel insisted on going to talk to the unit. Harif had Wedro carry the supplies to close and cover the injury, and walked with Kasiel, holding pressure on the freshly bleeding wound.

The khevarin's healer had moved on to stitching the cuts in Velara's neck. The last of the wounds that needed such treatment. She gave Tath leave to join them for no more than twenty minutes, stating that she could manage Velara's condition for that long.

When they arrived in the other room, the rest of the unit, except for Jethan, was there waiting. Rather than take advantage of a moment to rest and sit with Darro, Tath chased Harif away from Kasiel and took over tending his injury.

When Kasiel gave her a questioning look, she simply shrugged and said, "You're family."

"Thank you," he murmured. Then he swept the others with his gaze. "We have a new mission. It doesn't leave this room yet, but the group that bombed our wing of the palace also took Prince Kaden hostage. They're trying to blackmail the king and queen to call off the alliance with Vanris. We are going to go after him."

CHAPTER TWENTY TWO

They found nine more people involved in the attack and had the fires put out in the east wing before the company left to go after Prince Kaden and his captors. Kasiel's unit got a little sleep while Zafyr and a Charmer from another unit questioned the prisoners and the Delaphinians who would accompany them on their hunt. They wanted only those unconnected to the attack and who reacted positively to the idea of the alliance to ride out with them.

Arhk dispatched a messenger to Vanris to summon reinforcements, since several of the more seriously injured Vanrians wouldn't be able to travel for several days. Foremost among those being Velara, who wasn't conscious yet when they departed. With her injuries, she would be in considerable pain when she did wake. Kasiel wanted to be there for her, even if it wasn't his place, but he had assigned himself another task.

Kasiel's company took the two prisoners who appeared to have the most information about the attack and its execution with them. From the memories and thoughts Zafyr had extracted, they now knew a mixed group from Delaphine and Sarket were behind the bombing and abduction. Neither prisoner appeared to know who had organized the attack, but they knew the Delaphinian prince was being taken to a location in the nearby city of Coranthis. That was consistent with the direction of the trail Arkos and Niskenya had found leaving the palace grounds to the south. Unfortunately, Coranthis was the largest city in Delaphine.

With Jhanik staying behind, Kasiel couldn't risk bringing tethdraks with them. If something happened to him, the big reptilian predators would be uncontrolled in a densely populated area. Irith had bonded enough with Jethan and others in the unit that they could bring him to take advantage of his keen senses and usefulness as a fighter. Despite being in the room during the explosion, the cliff cat came away with only superficial scratches and some singed fur.

With no way to confine her at the palace, leaving Niskenya behind wasn't an option. Kasiel made one admittedly half-hearted attempt to persuade her to stay, but she would have no part of him heading into danger without her. She bombarded him with the conviction that he needed her protection, a stance his father agreed with.

"Make no mistake, Kasiel," Arhk had warned him, "all your accomplishments and your skill as a Feral have made you a primary target. Given the opportunity, they will not hesitate to kill you."

Words that convinced him having Niskenya with him was the preferable option, hence his lack of effort in deterring her.

General Itana led the Delaphinian unit, a collaboration that Kasiel found both disconcerting and curiously reassuring. The former mercenary may have destroyed his right arm when they fought each another in Sharith, but his courage in that encounter and watching him spar left-handed in the practice ring at Trenath had earned him her respect. With her and her unit accompanying them in their Delaphinian uniforms, the locals would be less apt to panic or react violently to the sight of Vanrians and his beasts in the area. They also gave part of his unit Delaphinian cloaks, to give the impression from a distance that a larger portion of the company was local.

It took less than a day to reach Coranthis. They deliberately approached the city well after dark, when there were fewer people about to witness their arrival. Jethan had been working with the two captives along the way. They were completely in his thrall. He made himself their confidant and one friend within the company. If he moved them out of obvious earshot of the group, they would tell him anything now, and Kasiel could eavesdrop through one of their horses. They started turning to Jethan when they felt threatened or anxious, something that occurred every time Kasiel approached on Niskenya. Perhaps they could sense his hatred, since he saw Velara lying covered in debris and blood whenever he looked at them.

If Kasiel had grown up among the Vanrians like he should have, what his tehnaak could accomplish with his ability when he had time to work at it might not disturb him so much. As it was, he could understand the increasing unease he saw in the eyes of the Delaphinian soldiers as they watched the transformation in the prisoners. The change made chills creep down his spine.

After spending time in the extravagant Summer Palace surrounded by the quaint town of Norvask, the prevalent architecture of Coranthis struck Kasiel as odd. The buildings looked like boxes of wood and stone piled atop one another and packed in so tightly that many of the alleyways between blocks were barely wide enough for a single person to walk along. The city occupied steep hillsides on either side of a busy riverfront. Many homes in the poorer districts near the dock warehouses looked like they might tumble into the water with a firm push.

The people in the streets at that hour represented a

diverse array of races from the southern kingdoms. Kasiel watched the city folk from a stand of trees on a hillside overlooking one end of the town with Darro, Itana, and her second, a bearded man missing one finger who rarely had much to say. Jethan was nearby, conversing with the prisoners. Kasiel wasn't listening this time. He knew his tehnaak would share any important information.

"Look at those people," Itana said. "Not a heathen in the bunch."

Kasiel gave her a sharp look. "Are you trying to say something?"

She grinned at him. Even at night, her teeth were bright against her dark skin. "As I understand, you Vanrians with your pretty pointed ears don't follow the teachings of Havaad."

His hackles went up at the mention of their pointed ears, making him cut his words off with a hint of a growl that Irith echoed. "I grew up in Fernwallow, in southern Fallend. More than half the people there didn't either."

"Nor do I." Itana chuckled. "So easy to get under your skin, little Feral. Is it true that your beasts make you more savage?"

He picked out her eyes in the darkness. "Are you trying to make this more difficult?"

"Apologies, Ahninveth, I am merely impatient to test my weapon this night."

"As am I, General, though I wasn't planning to test it on your pretty black hide."

Her deep laugh broke through his irritation. "It will be interesting to fight alongside you instead of against you this time." She tilted her head to point at something behind him with her chin. "Your brother approaches."

Kasiel glanced over his shoulder to see Jethan walking up. "What did your new friends have to say?"

A disgusted grimace curled Jethan's lips. "I can't wait to stop playing nice with them. Every minute I spend in their company, I'm reminded of what they did."

Kasiel put a hand on his shoulder. "Hopefully, it will end tonight."

Jethan glanced across the river at the old wooden dock that looked like it was ready to collapse into the water. The building tucked up against the hillside behind it didn't appear much more stable. "That's the one. A run-down looking warehouse along the river on the westernmost edge of town. Neither of them has been here before, but it's what they have as their rendezvous point after the attack in Norvask."

"Can you convince one of them to go in ahead of us without revealing that we're here?"

"I might convince Piers to do it, but how will we know if he betrays us?"

Kasiel smirked. "There are rats aplenty in that building. Besides, I plan to follow them. I just want to see if they can draw anyone out before we go in."

As they spoke, he was wandering the warehouse with a chubby rat, its long whiskers twitching as it sniffed the air. It was dark inside, with a single torch burning in the front section. A lot of crates and barrels were stored within, most coated with dust and linked with cobwebs, as if forgotten. The structure continued back into a big, two-story room carved out of the rocky hillside. That room was also inadequately lit, with a torch by the front door and another near the rear. More old crates and barrels sat on tall racks along the sides and in piles in the corners. Three tables arranged in the center had a few cleaner spots amidst the thick dust on them, suggesting more recent visitation. Two doors left the room at the back, one at ground level with the torch beside it and the other coming out above it onto a raised wooden platform. He couldn't locate any rodents beyond those doors to spy further with, but if there were people in the building, that was where they were.

He pulled back from the rodent and examined the warehouse through his own eyes. A small structure attached to the side of the building up against the hillside caught his attention. His initial assumption had been that it was a storage shed, but what if it connected through to the inside?

Reaching out again, he found a mouse creeping about near the buildings and sent it poking around until he located a crack in the wood siding. Inside, it was almost too dark to see much of anything, but he could make out enough through the rodent's eyes to find a door at the back leading into the hillside. He returned to himself again.

"We won't take everyone in. No more than five from each unit. The clutter in there will make it a hazard for more than that. I'll bring Jethan, Darro, Wedro, and Etris. The others can stay outside to keep watch for anyone trying to come in behind us or sneak out through that side building."

Itana nodded. "I'll get my team together."

As she walked away, he turned to Jethan. "Prepare your prisoner. Let's see if we can get a little closer to saving this alliance."

Twenty minutes later, their small group of ten stood in the shadows of a neighboring building, watching Jethan's enthralled prisoner, an eager young man named Piers, approach the warehouse. His dark eyes darted around as he warily approached the door. Kasiel waited, observing from his hiding spot and from inside through the eyes of another rat. Piers tried the door and, finding it unlocked, pulled it cautiously open. For an instant, Kasiel had the uncomfortable experience of seeing the man through his eyes and those of the rat at the same time, then Piers stepped inside and pulled the door almost closed behind him, not quite letting it settle back into the frame.

No one emerged while he made his way through the maze of crates and racks in the first room to the open doorway in the back. Once he was there, Kasiel signaled his companions, and they approached the warehouse. The rat watched their prisoner walk into the big room carved out of the hillside while Kasiel and the others crept inside and started sneaking through the entrance area. Piers was over halfway across the second room when a man with cropped brown hair emerged from behind the ground-level door in the back.

"Piers. You made it. Is it just you?"

A wave of tension moved through their unit. They froze in place, waiting to see how thoroughly Jethan had Charmed the man.

"Yes, I'm alone," Piers answered. "Where's everyone else?"

A soft, collective sigh moved through them, felt more than heard. Slowly, they advanced toward the big room again.

"There's only two of us watching this place right now."

This wasn't where they were keeping the prince then, though that didn't surprise Kasiel. They were using this location as an interim meeting spot in case someone gave it up under duress or was followed. It was the smart thing to do, but it meant they needed to get their hands on someone here to find out where to go next. They couldn't depend on Jethan's influence to last long enough to wait for anything else.

Kasiel signaled Darro, gesturing to his crossbow. The other man nodded and drew it, preparing a bolt as he moved to the front with Kasiel.

"I'm tired and hungry," Piers was saying. "When can I join the rest?"

"Only four others from the attack team have made

it so far."

A flush of pride suffused Kasiel at hearing that they had stopped that many from escaping the grounds. The tethdraks deserved considerable praise, though it also meant there had to be more traitors still walking free at the palace. He had no choice but to trust that Zafyr and the other Charmer would find them soon if they hadn't already.

"I'm not surprised. It was difficult getting out of there. The Vanrians are formidable with their beasts," Piers said, continuing to keep their presence hidden for now, though a tremor in his voice suggested that might not last much longer.

"What happened?" the other man asked. "I know the bombs went off, but the other four fled before verifying any kills. Are the Warden and his son dead?"

A chill moved through Kasiel. The man didn't ask about the khevarin first, or Velara, but him and his father. If there were only two of them in the warehouse, they had wasted enough time. He needed information.

Kasiel stepped out from his hiding place and walked into the room, Darro hurrying up by his side and leveling his crossbow at the stranger. The man's eyes went wide, and he dropped a hand to the axe at his belt, though he didn't draw it. Instead, he retreated a few steps toward the door he had entered through, watching as more of them came into the open.

"My father and I are not dead," Kasiel stated, his tone flat with disgust. "You're far more likely to get there ahead of us if—"

That was where the conversation ended. The upper door flew open, and a woman stepped into the doorway with a shortbow in hand, aimed at the ceiling.

"No! Don't!" the man on the ground shouted.

Kasiel looked up, spotting bombs tucked up into a crack in the rock above them. "Get out!"

The woman let her arrow fly.

Three violent explosions blasted overhead. Kasiel threw himself under one table as rock and dirt crashed down around him. He shut his eyes and put his hand over his nose and mouth to block out the dust and smoke that billowed into his hiding space. The legs on one side of the table collapsed, forcing him to pull himself in under the angled remains and hope the other two held.

When the crashing stopped, Kasiel glanced around his patch of blackness. Even through his hand, the thick smoke and dust raked at his lungs, forcing a cough from him. The remains of the table groaned under the weight of the rock on top of it. Niskenya's rage and panic slammed into him. Desperately reigning in his own desire to flail about in terror, he forced calm to her. In the current circumstances, what could she do? A kanodrak in the building would make the situation worse.

Kasiel reached out, finding a rat hiding between barrels in the entry area. He brought it near the feet of those who hadn't entered the room before the explosion and now stood staring in, trying to see through the slowly settling dust cloud.

"Kas!"

That was Jethan, standing in the doorway. He had a scrape on one cheek that was bleeding, but he looked otherwise unharmed. Given where he was, he must have been close enough to dive for the exit when it happened. Itana stood next to him. She spat blood onto the floor, her lip split and her dark eyes blazing with anger.

"Find some candles or torches," she ordered.

As the dust cleared and others returned with light, they could see the pile of rubble that covered the floor of the room. Sand and fragments of rock continued to trickle down from the destabilized ceiling. Through the rat's eyes, Kasiel could no longer see the table he was under, though he knew roughly where it had been. Where was Darro? Piers and the traitor had been farther in. A couple of Itana's soldiers had also come inside, but Kasiel could only care about Darro now. Darro was tehsheyn.

The dust forced another cough from him.

"Over there." Jethan started into the room, but Itana caught his arm.

"Be careful. More may collapse. And watch where you step. Your brother is not the only one buried in this mess."

Jethan nodded and pulled away, forging carefully into the rubble.

Itana turned to one of her remaining soldiers. "Get the others. Two can stay to watch the prisoner. The rest need to come and help move debris. Have the Vanrian healers prepare to tend the injured, if we are lucky enough to find any."

Kasiel could hear a few people picking their way across the rubble now. Pulling away from the rat, he closed his eyes and focused on trying to keep his breathing calm and shallow in his tiny, dust filled pocket of space. Extending his ability out, he turned some energy to reassuring Irith and Niskenya, finding that the process helped to do the same for him.

"There's someone buried here," Wedro called from another place in the room.

Their voices were strangely muffled now that Kasiel heard them only from within his enclosed space.

"Go help him dig." That was Itana. She was closer to him now. "Lord Jethan, do you think Ahninveth Kasiel could be alive? He was almost directly below the blast."

"He has to be," Jethan answered, very close now. "Niske and Irith would be tearing this place apart otherwise."

Kasiel smiled to himself. His tehnaak was no idiot. "Jeth," he called, breaking into a coughing fit as dust invaded his lungs.

"Kas! He's here. Help me."

Rock started moving above him. The table creaked.

"General Itana," someone called from near the entrance, "we caught this one trying to slip out through the side shed."

"Tie the bitch up outside and gag her. We'll deal with her when our people are all accounted for."

There was a rumble and some shouts. More rock crashed down. Kasiel held his breath, needing the others to be all right. He heard Kince cursing nearby.

"Be careful," someone warned needlessly.

More rock shifted, and a shaft of hazy torchlight cut into his space.

"Kas?"

"I'm all right." The sound of wood cracking next to him startled him. "Be careful. This table I'm under is ready to give."

"We'll get you out. Promise." Hands began shifting the rocks around the tiny opening.

"I found Darro," Kince shouted. "Merrin. Avris. I need your help. Now!"

A louder crack announced the collapse of the table as the two remaining legs snapped inward, a piece of one smacking Kasiel in the face before the rest collapsed on him. The weight crushed down, pressing the air from his lungs. Blood pounded in his skull. He could hear Niskenya's roar in his head, but he was past a place where he could calm her.

"No!" Jethan shouted. "Dig faster."

Yes. Much faster.

CHAPTER TWENTY THREE

Was that the sound of people digging or of more rock falling in?

Kasiel felt a hand on his arm, taking hold of him. He grabbed back, opening his eyes and blinking the dust from them.

Jethan barked out orders. "Get his other arm. Someone help Wedro shift the table."

Itana grabbed his other arm, and they pulled so hard it felt like they might dislocate his shoulders, though that still sounded better than being crushed under a pile of rock. Then the pressure lifted from his ribs and Jethan and Itana threw themselves behind another pull, yanking his legs free. The two fell over backwards and Kasiel landed partially on top of them. They all struggled to their feet on the rubble, and Itana rushed off to help elsewhere while Jethan pulled him into a tight embrace.

"Stop letting people try to kill you," he snapped.

"Letting?" Kasiel rasped, his throat still coated with dust. "Where's Darro?" Moving his mouth made him aware of the cut along his jaw where the piece of table leg had struck him. He could feel blood trickling warm down the side of his neck.

Jethan disengaged. "Kince?"

Kince was digging in the rubble. He didn't respond, his focus entirely on the figure he and a few others were uncovering.

Kasiel took a step in that direction, but Jethan stopped him with a hand on his arm. "No. You'll just pull the stitches from last night digging around in this. Go have Harif or Tath check you over and tend that cut. I'll help dig."

Kasiel hesitated. He didn't want them in this room with more rock threatening to fall. The more help they had, the faster they could get out. He coughed to clear his throat and shook his head. "I'm not leaving with any of you in here."

"We can't afford to lose you, Kas."

"Don't give me that shit again. Maybe you don't *want* to lose me, but I'm no more important than the rest of you, and I never would have gotten this far without you. I *will not* leave this room without all of you."

Jethan's lips pressed into a tight line. Arguments flashed behind his eyes, but he gave a shake of his head and gestured to where they were trying to dig Darro free. Merrin handed Kasiel a water skin that he drank from like it was life itself, then joined them pulling rocks away. There were others digging around the room, looking for two of Itana's soldiers. Piers and the traitor who had come out to speak with him were buried somewhere in the rubble, but no one searched for them. Whether they were alive or dead now didn't matter, they weren't worth the risk.

They finally got Darro out despite a few more small cave-ins and moved him to the camp in the woods outside of town. He was conscious, almost unfortunately so, given that he had a broken leg, a snapped collarbone, and some cracked ribs. They found one of Itana's missing men crushed to death. The other escaped with a broken arm and a severe head wound. He couldn't string sentences together coherently, a fact that worried the healers.

Tath focused her efforts on Darro. No one tried to

argue with that. Harif had Kasiel put pressure on the cut on his jaw while he helped stabilize Darro's injuries. When he finished that, he came back to Kasiel to clean and close the cut on his jaw and fix some pulled stitches in the one on his chest. Irith wouldn't leave Kasiel's side now, and Niskenya lay nearby, her intense gaze following every move he made.

Kince wandered over when Harif was done with him, his brows pinched with worry. "Thank you. For helping, and for what you said to Jethan. It means a lot, knowing how much our lives matter to you."

"This unit is my tehsheyn, Kince. I didn't like being treated like my life was worth more than the rest of you when you brought me back from Fernwallow, and I won't stand for it now."

He managed a tight smile. "Well, you're not the fragile son of the dhomvalen now. You've proven to be a lot more than that. I don't regret bringing you back. Not even a little." His gaze wandered to where Darro lay, a flicker of distress tightening his features.

"He'll be all right. Tath will see to it."

Kince averted his gaze, ducking his head in a quick nod. "I know."

"Come to admire our fearless leader's newest scar in the making?" Avris walked over and placed a hand on Kince's shoulder, Jethan, Merrin, and Wedro coming up behind her. "You do look sexier with a few scars, Ahninveth, but don't overdo it."

He managed a weary smile. "I'm working on a full-body set."

Itana joined them then. "I could help you with that."

Kasiel disregarded her words, choosing to focus instead on the respect in her regard. "Thank you for helping get me out of there."

She grinned, though the expression didn't come as

easy as before. Her unit had lost one soldier. She was sending two others to take the one with the head wound to medical facilities in the city, though there was little they could do for him beyond tending his obvious injuries. The soldiers had strict orders to say he had fallen off a nearby cliff, and not to mention the rest of the company or their purpose there. The way she looked at him as he was being escorted away told Kasiel she didn't expect him to survive his injuries.

"I considered finishing you off while you were vulnerable, Ahninveth. To take out the Warden's son would make me a hero to many people who are not ready to make peace." She swept her gaze over them, seeming amused by the defensive glares that answered her comment. "But having seen some of what you can do with your mind-crafting, I believe that, should this alliance fail, Vanris will grow weary of keeping us out and force the Pandrean Alliance kingdoms to heel. I see that your country has the power to do so, and I much prefer to be on the winning side. I have also noticed that your people are extremely devoted to you. It would be a shame to destroy such a rare thing."

"Thank you, I think." He offered her a respectful nod before turning his attention to their new prisoner, sitting bound and gagged next to where Niskenya lay. "We still need to find the prince. Are you up for talking to her, tehnaak?"

"Charming her, you mean?" Jethan grimaced. "Yes, let's get it over with."

Itana walked with the two of them to the woman who had set off the ceiling trap with her perfectly aimed arrow. Her defiant glare drilled daggers into Kasiel when he pulled off the gag. Jethan crouched in front of her.

"I'm not telling you mind-fuckers anything." She raised her lip in a disgusted sneer.

"Such language." Jethan waggled a finger at her

like a scolding father. "You really should try to be more civil."

"Havaad take you, Vanrian bastard. My god will protect me from you."

She spat at Jethan, but he shifted aside to avoid it. "Given how completely you failed at killing us, I think your god must be busy elsewhere. It's unfair of him to abandon you like this, isn't it?"

Jethan wasn't wasting time. The wave of soothing that rolled out with his last sentence was powerful enough that Kasiel started feeling drowsy and unsteady on his feet. Itana widened her stance beside him, clearly similarly affected. Moisture rose in the prisoner's eyes.

"Havaad can't be everywhere," she answered, the conviction fading from her voice.

"He has let you down a lot though, hasn't he?"

A tear raced down her cheek. It was cruel what Jethan was doing to her, but Kasiel had a hard time feeling bad for her. One look at Darro was enough to dispel any sympathy.

"I... I don't think he listens to me anymore. I've done bad things." Her voice cracked. More tears fell.

"Like you did today? You killed two of your own people in that room. I don't imagine he looks kindly on that, do you?" Jethan's tone was soothing, thick with false sympathy. He reached out and brushed a tear from her cheek like he might a child.

Kasiel watched the last of her stubborn will break. It was a subtle change. A softening in her eyes, the relaxing of muscles in her jaw. A desperate need to be understood finding a home in the forced connection his tehnaak had made with her.

"Please," she whispered, "please help me fix this."

"What's your name?"

"Ivette," she answered in a small voice.

Jethan managed a convincingly warm smile. "Help

us reunite Prince Kaden with his family. That should be an easy first step."

Ivette's brows pinched, and she gave a small shake of her head. "But Prince Kaden is the one leading us."

The air was sucked out of Kasiel's lungs. A ripple of tension moved through Itana next to him. To his credit, Jethan gave no visible indication that this came as a surprise to him.

"Against the wishes of his family. I know how important blood family is to Havaad. If you help us bring the prince home to reconcile with his parents, he and his followers might regain Havaad's love. That's a noble purpose, don't you agree? It could help you earn back Havaad's favor."

Kasiel marveled at Jethan's composure before the gut-punch of information she had given them and his knowledge of her religion, picking the perfect words to feed into her insecurities.

All along, through his conversations with Kasiel and his time spent courting Velara, Prince Kaden had been planning their deaths. He didn't want to marry her, but not because he was in love with someone else. The prince didn't want this alliance at all. For him, it was nothing but an opportunity to get close enough to destroy his enemies.

"You can't hurt him," Ivette was saying.

"Of course not." Jethan's smile was full of reassurance and kindness Kasiel was sure he didn't feel, though the expression was convincing enough to be unnerving. "We want to help him, and you, find your way back into Havaad's embrace."

She nodded, gazing at Jethan now as if he were an acolyte of her god, come to save her. "I can take you to him."

Itana beckoned Kasiel and Jethan aside. "I ask you to keep this information quiet for now. I made my decision about the alliance with Vanris, but there may be those among my unit who are not as certain. Knowing Prince Kaden stands against it could be enough to make them question their choice."

Jethan's dubious regard told Kasiel his tehnaak wasn't as confident in Itana's decision as she professed to be. He stepped in before Jethan could do something potentially damaging, like attempt to Charm her. "Your loyalty to the king and queen is unexpected, considering..." He trailed off, realizing what he was about to say could easily be taken as an insult.

Her eyes narrowed. "Considering I was a mercenary? I will forgive your words only because I have heard rumors that you were treated terribly in mercenary hands before. We are not all the same, but I know many who can be extremely cruel."

"You were willing to kill innocents in Sharith," Jethan pointed out.

"Those were my orders. If it looked like we would lose the town, I was to kill all the prisoners. It was not how I would have preferred things to go."

"And yet you didn't kill Kas," Jethan pressed.

"I am no fool, Lord Jethan. I knew well enough that, had I killed the Warden's son in front of him, I would not have survived the night. I had dealt him a debilitating blow, or what I thought was one. I have seen many a soldier's spirit broken by such an injury. I did not know that he would be so resilient. I certainly did not expect him to come back stronger than before." Her dark gaze shifted to Kasiel. "When I say that it is an honor to work with you, Ahninveth, I mean it."

Kasiel met her gaze. He believed she was speaking the truth. Jethan seemed willing to as well now, since he didn't question her further. "Select five of your most trusted soldiers to stay here with Tath, Darro, and the other prisoner from Norvask. Niske will help protect them. That should leave you with thirteen soldiers and me with seven plus Irith to go after Prince Kaden."

"It shall be done."

*

The prince and his band of traitors, those that weren't still trapped at the palace in Norvask, were hiding out in a manor well up on the hillside. With some more clever questioning, Jethan learned that most of the prince's supporters were gathering in the capital of Dekingham or traveling in search of people to recruit to his cause. He hadn't had a great deal of time to build up his following since learning of the proposed alliance with Vanris. That meant he didn't have a large group here, and many of those he had were still stuck in Norvask. This was the perfect time to go after him.

The hardest part of Kasiel's rough plan was convincing Niskenya to stay behind. It would be impossible to get to the manor unnoticed with the kanodrak, and she was too large to enter most buildings besides. He persuaded her that knowing she was in the camp watching over Tath and Darro would allow him to focus on the confrontation ahead. Since he was leaving them with Itana's men, he wanted someone he could fully trust there. His confidence in Itana was growing, but she was right in thinking that, if her men found out the young prince was behind the attack on the Vanrian company, it could sway anyone not fully committed to the idea of an alliance.

They struck out through the city on foot, separating into groups to avoid drawing attention. Some of the Delaphinian soldiers followed the directions Ivette gave them less discreetly, since they wouldn't appear out-of-place patrolling the streets. The Vanrian group took Ivette with them along a stealthier path she said they often used to avoid notice. Merrin and Kince crept out ahead to dispatch the watches Ivette warned Jethan about.

The manor was one of several sprawling, box-like structures built near the top of the steep hillside, looming over their less wealthy neighbors. Unlike the lower buildings, each manor took up a block unto itself and boasted details like ornate ironwork fences and window framing, along with cozy rooftop garden patios. The structures struck Kasiel as pretentious, especially given that they looked as likely to end up in the river someday as all the buildings below them.

When they were almost to the manor, the leaders of each group met up alongside another home, hidden from sight. Merrin and Kince rejoined them there to report the successful elimination of their targets. After a brief discussion, Wedro, Etris, and Kince went with some of Itana's soldiers around one side of the manor to look for alternate entry points. A second group including Merrin, Avris, and Irith made their way around the opposite side. Once the designated lookout for each group spotted Kasiel's team going in through the front, they would enter as well to clear out any threats they could find within.

Kas, Jethan, and Harif stopped in the shadows not far from the front door with Itana, and two of her Delaphinian soldiers.

Jethan turned to Ivette, waiting until she met his eyes to speak. "No matter who answers that door, don't tell them we're here. Tell them you have good news to report regarding the Warden's son. We need to handle this carefully if we want to make sure no one gets hurt, right?"

She answered with a sober nod. "You've got nothing to worry about."

"Good. Go now. Havaad watch over you."

"And you," she whispered back.

They waited as she walked toward the door, her manner convincingly casual.

"You really didn't know he was planning this?" Kasiel asked, stealing a glance at Itana.

She shook her head. "When you and I first met in Sharith—"

Kasiel breathed a laugh. "Met is a gentle word for what happened that night."

"Yes." She chuckled. "At the time, I had just been made general and had not yet met Prince Kaden. He asked me, after our visit to Trenath, if I regretted not killing you in Sharith. I told him I did not. That I thought you were an excellent warrior and a good leader, and it was a shame to waste such things. Knowing this now, I suspect that may be why he never brought me into his confidence."

While they spoke, Kasiel had part of his attention turned to finding rodents or other life within the manor. It was disturbingly free of such invaders. After spending time with him in Trenath and Norvask, perhaps it shouldn't surprise him that Kaden's hideaway was clear of eyes and ears a Feral could use against him.

The front door opened, and the man inside spoke with Ivette for a few minutes, then gestured for her to come in, glancing up and down the street before he pulled the door shut behind her. Their team moved, sneaking quickly up to the entrance. Kasiel checked the door, unsurprised to find it locked. He nodded to Jethan who pulled out a set of small metal pieces and made quick work of picking the lock.

"Your brother has unusual skills for a nobleman," Itana whispered.

"Unusual morals too."

As they snuck inside, Kasiel took a quick look through Irith's eyes, checking that the group on that side was heading in. Without a creature ready on the other side, he simply had to trust that they were moving as well. Ivette still waited in the entrance hall. She glanced back when they entered, and Jethan beckoned her closer.

"He's letting Prince Kaden know I'm here," she whispered.

"Excellent. Go back to wait," Jethan said. "Pretend we're not here."

Kasiel and Itana flanked the doorway as Ivette returned to her place before the door. Harif pressed himself against the wall behind Itana. Jethan stood close to Kasiel in a position where he could easily get Ivette's attention if he needed to intervene.

A moment later, the man who had answered the door walked in, dressed in civilian clothes with a short-sword at his waist. The way he entered, not looking to either side, spoke to a lack of military training.

"Prince Kaden is waiting in the study. He's eager to hear your report. Come with me."

Before he could turn, Itana stepped in and grabbed him with one arm. "Quiet now," she whispered, driving a dagger into the side of his neck.

CHAPTER TWENTY FOUR

Harif's eyes went wide and Kasiel jumped forward to throw a hand over Ivette's mouth, silencing the cry he saw forming on her lips. Keeping his hand there, he stepped to the side, letting Jethan address the alarm in her eyes while Itana eased the dying man down into a chair along the wall.

"It's all right. You know he was going to expose us." Soothing rolled out from Jethan in a powerful wave. "We'll do our best not to hurt anyone else."

Moisture rose in her eyes, but she gave a slow nod, and Kasiel cautiously took his hand away. When she didn't make any noise, he turned and gave Itana a hard look.

Her answering stare was equally fierce. She moved away from the others and beckoned for him to join her. "We cannot leave a trail of half-controlled thralls behind waiting to turn on us the moment they come to their senses," she whispered. "You should end that one too. We do not need her now that we are inside."

"Not yet."

Truthfully, he didn't want to kill the woman. For all the fighting he had done in the last year, he still hated ending a life. When he glanced at Ivette, he caught Jethan watching him with a hint of dread in his gaze. His tehnaak had no love of killing either. That was what made pragmatic soldiers like Merrin and Kince valuable in a unit. People who wouldn't hesitate to make tough choices. Only, he was supposed to be their leader. Shouldn't he be the one making those decisions?

Kasiel gave himself a mental shake. There would be time for such contemplations later. Now they had to get to the study before Kaden questioned the delay.

Itana touched his arm and leaned close. "Leave her with me if you do not wish to have her blood on your hands. There is no shame in not wanting to kill, so long as your hesitance does not jeopardize your people, Ahninveth. Something having her with us will do if fighting breaks out and your brother cannot manage her."

Kasiel drew a breath and called Jethan over. "Tell Ivette to stay here with Itana."

His tehnaak looked at the general, his eyes narrowing. "Kas?"

"It's too much of a risk to keep her with us. You know Kince and Darro would recommend the same."

"Shit." He walked back to Ivette. "We might need you again, but you'll be safer if you wait here." He punctuated the sentence with an icy look at Kasiel and Itana.

Ivette nodded, her gaze following him as he accompanied Kasiel, Harif and the two Delaphinian soldiers into a crossing hallway, letting the door shut behind them.

Itana joined them through a few seconds later, sheathing her dagger. "It is done."

Unwilling to dwell on it, Kasiel gestured for Itana and Jethan to each take one of Itana's soldiers and go into the side halls to check for guards or patrols. He waited until they disappeared around those corners, then eased open one of the double doors in front of him enough to peek through. They opened into a large two-story room with a sitting area to one side and a grand piano set in the near corner. A balcony extended around the perimeter of the room above them, with hallways and doors leading to other areas. For the moment, the space was empty, so he stepped in with Harif, clicking the door closed behind them. Halls entered on either side of the room and there were double doors in the opposite wall, designed to blend in with the carved wood paneling.

Jethan leaned in from the hall to their right, nodding to let him know the route was clear so far. He pointed up to indicate that he would investigate the balcony area, then vanished into the shadows. Seconds after he left, one of the double doors at the back of the lower level opened. Two men carrying weapons entered the room with Kaden between them, unharmed and clearly not being held against his will.

The prince stopped in the doorway, unease sparking in his eyes. "You are... not who I expected." His gaze jumped to the balcony, then shifted back to Kasiel. "In fact, I'm not sure words can express exactly how disappointed I am to see you here."

At first, Kasiel thought Kaden might have spotted Jethan above, but then a door along the balcony opened and someone stepped out. He dared a quick look to see who had come in to find a crossbow aimed at him, being held by a woman he had hoped never to see again.

Danica glared at him, a hatred in her eyes born of love betrayed. "Hello, Kas. I've been looking forward to seeing you again. We had some unfinished business."

"I believe you know Danica," Kaden said, smiling up at her. "She's one of my most devoted supporters. I found her on our trip back from Trenath. She was organizing a team to target mind-crafters in Vanris. She had a particular first target in mind. I admired her enthusiasm, so I brought her with me. She was quite upset when I told her tonight that you were probably already dead. Perhaps it is fortunate that you survived after all."

Kasiel met her eyes. "This won't make anything better, Dani."

"Don't call me that," she snapped. "You took everything from me. All I want now is to return the favor."

She raised the crossbow and Jethan sprang from the shadows behind her, shoving her arms as she pulled the trigger. The shot went wild, and Kaden cried out, staggering back into the room behind him. Danica dropped the weapon and twisted away from Jethan, drawing her sword. He did the same, and the two engaged. Kasiel didn't have time to worry about them. Three of Kaden's supporters came through another entrance to join the two already inside. One went after the prince while the others came for Kasiel. Behind him, Harif drew his sword, but Kasiel signaled him to stay back. These were armed civilians, not trained soldiers. He wasn't about to risk the only healer they had with them until he had no other choice.

Niskenya was far away, but not so far that Kasiel couldn't reach out to her and invite her in. He drew his sword as her wild, protective fury raced through him. For a heartbeat, he struggled to hold on to himself before that torrent. Then she merged with him, reluctantly letting him maintain control.

Kasiel sprinted forward, raising his blade as if to attack the first man. At the last instant, he lowered the sword and ducked under the man's axe. Bringing the weapon back up, he took the second man by surprise. His blade caught the hilt of that man's sword with enough force to rip it from his grasp. Keeping his momentum going, he plunged the weapon through the man's chest.

Before the man fell, eyes still registering the shock of his defeat, Kasiel spun and blocked a swing of the first man's axe. Out of the corner of his eye, he caught the other two moving in as three more people entered the room. Harif came forward, preparing to join the fray.

A loud cracking noise above drew Kasiel's gaze to the balcony as Jethan and Danica went through the railing locked in a grapple. Jethan hit the edge of the piano, the force of the impact breaking the top of the instrument and two of its legs. Danica hit the ground to the side of it.

Fear for his tehnaak sent a metallic taste across Kasiel's tongue. He lost track of the two for a few seconds, forced to focus on the man with the axe who rushed in with a volley of fierce swings, rage making him reckless. Embracing Niskenya's instinctive reactions, he parried, dodged, and came out forward and to the side enough to cut deep into the man's thigh. As the injured leg gave out, and the man tried to catch himself with the other, Kasiel brought his blade around into the back of his neck with enough force to eliminate the concern.

Itana charged into the room. Kince, Wedro, and a couple of her soldiers rushing through the doorway behind her. The group of them caught the attention of Kaden's supporters. With that concern taken away for the moment, Kasiel turned back to see Danica on her feet next to Jethan, who still lay stunned on the floor. She brought her blade up in both hands, ready to plunge it down.

"Danica!" Kasiel sprinted for her, his shout getting her to look his way.

She scowled and turned back to Jethan. Panic lanced through Kasiel like a bolt of lightning. He wouldn't reach them fast enough.

One of Kince's throwing daggers sank into Danica's left leg as she was bringing the sword down. She cried out and staggered to the side, taking one hand from her hilt to reach for the weapon buried in her thigh. It bought Kasiel the seconds he needed to slam into her from the side, sending her sprawling behind the partially collapsed piano.

"Harif," he shouted, gesturing to Jethan as he continued after her.

Danica lunged to her feet again, desperation giving her speed despite the injured leg. She raised her sword between them to keep him back.

"You chose him." Sorrow fractured her voice. "You took away all the family I had and abandoned me."

Kasiel stalked toward her, Niskenya's bloodlust and protective rage burning through his veins. "Your father and Edmund stole me from my family and made me their experiment for twelve years. Jethan helped me find a new family. You could have tried to do the same for yourself."

Danica lunged at him, her attack faltering when her weight landed on the injured leg. Taking advantage of her impairment, Kasiel struck her sword aside with his blade and kicked out to sweep her good leg out from under her. She went down again. To her credit, she still held onto her weapon. He stepped forward and brought his foot down on that wrist with enough force to draw a cry from her. Her hand spasmed open, releasing the sword. The point of his blade came to rest against her neck.

"Easy, Kas." Wedro stepped up next to him and placed a hand on his arm. "This is Danica. Once you kill her, you can't take it back. Besides, we may need her if we can't find the prince. She seemed to have his favor."

His words suggested he had overheard the conversation with Kaden before the fighting started. Kasiel tried to focus on his message. Wedro wouldn't caution him from killing her without good reason. His blade trembled. The drive to punish Danica for attempting to kill Jethan was nearly overwhelming. Niskenya urged him on to protect his family. Fighting for control, he made himself step off her wrist, and glanced around the room. They had soundly defeated the prince's other followers. Danica was one of only three still breathing.

The rest of the group Kince and Wedro had been with were trickling in now, a few escorting prisoners.

"Tie her up and gag her," Kasiel growled under his breath, turning to where he had left his tehnaak.

Though he was sitting up now, the color had drained from Jethan's drawn features. A bright smear of blood painted his lower lip. He was breathing shallowly, as if it hurt to do more. Kince knelt next to him alongside Harif, who was examining Jethan's left wrist. Jethan let out a grunt when Harif tried to move it, and he immediately stopped.

"This is broken. Let me give you something for the pain." Harif started digging into his bag.

Jethan shook his head. "Just splint it. I need my head clear."

Kasiel crouched on his other side. "What can I do to help?"

His tehnaak met his eyes. "Find the prince. We need him. When I interrupted Danica's shot, I think it hit him in the chest." He winced and his voice caught when he tried to breathe more deeply. Settling for a shallower breath, he continued. "He won't get far without help."

"You'll be all right?"

Jethan answered with a cautious nod.

Kasiel caught Harif's attention. "Make sure of it."

"I will."

Kasiel slipped behind Irith's eyes and turned to look over the group he was with. The cliff cat wasn't far. That team had scoured their side of the building and had a few prisoners with them. They were currently stalking through some nearby halls with their weapons ready. They appeared to be missing one of Itana's men and another was limping, but there were no other obvious injuries.

Avris glanced down at the cat, catching on to the change in his behavior. "Take him, Kas. We're fine."

Kasiel drew Irith to him, walking in the cat's direction in case the beast ran into any doors he couldn't get through. In a matter of minutes, the cliff cat was back at his side. He sent him images of the prince and led him to where Kaden had been when Danica's bolt struck him. They followed the scent across the study and through a door left standing ajar at the back of the room that led to a long, poorly lit hallway. Irith broke into a lope down the hall, Kasiel jogging after him. A few thick smears of blood along the wall didn't bode well for the prince's current condition.

Toward the end of the hall, a door on the right had blood on the doorknob. Irith stopped and scratched at it, leaving a deep set of runnels in the wood with his claws. Kasiel opened it, and they stepped out into the night, emerging toward the back of the property.

The cliff cat tracked Kaden a few blocks up the hill where they found him sitting against the side of a building with three of his people gathered around him. Blood had soaked his shirt and partway down his pants below the crossbow bolt still sticking out under his collarbone. The three with him jumped up and drew their weapons, turning to face Kasiel. Irith lunged at the rightmost opponent, his speed catching the man by surprise. The big beast bore him to the ground.

The one in the center spun as if intending to help his companion, but Kasiel leapt in, bringing his blade up at an angle. Realizing his error, the man stopped mid-turn and started bringing his axe around to block. He was too slow. Kasiel's sword cut up along the length of his arm, sheering away skin and muscle to the bone. The man screamed, his axe hitting the ground.

With Niskenya guiding him, Kasiel twisted around in time to parry the blade of the third opponent, this one a younger woman. Before he could take advantage of the opening, she struck out with a dagger in her other hand, and he turned sideways, sucking in to avoid what would have been a nasty wound. Giving himself more completely to Niskenya, he caught the back of her hand with a quick strike from the pommel of his sword. She yanked the wounded hand in with a hiss, keeping hold of the dagger.

Irith snarled behind him. A second later, the man whose arm he had sliced stopped screaming. Fear shone through in the way the woman's hands shook now. Both of her companions were down, and Kaden could do nothing to help. Kasiel met her eyes, Niskenya's snarl curling his lips.

The woman darted in. She was fast. Her dagger was quick to reach for any opening she could make by keeping him busy with her sword strikes. She also had a pattern, and Kasiel wasn't fighting with his senses alone. They exchanged a series of attacks. Parry, block, dodge the dagger, and repeat. A sharp sting in his hand vanished in an instant, the pain taken by Niskenya. Finally, catching the rhythm of her movement, Kasiel evaded her next sword thrust and twisted into her, knocking aside the dagger with his right hand and striking her in the jaw with his sword pommel hard enough to break bone.

The woman staggered back, pain contorting her features as blood began streaming from the now misaligned corner of her mouth. Kasiel didn't give her time to rebound. He grabbed his hilt with both hands and caught her with an angled upward slice below the ribs. The dagger dropped, and she curled in toward the wound. He brought the blade back around into the side of her neck. The light guttered out in her eyes before she finished falling.

All three now lay dead around Kaden's feet. The prince stared up at him, sweat beading on his furrowed brow. Kasiel cleaned his blade and sheathed it before going to crouch next to the prince. He eyed the bolt in the man's shoulder. Too much blood still flowed out around it, drenching his arm, chest, and the front of his pants.

"Our talk in the garden—"

"Was a diversion," Kaden spat. When he continued, his voice was strained, as if every word took considerable effort. "I wanted to be sure you and your beasts hadn't caught wind of anything amiss."

"It didn't have to be this way."

Kasiel was aware of footsteps as someone came up behind him. A quick glance through Irith's eyes showed him Itana, but the Delaphinian general made no move to interfere. She remained silent, her jaw set tight, her pitiless gaze locked on the fallen prince.

Kaden sucked in a shallow breath. "I would never share my bed with a Vanrian whore."

Red closed in around Kasiel's vision, his chest constricting. He ground his teeth, fighting the urge to hurt the man. Only one thing stopped him, and it wasn't the general standing behind him. "You're lucky you're already dying, because otherwise I would kill you slowly for calling her that. You were never good enough for her." He drew a breath. They didn't have time for emotions. "Do you know who was behind the attempt on her life in Trenath?"

"Both of your lives. We always meant to get rid of you. You and your fucking father." Kaden's head dropped back against the building.

"Who are you working with?"

"You'll need to look closer to home for those answers." His eyes slipped closed. "Her home."

"I need more than that." Kasiel reached out and shook the prince, but the man's eyes only fluttered, his breathing growing shallower. Another shake elicited no response at all. "Shit." He glanced at Itana. When she nodded, he yanked the bolt free, and blood gushed from the wound. "To the Break with you," he growled under his breath.

"We can carry his body."

Kasiel glanced around to find Merrin and Avris also standing behind him now, with Irith between them. The big cat was becoming almost as fond of his companions as he was of Kasiel, a notable difference of having a cliff cat instead of a tethdrak. Sylaryth had been devoted entirely to him. This was easier in some ways, though he would give a lot to have the tethdrak at his side again.

Kasiel stood. "I can help."

Merrin shook her head. "You should get back to Jethan."

"Is he all right?" That metallic taste spread across his tongue again, a shudder of dread moving through him.

"He's having some trouble breathing. Wedro ran to get Tath."

He glanced at Kaden. The prince was gone. "Thank you." When he started to turn away, Avris grabbed his wrist.

"Hold on. You're bleeding all over."

She wasn't wrong. The flash of pain in his hand had been the woman's dagger cutting into the side of it. The more invested he was in his connection to Niskenya, the more pain she could take from him. While useful in certain situations, it also led to a lack of awareness of his own injuries. He waited, feet shifting with impatience while Avris cut a piece of fabric from a dead man's shirt and firmly wrapped the wound.

"I will go with him," Itana said. "I have seen all I needed to see here."

Avris met Itana's eyes. "Thank you, General Kedran. Make sure he has Harif look at that once Tath gets there."

"I'll leave Irith with you two," Kasiel said, "in case any more of his followers are lurking around."

Merrin nodded before turning to deal with the prince.

"You were mad to come after him alone," Itana remarked.

"I'm never alone."

She said nothing to that.

Kasiel yearned to know what she was thinking after this turn of events, but right now, Jethan was his primary concern. As they hurried back down the hillside, he directed Irith to guard Avris and Merrin, then reached out to Niskenya. The kanodrak hesitated a moment before letting him see through her eyes. Tath was already gone. Niskenya paced restlessly near where Darro lay sleeping. A state Kasiel hoped Tath had induced. Itana's men were nearby, watching over things at a distance from the agitated kanodrak. He sent reassurance to her, though how convincing it would be with his overriding fear for Jethan remained to be seen. Niskenya wasn't that easily fooled.

"You didn't try to save him," Kasiel said.

Itana kept her eyes on the road ahead. "He had already lost too much blood. Had he not run like a coward, we might have saved him, but as it was, there was no hope for him. Besides, his actions were dishonorable. He betrayed his family and country."

Kasiel couldn't stop a derisive snort. "No offense, but you were a mercenary until quite recently."

"As I said before, your experience with mercenaries may color your opinion, but to me, a mercenary with no sense of honor is just a criminal looking for ways to monetize their violent inclinations. I was a professional soldier, not a thug for hire."

He glanced at her, seeing nothing in her expression to make him doubt her conviction. "I think I'm honestly starting to like you."

She grinned. "Good. There is much I could teach you."

They arrived in the room at the manor right after Tath got there. Jethan lay on his back now, eyes closed, his uninjured hand resting against his forehead. A splint braced his wounded wrist, but that didn't appear to be the chief concern anymore. Tath was carefully checking his ribs. Harif was a short distance away, finishing a tight wrap around the knife wound in Danica's leg while she glared at Jethan. The expression rekindled some of Kasiel's anger, an emotion Niskenya's distress fed into all too well.

Kasiel crouched across from Tath. "How is he?"

"Capable of speaking for himself, you callochs," Jethan answered, his voice strained. He drew in a shallow breath, not opening his eyes. "I'll be fine."

Kasiel looked at Tath. She would tell him the truth.

"I'm not sure yet. Could be broken ribs, could be his back. The fall wasn't terribly far, but the landing left a lot to be desired."

"The piano would agree with you," Jethan added, a grimace twisting his lips.

Tath looked Kasiel over quickly, her attentive gaze catching for a moment on the bloodied cloth wrapped around his hand. "Have Harif take care of that," she said, turning back to her patient.

"It's nothing."

Jethan opened his eyes. "Do what she tells you, blasted Feral. It's not like you can help with this."

Kasiel caught Harif's attention with a wave and beckoned him over. Then he sat on the floor beside his tehnaak and held up the injured hand as the other healer approached. "Tath wants you to check this."

Harif silently sat next to him and started uncovering the wound. Jethan let out a sharp gasp as Tath pressed along his ribs. Then she helped him roll up on his other side.

"Where's the prince?" she asked.

"Merrin and Avris are bringing his body down. The crossbow bolt killed him." He said it loud enough for Danica to hear, watching as she hung her head and squeezed her eyes shut.

Itana's brow furrowed. "His death is unfortunate, but perhaps we can turn it in our favor."

Kasiel frowned up at her. "How?"

"We say that his captors killed him." She glanced over at Danica. "Then we emphasize that he died supporting the alliance with Vanris."

"You're suggesting that we... Ah!" He flinched as Harif began messing with the cut on the side of his hand. "Easy, that's attached."

Harif gave him a flat look. "Then you'd best keep it still."

Kasiel scowled at him before turning back to Itana. "You want us to lie to the king and queen?"

"It is the story they will want to hear. The one that will give their hearts the most ease and save this alliance." She held his gaze unflinchingly.

"And if others come forward saying differently?"

She shrugged. "We make his death a rallying cry in favor of this alliance before they can do the opposite. We will need to kill any prisoners we have taken here if we are to get ahead of this and convince the king and queen it is true."

"I can't support killing people we've already defeated."

"I will not let it be your call, Ahninveth. This is my country," she said, her features set with determination. "If you want the alliance to work, you will not stand in my way."

Kince nodded agreement from where he leaned against the partial remains of the piano. Kasiel looked away, his gaze landing on Danica, who was watching them now with wide, fearful eyes.

Finally, he nodded. "Do what you must. Except for her. I'm taking responsibility for her."

Itana gave a sharp nod. She turned to where they had gathered the other prisoners on one side of the room. "Bring them."

Kince, Etris, and Wedro went to help Itana's men move the seven people they had captured out of the room to whatever place she had chosen for their deaths. Danica gave a hard swallow as she watched them go.

Kasiel cursed under his breath, a sick feeling in his gut. When Harif had finished tending and re-wrapping the injured hand, Kasiel got to his feet and walked to Danica.

He took off her gag. "Follow me."

She didn't move. "Where?"

"The study. We're going to have a little talk, you and I."

She glanced at the door the others had left through, then struggled to her feet, the process made more awkward by her bound hands. She hissed in pain a few times, but Kasiel offered no help. Once she was up, he walked toward the adjacent study, and she limped after him.

CHAPTER TWENTY FIVE

Kasiel gestured for Danica to enter the room ahead of him. Before he followed her in, Merrin and Avris arrived, lugging Kaden between them. Some of Itana's soldiers went to help them. Kasiel met Avris's eyes, drawing Irith to him when she nodded. He sent the cliff cat into the room and followed the beast in, shutting the door behind them. Danica stood to one side, her weight balanced mostly on the uninjured leg. She tensed when Irith went past her, but the cat ignored her.

Kasiel shut the rear door, then gestured to one of the two chairs in front of the desk. "Sit."

She lowered herself awkwardly into the chair, leaning to one side to keep pressure off the wounded thigh. He turned the other chair to face her and sat. Irith settled beside him, and Kasiel rested a hand on his head. For once, the big cat didn't start purring. Perhaps he sensed they were the aggressors here and wanted to play his part well.

"You should be dead." Kasiel gave his blunt words a moment to sink in.

Danica lifted her chin. "Why didn't you kill me then?"

Defiance had always looked good on her, but this time, it lacked the power to sway him. "Had Wedro not stopped me, I would have, but I wasn't talking about what happened tonight. I was naïve when I took you to Vanris. Naïve to think they wouldn't hate you. Naïve to think they would help you and let you go. If I hadn't chosen Jethan over you that day, they would likely have put us both to death." Her eyes widened, a glimmer of hope rising in them. He shook his head to discourage it. "Don't take that to mean I would have chosen you if the circumstances were different. Jethan is my tehnaak. I will always choose him."

His words brought her hurt and indignation back. "I don't understand. You've known him a year. We grew up together, Kas. How did that come to mean nothing to you so quickly?"

Nothing. Their history together meant so much more than nothing, but it was the past. Part of a life he hadn't chosen. "I can't explain it to you in the time we have, and it makes no difference anyhow. What I need you to understand is that, after I made that choice, they still intended to kill you, but my father took pity on me by letting you leave with the Alliance messenger. You shouldn't have gotten out of Vanris alive, but you did. You had a chance to rebuild your life, and you squandered it looking for revenge.

"And here we are again. I am the only reason the general didn't put you to death with the others. How long that remains true depends entirely on whether you have any useful information to give us."

"You would really let them kill me?" Disbelief lit her dark eyes even now.

He leaned forward, letting Niskenya's frustration feed his anger and drown the sympathy he might have felt for her. "Let me be clear. You tried to kill the one person I would do anything to protect. Right now, I'd consider killing you myself."

Tears welled in her eyes, but she clenched her jaw and fought them back. "What do you want from me?"

"Prince Kaden appeared to hold you in some favor."

She shifted her leg, trying to get comfortable, and avoided looking at him. "Only because I knew you before all this and wanted to see you pay for the things you've done. I told him everything I could about you in case any of it might give him an advantage."

He clenched his teeth. The things *he* had done. Even knowing that her father and Edmund had destroyed his family, she still held their deaths against him. "Before the prince died, he said that, to find who arranged the attack on Khesran Velara in Trenath, I would need to look to her home. Did he tell you who in Doran was behind the attempt on her life and how he found out about it?"

Her hands clenched and relaxed. "No."

Kasiel stood, Irith rising with him. "Good. That information should keep you alive as far as Norvask."

Her brows pinched. "I said no."

Kasiel forced an unfriendly smile. "I know, and you always clench your fists for a second when you're about to lie. The dhomvalen's Evoker can handle the rest." He gestured to the door. "Let's go."

She didn't move. "I don't want to go back to Norvask."

Velara's bloodied face flashed in his mind. Fresh anger pulsed through him. He caught himself before his hand closed on the hilt of his sword. Irith growled at her, and she shrank back in the chair.

"Admitting that you were involved in what happened in Norvask won't improve your situation. Get up. You're coming with us, and you are to speak to only me unless I tell you otherwise. If you do anything else, I will keep you gagged until we reach the Summer Palace, understood?"

"I hate you."

How much would it please his father and the khevarin to hear her say that? He swallowed against the twist of pain in his throat. "Good."

*

They had to spend the night in their camp. Jethan had a broken wrist and a significant enough injury to his back that Tath wanted to keep him off his feet. Darro wasn't in much better condition. Danica and one of Itana's soldiers both had leg wounds that would make it difficult for them to ride. They needed to find transportation for the injured and a respectful way to carry the prince's body back to his parents.

They kept the wounded as comfortable as they could through the rest of the night. In the morning, Itana and a few of her soldiers rode into Coranthis. They took possession of two enclosed wagons to transport the wounded and dead. The man she had sent to town for medical care had, not unexpectedly, died in the night from his head injury.

By late morning, they had everyone loaded and were on their way to Norvask. Kasiel had Danica ride in the front of one wagon where he could keep an eye on her. The wagons forced them to stick to roadways, and they stopped a few times to give Darro and Jethan a break from the jostling. Tath and Harif monitored them and kept them heavily medicated enough that they were barely aware of the journey. The Vanrians, and Niskenya in particular, caused a stir along the way. Itana kept her soldiers spread out around them to avoid conflict. The Delaphinian general was quick to defend their presence and praise their efforts in protecting the kingdom, though she was necessarily vague about how they had done so.

The journey was slower than Kasiel liked, but there was nothing they could do about that. They came into Norvask well after midnight. As soon as they entered the town, Kasiel had Etris try to reach the dhomvalen's

Speaker. Arhk needed to be made aware that his Evoker would detect several falsehoods in their story if they were taken to the king and queen before they could speak with him. Things he needed to let pass until Kasiel could explain the situation. They were entering the palace grounds when Etris finally confirmed that he had received the message.

A flurry of activity ensued as people had to be woken up and the injured moved into the palace. Kasiel ordered Danica gagged and taken to the Vanrian quarters to be locked in a room under guard. The prince's body they carried to the throne room, with Kasiel and Itana as escorts. The healers cleaned Kaden up as best they could before their arrival, presenting him with the dignity of a hero and not the traitor he truly was.

Queen Ceanna fell to her knees, weeping beside her son when they laid him out before the throne. King Mahlik met the pronouncement that his captors killed him with outrage, calming some when he learned that the combined company had dispatched all but one of them and had taken that one prisoner. Something in the king's reaction rang false to Kasiel, but he wasn't in a position to question it. The Evoker, Zafyr, whispered to the dhomvalen as he looked on, but Arhk stood at Khevarin Seylin's side without expression. Seylin gave her sympathy to the king and queen, offering to postpone discussing the political implications of the prince's death to give them time to mourn their son in private.

As they exited the throne room, Itana caught Kasiel's eye. He gave a slight nod, and she answered in kind before they went their separate ways. Arhk and Seylin led Kasiel along with Zafyr to Seylin's new rooms in the palace.

"The prince was behind this attack?" Arhk asked once they were behind closed doors. Zafyr must have gotten that much from reading their thoughts in the throne room.

Kasiel inclined his head to Seylin and his father before answering. "Yes. General Itana and I made the call to hide his involvement to protect the alliance and allow his parents to mourn the son they wanted him to be. We killed all but one of his followers in Coranthis. That one may have knowledge of who was behind the attack in Trenath."

"You suffered losses as well?" Arhk asked, his gaze flickering to the fresh cut along Kasiel's jaw.

The deep ache of worry he had been holding back broke free and spread through his chest. "No deaths in my unit, but Darro and Jethan were both seriously injured. They're being moved into a room so Tath and Harif can care for them."

A flicker of uncommon sympathy softened Arhk's features. "I will have Jhanik's healers sent in to help them. Bring me your prisoner and see to your unit, Ahninveth. Then get some rest." He gestured toward the door.

"No. With all due respect, Dhomvalen... Father, I would prefer to be involved in her questioning. I believe she'll be more cooperative with me there."

Arhk's eyes narrowed. "And why would you think that?"

Kasiel didn't waver before the sudden daggers in his father's gaze. "Because it's Danica."

Arhk's expression darkened, shadows creeping in at the edges of his eyes, then Seylin touched his arm and the darkness retreated.

"Trust your son, Dhomvalen. He has done well, and his eyes tell us he is not letting his former attachment to the girl guide his choices this time."

Her support caught Kasiel by surprise. Finding himself at a loss for something intelligent to say, he settled for a slight bow. "Thank you, Majesty."

The tension in Arhk's stance eased a fraction. "Very

well. There are only a few hours left of the night. Get what rest you can, and we will question her in the morning."

He bowed to Arhk this time before taking his leave.

The door had just shut behind him when Keyla came jogging up, dark circles under her eyes making it apparent she hadn't slept much since he last saw her. "How's Jethan? I heard he was hurt."

"He should recover, but it may take a while. You should be asleep. There's nothing you can do for him right now."

Her lips pressed into a tight, irritated line for a second. Then she took his wrist and drew him away from the door and the guards outside it. When she spoke again, it was in a whisper. "I can comfort him," she said, "just as you can comfort Velara."

"You know I can't." He took a step back, not quite able to make himself walk away, although he knew he should. "How is she?"

Keyla stepped closer to him again. "She needs you, Kas."

"I'm not her tehnaak."

"And I can't give her the kind of reassurance she requires right now. Trust me. You are who she needs."

Exhaustion, worry, and responsibility weighed heavily on his shoulders. "I can't. Besides, she should be resting."

"She was asleep almost the entire time you were gone. The noise of your unit's arrival woke her to a reality she isn't dealing with well." The desperation in her eyes tugged at something in him. "Please, Kas."

He drew a deep breath, his gaze lingering on the door to the khevarin's rooms. Then he met Keyla's eyes, recognizing the worry in them that reflected the concern he felt for Jethan. The difference was that she could visit Jethan without causing a scandal. And yet...

"All right, but I need you to look after my tehnaak."

"You know I will. Thank you." She grabbed his hand and led him to a door down the hall. The guards there eyed him, not shifting from their positions when Keyla stopped in front of them. "Let him in," she commanded.

"The khesran is resting," a female guard on the right replied, her blunt tone making it clear the conversation was already over as far as she was concerned.

"I know exactly what she's doing," Keyla snapped back, "I was just in there. Velara wanted to speak with Ahninveth Kasiel the moment he returned. It isn't your place to question her orders."

The guard scowled, but she opened the door. Keyla stepped back and gestured for him to go inside, lingering long enough to shut the door behind him. Velara lay on the bed, her pillows arranged in an incline to help limit swelling in her face and neck from the covered wounds there. The khevarin's healer sat in one corner, straightening slightly when he entered.

Velara opened her eyes, looked at him, then closed them and turned her head away. "Get out."

Her voice was soft, her lips barely moving as if speaking hurt, which he imagined it must, given the number of stitches in her face and neck. There was a mild slur to her words, probably from medications given for sedation and to lessen her pain. Kasiel glanced at the healer, who watched him in curious silence, offering no guidance, then he walked to the bed and sat in the chair beside it. Irith curled up near the foot of the bed as if expecting them to be there a while.

"I'm staying."

"I don't want you to see me like this." Her voice cracked and tears slipped out between her lashes.

The healer stood and walked over to hand him a soft handkerchief. When he took it and started gently wiping away her tears, being careful of her wounds, the woman stepped out, leaving him alone with the khesran. Not a move he expected, but one he appreciated, nonetheless.

Velara brought her uninjured hand up and tried to push the handkerchief away, the effort disturbingly weak. He caught the hand and pressed the back of it to his lips, then lowered it to her side as he brushed away more tears.

"I hate you," she murmured.

The same thing Danica had said, only this time he didn't believe it. "You don't."

Her hand squeezed his, and she opened her eyes. "Look at me, Kas. I'm hideous."

He met those bright silver eyes, a fond smile curving his lips. "I am looking at you, and you're beautiful."

"Liar," she growled under her breath. "No one will ever want me now."

He leaned closer. "I do," he whispered, placing a light kiss on her lips.

The tears came faster. As much as he wanted to hold her, her injuries denied him that. Instead, he stayed next to her, gently drying her tears so they wouldn't soak into her bandages. Exhaustion pulled at him, making his eyelids heavy, but sleep would have to wait a little longer.

When the crying stopped, she watched him for a moment, her gaze taking in the cut along his jaw and his struggle to keep his eyes open. "Don't leave me. You can sleep here. There's plenty of room."

"I thought you hated me," he teased.

"Calloch," she muttered. "You ruined that. Now I'll hate you if you go."

He glanced at the bed, knowing he should refuse. The guards were aware he was in here, as was the khevarin's healer. And yet, the need in her eyes had no care for such things. He walked to the other side and eased himself down next to her, wary of her injuries.

A trace of a smile touched her lips as he took her hand. "Thank you, Kas," she whispered, her eyelids drifting closed.

Smiling back at her was the last thing he remembered until the healer woke him a few hours later. She was careful not to disturb Velara, and he followed her example, easing off the bed so as not to wake the sleeping khesran.

When they stopped at the door, the healer leaned close to him and spoke in a whisper. "Your father was searching for you. I told him I might know where to find you. He said to have you meet him in the room with your prisoner."

"Why did you let me stay with her?" He ran his fingers through his hair, hoping the effort served to tidy it rather than doing the opposite.

"When she was awake, it was you she most dreaded seeing her like this. In her drugged sleep, it was your name she spoke. Sometimes part of being a healer is recognizing that your patient may have wounds that stitches and medicines can't heal. When you refused to let her send you away and were willing to dry her tears, I knew you were what she needed."

Kasiel watched Velara for a moment. She had spoken his name in her sleep. He was as wary of reading too much into that as he was of downplaying it. Her betrothed was dead, but what did that mean as far as he was concerned? She was still the khevarin's daughter.

He gave himself a mental shake and nodded to the healer. "Thank you. Take care of her."

"With everything I am," the healer said, moving aside to let him leave.

He found his father in the room where Danica was being kept, next to the one he should have taken his rest in. Zafyr was also there. They had dismissed the guards keeping watch over Danica. Despite his hostile interactions with her thus far, some of the fear left her eyes when he joined them.

Ignoring Arhk and Zafyr, Kasiel went to crouch down next to her. "You remember when I said I was willing to kill you myself because you tried to kill Jethan?"

The fear sparked to life in her eyes again. "Yes."

"He can't walk right now, thanks to you. I suggest you find some extremely compelling information for us in that head of yours, because it's the only thing that might save your life now."

Her lip curled in a disgusted sneer. "I despise you."

He ignored the comment. "Ahnvaris Zafyr is an Evoker. I'm sure you remember what they can do from your time with Ahndhomen Setera. Don't try lying or hiding anything, and you stand a chance of making it through this."

"What have they done to you?" Tears welled past the hatred in her eyes.

"They gave me back the life that was stolen from me. You're now just one of many people who have tried to ruin it." His heart ached as he stood and went to lean against one wall.

The faintest hint of a smile curved Arhk's lips when his eyes met Kasiel's. Then he turned his attention to Danica. "Prince Kaden was behind the attack here in the palace. Is that correct?"

Her lips pressed into a tight line, but she nodded.

"He also knew about the attack in Trenath?"

"I don't..." Danica looked at Zafyr and swallowed. "Prince Kaden said he spoke to one of the assassins the night before he departed."

One of? Then the one they had caught hadn't been the only one. That made sense if what Kaden said about him and Velara both being targets was true.

"Go on," Arhk prompted.

She started to turn toward Kasiel but caught herself

and stared forward between Zafyr and his father instead. "The man had been sneaking through the servants' passages and overheard Prince Kaden railing against the marriage and the alliance to someone in his rooms. He approached the prince the next night. When Prince Kaden convinced him they had a shared interest in stopping the alliance, the man admitted that he and another assassin were there to kill Khesran Velara and..." she paused, her gaze flickering his way, "...and Ahninveth Cavenos."

"Did he say who sent them?"

Danica cast a look of loathing at Zafyr before answering. "One of Khesran Karith's guards hired them in Doran."

Arhk glanced at Zafyr. The woman confirmed with a slight nod. Whether there was truth behind her words, they were at least what Danica remembered Kaden telling her. But that implicated Velara's older brother in the attempt on her life in Trenath.

"Ahninveth Kasiel." Arhk turned to him. "Go inform Khevarin Seylin that she is needed here. Then check on your injured soldiers."

Kasiel pushed away from the wall, his nerves sparking alight. After a brief inner struggle, he stopped himself from looking at Danica. This was too far above his rank and experience. He shouldn't be involved, and yet, a childhood full of memories tied him to Danica regardless of how dramatically their lives now separated them.

Arhk held his gaze without threat or anger, nor with any hint of understanding or sympathy. Nothing but the expectation of a superior officer issuing an order.

Kasiel's heart pounded in his chest, lungs tightening as he forced out the words. "Yes, Dhomvalen."

He didn't dare glance back until he was outside, shutting the door. When he did, he saw Danica watching him, eyes wide and damp with fear, her beautiful black braids snagged and in disarray. Her lip trembled and a single tear raced down one cheek. They both knew her life was out of his hands now.

CHAPTER TWENTY SIX

On his way to the rooms Seylin was now staying in, Kasiel spotted her in the Ruby Drawing Room, the khevarin a pale diamond amidst the deep red walls with their ornate white moldings separating every panel. Early dawn light crept in the windows. She sat across from Ahndhomen Aleren on an elegant ivory couch drinking what smelled like mint tea. Kasiel stopped in the doorway between the guards. A few servants passed in the hall behind him, the palace waking up.

"Come in, Ahninveth Kasiel," Seylin beckoned him with the graceful curl of her fingers.

When he entered, Irith didn't follow. The big cat stood in the doorway, snorting at the aroma of mint and rubbing at his nose on one foreleg. Kasiel started kneeling to the side of the table, but Seylin interrupted with an upward wave of her hand.

"You need not kneel. We do not doubt who you serve." Her crystalline eyes looked him over. "You could use a bath though," she observed. "How is my daughter?"

Kasiel's gut clenched, but he knew better than to lie to her. The healer may well have informed her of his visit. "Her injuries will heal. Her spirit may take more time to recover."

Her lips curved up a fraction, approval in her gaze, as if he had passed some test. "We both know this is not enough to keep her down, headstrong as she is."

Had his father told her about finding him with Velara the night of the attack? He doubted she would be this congenial if he had. Still, he had to fight the urge to avert his gaze. "Majesty, Dhomvalen Arhk is questioning the prisoner and has requested your presence."

One eyebrow arched, and she glanced at her tehnaak. "Requested our presence? Do you think Arhk would be so polite?"

"Not if he could help it," Aleren answered with a chuckle.

Seylin's gaze returned to Kasiel. "We appreciate your decorum, Ahninveth. Please, escort us to him."

Kasiel did as she asked, Irith taking up by his side again as they walked out. He stopped outside the room Danica was in when they got there, staying far enough back that he couldn't see her or she him. When the door closed behind Seylin and Aleren, he went to find where Darro and Jethan were being cared for, but he didn't make it far before one of the Delaphinian royal guards intercepted him.

"Ahninveth Kasiel Cavenos, General Itana would like to speak with you, if you please."

Kasiel drew a breath. He wanted to see his tehnaak then take that bath the khevarin mentioned. Now that she said something, he could feel nothing but the lingering grit of dirt and blood upon his skin. It appalled him to think he had lain next to Velara in such a state. More so that she had actually wanted him to. Still, given the events of the last few days, it would be prudent to see what Itana needed.

He compromised by stopping at his room to wash away the worst with a wet sponge from the basin and put on cleaner clothes before letting the guard lead him to where Itana waited. They stopped at a room on the second floor of the west wing. Two more royal guards stood outside, one opening the door to a large study, its dark blue walls laden with hunting trophies, weapons, and paintings of hunts. Irith let out a low growl as they walked in, and Kasiel settled a reassuring hand on the cat's shoulder.

They stopped a few steps inside the door when the king, standing in the far corner gazing up at the head of a boar, turned to face them. Itana, apparently not the one who had wanted to see him after all, stood on the opposite side of the room at silent attention.

Unease rippled through Kasiel. "Your Majesty," he greeted with a bow.

The door clicked shut. King Mahlik walked over behind a heavy desk, tapping a finger on its glossy wood surface. "General Itana tells me you are a good man, Ahninveth. I wish to believe her, just as I wish to believe that you both had our best interest at heart when you agreed to lie about my son's misdeeds."

The unease was more of a wave now. His gaze shifted to Itana, but she offered no insight. Looking back at the king, he said, "We intended no harm, Majesty, of that I can assure you."

"General Itana did not expose your secret. She did not need to. My son and I had many heated arguments regarding this alliance. I feared, when he finally agreed to the marriage, that his heart might not be in the right place, though I never imagined he had such plans as this." His dark eyes bored into Kasiel. "Whatever your motivations, I appreciate you sparing his mother the truth and allowing us the opportunity to bury him with dignity."

"We took those things into consideration when we made that decision, along with a shared desire to save this alliance, Majesty," Kasiel said, meeting the king's eyes. "I believe the alliance is necessary if our countries ever want to see an end to the bloodshed. I, for one, grow weary of seeing people I care about hurt or killed."

The king lowered his gaze, shifting a few items on his desk. "A motivation I cannot bring myself to disagree with, and one my eldest son, fortunately, also agrees with. Unfortunately, he is already married."

That wasn't unfortunate in Kasiel's opinion, not that he would ever say as much. "For what it's worth, I am sorry I could not bring Prince Kaden back alive, Majesty."

The king walked around the side of his desk, eyeing Irith thoughtfully. "But you brought back his body, and the woman whose weapon ended his life. I thank you for that. The dhomvalen has agreed to hand her over to us as a gesture of peace and cooperation when he and his Evoker finish questioning her. She will be put to death tomorrow as a traitor to the crown and as Prince Kaden's murderer."

Kasiel was suddenly lightheaded.

What other end could she have had? Danica was a traitor and executing her for the murder of the prince would allow the royal family to frame him as a martyr for the alliance. Nothing Kasiel said in her defense was going to save her from this, and appearing sympathetic to her now could weaken Vanris's position in negotiations. How eager had Arhk been to hand her over? To be fair, it was probably his only viable option if they were going to move forward with the alliance, but had he considered for a second what it would mean to his son?

The king was watching him intently now. "You will attend, of course, as the man who brought her in. A renowned soldier of Vanris seen acting in Delaphine's interests will gain considerable support for our alliance."

Kasiel swallowed against the panic that made him feel like throwing up. Part of him had expected her to die, had even accepted in the heat of battle that he might be the one to kill her. But he had no desire to watch while another member of his childhood family was publicly executed.

"Of course, Majesty."

The king nodded his approval. "You shall have a place of honor at the proceedings. Now, I imagine you have duties to attend to."

"I do, Majesty." Kasiel offered a slight bow.

He didn't look at Itana as he left, afraid she would see the horror in his eyes. Irith pressed close to him, enough so that it made the long walk back to where Jethan was more difficult. He didn't push the cliff cat away. Niskenya's presence wrapped around him, offering a comfort that couldn't penetrate the cold within.

When he found the room Jethan was in, Tath had recently dosed his tehnaak with something to help him rest and he was sleeping soundly. She insisted on checking the wounds on Kasiel's hand, shoulder, and jaw before letting him go with advice to return in around four hours if he wanted to speak to Jethan. He tolerated her ministrations, saying as little as he could get away with, and left the moment she finished, heading out through the gardens to where Niskenya could join him.

The massive kanodrak sank down beside him, and Kasiel climbed up on her back. She didn't have a saddle on, but he was comfortable enough riding her now that he could manage without it for this. Once she was up, they sprinted away from the palace and out into the surrounding woods.

No matter how many times he told himself Danica had orchestrated her own end, his heart blamed him for bringing her to Norvask, guilt clawing him apart from within like a beast trapped in his chest. He could have questioned her in Coranthis and let her escape, but he would have broken Itana's trust and that of his father and the khevarin had he done so. Now, she would die as Edmund had, helpless to save herself while he looked on.

Unable to escape the torture of his thoughts, Kasiel welcomed in all Niskenya's wildness, letting it drive out the emotion in him. The breeze they created with their speed dried the moisture on his cheeks. Irith dropped off to hunt on his own while Kasiel and Niskenya ran and hunted as one, all reality outside of them fading away. He wasn't sure how much time had passed when another kanodrak joined them at the edge of a lake in the woods. The blood of Niskenya's kill was still fresh on her claws, bloodlust from tearing apart the small deer coursing through them.

Niskenya snarled, baring massive teeth at the other beast.

"Easy, Ahninveth, I'm not your enemy."

With his identity submerged so deeply in the kanodrak, it took a few seconds for Kasiel to form words. He glanced at Jhanik, giving himself a shake. "You're sure of that?"

Jhanik answered with a wry grin. "Welcome back, you Break-blasted calloch. Seems like you got a bit lost there. No judgement," he added hastily, "I've been there myself, usually when I'm upset about something. I'd be careful though. Your kanodrak is powerful and your connection with her runs deep. Give over to her too much, and you may never come back."

He rested a hand on Niskenya's shoulder. "Sometimes that doesn't sound so bad."

Arkos pawed the ground, claws digging deep into the soil, releasing the scent of damp dirt and decaying evergreen needles. "I can't entirely disagree."

They sat in silence for a moment, the shifting and breathing of the kanodraks and the chatter of other creatures in the forest the only sounds. Things between him and Jhanik were becoming less hostile, perhaps simply because they shared a responsibility to Vanris to work together. Whatever the reason, Kasiel was glad he didn't have to add conflict with the other Feral to his current concerns.

"I should get back."

"Probably. The dhomvalen was looking for you."

Kasiel gave him a sharp scowl. "You could have led with that."

Jhanik's crooked grin reminded him unnervingly of Jethan for a second. "I told him you took Niskenya to do some scouting and stretch her legs. He looked concerned – an expression I've rarely seen on that man – and said to let him know if you didn't return soon. I thought maybe I should come check on you."

Kasiel glanced at the back of Niskenya's head, feeling her affection and wildness rippling around the edges of his mind. The weight bearing down on him was as heavy now as it had been when he rode out here. Their wild run and hunt provided nothing more than a temporary escape.

"Listen, I know your tehnaak and another of your soldiers got hurt pretty bad in Coranthis. I also get the feeling that isn't all that's bothering you, but if..." Arkos shifted from one front foot to the other and back, manifesting his companion's discomfort. "If I can help in..."

Kasiel nodded, saving him the effort of finishing the offer. "Thank you. I'll let you know." He reached out, finding Irith contentedly resting beside the stripped bones of some small creature. With a quick thought, he sent the cliff cat toward the palace, then looked at the other Feral. "You and Arkos up for a run?"

Jhanik grinned. "Always."

They turned their kanodraks toward the palace and Kasiel gave himself to Niskenya for a short time longer as they sprinted back. She maintained a slight lead over Arkos the entire way. The other kanodrak had shown deference to her in the past and didn't seem interested in pushing for more now. If that upset Jhanik at all, he kept his feelings to himself.

When they reached the palace, Kasiel didn't go in search of his father. Instead, once Irith rejoined him, he walked to the room Jethan was in. His wild wandering through the woods had gone on long enough that his tehnaak might be awake now.

When he walked in, Darro, propped up at an angle the way Velara had been, was softly arguing with Tath about how long he needed to stay off his broken leg. Unsurprisingly, he was pushing for a much faster recovery than she felt reasonable.

"That's ridiculous," Darro was saying.

"If you want full use of that limb again, you'll do what I say and stay off it."

Darro acknowledged Kasiel with a nod before turning his focus back to Tath. "Maybe with a little incentive, you could convince me to stay in bed longer."

She drew a deep breath and rolled her eyes at him. "I could break the rest of those ribs. How's that for incentive?" She softened her words with a kiss, though her steely gaze issued him a warning.

Jethan, awake now, but still flat on his back, gave Kasiel a smile that lacked his usual humor. "Good to see you, tehnaak. I heard you'd gone off in the woods on Niske a few hours ago and Jhanik went to find you. Did you all make it back in one piece?"

"Yes. He was unexpectedly tolerable." Kasiel sat in a chair by the bed. "How are you doing?"

He grimaced. "I hate this. It fucking hurts and I can't do anything to help you, or anyone else, for that matter."

Kasiel forced a smile. "Worry about recovering for now. I can handle things."

Jethan met his eyes. "Really? Because the dhomvalen

said they're executing Danica tomorrow and King Mahlik wants you to attend."

His gut twisted with a fresh wave of nausea. He hadn't eaten yet today, and now he wasn't sure he would. The knowledge that his father had spoken to Jethan about it brought a touch of comfort. Maybe he hadn't made the decision to give her to the king completely without remorse.

"I'm sorry I can't be there to support you, Kas. It's where I'm supposed to be." Distress pinched Jethan's brows together.

"And Danica's the reason you can't be there." If only he could summon forth more of his anger with her, but it eluded him right then. "I'll survive."

"I know. You're remarkably good at it. I just wish you didn't have to do it without my help."

They spoke for a while longer. A servant brought in food and Tath came to help Jethan into a position where he could eat with some small amount of dignity. By the time he finished, he was grimacing with pain, and Tath gave him something to help him sleep. Once he drifted off, Kasiel left. He caught a servant in the hall and asked for bath water to be brought to his room. On the way there, he spotted the khevarin's healer and waved her over.

"Ahninveth Kasiel," she greeted.

"Healer..." He faltered, realizing he had never asked her name. "I apologize."

"Don't. I like my anonymity as simply the khevarin's healer. My name, if you must have it, is Rihane." The corners of her mouth curved up as she searched his eyes. "And to answer your unspoken question, the khesran is doing a little better this afternoon."

He managed a smile. "Thank you."

"Another visit might help her more." Rihane regarded him expectantly.

"I'll come by if I get the chance. Perhaps after a bath."

"A wise plan."

She continued on her way, and Kasiel retreated to his room. When the bath was ready, he soaked in it for a long time, careful to keep the stitches below his collarbone above the water. For a while, he dozed, lulled by the heat. When he woke, it was only enough to stumble to the bed and let sleep claim him again. Irith was curled up over three-fourths of the bed when he woke later, shoving him to the edge. It was dark outside the windows, and hunger gnawed at him.

He dressed and slipped out into quieter hallways. It took a few minutes to find a Delaphinian servant.

The woman curtsied, keeping her eyes lowered and her hands clasped before her when she straightened. "Milord, what can I do for you?"

"You know where the prisoner is being kept?"

She gave a quick nod. "Yes, milord."

"I'll be taking over guard duty for a while. Can you bring my supper to her room, along with a mug and a decanter of wine? And a mug of water for the prisoner too, if you would."

"Of course, milord." She curtsied again and hurried off.

He took Irith out briefly to let the cat run and relieve himself, then went to the room alongside his. The Vanrian guards at the door let him in without question. Inside, Danica sat on the bed, her back to the wall, glaring at the two guards who sat staring sternly back at her.

Both guards stood when Kasiel entered. "Ahninveth Kasiel."

"You're relieved. I'll take over for tonight."

"Alone, my lord?"

At a quick mental prompt from Kasiel, Irith growled, and the guard took a step back.

"Apologies. I didn't mean..." He trailed off and

lowered his gaze. "Yes, Ahninveth."

When they were gone, Kasiel turned to Danica. Her bloodshot, puffy eyes told him she knew her fate.

"Did you come to taunt me?"

He shook his head. "Why would I do that?"

"Because you're getting what you want. I'm to be executed tomorrow."

He picked up a chair, carried it over to the bed, and sat down. Irith settled next to him, watching her with those vibrant blue eyes. "Why did you do it, Dani?"

She rubbed her face in her hands. When she looked up, her gaze came to rest on the cliff cat. "When you disappeared from Fernwallow, I was so afraid for you. I just wanted to help save you. After you chose to stay with the Vanrians in the woods that night, Edmund and my father told me they had brainwashed you, and I believed them. Why else would you choose strangers – enemies – over your family? Then we met in Katovan, and I realized you weren't coming back. I had to let go, but I felt so lost without you, Kas, especially know-ing Edmund and my father were lying to me. Using me." A quiet tear ran down her cheek, dragging a blade through his heart.

"Then your beast killed my father. I wanted to hate you. I tried so hard to hate you, but I just missed you. Nightmares plagued me, most with you or my father in them. They started haunting me even when I was awake. Edmund, despite the awful things I knew he had done, was the only one I had to turn to. In a strange way, staying with him helped me feel like I still had a connection to you. Then you showed up. You destroyed my new home and took Edmund and me to Vanris. I watched you with that woman, Nerith, and saw how at home you were with your beasts and companions. I finally understood that you had no need of me in your life, a fact you confirmed when you chose Jethan over me and watched them put Edmund to death."

She finally looked at him. "I could finally hate you. With nowhere left to go, I lingered around the border town where the messenger left me and found others who shared my hatred for you and your people. That eventually earned me Prince Kaden's attention and a path to revenge for everything you had destroyed. The sad thing is, in a way, I was still clinging to you. Now you can watch them do to me what they did to Edmund. You can finally finish erasing your past."

"I don't want to erase you, Dani, but I never belonged in the world we grew up in. Vanris is my home. I always hoped you might go back to Fernwallow or make a new home for yourself somewhere else. The last thing I want is to watch you die like this."

She leaned forward, a desperate hope sparking in her eyes. "Then help me. Tell them I didn't mean to kill Prince Kaden."

He shook his head. "I can't fix this. The king already knows you didn't mean to kill his son. It doesn't matter. You're still a traitor to the crown. The punishment is the same."

She fell back against the wall, her head hitting hard enough to make him wince. More tears spilled down her cheeks. Before he could think of anything to say, there was a knock at the door.

Kasiel went to sit near the table. "Come in."

One guard escorted a servant in, watching while she set down a tray with food and wine on it. She set a second mug full of water to one side, intended for Danica. Kasiel thanked her, then waited in silence while the guard followed her back out. When they were gone, he pulled the table over by the bed.

"Do you want this water?" he asked, handing her the mug.

She took it. While she drank, he poured himself a

mug of wine. When she started setting down her mug, he raised the decanter in offering. After a moment's hesitation, she lifted her mug to her lips and drank the rest of the water, then held it out for him to fill. He did so, waiting as she took a sip before gesturing to the platter.

"Eat with me?"

Her eyes narrowed. "Have my last meal with you, you mean?"

Kasiel held her gaze. "I'll leave if you want me to."

She lowered her eyes and shook her head. "No," she said in a small voice, her defiance crushed.

They ate in silence for a while, sharing the same utensils. When it was clear neither of them had much enthusiasm left for food, he refilled their mugs, pushed the table back into place and went to sit next to her on the bed.

He sipped the wine before resting his head against the wall. "Remember when we cut all of Barden's snares because we felt bad for the rabbits he kept catching?"

Danica giggled. "How old were we? Seven? Eight? He was so mad, I thought he was going to skin us and use our hides to make up for his losses." Her smile quickly faded. "I'm scared, Kas. I'm so scared."

He took her wine from her and set both mugs on the nightstand. Then he leaned back again and held one arm out. Danica slid over and put her legs across his, curling into his embrace.

"Don't leave me tonight," she whispered, resting her head on his shoulder.

He held her tight with one arm and wiped away a tear with his free hand. "I won't, Dani. Not tonight."

CHAPTER TWENTY SEVEN

Kasiel stayed with Danica throughout the night, as promised. When she dozed off, he sat and waited. When she woke up crying, he held her until she fell asleep again. In the end, he could no more stop her fate than he could stop the sunrise. When the guards came to prepare her, he made them wait outside a minute while he wiped away a few more tears.

"I love you, Dani. I always did." He gently kissed her forehead. "I'm sorry about everything."

"I love you too." She met his eyes, briskly wiping away another tear, and nodded, her jaw muscles working as she tried to fight more tears.

Kasiel watched them escort her away, Niskenya's strength and Irith's devotion bolstering him as he went to change into something more appropriate for the occasion. Avris met him in his room. She didn't speak as she waited while he changed, then helped him work a few braids into his hair and put on the symbolic ear cuffs. It reminded him of Nerith preparing him for Edmund's execution. A memory that came with a mountain of guilt.

They held the execution in a perversely beautiful, flower-filled square in the town. Delaphinian and Vanrian soldiers lined the perimeter, symbolically intermixed. The king and queen stood in places of honor upon a carpeted platform with the khevarin and dhomvalen beside them. Itana and Kasiel also held places of honor on either side of the group. Outside the barrier of soldiers, a crowd of townspeople gathered.

Danica stood in plain clothes, bound with her arms pulled out beside her to a roughly constructed wall of planks designed to prevent risk to people in the area. She was to be killed as Kaden was, by the bolt of a cross-bow. The hang of her head made it clear she had given up. Any confidence she had in her choices was gone. Kasiel realized he had stolen much of that from her by supporting her through the night. Now she stood before them defeated.

The king gave an extended speech, extolling the benefits of the alliance with Vanris and the false virtues of his son. Kasiel couldn't listen. He heard birds singing. The whisper of a breeze through the leaves of some trees at the edges of the square. The shuffle of feet and murmuring of the crowd. Arhk shifted closer, softly prompting him to offer a gracious bow at one point when the king had apparently recognized him for his efforts. He did as he was told, feeling as broken as Danica looked. The crowd's cheer rang hollow in his ears.

When the moment came, two Delaphinian soldiers with crossbows stepped up to the platform and bowed to the king. One asked, "Where shall we aim, Majesty?"

Itana's eyes met Kasiel's. Her gaze flickered from him to Danica and back again. She saw. He knew she did, but he couldn't bring himself to care.

The king's expression darkened. "She should suffer as my son suffered," he answered in a low voice.

As the two men started turning away, Itana held up a hand to stay them. She faced the king, inclining her head respectfully. "Majesty, if I may?"

"Speak, General."

"This is not merely an execution. It is a show of

unity and a movement toward peace with our new allies. If your people believe that violence is the only language you know, that is how they will always relate to you. Perhaps this is the time to begin teaching them a new language."

The king regarded her in silence for a few seconds. "You are advising that I show mercy?"

"I am, Majesty."

The king glanced at Arhk and Seylin, both of whom gave subtle nods of agreement. He drew a deep breath and considered Danica again. "Very well. Aim for her heart."

Kasiel watched in silence.

Did it matter that he had torn out her heart some time ago?

The two men took their positions and aimed. Danica looked up, her eyes meeting his. At the king's command, the crossbows fired with a snap that made him flinch. The bolts drove into her chest less than an inch apart, the force of their impact slamming her against the wall. She looked surprised, more than anything, mouth open, tears spilling down her cheeks. The pain registered in her eyes mere seconds before she convulsed and slumped unconscious in her bonds. Death would come quickly.

Kasiel could only stare, finding it hard to draw a breath. When the executioners confirmed her death, the king said his final words and dismissed them. Kasiel jerked away from the hand Arhk had placed on his shoulder at some point and strode from the square. He didn't go to Niskenya, though he brought her presence with him to his room in the palace, a place where no one could see him. There he sat on the bed and closed his eyes, pressing his hands over his ears as the snap of the crossbows firing sounded again and again in his head.

No one knocked before the door clicked open sometime later. He watched Velara shut the door behind her, her careful movements betraying her pain. After staring at her for a second, he slid across the bed and walked to her.

"Vel, you should be resting."

"Jethan told Keyla that the woman they executed this morning was someone important to you." Her voice was quiet, still trying to avoid too much movement that would pull on her stitches.

He shook his head. "That's irrelevant. You shouldn't be walking around. Why did you come here?"

Bringing up her uninjured hand, she gently traced a line of the tattoo on his cheek. "Isn't it obvious?"

He stared at her, a chill of apprehension whispering through him.

"I love you, you idiot. I won't let you suffer alone." A pained smile crossed her lips. "Don't worry. I don't expect you to say the same. I know your heart belongs to another."

Did it? He wasn't sure anymore. It wasn't something he could think about right now. He stared into her silver eyes, not resisting the urge to sink into them. Leaning in, he placed a careful kiss on her lips. Then he drew back a fraction, holding her gaze.

"I'm escorting you to your rooms."

"No."

Someone knocked on the door.

"Come in," he called, taking two steps back from her.

Healer Rihane entered the room, pulling the door shut behind her. Her chastising gaze fell upon Velara. "I leave you alone for five minutes, and you wander off. Your injuries are not to be taken lightly, Khesran."

"They're my injuries," Velara snapped back. Then she winced, her fingers going to the bandages on her cheek.

Rihane crossed her arms, brows rising.

Velara rolled her eyes. "Besides, aren't you the one always going on about the importance of caring for the injuries we cannot see?" She looked at Kasiel again, the concern in her gaze threatening to break through the numbness that shielded him from his sorrow.

The healer's arms unfolded, her shrewd gaze raking over Kasiel. "I'll give you half an hour. No more. If your mother finds you here, I will tell her you snuck out."

Velara didn't look away from him. "Agreed."

After considering them for a few more seconds, Rihane added, "I'm putting you in charge of her, Ahninveth." Then she left the room.

"Make me a comfortable place to sit and tell me about this woman."

He heard the snap of the crossbows firing in his head. "I don't—"

She put her finger to his lips. "I'm not asking, Kas. I want to know who she was. Tell me your favorite memories of her, and your least favorite. You have half an hour, so you had best get started."

He heaved a sigh and walked to the bed to arrange the pillows for her. "Danica's father helped Edmund take me from my family when I was five. He..." Kasiel trailed off when her hand came to rest on his shoulder. He turned to meet her eyes. She didn't have to say anything. He started over. "Dani and I grew up together. She was my best friend in Fernwallow, my partner-in-mischief."

Velara's careful smile warmed him a little. "What kind of mischief?"

For the next half hour, he told her some of his favorite memories from his childhood with Danica. When Rihane returned for her, his throat was raw with grief and his eyes stung. The crushing devastation wasn't gone, but his heart felt a little stronger somehow.

*

For the next three days, with Arhk and Seylin occupied with negotiations, Kasiel split his daylight hours between visiting Jethan and Darro or sparring to keep his mind off other things. The evening of the execution, he had sought out Itana to thank her for convincing the king to be merciful. She had shrugged it off and invited him to train with her, so that was what they did. From then on, he went out after every evening meal and eased away from Niskenya for a short while to spar with the Delaphinian general. The rest of the time, he practiced with Merrin. She was the only one skilled enough to keep him fully focused on combat when he had Niskenya on board, which he usually did. He could move past his sorrow as long as he had the kanodrak's presence there.

By the third day, the Vanrian healers, working with local craftsmen, finished construction of a brace for Jethan's back so that he could more safely move around. It felt good to have his tehnaak among the rest of his companions watching when he sparred with Itana that night. Darro had also come, with Tath and Harif keeping a close eye on the two injured men. It was the first time since they chased Kaden to Coranthis that the entire unit was together in one place. Except for Nerith. Despite everything, Kasiel still couldn't accept Harif as a permanent replacement for her.

Velara had the stitches in her face and neck removed. The healing cuts stood out vividly against her pale skin where they created that sideways V on her cheek, the lower line stretching up and over the bridge of her nose. Three jagged scars ran along one side of her neck as well. She spent a great deal of time trying to hide her face behind the curtain of her hair when he visited her after his late sparring sessions. A behavior he couldn't talk her out of no matter how often he told her he thought she was beautiful.

The fourth day, they left Norvask. One wagon they acquired in Coranthis became a transport for luggage so that the finer carriages, with their smoother travel, could be reserved for royalty and for the injured who still couldn't ride. Irith alternated between trotting beside Kasiel on Niskenya and lounging in the carriage with Jethan and Darro.

Kasiel knew little about the details of the alliance. It wasn't his position to know. All he knew was that Seylin and his father seemed satisfied with what they had accomplished, though a shadow hung over them, the khevarin especially. That didn't strike him as surprising, given the losses their company had suffered, and the possibility that her eldest son might have been involved in the attempt on Velara's life in Trenath. That situation still had to be addressed.

He touched the pouch on his belt with Sylaryth's claw in it.

It felt strange to be involved in things that could change the course of their country's future. About a year ago, the mercenaries had taken him captive, dragging him bound and gagged away from the life he had grown up with. He had been a different person then. If they tried to do the same to him now, they wouldn't have nearly as easy a time of it. Another life in another place, full of people who were gone now. Garrick, Edmund… Danica.

Kasiel straightened in the saddle when the Arhk rode up beside him, only two of his three guards surviving to return to Etrion with him.

"It seems unfair to ask Niskenya to carry the weight of such melancholy."

"She's used to my moods," Kasiel answered, managing a halfhearted smile.

"I know you must be tired, Kasiel, and heavy of heart, but—"

"But there's another mission," Kasiel finished for him. He glanced at his father, noticing that he also looked somewhat tired. "Doran?"

Arhk nodded. "Once our injured are safe within the walls of Etrion, I will head to Doran to follow up on the incident in Trenath. I want your unit with me. With two of your soldiers injured, you should consider if there is anyone you want to fill in those gaps for this mission. If not, I will assign soldiers to you."

"What of Jhanik and his unit?" It was disconcerting to realize he was asking because he had grown used to having the other Feral around.

"We will give both units a night to rest in Etrion, then we are sending his unit to reinforce a base farther west. An increasing number of Sarket troops have been spotted roaming the Break in that area. We are reinforcing the watchtowers there as well. Vanrian troops have also been sent to fortify Delaphine's towers near the western edge of their border along the Break so that they might focus on shoring up defenses along their border with Sarket."

"They expect more trouble?"

Arhk answered with a sharp nod. "I considered sending your unit west, but this will give your injured time to heal while you are away. If we must send you out into battle again, I prefer to do so with all your core unit functional. Your tehsheyn, as you call them."

Kasiel sensed something more resting unspoken between them. Another time, he might have let it go. Not now. "And?"

Arhk glanced at him, respect in his cool regard. "And there are few people I would rather have at my side for this."

Kasiel allowed himself the barest trace of a smile.

"My unit will be ready, Dhomvalen."

"The healers will check everyone over before we leave to be sure they are fit to go out again so soon, you included. Prioritize getting some rest when we arrive in Etrion." Arhk moved away, heading toward the carriage Seylin and Velara rode in.

When they reached Etrion several days later, Darro and Jethan went directly to the healer's building, sore and tired from traveling with their injuries. Kasiel imagined Velara felt the strain of the journey as well, though he'd had little chance to speak with her along the way. The unit split up, everyone exhausted and eager to rest, knowing they were heading out again. Kasiel had one task to complete before he could retire to his rooms.

He reached out through the city, relieved when he found Raxxa. That meant Kenna wasn't on deployment, though she wasn't with her companion at that moment either. He bounced from there out to the tethdraks, touching on the juveniles and adults until he found the other Feral in a separated area tending an injured female. After leaving Niskenya in the kanodrak canyon, he crossed through to the tethdrak habitat.

Kenna was out in a side enclosure trying to control a headstrong tethdrak long enough to tend a cut on one leg. Kasiel moved into the beast's head as he entered, kicking her out, and encouraged it to come to him.

Kenna watched it walk away, irritation and confusion bunching her forehead until she noticed him. Then she grinned and ran to the front. "Kas!" She threw her arms around him, slamming into him with a fierce embrace that made him stumble back a few steps.

He chuckled, returning the hug. "Nice to see you too. Want me to keep her still?"

A broad smile brightened her features when she stepped back, though the enthusiasm faded as she looked him over. "Yes, if you wouldn't mind." She knelt by the beast now that it was still to clean and put salve on the wound. "As exhausted as you look, I suspect you didn't come here just to visit."

"I'm afraid not. My unit needs two soldiers to fill in for a mission to Doran that's leaving tomorrow. I was hoping you and Therin might be willing."

She glanced up at him. "Please tell me no one's dead."

"No, but Jeth and Darro were both hurt badly enough they won't be making this trip."

She shot upright, a glob of salve still on her fingers. "But they'll be all right?"

Kasiel nodded. "I'm sure Jethan would welcome a visit."

"Speaking of visits, Nerith's back in the city."

A mix of pleasure and dread spun his stomach into instant knots. He closed his eyes briefly, searching for balance.

Kenna's brows crept up. "Not actually the look I expected in response to that news. What's going on?" She held up her hand before he could speak. "You know what? Don't answer that. I'll visit Jethan. You can figure out whatever that was."

"Thanks. I appreciate the support." He gave her a wry smile. "About the mission?"

"I'll check with Adnar. If he doesn't object, we'll join your unit."

"Thank you, Kenna. I'm going to..." He gestured toward the palace.

"Sounds like you have it all figured out." She gave him a wink. "Good luck."

He drew in a deep breath of cool evening air before taking his leave. When he got to his rooms, a meal was already waiting. Despite the ache of hunger in his gut, he took a few minutes to wash away the dust from the road and change into clean, comfortable clothes. He would only get tonight to enjoy the luxury of his own rooms, after all.

Halfway through a plate of food and his second pour of wine, a knock came at the door. He stood and walked over, unsurprised to find Nerith there, her lavender eyes gazing warily up at him. She didn't embrace or kiss him as he had both feared and hoped she might, saving him the trouble of figuring out how to respond to that, though her reservation increased his anxiety.

Uncertainty tightened her features when she searched his face, and she clasped her hands in front of her. "I ran into Jhanik. He said I might want to prepare myself because you had important news for me regarding our relationship, though he wouldn't elaborate beyond that."

The other Feral had shown unusual restraint. Kasiel would have expected Jhanik to have readily told her everything about his interactions with Velara, at least as much as he knew or suspected of them, perhaps with some embellishments. "I suppose I do." He stepped back to let her in.

She walked to the sitting area and faced him. "Before you say anything potentially upsetting, I wanted to thank you. I know you and Jethan were involved in Tath's offer to take me as her tehnaak. The council set aside my father's dispute in favor of her proposal. It gave me the escape I needed, and I am honored to accept."

"I'm glad it worked out. Your father shouldn't be the one making those decisions for you."

She nodded, her mouth slightly open as if she wanted to respond but wasn't sure what to say or how to say it.

He looked at her standing there, her silvery braid draped over one shoulder, her expression guarded, expecting to be hurt. He had never wanted to hurt her. Drawing a deep breath, he said, "I may have been unfaithful to you."

Her eyes narrowed. "You may have been, or you were?"

It was almost impossible to hold her gaze, but he made himself do so. "I was."

Her hands clenched at her sides. "Can I ask with whom?"

The guilt was crushing, but no matter how awful he felt for doing this to Nerith, he couldn't regret his time with Velara. A rush of moments raced through his mind. Velara asking him to kiss her, chatting with him late into the evenings in Trenath, listening while he remembered Danica, telling him she loved him. He knew when he began developing genuine feelings for the khesran. It was early on, when she expressed an interest in Sylaryth's claw and talked into the night with him about his lost companion.

"Khesran Velara."

Nerith drew a deep breath and blew it out. "By the Break, Kas, tell me you weren't sleeping with the khesran while she was being courted by the Delaphinian prince."

"She's still a virgin," he added lamely, as if that made it better. "We didn't take it that far."

She broke their eye contact, shaking her head. "Fool. Do you know what could happen if someone other than the woman you *pretended* to love found you out?"

"I was never pretending," he stated. "As for the other, we're past the getting caught point. My father knows. The khevarin may be aware, though with the attacks at Trenath and Norvask and the death of the prince taking up everyone's attention, I don't really know."

Her eyes widened. "Clearly, things have happened that haven't been shared with the general populace yet."

He ran a hand through his hair. "A lot of things."

She took a step closer, her gaze piercing into him. "Well, at least we've established that you're a horse's ass and an idiot."

"Thank you."

There was no humor in her regard. "I was being generous. I came to tell you that, after almost being forced to marry a man I don't love, I realized I am not ready for that step in my life, even if the man I thought I loved had wanted to wed me." Her sharp words cut into him, though no more than he deserved. "I was going to suggest slowing down our relationship while I figure out what I do want, but I guess you took care of that for us."

"I'm sorry, Nerith, I never meant—"

"I don't want to hear it. Maybe later when the urge to stab you has passed." Her gaze flickered to a sharp knife on the table. After a second, she faced him, unshed tears pooling in her eyes. "Odd as you may find the request right now, I wish to remain part of your unit as Tath's tehnaak, if you will allow it."

A flood of relief met her words. "You are always welcome in my unit, Nerith. You're an excellent healer and a remarkable person. I count myself lucky to have you."

"If only your actions supported those words." She gave him a shrewd look. "Forgive me if I'm not so impressed by you at the moment."

"That's fair."

"What isn't fair is that my father is going to get what he wants after all. If he hadn't forced me to remain in Doran, I might not have lost you so easily." She looked at the table again, one hand coming up to wipe at a few tears that slipped free. "I haven't eaten yet this evening. If you'll excuse me, Ahninveth, I'd like to go see if Tath is available. She can bring me up to date on the events in Trenath and Norvask."

He didn't want her to leave. With Jethan being treated for his injuries, the rest of his unit seeing to preparations for tomorrow, and her justifiably furious with him, he felt more alone than he had in some time.

Worse, he could see her struggle to hold herself together in the shake of her hands and the working of her jaw. He yearned to comfort her, but he had no right to do so or to seek comfort from her after what he had done.

"Yes." He lowered his gaze. "Of course."

She rushed out without another word.

Dhomen Aleren joined them when they left early the next morning for Doran. Arhk set a fast pace from the moment they exited the city gates. The absence of Darro and Jethan weighed on the unit, but they seemed happy to have Nerith back, though there were curious glances prompted by the new tension between her and Kasiel. Kenna and Therin filled the open spots, which meant Irith had company of his own kind for once with Kenna's cliff cat Raxxa there. Arhk had his two surviving guards, and, to Kasiel's surprise, Ahndhomen Setera riding with him.

When they stopped to camp late the first evening, Kince joined him while he was settling Niskenya and his ten tethdraks for the night. "I saw you trying to puzzle out Setera's presence," he said in a low voice. "The guilt of a royal has to be confirmed by at least two Evokers for an arrest to be binding."

Kasiel glanced at him, then toward the other fire where his father was speaking with the Evoker. The two sat comfortably close, a slight lean in their postures hinting at a desire to be closer still. Were they intimate, or perhaps moving in that direction? He didn't want to think about Arhk's personal life, but, lacking any memory of his mother, he felt no betrayal in his father seeking other companionship.

"That's why he brought Setera. They must really believe Khesran Karith could be involved?"

"I'd say the dhomvalen isn't taking chances. Although, watching those two together, that may not be the only reason he brought her specifically, but it is why he brought two Evokers."

Kasiel glanced over in time to catch Kince's smirk. He wasn't imagining the attraction between the two then. "If Setera and Zafyr both find surface thoughts implicating Karith, what happens next?"

"We arrest him. I imagine the dhomvalen has orders to take him to Etrion to stand trial. Though Khemron Genyith may object to that course of action."

"What if he does?" Kasiel's gaze lingered on his father, who was leaning over to whisper something in Setera's ear that made her laugh. Arhk smiled. An easy, almost warm expression. It was unsettling.

"Then Dhomvalen Arhk would have to dispute the issue with the khemron until they come to an agreement. That part is out of our hands, but the khevarin holds a great deal more power than her husband. With your father acting on her authority, I suspect things will go her way." Kince fell silent for a second, his gaze moving to the fire their unit gathered around. "Do you know what you're going to do about her?"

Kasiel followed his gaze, spotting Nerith sitting next to Tath, a subdued smile curving her lips as she watched Avris, who appeared to be recounting some tale of revelry. Her gaze shifted to him, their eyes meeting for an instant. The smile faded as she looked away.

"I believe I've burned that bridge." He turned his attention to Niskenya, who was watching over the tethdraks like some terrifying manifestation of a sheepdog with her flock.

"Is that really what you believe? Because I think the foundations are compromised, but the bridge is still standing." He arched a brow at Kasiel. "Or has someone else stolen your heart?"

Kasiel looked at him, searching for the intent behind his guarded expression. "Are you trying to get at something?"

"Yes. I think you should consider aiming for a target you can hit. Velara's injuries and Prince Kaden's death may alter her future, but she is still Seylin's daughter. If her brother is found guilty of trying to have her killed, there will be turmoil in the royal family that you would be wise to stay clear of." Kince started walking away, calling back over his shoulder, "You know where you belong. Come join your unit, Ahninveth."

Kasiel's gaze moved past him to where the others were. His family. Maybe there was wisdom in Kince's words, but he couldn't abandon Velara when she needed someone as badly as she did now. Should it matter if there was no future for him with her? What kind of person would he be if the only future, the only need, of importance to him was his own? He still cared for Nerith, but he didn't think he was what she needed anymore. Being held hostage to her father's wishes had sparked a desire to pull back from their relationship. That alone didn't preclude them having one, but in that same period of time, he had lost part of himself to Velara. He wasn't sure he wanted it back.

Join us, country boy.

The voice in his head was unmistakable. He met Therin's eyes, the other man's grin teasing a matching expression from him. Avris, now standing beside Therin, beckoned Kasiel with a wave of one hand. Niskenya nudged his back with her nose, the massive predator having somehow snuck up behind him. The gesture nearly knocked him over, and he chuckled, turning to press a hand to her forehead briefly before walking to the campfire.

"There he is." Merrin raised her mug to him. "Our fearless leader."

Even Nerith joined the quick cheer as the rest lifted their mugs in response, though she did so with a forced smile. Kasiel glanced toward the other fire as Wedro handed him a mug of his own, catching Arhk's approving nod before he turned back to his own company. This was where he belonged. Kince was right about that much.

They rode hard the next several days, the aggressive pace and long hours in the saddle bringing them to Doran midday on the fifth day during a spring rain. The rain gave them an excuse to keep their hoods up, which allowed Arhk, his two guards, and Setera to pretend to be part of the unit. At the entrance, Aleren's presence got them past the gates without questioning. They moved through the city in a column, with Kasiel and Aleren in the lead. The tethdraks created a barrier on either side between them and locals coming out to gawk. The formation and official bearing were enough to make it clear this was a formal visit.

People watched Kasiel on Niskenya with a glimmer of admiration in their eyes that made him sit straighter in the saddle. He represented something to them. A Feral kanodrak rider. A hero. A leader. All things he never would have dreamed of becoming back in Fernwallow under Edmund's isolating tutelage. The honor of those things lifted him as much as the responsibility weighed him down.

On the previous visit, he noticed they regarded Arhk with respect and fear. But that was the dhomvalen's place. That was what made him such a powerful weapon in the khevarin's arsenal. He handled the unpleasant tasks. The ones that might lose her the support of her people if she were to involve herself in them directly. He was the one they were expected to fear or hate if necessary. Somehow, Kasiel was becoming his counterbalance. The one they could love and admire. The one allowed to sacrifice everything for them, even his life, if it came to that. It seemed odd that father and son should serve such opposite purposes.

The flowers in boxes and planters along the cobbled streets were in full bloom now, raindrops making them dance in place. Though the architecture and size of the cities differed, Doran reminded him in some ways of Norvask. They weren't so dissimilar. Nor were the people when you looked beyond obvious traits, like skin tone and ear shape. They were very much alike. Although, in Norvask, they had watched him with fear for the same reasons people here regarded him with hope. With Niskenya, he was a visible representation of the strength of Vanris.

A group of harried-looking soldiers met them outside the palace.

"Watch the horses," Aleren ordered. "We may not be here long."

The woman in front bowed. "Of course, Dhomen. What of the beasts?" Her gaze swept over Niskenya and the tethdraks.

Kasiel beckoned Kenna over as Aleren said, "Ahninveth Kenna will stay with them for now. You need only concern yourselves with the horses."

"Yes, Dhomen."

They continued inside, leaving Kenna and Therin out with the animals. Kasiel could manage them remotely, but having someone physically there would put the guards at ease, and Therin could reach out to Etris if there were problems. They entered the palace, keeping their hoods up to continue hiding Arhk and the Evokers for now. Aleren seemed to have a destination in mind, leading the way with swift, purposeful strides. When they got deeper in, she intercepted a royal attendant.

The woman started sinking to one knee, but Aleren caught her arm, forcing her to stay standing.

"I must speak with Khemron Genyith and his sons immediately."

"Yes, Dhomen. If you will follow me."

The woman led them to a moderately sized audience chamber, stopping two other attendants along the way and sending them to find the two khesrans. Genyith, having apparently already gotten word of their arrival, stood near one of two ornate thrones, an air of dangerous tension radiating off him when they entered. Aleren approached the front, giving a partial bow as Kasiel and the rest, his father's group among them, knelt to one side.

Genyith glanced over at them, his brow furrowing, then focused on Aleren. "We heard of the attack in Norvask. They said Khesran Velara suffered dire injuries. Tell me, does my daughter live?"

Kasiel's respect for the khemron grew at that moment. It was clear by the faint tremor in his voice that the hardened warrior cared deeply for Velara. Aleren didn't indulge him, however.

"I have news, Khemron, but I feel it best to wait until your sons are here with you."

Before Genyith could argue, the doors opened and Khesran Nakhul entered, an intensity of purpose burning in his gray eyes. His features had some of the refinement and elegance that Seylin and Velara shared. He had his jaw-length white hair pulled into tight braids against his scalp on one side and flipped over, shading his eye on the other.

"Dhomen Aleren," he greeted, crossing the room with quick, anxious strides, "is my sister all right?"

Khesran Karith entered almost on his heels with his wife and tehnaak, Safya, a petite blond with eyes the color of pale honey, hanging on his arm. The eldest khesran glanced at Kasiel's waiting unit, his long red hair left loose around his slender features, green eyes narrowing when they settled on Aleren.

"You've returned, Dhomen. With good news, I hope."

Something in his voice contradicted his words and put Kasiel's hackles up. Irith tensed beside him.

Arhk stood and tossed the hood of his cloak back, not wasting energy on formalities. The rest of them rose with him. "Khesran Karith, did you attempt to have Khesran Velara killed in order to stop the alliance with Delaphine?"

"Dhomvalen." Karith took a step back, surprise widening his eyes. "Kill my sister? Absolutely not! What an absurd accusation."

Nakhul was glaring daggers at Karith now, and Genyith's brows pulled together as he watched the scene unfolding before him. Arhk calmly turned to Zafyr. The Evoker pushed back her hood and met his eyes, giving a single, condemning nod. A glance at Setera got the same response. A ripple of fresh hatred moved through Kasiel, and Irith's hackles went up. The cliff cat growled, sinking into an attack posture.

"Arrest him." Arhk ordered.

Karith's wife stepped back from her husband, hands coming up to cover the alarmed O of her mouth.

Setera gestured to Safya. "I suggest taking his teh-naak as well. Her thoughts suggest she has some knowledge of this." Her sharp gaze jumped to the attendant who had accompanied the two in. "All three of them."

Arhk nodded to Kasiel.

One of the khesran's guards drew his sword. In a flash of motion, Merrin was beside the man, her dagger at his throat.

"I advise against it," she warned.

The other palace guards hesitated, looking to the khemron for guidance.

"Dhomvalen Arhk," Khemron Genyith's booming voice brought stillness to the room, "what is the meaning of this?"

Tension rippled through the group. Only Arhk appeared at ease. He inclined his head in the barest gesture of respect.

"Apologies, Khemron, I would have spoken to you first if the element of surprise were not necessary to avoid giving our suspect a chance to prepare himself. Allow us a moment to secure the prisoners, and I will explain."

"This is ludicrous!" Karith shouted. "You can't allow this, Father."

Nakhul walked up close to his brother, staring into his eyes. "The only thing ludicrous was you thinking you could get away with this. Evokers don't make mistakes, Brother. Try not to make a fool of yourself."

Kasiel watched the two, standing back enough that he and Irith could be in a position to react if anyone else tried to intervene. When they were in Doran before, he had noticed a closeness between Nakhul and Velara that didn't appear to exist between either sibling and their older brother, but attempting to have Velara killed seemed an extreme manifestation of that division.

"Nakhul knows something," Zafyr whispered to Arhk, barely loud enough for Kasiel to hear through Irith's sharp ears.

Arhk glanced at Setera, who confirmed with a subtle nod.

Genyith's gaze moved over them all, lingering a moment on Zafyr before coming to rest on Setera. "Ahndhomen Setera, it has been some time since you last visited Doran."

She offered a respectful bow. "It has, Majesty."

"Is this truly necessary?"

"I am sorry to say that it is, Majesty. Evidence suggests

that Khesran Karith may have been behind the assassination attempt on Khesran Velara in Trenath."

The look the khemron gave Karith then could have melted iron. "Tell me, is my daughter alive?"

Aleren inclined her head to him. "Her injuries were severe, Majesty, but she is alive and recovering in Etrion now."

Karith's lip twitched into the barest hint of a sneer.

"It pleases me to hear that she survives." Genyith regarded his eldest son for several tense seconds before speaking again. "My guards will help you secure them. When you finish, Dhomvalen Arhk, Dhomen Aleren, you will find me in Seylin's drawing room." He frowned. "Someone ought to use the space for something." With that, he and four of his guards disappeared through the double doors at the back of the room.

Arhk turned to Nakhul while Kasiel's unit and the rest of the king's guards secured the prisoners. "You knew he was guilty?"

Nakhul cast a scathing glance at his brother before answering. "I had reason to believe he wanted her out of the way."

"You will submit to questioning."

"Naturally."

The implicated attendant they left to the guards to take to Doran's version of the deeps. Karith and Safya, they placed in separate secured rooms in the palace.

"No one enters or exits these chambers who is not part of your unit," Arhk told Kasiel. "We do not know yet who else might be involved." His gaze shifted to Nakhul. "And keep him here. If he tries to sneak off, lock him up as well."

Nakhul answered with a simper and a slightly mocking bow. "Dhomvalen."

"Yes, Dhomvalen." Kasiel bowed his head respectfully.

Arhk left them without sparing another glance for Nakhul.

They waited for the dhomvalen and the king to come to an agreement on how to handle the situation. Kasiel eventually had to deal with Irith's need to go outside. Nakhul asked to accompany him to stretch his legs. Kasiel allowed it, waving off Kince when the other man moved to join them. If he and Irith couldn't handle the younger khesran, they had bigger issues, and it would give him a chance to ask Nakhul a few of the questions burning in his mind.

"Why would your brother have Velara killed?" he asked the moment they were out of earshot. Information he should leave for the interrogation, but he had a personal interest.

Nakhul considered him thoughtfully, the same fiery spirit that Velara possessed burning behind his gray eyes. "Maybe it has something to do with what your father said to him."

"What do you mean?"

"When you came here to escort Velara to Etrion, the dhomvalen told Karith he might be destined for a more superficial rule. If the alliance worked out to be the first step in bringing peace to Pandrea, we could go back to the leadership of a council with the positions of khevarin and khemron becoming figureheads."

His father had said that? Had he expected Karith to like the idea of being a mere figurehead of a country at peace? It didn't sound bad to Kasiel, but if power and control appealed to the elder khesran, such a comment could have driven him toward interfering in the alliance effort. Could Arhk have been trying to stir things up? After all, a time of peace would also diminish the role of the dhomvalen.

Kasiel shoved the thought away. He had to believe his father wouldn't deliberately provoke conflict in the royal family. That would be treasonous. Given how closely he and Seylin worked together, he couldn't imagine Arhk doing anything that might lead to the loss or imprisonment of one of her children. More than one of them, had the attempt on Velara's life been successful.

"Do you think Khesran Karith wanted to have the level of influence over Vanris your mother has when he assumed the throne?"

"Maybe." Nakhul shrugged his slight shoulders. "Karith is a greedy calloch, and he and Vel have never gotten along. I can't see him shying away from hurting her if he thought it would get him what he wants."

"Why is there such hostility between them?"

"Among other things, she got something Karith believes should have been his. Mind-crafting ability runs in bloodlines, but no matter how many children a mind-crafter has, it only ever manifests in one of them. Most of the time, the first-born child is the one who gets it. Our family is one of the rare exceptions."

It struck Kasiel as foolish to hate someone for something they had no control over. Then again, if emotions were rational, he wouldn't be in the mess he had gotten into with Velara and Nerith. There was still more to dig out here, though.

He pinned the youngest khesran with a shrewd gaze. "How did you know Karith wanted to harm her?"

"Oh, palace life can get dreadfully dull, so I invest many hours into finding hidden places to eavesdrop from. Vel and I practically perfected the art together." He gave a conspiratorial wink as if it were all a big game. "I heard my brother whispering with Safya about how he hoped he had finally gotten rid of Velara."

Not good enough. "Why didn't you tell someone?"

"Because that was yesterday evening. We had only just gotten news of the attack in Norvask. I was furious with Karith for dismissive reaction to Velara's narrow escape in Trenath, but I assumed he was being petty and cruel because of their rivalry, as usual. Then I noticed the hint of pleasure in his eyes when we got word of the incident in Norvask and the messenger did not know if she would survive her injuries, so I started spying on him."

"What happens if he's found guilty?"

Nakhul glanced at him, a hint of surprise drawing up his brows, as if he had assumed Kasiel would know more about the workings of Vanrian royalty. "They *will* find him guilty. I expect a death sentence, or at least life imprisonment." The flicker of sorrow that subdued his expression was reassuring. A sign that the potential loss of his brother might upset him at least a little. "If Prince Kaden really is dead..." He looked at Kasiel, waiting for a nod of confirmation before continuing. "Then Velara will become the official heir to the Vanrian throne."

A stab of disappointment moved through Kasiel. If anything was going to end the relationship, or whatever it was he had with her, becoming the khevarin's heir would certainly do it.

Nakhul startled him with a laugh. "You do fancy her. I knew it."

Kasiel schooled his expression, choosing to dodge that line of conversation. "Why does the prince's death matter?"

"If they were moving forward with the marriage as part of the alliance, she could not take the throne. Our people would never tolerate a foreigner as khemron. Not to sound callous, but I am glad the prince is out of the picture. I don't want the Break-blasted throne. I don't know if Vel wants it either, but I doubt mother plans to give it up anytime soon, so she'll have time to learn and grow into it."

It was a little late to worry about sounding callous. "This is all information you should be sharing with the dhomvalen and your father, not me." Kasiel opened a door leading out to one of the less decorative gardens. Not the perfect place to take Irith out, but it would have to work for now. He didn't want to wander too far from his post.

"You are the dhomvalen's son. I see no harm in..." He trailed off, gazing down the crossing hall behind Kasiel.

Peering through Irith's eyes, Kasiel spotted two guards approaching, their attention fixed on Nakhul. Transitioning to his own vision, he faced them. They stopped a few strides back, offering quick bows.

"Khesran Nakhul, Khemron Genyith and Dhomvalen Arhk require your presence."

Nakhul gestured down the hall, a hint of sarcasm in the flourish of his hand. "Lead the way."

The guards gave Kasiel respectful nods before escorting the young khesran away. Nakhul glanced back, waggling his fingers in an almost playful wave as he departed.

CHAPTER TWENTY NINE

Nakhul didn't return, and Kasiel wondered if he remained with the khemron and Arhk, or they let him leave on his own. Khesran Karith and his wife were called in separately for questioning over several hours. Kasiel left for a short time to take his tethdraks and Niskenya out to the enclosures where they could hunt and run in case they didn't get back on the road before the end of the day. It turned out to be a good choice.

Khemron Genyith stayed in the room with Arhk and the two Evokers through the night, questioning those implicated in the attempt on Velara's life and anyone closely connected to Khesran Karith. Nakhul eventually returned under guard and they placed him in a room next to his brother for safety reasons, though no one clarified exactly whose safety they were most concerned about.

Arhk refused to let anyone guard Khesran Karith and his wife who wasn't part of Kasiel's unit. Until they knew who else could be involved, he didn't want anyone having contact with the khesran who might be sympathetic to his cause. Kasiel set up his unit to work in shifts with four to a shift. Counting Irith and Raxxa as soldiers let him break up the night into three shifts. He assigned Tath and Nerith to stand watch with him, mostly to keep tehnaak pairings together and make sure the other two teams each had a Speaker capable of reaching out to Arhk's Speaker in case of trouble on their watches. His team took the shift from midnight to three.

Having Nerith there led to initial discomfort, but Tath engaged her in a discussion about the injuries Jethan and Darro were recovering from. The two healers quickly became absorbed in the conversation. He appreciated their expertise on the subject from the opposite side of the hall, trusting Irith to be an early warning if anything seemed amiss. The hours swept past.

The next two days went much the same, with Kasiel waiting for updates while managing his unit's shifts to guard the three rooms. Arhk forbade them from leaving the palace grounds except, in Kasiel's case, to check on the tethdraks and Niskenya a few times. Orders also came from him directing them not to speak with anyone regarding their purpose there or the ongoing investigation.

Had he expected to be in Doran for more than one night, Kasiel might have broken up the guard shifts differently. As it worked out, he and Nerith lapsed into a more comfortable place with each other by the third night, primarily out of habit. They kept a physical distance between them, but their manners and conversation relaxed to a place of familiarity.

That night, when Wedro, Etris, Merrin, and Avris arrived to take the last shift, Arhk also made an appearance.

"We depart at dawn," he informed them. "Khemron Genyith's Evokers will continue questioning people here. Khesran Karith and his pairing, Safya, will be returning to Etrion with us for further questioning and sentencing. Khesran Nakhul is free to go."

"He's not involved then?" Kasiel asked.

"Nakhul?" Arhk shook his head. "He may be spoiled and eccentric, but he adores his sister."

Perhaps Kasiel had something in common with the youngest khesran after all. "We'll be ready to go at dawn, Dhomvalen."

Arhk met his eyes. "I know you will."

Before they left the palace, Nakhul gave Kasiel a gift for Velara. A tiny, polished wood box containing two silver, claw-shaped earrings with dangling teardrop gemstones the same deep red color as her hair.

"Give these to her with my love. Or yours, if you prefer." He winked at Kasiel. "So long as it's love she gets."

Kasiel promised to do so, tucking them in the pouch with Sylaryth's claw.

To avoid drawing too much attention, they acquired the nice, but simple carriage of a lesser nobleman for Karith and his wife to travel in. The carriage restricted their speed, forcing them to keep a more restrained pace than they could maintain with only horses and beasts. Safya claimed to not feel well a few times on the third day, her illness further slowing their journey. They reached the jagged crags of Vareyl's Warning north of Etrion as dark was falling on the sixth day. Arhk stopped them at the foot of the path that wound up through the towering spikes of black stone. He gave no order to set up camp, so the column stayed in formation and waited. Their tired mounts stood still, taking advantage of the opportunity to rest.

Kasiel urged Niskenya forward with a thought. Arhk's guards shifted to the sides, making room for the kanodrak as he rode up beside his father. "You want to push through tonight?"

Arhk spared him a brief glance. "I would prefer to camp on the south side. It would set us up for an early arrival in the city tomorrow."

"It'll make for a late night, and little sleep."

Arhk twisted in the saddle to look over the column.

"You know them best."

Kasiel didn't look back. "I know they're eager to be home."

Arhk nodded.

They set the column moving again, Kasiel falling back with half of his unit in front of the carriage. The rest brought up the rear with the tethdraks arranged in two lines along each side.

Kince glanced over at him. "Pushing through."

"Yes."

"Good. I'm sick of being on the road."

Kasiel breathed a soft, tired laugh. "You and me both."

They wove along the roadway that ran through the crags, the spears of black stone angling up out of the ground around them. The rugged landscape took on a more ominous, hostile feel as the shadows grew deeper and darker with the setting of the sun. They were less than halfway across when a ripple of tension moved through the beasts. Kasiel spread a quick mental touch among them, feeling their unease and the sudden hyper-awareness tuned toward the rocky landscape around them.

"We're not alone." Niskenya shifted closer to Etris as Kasiel looked at the Speaker. "We've got company hiding out in the crags."

Etris answered with a sharp nod, her gaze turning inward as she relayed the message to Arhk's Speaker. He saw his father reach for his sword, then chaos erupted. The horses panicked, rearing and bucking to fight their riders. Armed fighters rushed out at the front of the company and along the sides of the narrow roadway. They had a Feral among them, whoever it was undoubtedly hanging back somewhere out of immediate danger. Kasiel could feel the individual struggling to push him out of the heads of the tethdraks when he turned some of his focus to trying to regain control of their mounts.

"Kenna, the horses," he shouted.

Unsurprisingly, she was the only one in the group who currently had their mount in hand. She nodded, her focus turning distant as Raxxa charged a fighter coming at them. Kasiel sent Irith to join the other cliff cat while he secured his hold on the tethdraks. Whoever the enemy Feral was, they were skilled, but not strong enough to wrestle his beasts away from him.

Kasiel sent the tethdraks into the fray, defending those who still struggled with their mounts or had been thrown. Merrin, Avris, and Kince went galloping past, their horses apparently reclaimed by Kenna. He felt the sudden pressure of Arhk's ability sweeping out, but it vanished just as quickly when a cliff cat that wasn't one of theirs sprinted out of the darkness and lunged over the back of Arhk's stallion, taking him to the ground with it. Kasiel struck out with his ability, violently ejecting the other Feral from the cliff cat that had his father. Seizing control of the beast, he sent it after one of the fighters attacking them.

The aggressive ejection had the desired effect of not only getting the beast off Arhk, but of disrupting the other Feral's hold on their horses. The remaining animals came under control again, and the rest of his unit charged into the battle. Kasiel kept the tethdraks on the offensive, already nudging the fight in their favor while he and Niskenya held position, trying to pinpoint the location of the hidden Feral.

Niskenya's ears flicked back, her energy shifting that way, and Kasiel turned to see the door of the carriage standing open. Later, he could take time to kick himself for not leaving a few of his tethdraks there to guard it. Right now, he needed to keep their prisoners from escaping.

Niskenya spun and galloped back the way they had come. They didn't have to run far to spot the group of riders driving their mounts hard away from the fight. Karith and Safya rode at the center of around ten other Vanrian traitors. A quick jump behind Irith's eyes told Kasiel enough that he felt comfortable drawing on some of his tethdraks to join the chase. Then he reached ahead into the minds of the horses, running up against the presence of the other Feral. For the moment, he wasn't vying for control, but fishing for a reaction, and he got it.

One rider near the middle glanced back the second Kasiel touched on the horses' minds, his eyes widening. Kasiel grinned and Niskenya sped up. More than a match for the horses. He tightened his hold on the saddle grips and leaned low, squeezing his legs into the molded seat.

Niskenya sprinted up along the side, gaining ground with ease. They ignored the riders they were passing. The one they wanted was just ahead and riding one in from the outside. With a burst of stunning power, the kanodrak lunged, angling away from the group. She leapt up against the side of a spire of black rock, using the solid structure to rebound off and send them over the top of the outside rider. Her massive claws latched onto the Feral and his mount. A flash of warning hit Kasiel, and he disengaged, leaping clear as Niskenya took both horse and rider to the ground with her.

Their crash in the middle of the group took down many of the others with them. Kasiel caught hold of another rider as he flew through the air, slamming into the ground with her and her horse. The impact hurt, both because of how hard he hit and because he felt Niskenya's collision with the ground and all the strikes she took as other horses that didn't have time to stop plowed into her and her prey.

Dead or not, the enemy Feral no longer had influence over the animals. Kasiel took charge as he struggled free of the mess, stopping the horses. He moved them out of the way and drew his sword. The rider he had gone down with wasn't getting up. She lay at his feet, gasping for air, blood on her lips. He left her there, turning his attention to those who hadn't fallen into the pileup.

Four were on their feet moving toward him now, weapons ready. Not great odds, but he didn't have to keep them busy for long. The tethdraks were almost there. One of the four rushed him and Kasiel narrowed his focus, meeting the attack with very little help from Niskenya. Most of the kanodrak's attention was still on getting untangled from the horses and riders that had fallen over her and her victim.

He parried another strike and retreated, trying to stay aware of the other three moving to flank him. The effort was futile. He couldn't keep eyes on all of them at the same time. They were surrounding him. Desperate, he changed direction and lunged into a slender man on his right, hoping he could overpower him if they collided. The man leapt to the side, giving himself room to swing his axe. His weapon hit Kasiel's ribs toward the back as he barreled past, deflected by one of the dark metal plates affixed to his black leather armor. The strike was still powerful enough to hurt and make breathing harder for a few seconds.

Niskenya's awareness moved through him then, helping him refocus as he spun and engaged the slender man. The burst of intensity and speed caught the man by surprise. He twisted to avoid a strike and stumbled. Kasiel didn't think or hesitate. With a quick lunge, he drove his sword into a gap in the man's armor above the waist, sinking half the blade through his gut. The man dropped his weapon, the horror of his own certain death contorting his features. A death that would be slow and agonizing if no one intervened.

The attack eliminated one opponent but gave another

a chance to get a strike in, catching Kasiel with a glancing slash to his arm. His quick retreat made it a superficial injury, the sting of it heightening his focus. Another fighter who had gotten free of the mess was coming over to take the fallen man's place.

Before he could pick his target, three of them rushed him at once. By some miracle, he blocked and dodged their initial attacks, but a boot to the gut caught him by surprise, followed quickly by a second kick to the chest that sent him sprawling. He kept hold of his dark metal blade, but his opponent's foot came down on his forearm, rendering it useless. The woman touched the point of her sword to his neck and smiled.

"Arrogant, earless bastard."

She drew her arm back a fraction, ready to drive the point home, hesitating a second when Kasiel grinned at her. A tethdrak slammed into her from the side. Two more charged in behind the first, taking care of the rest of his problems.

Wedro arrived just behind the beasts and helped Kasiel to his feet. "I thought you might need assistance, but you appear to have it under control."

"That makes me no less happy to see a friendly face," Kasiel said, pulling the tethdraks back before they could kill everyone.

In the middle of the roadway, two horses lay dead, along with the Feral, another fighter, and Safya. Karith knelt in the dirt, cradling her limp form in his arms. He had several scrapes on his face, his tears mixing with the blood on one cheek. Kasiel squeezed Wedro's shoulder as he walked past to approach the khesran.

Karith glared up at him. "Look what you've done!"

Kasiel crouched next to him and looked at Safya, an ache spreading in his chest for her pointless death. "No, Karith, you did this," he whispered. "You did it."

Their side suffered no fatalities, though Zafyr and

Avris took severe enough injuries that they moved to the carriage once they were stable. Karith and two other survivors from the group that attacked them were bound on horses to finish the journey home. Arhk had four deep gouges in the back of his neck where the cliff cat would have bitten through his spine if not for Kasiel's intervention. Despite the seriousness of the wounds, the dhomvalen insisted on riding once Nerith finished cleaning and bandaging them.

It took almost an hour to deal with the aftermath of the battle. When they finished, they continued for the city. No one had any desire to set up camp tonight. They wanted to be back where they could receive proper care for their injuries and lock the traitors up to await their fates. Kasiel's unit was tired. Arhk and his group were as well. It was time to be home.

Kasiel's whole body ached from the fall in the roadway and the fight, but none of his injuries were life-threatening. His father, on the other hand, looked ghastly pale and unsteady, the wounds clearly causing him significant pain. Yet he stubbornly persisted, refusing to allow himself the ease of resting with Avris and Zafyr.

"Are you sure you don't want to ride in the carriage?" Kasiel asked, urging Niskenya up alongside him.

Setera, riding on Arhk's other side, let out a derisive snort.

"I will manage."

"Of course you will." Kasiel gave him a wry smile. "You're the Beast of the Break. Stubborn calloch that you are."

Arhk gave him a sharp look, though a glimmer of affection showed through in it. "Do not let your victories go to your head, Ahninveth. I still significantly outrank you."

Kasiel grinned, the expression fading when Arhk

sucked in a sharp breath. Nothing he said was going to get the man to take the less painful option, even though fresh blood had started seeping through the bandages on his neck. The best he could do was hope to distract him.

"How did you meet Ellaris?"

Despite the pain tightening his eyes and jaw, a genuine smile curved Arhk's lips. "Your mother beat me in a tournament in Doran when I was about your age. I believe I fell in love sitting on my bruised ass staring up at her when she offered to help me stand."

"She beat you?" Kasiel couldn't keep the surprise from his voice.

Arhk's smile warmed, his gaze turning inward. "She beat me soundly. I did not have half the fighting skill then that I have now, but she did."

"Tell me more about her."

He glanced at Kasiel out of the corner of his eye, not up for turning his head again. "You are far more like her than I would have expected. She would do anything to protect the people she cared about. I suppose that goes without saying, since she died trying to protect you. I believe if she could see you now, she would be incredibly proud."

Kasiel ducked his head and faced forward, hiding the moisture rising in his eyes. With a little more prompting, Arhk talked about Ellaris until the pain of speaking forced him to silence. That he had loved her deeply was apparent in the affection that infused every word and the faint smile that touched his lips.

When they reached the city, a few hours after midnight, Kasiel sent Tath, Nerith, and Merrin to accompany Avris and Zafyr to the healer's building. Kenna split off to deliver the tethdraks to the habitat. She also took Raxxa, Irith, and the dead Feral's cliff cat to their enclosure. Once they had the prisoners secured, Kasiel released the others to rest and tend any minor injuries, and Arhk finally allowed the khevarin's healer to lead him away to have his wounds properly cared for.

After getting Niskenya settled, Kasiel wandered to the private quarters in the palace. He stumbled his way to his tehnaak's room, slipping quietly into the sitting area outside Jethan's bedroom. There, he settled on the couch and fell asleep.

Kasiel startled awake to a sprinkle of water on his face. He sat up, groaning at the stiffness in his muscles from the abuse he had taken in the fight.

Jethan stood by the couch, part of the back brace showing under his loosely laced shirt, his fingers poised to dip into the mug of water he was holding again. "Morning. I see you made it home, but you missed your room by two turns and at least five doors."

Kasiel rubbed his face, trying to wake up. "I just wanted to see how you were doing. Besides, given how many times you've slept on my couch, I didn't think you'd mind."

Jethan tilted his head, glancing at Kasiel's arm. "Normally I wouldn't, but I've never bled on your couch. Has anyone looked at that?"

Kasiel tugged at the hole in his shirt, eyeing the shallow cut beneath. "Huh. I forgot about that."

"Lucky for you, I requested hot water for a bath, followed by food and a healer to be sent to your room. I'll join you for breakfast while they clean my couch." A fond smile curved his lips then. "I'm glad you're back. I hated not being out there with you. And I don't know what happened, but you clearly took a beating. Anyone else get hurt?"

"Avris, Zafyr, and my father all got hurt fairly badly, but they'll recover." Kasiel got stiffly to his feet, discouraged by how achy his battered body was. "I like your plan, tehnaak. I'll tell you the rest over breakfast."

"I'll have them add some sweet mead to the order."

"Excellent idea."

A few hours later, bathed and dressed in clean clothes, he told Jethan of their journey to Doran and back. Iatan stopped in to tend the cut on his arm. The rest of his injuries were bruises and scrapes that would heal without intervention. By the time all of that was done, the mead and lack of sleep lulled him. Jethan excused himself, and Kasiel stumbled to his own bed for a few more hours of rest.

When he woke in the afternoon, he dressed and wandered to his father's rooms. The visit was unannounced, and there were no guards at the door, so he tried knocking.

Setera answered. "Ahninveth Kasiel, do come in."

"Ahndhomen Setera." He inclined his head. "If this is a bad time—"

"Come inside, Kasiel," his father's voice called from within.

Setera stepped to one side to let him enter, then shut the door before going to sit in an elegant chair next to the couch Arhk sat on. An almost empty glass of wine waited for her beside a tray of fruit and cheeses. Fresh bandages wrapped the back of the dhomvalen's neck, and he looked tired, but otherwise appeared no worse for wear, which was surprising given the injury he sustained.

Arhk gestured to the chair Kasiel had stopped behind. "You are welcome to join us. There is plenty. And someone should enjoy my wine. I am not allowed any."

"Healer's orders." Kasiel shared a brief, tentative smile with his father at that. "Thank you, but I was just checking in to see how you were faring."

"The group that tried to free Karith last night had been hiding out south of Vareyl's Warning. Someone from Doran rode ahead and alerted them to our approach. I suspect Safya's claims of feeling unwell on the journey were merely a ploy to buy them time to get into position. The group was there planning an attack against some Delaphinian watchtowers. By using a Feral in an assault against Delaphinian forces, we could not deny that the attackers were Vanrian. Another attempt to break down the alliance thwarted by you, Ahninveth."

Kasiel lowered his gaze. "Not alone, Dhomvalen."

"Your humility has its place, Kasiel. Now and then, you are allowed to be proud of all you have done."

Kasiel looked up, his gaze going to Setera, because that was somehow easier than facing his father's praise. A smile curved her lips, and she offered him a small nod before taking a sip of her wine.

"I should..." He glanced at the door, then back at his father. "Is there somewhere in the palace I might arrange an evening with my unit? Maybe dinner and a place to gather after?"

Approval shone in Arhk's eyes. "Ask an attendant to take you to the inner court. I think you will find the rooms there meet your requirements. I shall send word to the palace kitchens that you will be holding a private dinner there. Provide them your numbers and your needs and they will handle the rest."

"Thank you, Dhomvalen." He hesitated a moment. "Father."

Arhk offered the barest hint of a nod, his movements restricted by his injury. "Enjoy your evening, Kasiel."

The unit met for supper in a private dining room in the inner court, an area reserved for palace residents to hold more intimate gatherings. It had a square table big enough to accommodate all of them, including Kenna and Therin. He invited Harif, Keyla, and Velara to join them as well. A sitting area took up one half of the room with several couches and chairs for lounging and conversation set before a large fireplace. He wanted them to spend time together without the stress of travel or distraction of the tavern. Even Darro and Avris, the latter of whom had suffered a deep laceration across her ribs, showed up, though Avris didn't arrive until after the meal. She opted to come for the socializing, knowing she might not have the fortitude to stay long.

Keyla also arrived after the meal was done. When Jethan inquired into Velara's absence, she sank beside him on the couch and exhaled a troubled sigh.

"Vel said it's because her ribs are still healing, but I know that's not it. It's the scars. She pretends everything's fine, but I've caught her several times staring in the mirror like she loathes her reflection. She's not happy, and I don't know what else to say or do for her." Her gaze drifted to Kasiel, pleading and hopeful.

"No." Jethan held up a hand between them. "He can't help. The royal family is in upheaval right now, and she and Kas have already pushed things farther than they should have. It's time to put all of that in the past, right, Kas?" Jethan's gaze shifted to him, a little more insistent than hopeful, but somehow strikingly similar to the look Keyla was giving him.

He reached into the pouch where he kept Sylaryth's claw and pulled out the small wooden box Nakhul had given him. He looked at his companions, some laughing or in deep conversation, others simply enjoying a chance to relax together. Tath and Nerith had Avris's shirt pulled up enough to show the long bandage there to Harif. The three healers were deep in a discussion about wound treatment in the field. Avris chatted with Merrin and Wedro over their heads. Darro and Kince sat together in companionable silence, Darro watching Tath while Kince drank his mead, looking content to be back in his tehnaak's company. Etris and Therin were still sitting at the table laughing, though neither Speaker had uttered a word out loud in some time. Kenna rolled her eyes at them and approached Kasiel's group. When she reached them, he stood and offered her his spot.

"Kas, where are you going?" An edge of warning sharpened Jethan's tone.

He looked at the box in his hand. "Khesran Nakhul asked me to give this to Velara."

"In that case, let's all go see her." Jethan moved to get up and Keyla caught his arm, pulling him down.

"Give them a chance to talk, Jeth. Kas can help her. I know he can."

Jethan's nostrils flared, and he looked for a moment like he might fight her. Then he settled into the seat, turning a stern gaze on Kasiel. "Tell me you won't do anything stupid."

"No more so than usual."

He narrowed his eyes. "You must know how reassuring that isn't."

Kasiel grinned and faced Keyla. "Take care of him until I get back."

She smiled. "You take care of mine, and I'll take care of yours."

"It's a deal."

Velara's chambers in the private quarters were easy to find, being one of two rooms under constant guard after the recent attacks, Velara's and Seylin's. He walked confidently to the door, only to have a guard step into his path.

"I just need to speak with the khesran."

"Apologies, Ahninveth, but she is resting."

Kasiel frowned at the woman. "I'm willing to bet she isn't." He gestured to the door.

The guard considered him for a few seconds with her lips pressed into an irritated line, then she knocked.

His uncertainty vanished when he heard Velara call, "Who is it?"

"Ahninveth Kasiel is here to see you, Khesran," the guard answered. "Would you like him sent away?"

He narrowed his eyes at the woman, but she ignored him. The long silence that followed brought the uncertainty back, and the guard started to wave him off when Velara called out again.

"Let him in."

Now it was the guard who frowned, but she opened the door, gesturing for him to enter, and followed him in. Velara stood near the fireplace in a simple black and silver dress, her back partly to the door, blood-red hair falling in a loose cascade over her shoulders. She started to look at them, catching herself before she turned far enough for the scars to show.

"Ahninveth Kasiel is one of my personal guards. I would like him to debrief me on the recent events with my brother. You may leave us." Her usual sharp confidence sounded forced, undermined further by her refusal to meet the guard's eyes.

"As you wish, Khesran." The woman bowed, gave him a look of warning, then left the room, closing them in together.

Kasiel walked to where Velara stood, stopping a few feet from her. She still wouldn't face him.

"Nakhul sent a gift for you." He presented the box.

Velara held a hand back to him, and he stepped forward to place the box in it. She pulled away abruptly when their fingers touched. One thumb brushed the top of the wood surface, a palpable sorrow hanging over her. After a moment, she opened it, and the visible corner of her mouth curved up a little.

"They're beautiful." The smile faded, and she set the box on the mantle, still open. "Too beautiful for this." She gestured to her face.

"Look at me, Vel."

"No."

"I'm not leaving until you do. I've already seen your scars."

"You have, but you lie to me about them. I'm not blind. I can see for myself." She gestured roughly to a small, broken mirror discarded on the couch. "I'm supposed to speak before everyone at a ceremony tomorrow evening." She finally faced him. "How can I show myself to them looking like this?"

He took another step closer, bringing a hand up to cup her jaw. His thumb lightly traced the upper line of the long, V-shaped scar on her cheek. "I'm not lying to you. You are so beautiful, Vel. I wish you could see yourself through my eyes. The scars make no difference to me."

Tears welled in her eyes. "You don't mean that."

"I do." He moved his hand until one finger remained under her chin, then tilted her head up and kissed her. A lingering, gentle kiss.

When he drew away, her hands slid up his arms, wonder and a cautious hope shining in her silver eyes. "You still want me? Even like this?"

"More than you can imagine."

At his words, a spark of hunger lit her eyes. "Wait a moment."

He watched her walk to the door and lean out, feeling the overflow of soothing as she Charmed the guards into agreeing that their important meeting must not be interrupted. When she came back, her deft fingers started undoing the laces of his shirt.

He caught her wrists. "You're still healing. I don't want to hurt you."

"Remove your hands."

When he did so, she reached up and pushed the jacket off his shoulders before returning to the laces.

He let her pull off his shirt, watching her gaze move over him, taking in the scars and tattoos that told their people who he was. Her hands slid back down his now bare arms. One fingertip traced the scar on his left arm where Edmund had bled him. Then she looked at the other arm, caressing her fingers lightly over the scars where they opened his arm to repair the damage from Itana's mace. Finally, she took his hands and started backing toward the doorway to the bedroom.

"I guess you had best be careful then, if you're so worried about hurting me."

He took a quick step forward, catching her in the doorway and sliding his hands around her waist to pull her gently closer. He claimed her mouth in a demanding kiss. She had been drinking a sweet wine. He could taste in on her lips and tongue.

When they parted, she gazed up at him, pulling away. "What about Nerith?"

He didn't let her go. "I told her about us."

She placed a hand on his chest to hold him back when he leaned in for another kiss. "Is there an us?"

"I don't know. I just know I love you."

Her eyes widened for an instant, then a smile curved her lips. She ran a finger lightly down his chest, stoking his desire with her caress. "You know that line we've never crossed? I want you to come to my bed and cross it with me."

He met her eyes. All the reasons not to do what she was asking raced through his mind, but he only cared about one. "You're sure this is what you want?"

Pressing her body against his and bringing her lips next to his ear, she whispered, "I want to feel you inside me, Kas. I want to be joined as completely as it's possible for two people to be."

Her words and the caress of her breath over his ear as her hands touched him elsewhere erased any lingering objections. He kissed her, moving forward into the bedroom as his fingers went to work on the fastenings of her dress. With one foot, he nudged the door closed behind them.

Later, when they lay twined together on her bed, Velara shifted back on the other pillow to look at him. "Do you really love me?"

He reached over to brush his fingers through a tangle in her hair. "Would I have said it if I didn't?"

"Men will lie when they want something."

He arched a brow. "So will women."

She sat up, her careful movements attesting to the lingering pain in her ribs. "I would tell all kinds of lies if I thought they would let me keep you here. However, I suspect we are in danger of arousing suspicion amongst my guards. We should be careful, at least until I'm officially recognized as my mother's heir."

She slid off the bed. For a few seconds, he lingered, watching her walk naked toward the bathing room. Then he got up and followed her, curiosity and a desire to continue observing her luring him on.

"Are you being recognized as her heir?"

She glanced over her shoulder and nodded. "That ceremony tomorrow evening is at least partly for that. I asked for you to be one of my escorts at the event, but they apparently have other plans for the Hero of Vanris."

Plans no one had shared with him. "Don't call me that." He stepped up behind her when she stopped at the basin and got a cloth wet to wipe away the sweat of their coupling. Sliding his arms around her waist, he asked, "What does that mean for us?"

"It means I either have more freedom, because my status will have risen, or less, because I will be under closer scrutiny. Maybe some combination of both." She turned, placing herself in his embrace, and ran the cool, damp cloth over his chest. "Either way, I will find ways to be with you, in secret if I cannot do so openly." Pausing her ministrations, she met his eyes, determination rising in hers. "I love you. They will not keep me away from you."

"What if your mother has someone in mind for you now that you'll be taking her—"

Velara interrupted him with a kiss. "Let's not talk about it now. We need to get you back to your unit."

"If they're still there."

"Is there wine, mead, and comfort?"

He smiled. "You're right. They'll be there most of the night." When she started turning away, he caught her shoulders, stopping her. "Come with me. Keyla would love it if you did. I would love it."

The confidence and determination that had re-emerged in their short time together vanished, and she folded into herself, averting her gaze. "I can't."

Kasiel brushed the backs of his fingers over her scarred cheek. "Tomorrow, you have to face everyone. How are you going to do that if you can't even face my unit? You couldn't find another group less likely to care about your scars in this entire city."

He opened his hand, cupping her cheek, and she pressed into it. Her eyes closed, lips thinning into a tight line. Distress etched itself in furrows along her tattooed brow. He placed a soft kiss on her forehead and another on her lips. When she opened her eyes, he offered her a gentle smile.

"Twice they tried to kill you and failed. These scars are the symbol of your strength. Of your will to survive. Don't let anyone try to make them into a weakness, yourself especially."

Her gaze wandered over him, lingering on the scars on his ribs, his cheek, his arms, the still healing cut along his jaw. "Twice I would have died if I hadn't been with you."

He grinned. "That sounds like a compelling argument for coming with me."

Velara backed up against the counter and threw the rag at his face. "Calloch."

He caught it and winked at her.

When they arrived at the private dining room, the others had settled into a single large group around the fire, several bottles of mead and carafes of wine on the table already empty or well on their way. Tath and Darro sat together now. Therin and Etris had taken seats on separate sides of the sitting area, though their occasional shared grins suggested an ongoing conversation that the rest of them weren't privy to.

A bright smile lit Keyla's face when Velara entered the room. No one questioned their arrival together or what they had been doing for the last hour. Jethan shook his head and took a swig of his drink before moving over to make room for them on the couch he and Keyla shared.

With no other options, Kasiel and Velara sat together, keeping a couple of inches between them for propriety's sake.

"Kas, where are they sending us next?" Darro asked, his braced leg resting on a table. He could use the arm on the side with the broken collarbone some now, though it was the other arm he put around Tath's shoulders.

"No new orders yet. You, Jeth, and Avris need time to heal, so I'm hoping they'll give the rest of us a break too, rather than send us out without you again."

Darro sank deeper into the couch, letting his head fall back.

Kince raised his mug. "Good answer, Ahninveth."

Wedro sat forward, eyeing Kasiel and Velara. "Hold on. You two need something to drink."

"I'll get it." Merrin stood and walked to the table. She returned a moment later with two clean mugs and yet another bottle of mead that she set in front of them.

"Thank you, Merrin." He poured the mead and gave one mug to Velara before taking the other for himself.

"To the Hero of Vanris," Wedro said, lifting his mug.

Kasiel stood, stopping the others with a gesture when they moved to join the cheer. "Not this time. This time, we recognize all the companions, those here now and those we've lost along the way, without whom I would still just be the dhomvalen's missing son. Everything I am and everything I have I owe to all of you."

"Well spoken. To all of us, here and gone." Tath led them in raising their mugs to each other.

Nerith joined in, though her manner was more subdued. Through some unspoken accord, they had both told anyone who asked that they separated for personal reasons. Only Jethan and Kince knew the deeper truth, though neither knew how far it had gone now. Some of the rest undoubtedly had their suspicions, but if so, they kept quiet about them.

"Can we talk about the big issue now?" Wedro asked once they had all taken a drink, and Kasiel returned to his seat. "How is it that Velara's scars made her more alluring somehow, and I got stuck with this unsightly mess?" He gestured to his face with the scar running down it that left a slight split in his upper lip.

Kasiel tensed, but he stifled the urge to shield Velara. The possibility of being forced to confront her scars was part of the reason he wanted her here. He could see her pulling into herself, so he slid his hand over to touch hers.

The contact snapped her from her retreat and she rallied, a smirk, forced though it was, curving her lips. "Have you considered that maybe it has more to do with the starting canvas than the strokes of the artist?"

"Ouch!" Jethan exclaimed.

Laughter rang out around the group. Even Wedro barked a laugh, looking both shocked and amused.

Merrin put an arm around his shoulders. "Don't take it to heart, darling. You're as endearingly awkward now as you ever were." She kissed his cheek.

The comment earned more laughter.

"You're all terrible people," Wedro said, his grin belying his words as he took another swig of mead.

Velara settled next to Kasiel, a tentative smile curving her lips.

He leaned closer to her and whispered, "It's nice when you find a place you belong, isn't it?"

She faced him, the affection in her silver eyes drawing him in. "It is," she murmured back.

Kasiel slept until almost noon the next day before an attendant woke him. He sat up, struggling to shake off the fog caused by their late night. The effort made his head hurt and his stomach turn.

"What is it?" he groaned.

"Lord Kasiel." The attendant stood in the bedroom doorway as he spoke. "I had orders to wake you so you might have time to eat and bathe before you visit Ahndhomen Adnar to prepare for the ceremony this evening."

He rubbed his temples with the thumb and forefinger of one hand. "How prepared do I need to be?"

"I only know that you are being honored, and that Khevarin Seylin is making an important announcement."

Kasiel squinted at him. "Honored for what?"

The attendant chuckled. "Any one of your remarkable accomplishments would make you worthy, Lord Kasiel. Taken together, most of us are surprised you haven't been publicly honored before now. I sent for bath water and food. Is there anything else you need, my lord?"

Kasiel groaned and flopped back on the bed, staring at the ceiling while his head and stomach continued to complain about the quantity of mead and wine he had consumed.

"I'll have something sent to address the effects of

your overindulgence last night, as well."

It was Kasiel's turn to chuckle. He glanced at the man. "Thank you."

The attendant bowed his head. "My lord."

Kasiel didn't bother getting up until they delivered the bath water along with a tincture meant to ease the nausea and headache. He downed it in one swallow and went to soak his aching body in the bath. By the time he got out, the tincture had done its work, and a new, long jacket was hanging on the outside of his wardrobe.

He put on something simpler for visiting Adnar. When he wandered out into the sitting area, Jethan was there picking at the food. Kasiel sat and began piling a selection of items on a plate.

Jethan watched him, a scowl tugging down his lips.

"I didn't do anything that foolish last night, did I?" Kasiel tossed a grape into his mouth.

"Other than taking the virginity of the future khevarin?"

He choked on the grape. After several seconds of coughing, he finally croaked out, "What makes you think we went there?"

"I'm not an idiot, Kas. I grew up with Vel. The others may not have caught on, but she read like an open book to me. A book my tehnaak had the audacity to open no less."

Gathering his composure, Kasiel popped another grape into his mouth and chewed it slowly. Jethan stared at him, his expression darkening. When he looked like his patience was about to snap, Kasiel swallowed and said, "Someone was going to get between her pages eventually."

"You calloch!" Jethan's face reddened, and he popped to his feet, hands balling into fists.

"Hold on!" Kasiel threw his hands up in a gesture of surrender. "I was joking. Sit down before you hurt your back."

Jethan shook his head. "Someone was going to get between her pages. I can't believe you even said that."

"You're the one who turned her into a book." He waited for his tehnaak to sink down on the couch. "I thought it was rather humorous."

"You're an ass." Despite his words, Jethan breathed a small laugh, though his expression quickly turned serious again. "You realize that if the wrong people find out, you could both be in a lot of trouble. You more so than her."

"I love her, Jeth. I know that's foolish, and I know what we did was probably foolish too, but it's not like we can take it back. Besides, is it so unbelievable that I might be a good match for her?"

"That's not a question you should be asking, because it's not your decision. Hers either, unless my aunt decides to grant her that freedom, which I don't see happening." Jethan leaned back, the brace keeping his posture rigid. "There are plenty of noble families in Vanris who had hoped to have their sons court her before the political marriage with Prince Kaden landed on the table. With him dead and her about to become heir to the throne, every noble family with an eligible son is going to be vying for that honor. No insult intended, but offering her hand to someone raised in the south would have gotten some hackles up before. Setting you up to become the next khemron of Vanris could bring considerable strife at a time when we need to be united. Not to mention, some might see it as a power grab by your father."

Kasiel set his plate down, his appetite suddenly gone. His chest felt heavy, as if someone had set a great stone upon it. Becoming khemron held no appeal for him, he only wanted to be with Velara. Those two things were about to become inseparable.

Jethan's expression softened. "I'm sorry, tehnaak.

You claimed something that wasn't yours to take or hers to give."

"So, what happens now?"

"You cease all inappropriate contact with her and hope no one learns the truth."

Niskenya's protective warmth moved through him. Getting up, he grabbed a jacket that lay draped over the back of one chair and put it on.

Jethan stood. "You should eat something."

"Maybe later. I need to talk to Adnar and check on Niskenya."

"If you don't mind the company, I could use some exercise."

"Why not? I can always use someone around to remind me of my place." He walked to the door, glancing back when he realized Jethan hadn't moved. His teh-naak stood by the couch, eyes downcast. Guilt twisted in his chest. "Sorry, Jeth. I'm just frustrated. I don't mean to take it out on you."

"I know." Jethan walked toward him, a sparkle of mischief pushing past the hurt in his eyes. "Had you stuck with the book of Nerith, you wouldn't be in this mess."

"This might come as a surprise, but pointing out where I erred in my reading selections doesn't help much." Kasiel opened the door. "Also, the book analogy is still awful."

Jethan grinned as he walked past. "I know. Why do you think I stuck with it?"

Kasiel gave an exaggeratedly dramatic sigh and followed him out, trying to embrace a sense of humor and let go of the ache in his chest.

*

Kasiel's sandhawk perched on the rooftop of the tall building at the back of an enormous half-circle amphitheater carved into the ground with much of the population of Etrion lining its stone seats. A wide aisle extended from the entrance to a set of broad stone stairs that split and came around either side of a raised platform in the front, currently lined with palace guards. In the fading light of evening, he picked out his unit through the raptor's eyes. They sat in the second row to the left of the aisle, behind a row of dhomens and ahndhomens. The group of them were his story as much as the ke'hanoath tattoos upon his skin.

Jethan leaned over to say something to Darro, pointing at the raptor. The message rippled along the line and several of them waved at the sandhawk. Kasiel chuckled and patted Niskenya's shoulder. The kanodrak huffed. She didn't like being confined, even as in the spacious staging area of the building they waited in. Irith, who had managed to sit patiently for at least thirty-five seconds, pounced on an unsuspecting spider, his tail lashing with excitement. Kasiel smiled, shaking his head at the big cat.

"Welcome, people of Vanris!"

At the sound of Seylin's voice and the responding cheer, Kasiel focused through the sandhawk's eyes again. The khevarin stood at the front of the platform, her hands upraised. Long silver fabric cascaded over her arms, catching the light of the torches around the amphitheater, casting her in a pale silvery glow. A delicate crystalline crown settled light upon her brow, sparkling even more brightly than her gown. The crowd had risen to greet her.

Arhk stood on her left flank, opposite Seylin's tehnaak, Dhomen Aleren. The dhomvalen wore elegant black attire under one of the long jackets he favored, accented with thin plates of dark metal to evoke the idea of armor. This version had far more silver embroidery work on the cuffs and along the lapels than his usual. The jacket was similar to the one Kasiel wore over his black leather and dark metal armor, only Arhk's was a sleek black, rather than the charcoal of Kasiel's that had an almost metallic luster to it.

When the cheers died down, the khevarin gestured for them to sit. They did so instantly. Obedient and devoted. Perhaps influenced by her Enkindler ability. Kasiel felt no overflow, but unless she was being aggressive, he likely wouldn't notice.

"As many of you may already know, Khesran Karith has chosen to remove himself from the line of succession through acts of treason meant to kill his sister and undermine our newly formed alliance with Delaphine."

A wave of angry noises rippled through the crowd, but Seylin merely smiled and silenced them with a gesture. "We shall deal with him another day. We have called you here this evening to celebrate the creation of an alliance that represents a push toward peace for our future generations and to recognize a new heir to the throne."

Cheers rang out louder, though Kasiel knew not everyone here favored the alliance with Delaphine. He suspected the khevarin was rallying them this time, helping people who might be less enthusiastic feel the same excitement as those who wanted this. It didn't matter in the crowd. This was the moment they would profess their support and devotion to the khevarin and Vanris. Dissent was for more private settings.

The khevarin let the cheers fade, then she smiled at the crowd. "Before we get to those things, we would like to recognize a young man who, despite being stolen from Vanris as a child and raised in the far south, has demonstrated a degree of valor and loyalty to this country that we should all aspire to. We call forth Ahninveth

Kasiel Cavenos, son of the honored High Lord Arhk Cavenos, Dhomvalen of Vanris."

That was his cue. Two guards pulled open the sliding doors, and he rode Niskenya out, turning down the aisle of the amphitheater at an easy trot with Irith loping beside them. He had two braids woven in his hair along his scalp on both sides, displaying the symbolic ear cuffs the khevarin had gifted him with. The rest hung loose over the top and back.

He wasn't convinced the cheer that went up had that much to do with him, though the number of respectful nods he received as he moved up the aisle surprised him. Niskenya passed encouragement and pride through to him, helping him sit tall in the saddle. They rode to where the stairs split and around to the right, stopping at the edge of the platform. Niskenya passed him a quick warning, and he tightened his grip with his thighs as she reared up on her hind legs and let out a startling roar.

Arhk struggled to hold back a smirk, and the khevarin arched a brow at them, but the kanodrak knew her audience. These were mostly soldiers. Men and women who considered fighting alongside such a creature one of the greatest honors. The roar of approval that went up easily surpassed all the previous cheers. When her front paws returned to the ground, Kasiel slid off, patting her shoulder and passing along the amusement he kept hidden from his expression. The noise died down as he went to kneel beside Seylin and bowed his head.

"This young man has proven that the blood of Vanris is stronger than our enemies could have ever imagined. In the year since his return, he has bonded to one of our revered kanodraks and become one of the most accomplished Ferals in our country. Under his leadership, his unit defeated the greatest threat we have faced since this war began, destroying the production of the elixir that rendered southern soldiers immune to our mind-crafters and bringing its inventor here to face our justice. He risked his own life to protect Vanrian prisoners in Sharith and our beloved daughter, Khesran Velara, in Trenath and Norvask. His unit helped hunt down and defeat the insurgents who attacked us in Norvask and murdered Delaphine's second son, Prince Kaden. Most recently, when traitors attempted to keep Khesran Karith from being brought here to answer for his crimes, it was Ahninveth Kasiel and his unit who prevented his escape.

"In the course of a single year, he has accomplished all of this and more." She faced him then. "Rise, Ahninveth Kasiel Cavenos."

He managed to do so with some semblance of grace, primarily because Irith and Niskenya offered him their strength to calm the dancing of his nerves and the anxiety twisting in his gut.

The double doors at the back of the platform opened to let Adnar through. The Feral ahndhomen carried a kanodrak saddle in his arms the same charcoal color as Kasiel's jacket, with similar dark metal accents. He stopped behind them, the saddle visible to the audience in the space between Kasiel and the khevarin. Up close, Kasiel noticed a decorative dark metal emblem affixed to each flank.

"Heartsmith Ganok will add another mark of our recognition to your ke'hanoath. Additionally, we present you with this kanodrak saddle as a gift to honor your dedication to Vanris. The two emblems you see are gifts as well. On the right is a piece fashioned by a smith in Sharith, whose son was one of the prisoners you saved."

Kasiel couldn't stop a slight smile. The finely crafted emblem showed a mace shattering against a man's arm. If only it had really worked that way.

"The emblem on the left is a gift from King Mahlik

Durmond of Delaphine in recognition of your efforts there."

The second emblem showed the head of a kanodrak with the raptor of Delaphine in its eyes. The details on the fine metalwork were stunning.

Kasiel bent in a deep bow. "I am greatly honored, Majesty."

"It is you who has honored Vanris. May you, your kanodrak, and the soldiers you lead continue to be an inspiration to all of us." When she held out a hand to gesture to him, the gathering cheered again.

Kasiel waited until those cheers died down, then he turned to follow Adnar to where Niskenya stood. Behind him, Seylin asked them to welcome Khesran Velara Markanis. The doors at the back opened again and Velara walked through amidst another roar from the crowd. Her eyes were downcast, her head bowed so that her hair fell forward over her scars.

Kasiel angled his path so that they would pass within a foot of each other. "You are the most beautiful, most amazing woman here. Don't hide that."

She faltered a step, lifting her eyes to meet his. Their gazes locked for a few eternal seconds. Then she continued forward, her chin raised now. Kasiel smiled and went to join Adnar. The ahndhomen helped him quickly swap out the saddles while the khevarin extolled the virtues that would make her daughter a worthy leader to Vanris.

When the saddle was in place, Adnar carried the old one away and Kasiel went to stand beside his father, who had moved back to give the khevarin and khesran their moment. Velara was sinking to her knees to allow her mother to present her with a tiara that symbolized her new position as the heir to the throne of Vanris. Though her hands trembled at her sides, she didn't try to hide her scars again.

Arhk stepped closer to him. "With Niskenya and your many accomplishments, you have become the symbol of Vanris's might. Even Seylin had no choice but to acknowledge you. With very little effort, you could win the heart of this country."

Kasiel watched Velara, the uncertainty fading from her bright silver eyes as the tiara settled on her head and her people cheered for her. She glanced at him out of the corner of her eye and a faint smile touched her lips. Then she rose and faced the crowd, now as Seylin's official heir.

"I already have," Kasiel murmured to himself.

Arhk smiled and nodded as if he had heard and expected those words. For a moment, Jethan's warning that people might suspect the dhomvalen of making a grab for power jumped to mind. Focusing on Velara, he pushed the thought away. He knew what should happen next according to the plan. Adnar told him an array of guards would escort Velara down the aisle, giving her a chance to meet the eyes of the people she would one day lead. He was supposed to ride Niskenya behind them.

Kasiel swung up in the new saddle and, aware of his intent, the kanodrak moved up alongside Velara as she was turning to join her guards for the walk down the aisle. She glanced up and met his eyes, a smile blossoming across her lips when he hopped off and offered his hand to help her climb up. Niskenya lowered her stance to make it easier for the khesran. The moment she was on the kanodrak's back, the crowd roared. He caught a brief look at Seylin. Her icy gaze narrowed, but she would say nothing. Their audience was far too enthusiastic. Arhk appeared pleased.

Staying on the ground, he walked down the aisle beside Niskenya, allowing Velara to be the center of attention. The guards who were supposed to be escorting Velara now followed behind them. From her perch on the kanodrak's back, Velara waved to the surrounding people, producing more cheers. When they reached the end, Kasiel stopped and looked up at her.

"Where to?"

"The palace."

He climbed up in the saddle behind her, and they headed in that direction, her guards and Irith staying close around them. He sent the raptor above to watch for any threats between them and the palace. After everything that had happened, there was no point taking risks, even in Etrion. The moment they were out of sight of the amphitheater, she rested back against him. The khevarin would be dismissing everyone to continue the festivities by enjoying food and drink being offered free at taverns around the city. When they reached the palace, he had Niskenya wait out front while he and Irith walked with the guards to escort Velara to where Seylin and the others were coming in through a secure side entrance.

The khevarin gave him a sharp look before turning to Arhk. "Speak to your son about his impulsiveness. I have things to discuss with my daughter." She gestured ahead of her, her expectant gaze moving to Velara.

Without a glance in his direction, Velara went with her mother, the rest of the escort, except for his father, following. He watched them for a moment, smiling to himself when he heard Velara pointing out to the khevarin how much the crowd loved her exit.

When they disappeared around the corner, Arhk turned to him. "Is your unit meeting at a tavern?"

"No. With so many still recovering from injuries, we decided to avoid the crowds. We're meeting in Jethan's rooms." He braced himself, waiting for the lecture Seylin's words suggested should be forthcoming.

Arhk inclined his head. "Enjoy yourself then. You have much to celebrate."

"That's it?"

"Were you hoping to be reprimanded for your brazen disregard of Velara's planned exit?" When Kasiel said nothing, he continued. "I, for one, preferred your improvised version, and I believe your audience did as well. I am not here to prevent you from making your own choices."

"Just to nudge me in the directions you'd like me to go."

Arhk's shrewd gaze took his measure. "Only when necessary. Enjoy the chance to relax with the people you care about. Such opportunities can be rare."

Kasiel wanted to question the secrets hidden behind Arhk's calculating gaze, but his unit entered the hallway then. That conversation would have to wait for another time, especially since he could feel Niskenya's amusement at the alarmed reactions of people arriving at the palace to find a kanodrak out front with no Feral in sight.

He nodded to Arhk. "Goodnight, Father."

Arhk returned the gesture. "Goodnight, Kasiel."

Kasiel faced his unit as his father walked away. Tonight, they would gather as the original unit, with Etris and Nerith filling in where Ahrin and Chander had once been. Nerith and Tath would join as a tehnaak pairing soon. He wasn't sure Wedro would ever accept someone else in Chander's place, but maybe... someday.

"I'll meet you in Jethan's rooms. I need to take Niskenya and Irith back." He broke into a jog for the entrance.

"Don't get caught up by that fancy new saddle and forget to come back," Darro called after him.

Kasiel glanced back, grinning. "Never."

He did gallop Niskenya around to the kanodrak habitat entrance for the simple pleasure of doing so. Not to follow orders or protect anyone, just to feel the wind and enjoy their connection.

When he rejoined the unit lounging in Jethan's sitting area, Avris winked at him. "Hard to believe our little country boy is running around on a kanodrak and receiving accolades from the khevarin."

Wedro smirked over his mug. "I honestly didn't think he would make it a week here."

Kasiel tossed a slice of cheese he had picked up as he was sitting at the other man.

"Hey! No throwing food in my room," Jethan declared.

"What do you care?" Darro tossed a tart at Jethan that he managed to catch, though it squished in his hand. "You have people to clean up for you."

"Fine. Do as you will." Jethan proceeded to eat most of the crushed tart before taking the cloth napkin Kasiel offered him to wipe away the rest.

Kasiel watched them quietly for a time. The people who had raised him were gone. Knowing what Garrick and Edmund had done made it easier to let them go, especially with his new family around him. Danica remained a painful scar upon his heart. She deserved to be remembered as much as Ahrin and Chander did.

Nerith caught his eye, her expression guarded, but not openly hostile. He wasn't foolish enough to take that as a sign of forgiveness, but in time, maybe they could heal the wounds between them. For now, they were soldiers in Vanris's army. He hoped that commonality of purpose would give them a foundation to start over from. And she was part of the unit now. A place she chose despite what he had done. A place she belonged.

Someone knocked at the door, and Jethan called for them to enter.

An attendant stepped in, offering a slight bow to the group. "Ahninveth Kasiel, the dhomvalen would like to speak with you."

Kasiel sighed and set his mug on the table. Perhaps he would get that lecture after all. "Save me some?"

"A sip of mead and a wedge of a tart shall await your return," Tath answered, grinning.

"So cruel," Darro said, a distinct hint of admiration in his voice.

The others laughed as she leaned over to kiss him.

Jethan touched Kasiel's arm as he walked past. "Don't be long, tehnaak. I'll defend your mug as best I can, but I am injured."

Kasiel smirked and glanced at Darro. "I'm pretty sure you can take the guy with the broken leg. Good luck with the rest."

Kince raised a mug to him. "Good luck with your father, danro."

Kasiel followed the attendant toward his father's room, hesitating when the woman turned one hall too soon. Curious, he continued after her, his suspicions confirmed when she led him to Velara's rooms.

He caught her attention before they got too close to the guards. "The dhomvalen?"

She met his eyes, something off about her placid smile. "Yes, my lord." She pointed at Velara's room.

"Thank you. You can return to your other duties."

When she left, he continued to the room. One guard stepped forward to open the door for him. Velara was sitting in a chair before a warm fire, the flickering of the flames giving motion to her blood-red hair. She stood and walked to him, sliding one hand behind his neck to pull him into a lingering, sensual kiss. When she finally released him, it took a moment to put his thoughts back in order.

"I..." He gave himself a small shake. "Did you Charm the attendant?"

Velara's grin admitted her guilt. "That reminds me, I need to speak to the guards a moment."

Releasing him, she went to the door and leaned out. He felt that familiar soothing sensation as she told them he had stopped by for but a moment and already left. Once they both confirmed her words, she shut the door, slid the bolt home, and walked to him again, resting her arms on his shoulders.

"What happens when I really leave?"

"The next shift arrives in half an hour." Her shoulders lifted in a slight shrug. "I guess you'll have to stay until then. I'm sure your tehsheyn will wait. Since you're stuck here, what would you say to making love to the heir to the throne?"

He forced a tone of teasing indifference. "I made love to the future heir to the throne just yesterday."

"Oh, this will be better."

He yearned to sweep her into his arms and carry her to her bedroom, but he held himself back. "Will it?"

She pressed her body to his and ran a finger along his lower lip. "Much," she whispered.

"I'm not sure I believe you."

"I guess I'll have to prove it to you, Khemron Kasiel."

Unease rippled through him. "No. Just Ahninveth," he corrected, placing a gentle kiss on her forehead to stop the fading of her smile.

"Make love to me, Kas."

He looked into her eyes, the sudden intensity of her gaze stealing his breath away. This amazing woman had given her heart to him. The heart of Vanris.

"You need only ask."

THE END

<u>Kasiel's Glossary</u>

Vanrian terms I've learned

Calloch
Rank ball of monkey shit. A favored insult in Vanris.

Company (military)
The units and unions under the command of a single dhomen or ahndhomen.

Crack a stone
Popular Vanrian phrase meaning to open and drink a stoneglass bottle of Vanrian Black Mead. Vanrians love that stuff.

Danro
Someone who is lost / out of place / doesn't fit in (me).

Evalis
Black fruit used to make Vanrian Black Mead. Imported from the original Vanrian homeland.

Ke'hanoath
Each Vanrian's individual story represented in symbols tattooed somewhere on their person.

Kenis Seed
Medicinal plant component used for sedation.

Melinar
Medicinal plant extract used for sedation. Considered too strong to use on humans.

Mindcraft	Unusual abilities possessed by some Vanrians to manipulate the minds of humans or animals.
Mind-crafter	Someone with a mindcraft ability.
...na sek	Appended to an officer rank when a promotion is temporarily granted for a specific mission.
Sheyvyosk	Stinky smegma.
Stoneglass	An light metal alloy that looks like stone and is extremely durable. Primarily used to make bottles for Vanrian Black Mead... naturally.
Tehnaak	Spirit siblings, bound to each other through a ritual of some kind and raised together.
Tehsheyn	Spirit family.
The Deeps	Vanrian solitary confinement.
Union (military)	A grouping of three regular units combined under a third or fourth level ahninveth or inveth.
Unit, Regular (military)	A group of thirty-nine soldiers under a single inveth or ahninveth.

Unit, Feral (military)	A group of nine soldiers and up to twenty beasts under a single Feral ahninveth.

RANKS & TITLES:

Khevarin	Ruler of Vanris – the rough equivalent of a king or queen.
Khemron	Spouse of the ruler of Vanris, shares some of the leadership.
Khesran	Child of the khevarin and khemron – basically a prince or princess.
Dhomvalen	Protector or warden. A Vanrian military leader who answers only to the khevarin. (My father.)
Dhomen	A Vanrian officer – the rough equivalent of a general in the southern kingdoms. There are four levels.
Ahndhomen	A Dhomen who is also a mind-crafter (slightly outranks a dhomen). There are four levels.
Inveth	A Vanrian officer – the rough equivalent of a captain in the southern kingdoms. There are four levels.
Ahninveth	An Inveth who is also a mind-crafter (slightly outranks an inveth). There are four levels.

Inren

A Vanrian common soldier. There are four levels.

Omren

A Vanrian mind-crafter common soldier. There are four levels.

Idrek

A Vanrian recruit – soldier in training.

Odrek

A Vanrian mind-crafter recruit – soldier in training.

Other things of interest

Anso nut butter

Made from tree nuts grown in Fallend. So creamy. I wish they had this in Vanris.

Havaad

A god worshipped in parts of the southern kingdoms, particularly in Sarket.

Pandrean Alliance

An alliance formed between the three southern kingdoms of Delaphine, Sarket, and Fallend to fight Vanris.

Mindcrafting disciplines

Charmer

A mind-crafter who can manipulate an individual or small number of individuals to go along with their suggestions.

Dampener — A mind-crafter who can interfere with the way people's minds perceive their senses, effectively taking away the sight, sound, smell, and/or touch of individuals or groups.

Enkindler — A mind-crafter who can inspire positive or negative emotions in individuals or groups.

Evoker — A mind-crafter who can see and sometimes alter a single individuals surface thoughts and memories.

Feral — A mind-crafter who can connect with, influence, and control the minds of animals or groups of animals.

Frightener — A mind-crafter who can access the fears of individuals or groups and cause them to see terrifying visions, sometimes permanently scarring their minds.

Heartsmith — A blind mind-crafter who can tap into people's deepest thoughts and emotions in an abstract way to read the story of who they are in order to tattoo it upon their skin.

Speaker A mind-crafter who can speak into the minds of individuals or groups, limited somewhat by range and visibility (less so if their subject is also another Speaker).

New creatures I've encountered

Cliff Cat Large wildcats native to the mountains in Vanris. Some Ferals use them in combat. They have a deep blue-gray coat with darker blue stripes down the spine along either side of a ridge of longer hair. Their eyes are sapphire blue, and their tails end in a puff of hair the same blue as its stripes. They tend to be around waist high to a man at the shoulder.

Kanodrak Impressive Vanrian predators brought to Pandrea from the original Vanrian homeland. Taller than a horse and used as mounts by a few Ferals. Vaguely feline with a silver-grey, scaled hide and milky white eyes. They have bone armor plating that starts at the nose and runs along the spine to the base of their long tail. Their massive upper canines extend well below the lower jaw.

Sandhawk — Desert hawks commonly seen in southern Vanris and around the Crimson Break.

Tethdrak — Vanrian predators brought to Pandrea from the original Vanrian homeland. Some Ferals use them in combat. Built a little like a hound, but reptilian. Adults are mid-rib high to a man at the shoulder. The thickly muscled limbs and torso are covered in light shades of red and brown scaling with spiked plates along the length of the spine and thick tail. Two backswept horns extend from the head and their massive jaws bristle with sharp teeth.

Werdyn Cat — Large wildcats common in northern Sarket. Broad swaths of charcoal fur tipped in white puff out around its face with tufts of white at the top of its ears, giving it an owl-like appearance. They have scales beneath their fur and a coat that repels water. Tend to be more active in inclement weather.

Places

Andaro — Capital city of the kingdom of Sarket.

Coranthis — One of the largest cities in Delaphine. (falling down the hill)

Crimson Break — War-devastated, desert region between Vanris and the southern kingdoms.

Crimsondale — Town where the incident that started the war happened. Now part of the Crimson Break.

Daco — Town south of the Crimson Break in Sarket. Some animal in this region probably found and ate the missing tops of my ears.

Dekingham — Main capital of Delaphine.

Delaphine — Western kingdom on Pandrea. Home to the Delaphinian people.

Doran — The northern capital of Vanris.

Etrion — My home. The southern capital of Vanris. (Do you really need two capitals?)

Fallend — Southern kingdom on Pandrea. Home to the Fallenese people.

Fellenvar — First town north of the black crags in Vanris.

Fernwallow   Small village in Fallend where I grew up.

Katis   Vanrian military base slightly southeast of Etrion.

Katovan   Destroyed town in the Crimson Break. The Hall that survived there is in an agreed upon neutral zone sometimes used for negotiations.

Norvask   Northern capital of Delaphine – summer palace. (Maybe you do need two capitals.)

Pandrea   The continent.

Riftwater   Abandoned town in the Crimson Break southeast of Etrion.

Sarket   Western kingdom on Pandrea. Home to the Sarketi people.

Sharith   Vanrian town east of Etrion.

Vanris   Northernmost kingdom on Pandrea. New home to the Vanrian people after volcanic activity drove them from their original island home.

Vareyl's Warning   Black crags that create a natural border between northern and southern Vanris. Called Vareyl's Gift before the war.

People

Adnar	Vanrian ahndhomen (a Feral / Nevias's tehnaak)
Ahrin	Vanrian inren (Tath's former tehnaak – a healer)
Aleren	Vanrian dhomen (Seylin's tehnaak)
Andross Gaverin	Nerith's father
Arhk Cavenos	Dhomvalen of Vanris – My father (a Frightener)
Avris	Vanrian inren (Merrin's tehnaak)
Barden	Leatherworker in Fernwallow
Branith	Dhomen of the city guard in Etrion
Ceanna Durmond	Queen of Delaphine
Chander	Vanrian inren (Wedro's former tehnaak)
Danica Traven	Blacksmith's daughter, my best friend and first crush in Fernwallow
Darro	Vanrian inveth (Kince's tehnaak)
Edmund Danovan	Man who raised me in Fernwallow

Ellaris	My deceased mother – killed when I was taken
Erikson	Delaphinian watch captain
Etris	Vanrian omren (a Speaker)
Farren	Vanrian dhomen and combat instructor
Ganok	Vanrian Heartsmith
Garrick Traven	Blacksmith in Fernwallow
Genyith	Vanrian khemron (Seylin's husband)
Harif	Vanrian inren (a healer)
Iatan	Vanrian inren (a healer)
Itana Kedran	Delaphinian general (former mercenary)
Ivette	Delaphinian insurgent
Jethan Markanis	Vanrian omren (my tehnaak – a Charmer)
Jhanik	Vanrian ahninveth (a Feral kanodrak rider)
Jorgan Birk	Delaphinian captain.
Jortan	Vanrian history instructor in Doran
Kaden Durmond	Second prince of Delaphine

Karith Markanis   Vanrian khesran (Seylin's eldest child and heir)

Kasiel Cavanos   Vanrian ahninveth (a Feral kanodrak rider – me)

Kastus   Vanrian ahndhomen (an En-kindler)

Kenna   Vanrian ahninveth (a Feral / Therin's tehnaak)

Keryk   Vanrian inren (Jhanik's teh-naak)

Keyla   Velara's tehnaak

Kince   Vanrian inveth (Darro's teh-naak)

Leysa   Vanrian inren (Nerith's for-mer tehnaak)

Loak   Mercenary (bad person)

Lorin   Mercenary (also bad)

Mahlik Durmond   King of Delaphine

Merrin   Vanrian inren (Avris's teh-naak)

Nakhul Markanis   Vanrian khesran (Seylin's youngest child)

Nerith   Vanrian inren (a healer)

Nevias   Vanrian dhomen (Adnar's tehnaak)

Nix	Mercenary (she's bad too)
Nok	Barkeep at The Twisted Vine in Etrion
Piers	Delaphinian insurgent
Rihane	Khevarin's healer
Safya	Khesran Karith's wife and tehnaak
Setera	Vanrian ahninveth (an Evoker)
Seylin Markanis	Khevarin of Vanris (an En-kindler)
Sorval	Vanrian dhomen
Tarik	Vanrian city guard inveth
Tath	Vanrian inren (a healer)
Therin	Vanrian soldier (a Speaker / Kenna's tehnaak)
Treya (Ilsa)	Vanrian omren (a Charmer)
Velara Markanis	Vanrian khesran (Seylin's middle child)
Wedro	Vanrian inren
Zafyr	Vanrian ahnvaris (an Evoker / one of Arhk's personal guards)

ACKNOWLEDGEMENTS

If you've been in my life while I was working on this series, you know how completely it pulled me in. Kasiel's story has been an extraordinary adventure for me as well as an escape from difficult things. I am grateful to him and his companions for the joy they brought me while I shared their story on these pages. There are also many people who deserve my appreciation, so I will try to capture them all here.

To Linda, who was my first reader as always and provided so much support and valuable feedback throughout the process. I can't imagine doing this without you.

To Kai, who took the brunt of dealing with my constant distraction and obsessive need to write at all hours of all days, and still allowed me to read the book to him out loud. Thank you for your patience.

As always, my best friends and beta readers, Rick and Ann, who somehow continue to stand by me regardless of where my crazy goes. You are now, and always will be, my tehsheyn.

To my additional beta readers, Todd and Jordan, your feedback was invaluable. You are greatly appreciated. And to all the ARC readers who have joined me on this journey, thank you!

As always, I want to acknowledge the fantastic team who helped me put together the finished book. Robert Crescenzio, my incredibly talented cover artist whose vision helps bring these books to life in his art. Melissa Nash, the fantastic map designer who helped realize Kasiel's vision of Pandrea. Alexander Lockwood, my fantastic editor, fellow author, and now friend. Brian Short, my amazing formatter, whom I would also like to thank for your excellent company on many coffeeshop writing days. I love working with you all.

To my other friends and family, know that I love you and value your place in my life even if I don't call you out specifically here.

Last, but certainly not least, to my readers. To me, books are a collaborative effort between the author and their readers. Without you, this world would only ever come to life in my head. I hope you enjoy experiencing it as much as I did and will continue along the journey with me through the rest of this series.

AUTHOR BIO

Outside of my career as an author, I am a professional technical and creative writer, spider wrangler, animal lover, and devoted cat mom. Writing fantasy and science fiction stories has been a lifelong passion for me. I love to include in my work the diversity I see around me and draw upon my myriad life experiences doing everything from wild cave exploration and horseback endurance riding to practicing iaido and archery.

•

Thank you for taking time to read this novel. Please leave a review if you enjoyed it.

•

For more about me and my work visit me at http://elysiumpalace.com.

OTHER NOVELS by NIKKI McCORMACK

CLOCKWORK ENTERPRISES
The Girl and the Clockwork Cat
The Girl and the Clockwork Conspiracy
The Girl and the Clockwork Crossfire

FORBIDDEN THINGS
Dissident
Exile
Apostate

ELYSIUM'S FALL
Dark Hope of the Dragons
Dark Savior of the Dragons

STANDALONE WORK
Golden Eyes
The Keeper

SILVERBLOOD RAVEN
A Path of Blood and Amber
A Path of Secrets and Dreams
A Path of Storms and Reckonings

THRONE OF VANRIS

Kasiel soared high over the Crimson Break, using his Feral ability to look out through the eyes of a sandhawk. It was one of two raptors he had started working with consistently over the last couple of months. He had finished investigating Sarket's military company from above. They were gathered on the far side of a plateau south of an enormous black Vanrian watchtower, preparing for an attack. The same watchtower the company Kasiel had come with was now camped alongside. With the sandhawk's superior distance vision, he was able to scout out the Sarketi force's numbers and armaments while keeping the raptor out of range of their arrows. The enemy knew he could use birds this way now, which made the innocent creatures popular targets for their archers.

With the scouting run complete, he had turned the raptor out over the plateau, coasting on wind currents. The war-torn desert landscape glowed with rich reds and golds in the late afternoon sunshine. This place, an area typically associated with conflict and death, became beautiful in this light.

"We need to talk about my cousin." Jethan's voice startled him from his musing.

Falling back behind his own eyes, Kasiel encouraged the raptor to return to him and glanced over at his tehnaak. "Is now really the time for this conversation?"

"Why not. You weren't scouting anymore. I could tell by that contented smile you always get when you're just flying along for fun. And we're well away from Etrion and the source of the problem. Seems like the perfect time."

Kasiel held up his arm, giving the returning raptor a perch upon which to land. He frowned at Jethan as the bird's talons dug into the leather gauntlet he wore for that purpose. "Velara isn't a problem."

"Isn't she? If my aunt finds out that you two are sleeping together on a somewhat regular basis, she might just have you beheaded." He gave a meaningful glance toward Kasiel's groin. "Or be-something-elsed."

Kasiel chuckled. "You always have a way with words, tehnaak."

He launched the raptor again, sending it toward camp while he walked to where his kanodrak, Niskenya, waited near Jethan's carefully controlled mount. The horse was getting used to the massive, vaguely feline predator, given how often they rode together, but it was easy enough to keep a light mental leash on the animal as a precaution.

Jethan walked with him. "Kas, I don't want to see either of you hurt."

Kasiel blew out a heavy exhale, his elation from the flight fading. "Does it matter that we love each other?"

Jethan swung up into the saddle, the unwanted sympathy of his gaze falling on Kasiel once he was settled in the seat. "Not to the khevarin or any of the suitors lining up to try for Vel's hand."

"We can talk about this later."

Jethan frowned at him. "A succinct way of saying you're going to ignore my concerns and keep doing what you're doing."

Kasiel swung up on Niskenya, her silver-gray scaled hide surprisingly smooth under the hand he placed on her shoulder. The kanodrak's view on the subject was simple. She was an alpha of her species. As the Feral bonded to her, he should have similar privileges, at least as far as she was concerned. That meant his choice of mates and the freedom to pursue whatever he wanted to do, among other things. The finer details of human social structure were inconsequential to her. The more time he spent connected to her, the harder it was to remember what rules he was supposed to be following and why.

"We'll talk about it later," he restated.

"Sure, we will." The roll of Jethan's eyes said he didn't believe that. "What are your thoughts on our new friends from Sarket hiding behind that plateau?"

Kasiel gave his tehnaak an appreciative glance before answering. "I think I have an idea on how to welcome them."

*

As dusk started sinking over the Break, Darro woke Kasiel and Jethan from a short nap. They grabbed some food before heading out again. The entire unit came with them this time, setting up a small camp with no fire on the plateau. Niskenya settled on ground that still radiated warmth from the day, curling around Kasiel to give him something to lean against. Jethan sat cross-legged close by in case he needed anything. The rest of the unit took shifts standing watch, most in their spirit sibling pairings; Kince and Darro, Merrin and Avris, and newly bonded Tath and Nerith. Wedro and Etris remained unpaired and Kasiel wasn't sure if they ever would be, at least with one another. They had similarities, but those were all things they somehow seemed to find annoying in each other. Their differences, like Etris's Speaker ability, also resulted in friction between them.

In truth, Merrin seemed to be the only one Wedro really connected with since his tehnaak's death, though there didn't appear to be a romantic element there as with Darro and Tath. His gaze drifted to Nerith, recalling in vivid detail the intimate moments they had shared. How often did romance blossom within units like this one? Given all the time they spent together and how stressful missions could be, he suspected it happened with some regularity.

Nerith met his eyes and Kasiel realized he had been staring at her for at least a minute. At the way the light from the sliver of moon gave a soft glow to her silvery hair. He pulled his gaze away. He had made his choice. It wasn't fair to Nerith or Velara to let his mind wander.

Closing his eyes, Kasiel turned his focus to his beasts and the creatures of the desert, where it belonged. He started by moving a few small songbirds into the Sarketi camp near the command tent while there was still enough light for them to be seen. Then he waited, watching and listening. As expected, it wasn't long before someone came asking after the general.

The general, a stern looking man with chestnut hair and a well-trimmed beard showing hints of gray, emerged and scanned the area. The soldier who asked for him had barely started to speak when the general's dark eyes lit upon the songbird perched on a rack of weapons, showing that he at least had perceptiveness worthy of his rank. He snapped a hand up to silence the other man.

"How long has that bird been there?"

"What bird, General?" the soldier asked as he and the two guards standing outside the tent followed the direction of the general's gaze.

"You thrice-cursed idiots! I told you to keep this place clear of wildlife. That includes the avian variety." The general produced a dagger from somewhere, throwing it with shocking speed, but the bird was faster, flitting quickly up out of the way.

Kasiel grinned.

Next to his physical self, Jethan asked, "How's it going?"

"Just saying hello," Kasiel answered.

While continuing to watch through the eyes of the bird, he reached out to a pack of desert dogs, drawing them toward the Sarketi camp. When the dogs were close enough, he set them to howling. The general fell silent, him and the men he had still been reprimanding turning to stare out into the deepening darkness. All through the camp, conversations faltered.

"Look at the horses," a soldier next to the general whispered.

Kasiel had reached out to their horses, making them all turn and stare at the central tent, rather than out toward the noises of predators as they normally would.

"Shit," the general muttered under his breath.

"It's him, isn't it?" one guard asked. "The Warden's son is here."

The general turned on the men with him. "Are you soldiers or children?" he shouted. "If you're soldiers, I expect you to get back to your duties or get some sleep. We march on the tower at dawn."

Kasiel moved the wild dogs to the southern edge of the enemy camp to continue their chorus. Then he brought some of his tethdraks out as full dark fell over the landscape, guiding them to different points around the enemy camp and getting them to call out to each other periodically with their distinctive shrieks and clicks. Soon the Sarketi soldiers were all staring out at the darkness, meals and conversations forgotten, many of them flinching whenever a shriek sounded in the night. They whispered to each other. Some kept their volumes up, trying to appear brave, but Kasiel could hear the tremor in their voices through the ears of his beasts.

Kasiel smiled and settled in for a long night of tormenting their enemies. Laying her naturally armored head on her paws next to him, Niskenya purred.

After a few hours of Kasiel strategically moving beasts around the camp, getting them to make noise whenever the enemy soldiers had a chance to start relaxing again, Niskenya perked up. His cliff cat Irith did as well, letting out a low growl where he lay stretched at Kasiel's feet, one front paw draped possessively over Jethan's leg. Kasiel drew back some of his ability, investing in Irith to hear what had gotten his and Niskenya's attention. A few seconds later, he caught the faint sound of something moving at the edge of the cliff near where they were sitting.

At his prompting, Irith extended his claws, getting Jethan's attention with a slight prick of those sharp points against his leg. Jethan opened his eyes, looking into the cliff cat's bright blue ones. He sat silent for a few seconds until the faint sound of something shifting caught his attention, then gave a subtle nod.

Irith stood, padding silently into the stunted, thorny brush nearby. Jethan, his movements careful and quiet, took his sword and went around the opposite direction. He gave a subtle gesture toward the cliff with one finger by his leg to Merrin who stood watch a short distance away. Kasiel lost track of them after that, turning his efforts back to managing his psychological assault on the company from Sarket. It wasn't until a few minutes later, when he heard the soft creak of a bow being drawn, that he pulled his attention back to his current location again.

Someone cried out. An arrow whizzed past a few feet in front of Kasiel, making his heart jump in his chest. He glanced toward the bushes at the cliff's edge.

Jethan and Merrin emerged after a few seconds, intermittently leading and dragging a Sarketi scout between them. The young man had blood running from a split lip and a small cut above one eye. Jethan was holding a Sarketi shortbow in his free hand. Irith came out of the brush behind them, ears perked and looking quite pleased.

Niskenya raised her head, snarling as they shoved the man to his knees in front of Kasiel. The youth cringed away from the big predator, his breath coming in quick, panicked gasps.

"What would you like done with him?"

Kasiel struggled at maintaining his awareness of the many beasts he was controlling while dealing with the current situation, but he managed to fake a reasonable level of composure. "You were after me?"

"Who else would I be after? Mind-crafter freak," the man hissed, showing some courage until Niskenya growled again, at which point he almost fell into Merrin trying to shy away from the kanodrak.

"Kill him?" Jethan asked, his tone deceptively casual.

"Oh, can we please?" Merrin infused convincing enthusiasm into her voice.

The Sarketi scout twisted away from her now, then from Jethan, looking every bit like a cornered animal about to panic. Irith stepped close behind him and growled. This time the youth tried to lunge to his feet, catching himself on his hands inches from Niskenya's face when Jethan swept his legs out from under him. He froze, trembling as the kanodrak stood and snarled, her nose inches from his face.

"Tie him up and keep him quiet for now. We'll decide what to do with him in the morning. Maybe Niske can eat him." Kasiel closed his eyes, returning to the collection of beasts he had gathered almost before he finished speaking. Some part of him was distantly aware of the protests of the frightened youth as they took him away.

When the first hints of dawn crept over the desert, Kasiel watched several groups of Sarketi soldiers sneak away toward the south. He let them leave, struggling to hold onto his focus through a rapidly worsening headache. When there was adequate light for them to be seen, he urged his tethdraks and the other beasts back from the camp, silencing the noise that had plagued the enemy soldiers through the night.

A few other units in the Vanrian company joined them on the plateau. Darro and the rest of Kasiel's small unit mounted up and rode back down with them, heading out around the plateau. They took the Sarketi scout, throwing a cloak over him to keep his presence hidden in their ranks. Irith and Niskenya stayed with Kasiel. As the others departed, he and the two beasts moved closer to the southern edge of the plateau. Using only a raptor now, he watched the slightly reduced Sarketi company pull together to make their march north. They had barely gotten into formation when a warning blared from a horn one of the Sarketi scouts carried.

The Vanrian force, with Darro and Kince at the lead, came into view along the side of the plateau. The Sarketi general, his mouth set in a grim line, led his company out to meet them. The two sides stopped about ten yards apart. Sarket still had a greater number of soldiers, even after some defections. But that only gave them the advantage if they didn't count the combat ability of the tethdraks now emerging from the surrounding landscape, their reddish-brown scales allowing them to remain hidden until Kasiel was ready for them to be seen. As he guided them out around the enemy company, he had the raptor shriek a warning to Kince, then landed on the arm the man held out. The perch gave him a nice vantage through which to watch the rising fear in the eyes of the Sarketi soldiers as the tethdraks made their presence known.

"It looks as if your company shrank in the night, General," Darro called out.

The man's eyes narrowed. "Where's your captain?"

"Our ahninveth?" Darro corrected with a bitter smile. "He is exactly where he needs to be. Out of your reach, but plenty close enough to manage these beasts."

Kasiel drew two packs of wild dogs out into the open on the flanks of the Sarketi company. As he did so, he moved through the enemy horses, making them stand statue still, heads lifting to look toward the top of the plateau. Then he urged Niskenya to the cliff's edge, having her stand where they would be able to see the kanodrak with him on her back, well out of range of their arrows. Several enemy soldiers started trying to pull their horse's heads down, but the animals didn't respond.

Through the raptor, Kasiel could see fear in the general's hazel eyes as he stared up at the distant figure on the plateau. Now to see if his plan worked and all that effort throughout the night was worth it.

"I have orders to allow your company to leave here unharmed if you agree to ride directly south out of the Break," Darro said, a cutting edge in his tone. "An extremely generous offer, considering our tethdraks alone could decimate your company."

"There are other fronts we can attack on." The general glowered up at Kasiel when he couldn't get his horse to lower its head. "The Warden's son can't be everywhere at once."

From the raptor's vantage on Kince's arm, Kasiel could see the wicked smirk that curved Darro's lips. "Is that your final answer?"

Was this the right thing to do? The Vanrian company was primed to fight. The tethdraks wanted it too, bloodlust resonating through them. But just because combat was what they were all trained for–what they expected–didn't make it the best option. How would more killing bring them any closer to ending the war? His unit was his family. He would rather see them struggling to find their place in a peaceful Vanris than lying dead on a battlefield.

The Sarketi general's hand moved toward his blade. Kasiel's answering rise in tension sent a ripple of growls through the tethdraks and desert dogs. He felt Niskenya's muscles tighten as she prepared to move. The man's gaze swept over the snarling beasts partially surrounding his company. His hand sank away from the weapon.

"Tell your ahninveth we accept his offer, this time."

Kince smiled at the raptor. "He already knows."

Proving the point, Kasiel urged the tethdraks and desert dogs to back away, giving the Sarketi company room to retreat. Then he relinquished control of their horses.

"Until next time." Darro inclined his head to the general.

"Oh, general," Avris called out, reaching down to cut the bonds on the youth she and Merrin had kept obscured with their horses. "I think this is yours." The Sarketi scout wove his way quickly through the Vanrian force back to his company. "Gutsy little calloch. You might want to promote him."

The general only scowled at them while one of his soldiers gave the scout a hand up on back of his mount.

Kasiel gripped Niskenya's saddle. Pain speared through his head now, making his stomach turn. When the Sarketi general ordered his company to retreat, Kasiel moved the desert dogs out and set them free. He held the tethdraks in place until after the enemy soldiers were on their way and the Vanrian company began to pull back. Then he called the reptilian beasts to him and urged Niskenya away from the cliff face to where he could dismount and throw up in privacy.

The pain got worse then, continuing to spike out of control. By the time his unit reached him, he was kneeling in the dirt next to his own vomit, clinging to the stirrup of his distressed kanodrak's saddle to keep from falling over. Nerith and Tath rushed to his side, helping him to his feet and moving him away from the rejected contents of his stomach.

"You overdid it, didn't you?" Tath asked, going to dig through her packs after Jethan took her place, helping Nerith guide him to a seat on a nearby rock.

Kasiel closed his eyes to the pain, straining to maintain a visual link with the raptor he had watching the enemy company to be sure they departed as expected. "I didn't know that was possible."

"It depends on how strong your ability is." Nerith rested a hand on his arm as she reached out accept the flask Tath brought over. She opened it and held it up to his lips. "Drink this. It should take the edge off and ease some of the nausea."

When he squinted his eyes open, Tath was scowling at him, her hands on her hips. "You've been running a large number of beasts for over twenty-four hours without a break. You need to rest, Kas. You aren't invincible."

Irith pushed between Nerith and Jethan, coming up to headbutt Kasiel affectionately in the face hard enough that it almost knocked him down. He wrapped an arm over the big cliff cat's shoulders to steady himself.

"Thanks, Break-blasted brute," he muttered, grimacing at the persistent ache in his head.

Niskenya came up behind Tath, one of her elongated front fangs almost touching the healer's shoulder. She made a distressed sound deep in her throat.

Tath startled and stepped to the side. She gestured to the massive predator. "See, Niske agrees with me.

Kenna's at the watchtower. She can manage the teth-draks while they're idle and give you a chance for some real sleep."

He shook his head, keeping the motion slow and small to avoid aggravating the pounding in his skull. "That's not necessary."

Nerith's lavender eyes flashed. "Do you want to keep this headache?"

Kasiel looked at her. She was always the most beautiful when her fierce side came out.

Nerith averted her gaze and he cringed inwardly. They weren't a couple anymore. He couldn't look at her that way. This was what he had been afraid might happen when he agreed to have her stay in the unit as Tath's tehnaak, but she was someone he trusted and a good healer. He was going to have to adjust to the idea that their relationship was different now. Preferably before he drove her out of his unit.

His head throbbed. Turning away from Nerith, he found Jethan staring at him with a look that would accept no more arguments. "All right. Let's go find Kenna."

Jethan nodded approval and came to help Kasiel to his feet.